The Silk Weaver's Daughter

Elizabeth Kales

Acknowledgements

With gratitude to my own Huguenot ancestor, Pierre Gastineau, who sometime around 1685, made the brave decision to flee France with his wife, Elizabeth Hebert and their children. His desire was to worship the Creator in the way their conscience dictated. Since we are all accidents of history, it is partly to him, and his descendants, I owe my existence

I would also like to thank Didier Pothet, my 9th cousin once removed, for sharing with me the story of his Gastineau ancestors; how they chose to stay in their beloved France and be secret Huguenots, a very dangerous thing to do. It was speaking with Didier that gave me the idea for this novel.

I wish to give a special thanks to graphic designer, Jeff Fielder, http://www.jallenfielder.com/ for his wonderful cover design and to R. Gino Santa Maria http://shutterfree.com whose photograph was exactly how I pictured Louise.

Last but certainly not least, a heartfelt thank you to my husband, who has supported me in every way possible. His encouragement and help gave me the opportunity to accomplish my dream.

PROLOGUE

"Death where is your Victory? Death where is your sting"
The Apostle Paul

Southwestern France

July 1685

T hat's not Guilliame. Who can it be?" the old woman exclaimed to her husband. She stopped eating as the pounding of horses' hooves and the harsh voices of men in the courtyard alerted them to visitors.

"*Voila*," they heard one of them yell. "This is the place."

Her voice shook as her hands clutched at her breast. "Lucien! Do you think they have discovered us?"

"I don't know how, Mathilde," he whispered. "Unless we have been betrayed."

Monsieur and Madame Garneau had waited all evening for their guest to arrive. Once the sun disappeared behind gray-pink clouds in the western sky, and he failed to appear, they decided to start their evening meal. In spite of their disappointment, they bowed their heads, thankful to God for their blessings. The small garden plot they cultivated thrived and the few animals they nurtured grew fat and healthy. There were worshippers still brave enough to come to the secret meetings they held in their humble farmhouse outside the town of Lusignan. All had seemed well.

Now, there was a crash, as several armed men broke down the door and barged into the room. They wore the uniforms of the dragoons authorized by King Louis XIV to round up the disobedient clergy. Mathilde screamed as a soldier grabbed her by her long, braided hair and hauled her outside. With great courage, but flagging strength, the old man tried to resist. They soon subdued him and dragged him towards a wagon positioned under a large oak tree.

"You had a choice," the dragoon captain snapped. "The authorities warned all you Huguenot pastors to leave the country. You would have been wise to obey."

Another of the men forced the aged couple to stand on the wagon. He looped ropes around their necks and tied the other ends to one of the strongest branches. Lucien cried out to his God, but a dragoon stuffed a wad of cloth into his mouth. Madame Garneau whimpered; her lips moved in prayer.

The dragoon whipped the horses, causing them to bolt. As the wagon lurched forward, the pastor and his wife hung suspended in the air. They thrashed wildly for a few minutes. Then, as the life force of each ebbed away, they were still. For a moment, an eerie hush prevailed, broken only by the creaking of the ropes, as the bodies swayed in the slight evening breeze. Even the soldiers were silent.

"Well, those heretics are taken care of," the captain finally muttered.

"What about their animals?" one of the men asked.

"Leave them. Burn them with the buildings. Let this be a lesson to all who would defy the King."

Departing the horrendous scene, they failed to notice the middle-aged man, cringing with fear and despair, hidden in a small grove of firs.

PART 1
The Huguenot Family

"It is nowhere forbidden to laugh or to eat one's fill or gain new possessions or enjoy oneself with musical instruments or drink wine."
Jean Calvin

Chapter 1

One Week Later

Forty miles southeast of La Rochelle, in western France, a small Huguenot village sat half-hidden in a valley. One narrow track passed by some insignificant farms, then dropped down to the center of the settlement consisting of a few small shops and a neglected chateau. For several hundred years, the hamlet had been there—encircled by lush woodlands of oak and beech. However, its isolation had not saved it from the terrors of the last century. Nor would it again should trouble arise.

Once beyond the town site, the lane climbed a slight slope, crossed a bridge over a meandering river, and terminated at the most prosperous-looking farm in the area. Located behind two stone buildings, were a vineyard; a substantial orchard; and fields of grain that continued to the edge of the surrounding forest.

The owner, Pierre Garneau, stepped out of his house into the morning sunlight. He surveyed the familiar surroundings as he had done almost every day since his youth. Always, he marvelled at the beauty of it. How blessed I am, he thought. One of God's Elect, for sure.

No ordinary farmer, Monsieur Garneau was a master silk weaver, a trade that brought him an excellent livelihood and made him a relatively wealthy man. Nevertheless, rumours circulating the countryside worried him. It seemed that King Louis, the Sun King, wished to rid himself of every Huguenot in the land. They had been a thorn in the side of his Catholic cohorts for over one hundred years. The Edict of Nantes established by King Henry in 1598 had given some protection, but now Louis wanted it revoked, and the Protestants gone.

Pierre, serving as the village *consul* or mayor, reported to the Catholic *seigneur* in the nearest town five miles away. Word often filtered through to him about problems Huguenots experienced with the King's dragoons in other parts of France. Fortunately, up until now, Father Leger had been lenient towards the Calvinists in his area. What changes this new decree

5

might make to both Pierre and his villagers did not bear speculation on such a perfect morning.

On this day, life in his hidden valley appeared idyllic. The sun's rays came streaming through the verdant growth, and filled the cobbled courtyard with a warm glow. Scents and sounds of early summer enveloped him; the sweet aroma of the roses growing up the whitewashed walls; the bird songs as tiny lovers warbled to each other; the buzz of bees seeking sweetness in the honeysuckle vines. In spite of his tranquil surroundings, this gossip about the king's plans seemed ominous to him; like storm clouds gathering in an evening sky. If it proved to be true, the life of every Huguenot in France could change in an instant.

And how could I ever leave this valley, he thought?

Behind him, noise generated in the kitchen signified a flurry of activity. The family had finished breakfast, and the preparations for guests coming from La Rochelle had begun. His second daughter, Catherine, stood at the table peeling vegetables for the feast. Claudine, his wife, kneaded dough for fresh bread to go into the bake oven, while Suzette, their maid, basted the lamb roasting on a spit in the great fireplace. Even his small, four-year-old daughter, Jeanette sat on the floor zealously shelling peas. Through the open door, savoury aromas of garlic and rosemary emanated from the room.

He gazed over at the river winding through their farm to where his oldest daughter sat on a large, flat rock, a pensive expression on her face. Lovely like her mother, Louise had the same oval face with a small, straight nose; golden-blonde hair; and dreamy, grey-green eyes. He treasured her dearly. However, she presented another problem.

She spends too much time in a world of dreams and fantasy, he reflected. Is this natural in a girl of almost seventeen? She should be in there helping with the preparations, but there she sits, most likely thinking of Marc. He sighed in frustration.

The son of Jacques Garneau—his cousin and best friend—was not at all what Pierre wanted in a husband for Louise. Marc had far too worldly an outlook for a devout Huguenot. Moreover, like his father he was a travelling merchant. Pierre did not want his beautiful daughter marrying a man who ventured away from home two or three years at a time. Too much temptation, he believed.

Now, Jacques and his family were coming for a visit, and Pierre determined he would keep those two apart as much as possible during their stay.

Louise loved to sit and dream by the lazy river. Knowing they would be extremely busy this morning, she had arisen early to have a little time to herself. Only the day before, she heard the rumours about the king's intentions and they worried her. She remembered that her cousin, Marc had once told her of past Huguenot troubles.

Now, looking at the ruined chateau, she shivered, reflecting on the atrocities it had seen. When they were children, she and her younger brother, Jean Guy, went with Marc to explore the abandoned building. Five years her senior and very self-assured, he had explained to them what had happened at the chateau. How, years before, a group of Catholics determined to take over the town from the Huguenots, killed both their grandfathers there.

Marc's father was one of the prominent and wealthy merchants of La Rochelle. His travels had taken him all over the world, and his sons were extremely well educated. Marc's schooling had been first in a monastery and then the University in Paris.

Thoughts of her cousin always made her heart beat faster. He was a twenty-two year old man now, and along with his father had just returned to France from a trading journey in the Americas. During that time, there was not a night went by she did not dream of him. They were second cousins, so the relationship allowed for marriage. Certainly, both his parents and her mother would agree to such a union. However, she was concerned that her father did not seem as enchanted with the young merchant as the rest of them.

I fear he isn't serious enough, and much too adventurous for Papa's taste, she admitted to herself.

Hearing the kitchen door open, her attention turned to her father standing in the morning sunlight. Like all the Garneau men, he was agreeable to look at, with a tanned skin, bright blue eyes, and shoulder-length, black hair that shone like polished ebony. He was far more serious than his lively cousins. Nevertheless, she loved him deeply. He was strict, but always fair and kind. She knew he would die before he would let any harm befall them.

She watched with affection as he surveyed his surroundings, almost knowing what he was thinking. After a short time, he looked over at her, waved a 'good morning', and went into the kitchen for a few moments. Emerging with two pewter mugs full of hot coffee—the last of their precious supply Uncle Jacques renewed each visit—he approached and smiled at her.

"*Bonjour, ma fille*," he greeted her, handing over one of the beakers. "Maman and the others have started the preparations for tonight's meal. I expect you'd better go in and help them. You seem so preoccupied sitting here, though. Is something troubling you, child?"

"Yes, I know I must help. But in the village, I've heard the rumours about King Louis' plans and they worry me. Why do the Catholics hate us so much, Papa? What started all this anyway?"

He put a comforting arm around her shoulders. "You don't remember the history of our people? Did we really neglect such important events in your lessons?"

"I can't recall learning about it."

"Yes, well, perhaps I thought it best forgotten since we were supposed to be protected by the Edict. It's far too complicated a subject to go into in any depth just now. I can tell you, however, it began a long time ago. Something Catherine de Medici started over one hundred years ago. You've studied about Henri of Navarre and the wicked Catherine?"

"Yes," she replied.

"Well Henry, who was the heir to the throne then, was marrying Catherine's daughter, and Catherine had an intense fear of all Huguenots. They had a great deal of political power in those days. Once she was in the royal family, she instigated a huge slaughter. So many of our people were killed, they called it the St. Bartholomew's Day massacre. Henri wasn't happy about it and when he came to the throne, he instituted the Edict of Nantes that stopped the persecution of our people for many years."

"Do you really think King Louis would dare to cancel such an edict then?"

"He has the power. If he wants to do it, there's no one who could stop him."

"Then what would happen to us? Will you become a Catholic?"

"Become a Catholic? Never. Under no circumstance, could I do that." Her father's expression became even more serious than usual. "I didn't want to tell you this yet, and I'd rather you don't mention it to the other children. However, being the oldest perhaps you should know. It's possible we may have to leave France."

"Leave France?" Her heart sank. "Papa, where would we go?"

"I'm not sure, Louise, and I don't want you fretting about it today. There's too much work to do with your uncle's family coming. Now we must think of our guests and Maman does need help with the dinner. In any event perhaps it won't happen—perhaps the king won't change anything."

"Oh, why is everything so unpredictable?"

"Unpredictable? No, my child, right now it may seem so to us. Nevertheless all things are preordained—we have little control—so we must accept our destiny. Nevertheless, to please God, we must also work hard. Then we're assured of our reward."

"Why, Papa? If it's all arranged anyhow, why should we have to work hard? Sometimes predestination doesn't make any sense to me at all."

Gulping down the coffee, she stood. Then without waiting for an answer, she flounced into the house.

"Louise," her mother scolded. "Whatever have you been doing? Dreaming again, while we are so busy? Did you eat anything at all? Jean Guy and Claude have gone to the manufactory to make room for the bundles of thread Uncle Jacques will be bringing. I need you to get water for me. Now on with you, girl. There's no time to waste."

With a sigh, she bestowed a light kiss on her mother's cheek, then picked up the buckets and headed for the well.

Chapter 2

The clip-clop of hooves in the courtyard and the commands to the horses sounded the arrival of the party from the coast.

"They're here." Louise called to her family. Her heart racing in anticipation, she ran out the door to greet them followed by her family, with the exception of eighteen-month-old Andre.

They had not seen their cousins for over two years. Marc had a brother, Philippe, the same age as Louise, and two younger sisters. Besides the carriage carrying Jacques and the women, Marc and his brother each drove a cart filled with bundles of silk thread they had purchased for Pierre in Lyon. Much hugging and kissing ensued, and she sensed herself blushing as Marc brushed her cheeks, holding her close for a second.

At twenty-two, he now had a muscular build and was even more handsome than she remembered. With his black curly hair and eyes the colour of Persian pottery, he resembled his father, an extremely attractive man. However, Uncle Jacques sported a neat goatee and a carefully trimmed moustache, which gave him the distinguished and rather dashing look that Marc had yet to acquire. Standing beside his debonair father, the son still appeared charmingly boyish.

"Come along, Marc and Philippe," Uncle Jacques directed. "Let's help Pierre and Jean Guy moves these bundles into the manufactory. I want to see what they have ready for us to take to England on our next trip. Good news, Pierre. There's an enormous market for fine French silks there now. The English have many weavers but so far they can't meet your quality."

As unnoticed as he was in his own country, Pierre's name was renowned in London as one of France's best silk weavers and designers; and the lustrous materials his manufactory produced were in constant demand.

After attending the Huguenot University in Samaur, he had gone to Tour to apprentice as a silk weaver. However, he inherited the farm from his Grandfather and, since it had been his childhood home; he chose to live and work from there. He built the small manufactory on his land, taking on apprentices from the surrounding area. This enterprise helped the economy of the Huguenot hamlet a great deal. As he told his family, he was thankful the village was a long way from the eyes and ears of the King.

After all the bundles were stored in their allotted corner and Jacques and Marc had inspected the rolls of material ready for trade, Pierre led the party into the orchard. Louise and Catherine followed with Marc's sisters in tow. "Take a look at these," he said to Jacques.

He pointed to a grove of about eighteen young trees with beautiful green, shiny leaves and full of fruit resembling unripe blackberries. His daughters appreciated how proud he was of this special orchard.

"Hmm, they certainly look healthy," Jacques said. "But why mulberry trees, Pierre?"

"My plan is to raise silk worms, so I'll need the leaves to feed them. I know you bid well for the silk thread in Lyon but perhaps I'll be successful in growing my own cocoons right here as well."

"You realize that working with cocoons is difficult. Everything must be exactly right—the temperature, the light and those worms, they constantly need feeding. Do you really consider it worthwhile?"

"I know. It won't be easy. Still I want to try. Times are difficult for Huguenots out here in the country. The Monarchy forbids many occupations to us now, and people in the village have trouble making enough money to survive. Whatever work I can find for them here helps."

"Well, then. May God be with you on this. Everything else you do has been a success. I pray there will be the chance for you to achieve this as well."

"Thank you, *mon ami*. Now let's go in and try my new vintage. Last year was extraordinary for the *pineau*. Smiling at his daughters, he added, "And the women have created a delicious feast—roast lamb, I believe."

As Louise followed them inside, she pondered on her uncle's last words. He didn't sound very positive about Papa's idea, she thought. That's not like Uncle Jacques. I wonder if he knows something, he hasn't told us yet.

The residence Pierre ushered them into was a handsome structure built in the 16th century—long and low, with an upper gallery for the bedrooms and an attached barn for the animals. A staircase led up from the main salon, which was a large room with stone walls and dark wooden beams. Because of the visit, his two oldest girls had polished everything until it shone. The room presented a warm and appealing ambience, with woven tapestries hanging on every wall and small, silk carpets adorning the ancient, flagstone floors.

After the meal—a tasty fish soup; the roast lamb with herbed vegetables; and a mouth-watering, apple *clafoutis*—they settled into the comfortable lounge, and Jacques told them about the visit he and Marc had made to Versailles.

"We became acquainted with a most important person—the man who oversees the *Compagnie des Indes Orientales*—the French East India Company," he explained. "He has been extremely helpful and now he took us to meet King Louis."

"You were presented to the King? At court?" exclaimed Claudine. "You mean you went to Versailles? Is it as wonderful as they say?"

"Magnificent. The palace and grounds cover over nineteen hundred acres. The rooms are spectacular, especially the Hall of Mirrors. You can't believe that room. It is well over two hundred feet long, with mirrors lining both walls. The reflections—they go on forever. The chandeliers alone must have cost a king's ransom. In fact, no amount of money has been spared anywhere in the palace."

"Why were you there, Uncle?" inquired the practical Jean Guy.

"It has to do with the trading company. Because we're assigned to India to help with the building of a French fortress, they invited us to attend a banquet of executives, mostly nobles and merchants. We took gifts to King Louis, of course. Furs we got on our trip to Canada—beaver skins and silver fox. His Majesty was entranced with them and treated us quite royally." He laughed at his own pun.

"What was the food like? Did they feed you well?" inquired Claudine.

"But, of course, my dear." Jacques turned to her still smiling. "In fact, the meal was ludicrous—much more than anyone could eat. And a good deal wasted, I'm afraid. Afterwards we danced. There's a new one at court, which has everyone enchanted. Even the king tried it. They call it the *passé pied,* and since it came from Brittany, it's quite lively. In the candlelight, and with the reflection of the dancers in that great hall—*zut*, it was a sight to behold."

"Oh, I would love to dance at Versailles," exclaimed Louise.

"Well, why not try it right here, *Cherie*? Show her how it's done, Marc. Your mother knows the music. May Marie play it for you?" Jacques asked, turning to Pierre.

He hesitated a moment before replying. He wasn't against dancing. King David danced, he reasoned. However, having been an elder in a Calvinist church, he wasn't happy about emulating what went on in a Catholic court. Still he never could resist the *bonhomie* of his charming cousin and as a rule went along with whatever he asked.

"Of course," he finally said.

Jacques' exquisitely dressed and coiffed wife, Marie, settled herself at the *epinette* and began to play the spirited melody.

Pierre watched the couple as Marc made a leg, bowing in courtly style to his daughter. Eyes twinkling, the young man took her hand and proceeded to twirl her around the floor in a dance rather like a fast minuet. It took only a few seconds for Louise with her natural agility to work out the steps. They danced gracefully together, and the rest of the family appeared delighted by the energy and attractiveness of the good-looking couple.

As they danced, Marc managed to whisper something in Louise's ear. She blushed, nodded, and smiled into his eyes. Pierre's lips tightened with annoyance although he said nothing. When the music ended, Marc handed his cousin, flushed and laughing, back to her chair. With the exception of Pierre, they all clapped enthusiastically.

"*Très bonne, mes enfants,*" exclaimed Jacques, before going on with his account of the court visit. "After the dancing, the ladies retired, and we merchants were ushered into a room with card tables where we were offered the best brandy and played Primero until morning."

"Was the king still there?" Pierre asked.

"No, no. King Louis left after the dancing. He always has many documents to sign, and he goes to bed early, so they tell me. They're saying he has married again."

Jacques chuckled and continued. "It was officers from the company and some of the other merchants," he continued. "We had much to discuss regarding how we can compete against the Dutch and the British in India. They are most successful. We believe France can be, as well. We already do well in the Caribbean. Now we want to break into the oriental markets. After our trip to England, Marc and I will travel to Pondicherry in the southeast of India. I'm to be in charge of some of the construction work there."

"Does the King or these officers realize you aren't Catholic?" Pierre again questioned. Something worried him about Jacques' story—something that wasn't right—he couldn't quite put his finger on it. He had noticed his cousin avoided looking at him.

"No, no. It is my belief that what they don't know won't hurt them. We have an excellent business relationship, which I don't intend to spoil, at this moment. You know how King Louis feels about the Protestants. In fact, he is considering ways to get rid of them. No, none of them needs to know about this matter at all."

Yes, there is definitely something wrong, Pierre thought. He's been trying to keep up his usual *joie de vivre.* However, there's a tension there. I must speak with him alone. Tonight.

Chapter 3

For the first time since their relative's arrival, a lull occurred in the conversation. It was late, so Claudine stood as if to end the evening. She and Louise led Marie and the children upstairs for the night. Jean Guy, Marc, and Philippe excused themselves to go and look at the horses. The two men were left by themselves, with Jacques looking rather downcast.

"You seem so preoccupied tonight, Cousin," Pierre said as they stood to leave the room. "The rumours are true then? Do you envision more trouble ahead for Protestants?"

"Regrettably, yes. I didn't want to say anything in front of your family but the situation has deteriorated. Cousin Guillaume came down himself from Lusignon to inform me of the latest. The dragoons, Pierre..." His voice choked up. "I'm sorry to tell you this—they've killed his mother and father."

Pierre went cold. "Oh, no, Jacques! Uncle Lucien—they've killed him! And Aunt Mathilde! Dear lord. How was it done?"

"They came in the evening—right after dinner—took them out and hanged them. On an oak tree, in front of the cottage. Guillaume watched some of it from the forest. He was on the way to visit them when he heard the soldiers coming, so he hid in the grove. He blames himself for not helping them, of course, but what could he do. There were at least a dozen of them. They burned the house—the animals—everything. What an unspeakable thing for him to witness."

The cousins stood for a moment, tears running down their cheeks.

"A pastor! What harm did Lucien ever do to anyone?" Pierre's voice trembled with emotion. "And dear, old Mathilde! Oh, the poor souls—they are martyrs no doubt. It's too horrific even to think about. What could make King Louis order such a thing?"

"I don't know what to think about the king anymore. Someone must be manipulating him. I can't imagine he would think to do it on his own. Now they say by autumn he is certain to revoke the Edict. Right now, it's ministers. If it goes through, they will surely kill any who don't convert."

"*Fichu,* this is shocking. What should I do?"

"I can keep my ears open. If anything else momentous happens, I'll ride back myself to keep you informed. I believe you must now warn both your family and the towns' people of what may lay ahead, Pierre. It's only fair to let them know."

"Yes, you are right. I have prayed it wouldn't come to this but what will be, will be."

With that, Pierre soberly escorted his cousin upstairs, and they parted for the night.

Louise had not gone to bed after leaving her mother. She listened until the murmuring of voices and other sounds in the house stopped. Then she opened her door and as quietly as possible sped down the stairs. Just as he promised during their dance, Marc waited in the workshop for her. In his hand was one perfect red rose. He held it out to her. "Do you remember? Red roses are for true love, they tell me. This comes from my mother's garden in La Rochelle. I brought it just for you."

Without hesitation, she walked over to him, and taking the beautiful rose, smiled up at him. A cloud of curly black hair framed a face bronzed by the sun. His Persian blue eyes danced with merriment. How handsome he is, she marvelled to herself. But I'm so afraid Papa doesn't approve of him.

Marc was tall for a Frenchman, nearly six feet, so the top of her head came under his chin. He put his arms around her and drew her close. Only once before had he kissed her as a lover. She had relived the moment a thousand times. It happened before he left on his merchant trip. Somehow, he managed to be alone with her in the courtyard garden. He plucked one of the red climbing roses, and carefully tucked it behind her ear. His marvellous eyes softened, as he looked deep into hers.

"I want to go on this journey very much," he had said. "My only sorrow is I won't see you for over two years. You will grow up in the meantime, and you are already so lovely. Will you wait for me to return? You won't go getting betrothed, I hope."

"Of course I'll wait, Marc," she whispered, overcome with emotion and sudden shyness. "I'll think of you every day."

He leaned over then and brushed her lips with his. It had been the most glorious moment of her life.

Now, her heart again beat wildly as he looked at her in the way she remembered. "Did you keep the promise you made two years ago?" he inquired. "Are you still mine?"

"There has only ever been you." She lowered her gaze.

I think I have loved you all my life, Louise," he murmured. "We must marry as soon as your father allows it." His lips brushed her eyes, then her cheeks and came to rest gently on hers, first softly, then firmer as she responded to him.

She could hardly breathe; in her whole life, she never experienced a feeling like this. Although she often dreamt about her first real kiss, it was far more intoxicating and all consuming than she had ever imagined. New sensations surged through her in a way she could not quite comprehend. Yet, she did not want him to stop.

When he finally pulled away from her, his face was serious, his voice husky. "I hoped to speak to Uncle to arrange our betrothal on this visit, my *Cherie*. Now I'm afraid it must wait a little longer. I'm told the trouble between the king and the Huguenots is finally exploding."

"Oh, no. Do you really think it is?"

"I'm afraid so. It's his mistress Marquise de Maintenon—perhaps they *are* married by now. No one is sure. She was a Huguenot who turned Catholic, and now she hates us to the core. They say she is the one who encouraged Louis to revoke the Edict of Nantes. He wasn't particularly religious up 'til now."

"Then Papa was right. We might have to leave."

"If the king retracts it, it means all freedom is gone. No Huguenot will be safe here in France unless he renounces his faith. I'm sure my Father spoke to Uncle Pierre about this tonight, so I don't think now is the right time to break our news to the family. There'll be too many other things to consider for awhile."

"Papa did tell me not to worry about it. He must have some idea of what we should do. Well, I don't mind keeping our secret to myself a little longer, Marc. I won't be seventeen until November, so it's fine if we wait a little. As long as you don't stop loving me."

"That, *Cherie,* is something that will never happen. Now you must get to bed. We'll be leaving early in the morning. With all this uncertainty in France, my father will want to be back in La Rochelle. But I'll return to speak to your father as soon as possible."

Nodding, she hugged him once more, and then stealthily made her way back to the house.

PART II
Choices

"Men at some time are masters of their fates; the fault, dear Brutus, is not in our stars, but in ourselves..."
William Shakespeare

Chapter 4

Pierre sat, head in hands, at his desk in the silent silk manufactory. Most days the room was noisy with the clickity-clack of the looms. As well as his older sons, four young boys from the area served as his apprentices. He kept them all very busy.

However, today was Sunday and, as a strong Calvinist, he allowed no work done on the Sabbath. Instead, he spent part of the morning walking around his productive farm, wistfully surveying all he had created over the past twenty years.

Jean Calvin's philosophy appealed to Pierre's sensitive spirit. By nature a pacifist, he wanted to live his life quietly, creating beauty in both his surroundings and the astonishing tapestries and silken materials his small manufactory produced.

Embedded deep within his heart was the teaching of predestination. It went against this viewpoint to imagine the political climate of the country could change so quickly by the whims of the king, unless it was God's will. But why God wished such a thing, puzzled him.

The idea that they would be forced to leave France, and everything he had laboured for, filled him with a heavy depression. Still not sure what he should do, he deliberated his dilemma, considering his options. So many questions ran through his mind. Was this in fact God's purpose for his family—to leave everything behind? How bad would it be just to sign a meaningless paper? He could pretend to become a Catholic. Whom would it hurt?

It would be a lie, of course. To lie was a major sin, punishable by the fires of hell. And Pierre believed with certainty that his destiny was heaven. No. No, he mused. It is impossible. Not even to save my inheritance can I tell such a lie. We must go. There is no other choice for us.

It was not quite a week since his cousin's visit that brought the dreadful news of the death of their uncle. The following morning, after Pierre told his family, a pall had settled over the gathering. As soon as the bundles of silk intended for London were loaded on the wagons, their guests left for La Rochelle.

Now, an unexpected sound in the courtyard alerted him to the arrival of a horse and rider. He looked out the window and saw Jacques dismounting. After their serious conversation, he had anticipated his cousin's return with more news of the impending trouble, although not this soon. Pierre's heart sank as he viewed his relative's face. Once more, his usually cheerful countenance appeared gloomy.

"You're here early in the day, Jacques. How far have you come?" he queried, as he hurried out to the courtyard.

"About fifteen miles—from my friends in Sugères. I stayed overnight there since I wanted to get here as fast as I could." Jacques tethered his horse near a grassy patch and strode towards the door.

"Well, you must have some refreshment. Claudine has brought out wine and cheese for me. Come, sit at the desk."

"I think what Pharos and I need most is some water. I've been riding him rather hard. But yes, I could use some food as well."

After both man and beast had quenched their thirst and the horse fed some oats, Pierre ushered his cousin into the workshop where a small luncheon was set on the outsized worktable. Jacques sat down and took some bread and a piece of cheese along with a goblet of the *pineau.*

"Now, Jacques, tell me, what news do you bring?" Pierre asked him when they had eaten a little. "You look sorely troubled. It is bad then?"

"Yes, I'm afraid it's even worse than we feared. The dragoons, by King Louis' order, have already moved into some of our friend's homes around La Rochelle. They do whatever they please and the owners have no recourse. They must put them up in beds and feed them. There are already some bands of soldiers headed inland. I'm worried it won't be long until they reach this area."

"*Maudit.* What fiends they are. Then we'll have to leave. I can't give up the faith of my ancestors. For over one hundred years, our family followed the teachings of Jean Calvin. Where should we go? How much time would you say we have?"

"Pierre, you are not only my cousin, you are my dearest friend. I hoped someday Marc and Louise would make us truly brothers. I must tell you— although I'm sure you are aware—I've never been as inclined to religious conviction as you."

He faltered, as if trying to collect his thoughts, which Pierre found strange. Jacques was never at a loss for words. "This is difficult to say to you," he continued, "I—that is, my family—we won't be going with you. Right now, France offers me everything I've wanted in life. I'm much too involved with the trading company to leave, and I've worked too long and hard to get this far. I can't give up my position with this government for an ideal—at least one I don't accept in every respect."

Appalled, Pierre opened his mouth to speak. It was almost a gasp.

"No. No." Jacques put up his hand. "Hear me out. I've never told you this before. Marie and I made our choice a few years back. We both agreed to renounce Calvinism and convert to the Catholic Church. You understand, it was the only way for my sons to go to the university in Paris. We do it without sincerity, of course. No matter, I have no regrets. Now it saves the lives of my family. For all of them, I do this thing."

"Jacques, Jacques, no." Pierre cried in anguish. "I can't believe it. Are you certain of this? Yes, it saves you now; but it may mean your eternal life. Jean Calvin has shown us the Way. Have you gone back on your vow to serve God in truth?"

"That's the other thing, Pierre, I'm not sure the Way of Calvin *is* the absolute Way of Truth. He would have us believe all things are predestined—that we do nothing of our own accord—that some are predestined to be evil and others to be good. *This* idea—to be condemned to a burning hell with no choice in the matter—no, no, Pierre, this I cannot accept."

"The priests also teach hellfire."

"Yes, they do, although at least they give you the chance of repentance. I wouldn't condemn a mad dog to such a fate, and to be predestined to it— you think a loving Creator would do so? Calvin's teaching offers no chance of redemption. Even Grandfather had trouble with this doctrine."

"But—our destiny—we can't change it. It's all foreordained."

"I don't believe so, Pierre. Have you read anything of Shakespeare?"

"Of course not. You know my knowledge of English is limited. What does he have to do with this?"

"He writes an interesting speech in a play about Julius Caesar. Makes one think. Caesar says to Brutus, the man who betrays him, 'Men at some time are masters of their fates; the fault, dear Brutus, is not in our stars, but in ourselves...'"

"And what does that mean, dear cousin?" Pierre asked, with some sarcasm.

"Shakespeare is saying that, for the most part, it's a matter of choice— every choice we make eventually affects our destiny. That's what I believe. Not all Huguenots have believed in predestination, you know. In any case—I've never been a good Huguenot. I expect I'll not be a good Catholic either. Truth be told, I hope only to be a good man."

Pierre was shocked speechless. Forgetting that, less than an hour ago, he also had considered renouncing his faith; he felt his beloved cousin had forsaken everything that was dear to him. He stood up and walked over to the window of the workshop. Looking through the thick glass, he caught sight of the abandoned, medieval chateau standing on a slight rise in the village. Imposing as it was, it had seen much violence in the past. Like a young lad shorn of his curls, Catholics had torn down its beautiful turrets in a religious conflict, and replaced them with an ugly, slanted roof. Now, the villagers called it *Chateau a recadre*, the close-cropped chateau.

He never looked at it without thinking of the father and uncle he could not remember. Their deaths in that battle resulted in his grandfather bringing Jacques and himself up together as brothers. Gesturing towards the chateau, Pierre reminded Jacques. "How can you go back on our faith when so many have died defending it—our own fathers even? Do you also no longer believe in God?" he asked, despair in his voice.

"Of course I believe in God. It's just some of Jean Calvin's teachings, I question. After all, he is only a man. I'm not going to ruin all our lives for something I don't agree with, Pierre, and at present it is most expedient for me to accept the Church."

Pierre shook his head as if still trying to grasp the magnitude of this decision. Jacques' revelation explained what had puzzled him about his cousin's position at court; nevertheless, it had been a tremendous blow. He loved this man better than he loved anyone, other than his wife and children, and now they were to be torn apart, not only physically, but spiritually as well.

"Listen to me," Jacques said. "If you are definite about your choice, I will do anything I can for you and your family. I love them as if they were my own and nothing would please me better than our children should marry some day."

"And Marc? Has he made this decision too? I could never let my daughter marry a Catholic."

"For now, it isn't necessary for him to choose. Since the Church educated him, they assume he inclines towards them. I know he is in love with Louise. On our trip, he spoke of her every day. However, that discussion is for another time. Now we must concentrate on getting you out of this country. There is no doubt, Pierre, if you won't sign, you will die."

Chapter 5

"Have you given any thought to where you would want to go," Jacques asked Pierre.

"I have been considering New France—Canada, as they call it. One hears much about Ville Marie being a flourishing centre. You were there. It's an opportune place for a Frenchman, no?" As Pierre spoke, he returned to the table and refilled their wine goblets from the decanter of *pineau*. He moved like a man in a daze.

"If you are a good Catholic, yes," Jacques replied. "The priests are in charge, and they have barred the Huguenots now. Anyway, it's cold there; cold like you can't even imagine, Pierre. I feel it would be best to take your family to England. King Charles has promised sanctuary to the followers of Calvin. I'm often in London, so I would be able to see you. Trust me, it would be easier and much safer to get your family there."

"I've heard it's a large city and costly. What would I do for money? Those who've already left took little with them. We aren't even allowed to sell our homes anymore."

"True, but your silks are already well-known in London. I'm sure your business would flourish there. I have an excellent agent in the city; a goldsmith by the name of Hypolite Thibault—descended from a Huguenot family. Paul, they call him in England. I've banked much of my gold with him. He's a most trustworthy man with a reputation for honesty. I'd be happy to exchange a fair sum in London for you, in return for your farm. Is it still in Grandfather's name?"

"Yes, with all the problems we Huguenots were having, I never enquired about changing the title legally. I didn't want to call attention to myself. What in the world, would you do with this farm, Jacques? I thought you fancied the travelling life."

"I'll give it to Philippe. It will be his inheritance. He loves it here, and since we named him after Grandfather, there should be no title problems. I'll give you a letter of credit for Hypolite—or Paul, I should say. I know you'll like him."

Pierre's mind raced with all these new ideas. He was a prudent man who generally needed to mull everything over. However, he knew time was running out, so he listened as his cousin continued.

"In the meantime, I must get back to La Rochelle. I'll arrange with a captain that I trust, to take you across the Channel in his merchant boat. Of course, you'll need your looms when you get to London. For that, I'll put them on board the packet boat with this batch of silk. Since I'm also taking cognac, perhaps they can go in some empty wine barrels. That won't look suspicious."

"But the English," Pierre spoke, continuing his own line of thought. "Their ways are so different from ours. They don't much like the French, and I know only a little of their language. Do you actually think we can make a life among them?"

"I do. There are many Huguenots in England. In fact, in the area known as Spitalfields, you will hear only French spoken, and they hold meetings freely. You'll be able to worship as you wish there."

He took another swallow of his wine.

"Really, Pierre, it will be much less of an ordeal for your family to go there. If you're determined to do this, then it must be soon. I would say no more than a week or two at the most. The trouble escalates by the day, and once King Louis signs the new Edict, the sky will fall on those who insist on remaining in the faith."

"And you—you're positive you'll be safe here?"

"Believe me, I'll be fine. I'm a card player, and good at 'bluff.' No, they'll never doubt my sincerity. In the meantime, I'll not forsake you, cousin. I'll see that you get to England unharmed. Now, go and tell your family what the plan is, and I'll return to La Rochelle to work out the arrangements." He stood and turned towards the door.

"It's a long, hard ride back," Pierre commented, still somewhat in shock. "You should at least stay for a meal and rest overnight."

"No. I'll go back to my friend's chateau for the night. I wish to speak with them again in any case. You had better be ready to leave by next week. I'll come back then with a load of wine barrels. For the time being, say nothing of this plan to anyone else. It's difficult to know whom to trust anymore." He swept on his large hat. "Take care, Pierre. God be with you."

The cousins embraced and, after watching Jacques depart, Pierre turned towards the house with a forlorn expression. Jacques' revelations had torn his whole world apart, and now somehow he must tell his wife and children.

When the family gathered later in the day for their evening meal, Pierre told them about Jacques' short visit. He described the horrors that lay ahead for any who refused to renounce their faith, and explained some of the details of his cousin's plan to get them out of France.

"It will be a dangerous undertaking," he added. "However, it will be even worse if we stay here and refuse to convert."

"Then, we'll have to go," Claudine agreed. "I could never abandon my faith in Jean Calvin's teachings to please the king, or to save my life for that matter."

"Will Uncle Jacques' family come with us?" Jean Guy inquired.

"No, they want to stay in France. Nevertheless, they'll be safe, as they have no compunction about abjuring the faith. It is sad they're not true believers, although I don't think they believe in the Catholic faith much either. Jacques has his own strange thoughts on religion. Mainly he likes the position he holds in this country. Perhaps it's his destiny. However..."

"Papa," Jean Guy interjected, cutting off his loquacious father, "how will we live?"

"The silk looms are essential. I must have a way to support us, so we'll take them with us. Other than that, we can each take a few items of clothing."

"Oh, Pierre," Claudine replied, with a sob in her voice. "I must take our wonderful Baroque clock. It was a wedding gift from my parents. Could we take it? I'll bring only the clothing I'm wearing." Two large tears rolled down her cheeks.

Pierre looked at his lovely wife. Should he deny her such a small favour? He appreciated how much she loved her delightful home and her existence in this pleasant little village. No doubt, she would find it difficult to adjust to any other way of life. He had been mentally preparing for it for some time and still it wasn't easy to accept they must leave behind everything they loved.

"Don't worry, my darling. I think we can manage the clock," he said. He turned to the others. "And each of you pick one thing you love the most to take with you. Uncle Jacques is bringing us a load of wine casks. We'll take the looms apart and place them inside the barrels. I'm sure there'll be room for a few small items."

Louise had been strangely silent during the discussion. Now she spoke up. "I don't want to leave France, Papa. I'd like to stay with Aunt Marie in La Rochelle until Marc comes back. I'll be old enough for us to be married by then."

Everyone around the table looked at her in amazement. Pierre was the first to speak. He felt his face flame with anger. "What are you saying, girl? Stay here in France with a Catholic family. Never!" He banged the table with his fist.

"And what makes you think you're going to marry Marc?" he roared. "He's hasn't spoken to me about this, and I would certainly set him straight if he did. You will marry whomever I say, and it's not going to be the son of a Papist—even if he isn't a sincere one."

No one at the table dared to speak, while Louise, who had gone pale, sobbed quietly—her shoulders shaking in distress. Four-year-old Jeanette began to wail. The children had rarely seen him this angry, and he realized his outburst had shocked them all. His hand trembled as he put his fork down and took a sip from his goblet of pineau. He felt somewhat ashamed.

What is wrong with me, he wondered? I'm distraught about this whole situation, but I shouldn't be taking it out on Louise like this. It's only that I love her, and I don't want to lose her to a man I know isn't right for her.

When he spoke again, it was in a softer tone. "You may leave the table now, daughter. I think you should go to your room and think about this conversation. Your mother will speak to you later."

Turning back to the others, he continued. "Jacques is taking over the farm, and in return, he'll give me a note entitling me to a sum of money in London. We should be thankful, my dears. We'll be a lot better off than many who have fled France with only the clothes on their back."

"Yes," Claudine said, her voice strained. "Since you warned them, some of the villagers have already gone and left everything behind. Suzette leaves in a few days. She told me, they can take nothing with them."

Pierre shook his head sorrowfully, "We have a lot to consider. This is a difficult time for all of us. Right now, I believe we should have some Bible reading and a prayer. Beyond doubt, we must have God's help to strengthen our faith, and to give us the courage we need to escape this country alive."

So they sat and listened once more to the story of Moses leading the Israelites out of Egypt; and, as Pierre read the familiar words, he reflected on the dangerous journey on which they too were about to embark.

Chapter 6

In the last week of July, the day came when Pierre realized they could no longer delay; they must leave their village forever. Jacques and Marc arrived with two wagons—one loaded with wine barrels—the other a hay carrier. They reported the horrifying events happening throughout the country, and Jacques cautioned that the tyrants were quickly approaching their pleasant valley.

"These soldiers move into peoples' houses without permission," he explained. "And then the persecution begins. In some cases, they beat them with clubs, and then burn everything combustible in the fireplace, until it chokes them with smoke. Others, they stab all over their bodies with pins; or they pull out their hair and whiskers by the roots."

"*Maudit*, do these bullies have no mercy for their fellow man?" Pierre exclaimed.

"No, my cousin, there's no end to what they inflict on people to get them to renounce their faith. Even worse, they are now raping Huguenot women."

As well, around La Rochelle, the dragoons had hanged several more Protestant ministers who refused to leave the country. On the other hand, they killed regular parishioners if they caught them trying to flee. The only way a Huguenot could be protected was to sign they would convert. Even then, they were under suspicion, and their actions watched for months.

"Cousin Guillaume and his family are on their way to Geneva," Jacques continued. "He came to see me again before he left. He says there are people along the way who will help him. When they reach safety, he'll send Marie a letter. All we can do now is to pray for them."

These stories horrified Pierre. With heavy hearts, he and his family went about packing. They took the looms and the clock apart and carefully placed the pieces inside the wine barrels. On the second cart, they piled fresh-cut hay.

"You will all have to lie at the bottom of the cart and be covered over by the hay," Jacques explained to Claudine and the children. "Men alone probably wouldn't have any trouble. However, they would show no mercy if they capture a whole family of suspected Huguenots driving to the coast. I'm sorry it won't be comfortable, but it's the only way."

"How far will we go like this, Jacques?" Pierre asked.

"We'll travel most of the night until we reach Sugères. My friends, the *Compte et Contesse de Colbert* own a chateau there, and they have said you can stay for the day. They are Catholics. But they don't agree with what the dragoons do to our people, so they've offered to help. It's a brave thing they do."

"You're sure you trust them? We wouldn't be walking into a trap, would we?"

"Definitely not. I've represented their cognac in cities all over Europe and handled thousands of francs for them. They've been my good friends for many years, and I trust them—both with my life and yours."

"They take a huge chance then, no?"

"Yes, they do. If discovered, they'd be tried for treason—not just hung—drawn and quartered, as well. I suppose that could be my fate too," he added with a grim smile.

"Oh Jacques, I'm afraid we ask too much of you," Claudine exclaimed.

"Not at all. I'm used to danger. It's what I do. Now perhaps you two would like to look around once more before you start. I'll leave first, and you and Marc follow in about an hour. It's too perilous for us to travel close together, so I'll meet you at the chateau. May God be with us all, this night!"

He snapped the reins and started the horses hauling the load of wine barrels towards Sugères.

"Pierre. To leave all this. I do feel like my heart will break." Pierre and Claudine walked hand in hand through the house, and into the workshop, taking one last look at the lovely home they had created together.

"Claudine, dearest, when we married, I made a solemn promise to your father that I would always take care of you, and I pray I never go back on it. Thanks to Jacques, we'll be fine in London. It will be a new way of life, of course, but our children will be with us, and we can do this thing. Please, my dear, try not to be so unhappy. For their sake."

"Yes, you're right." She sighed, and then smiled up at him. "And if it's God's will for us, it must turn out for the best."

"That's the right attitude." He kissed her then, and held her for a moment before guiding her out the door. "And now we'll begin our journey and leave it in His hands."

They returned to the wagon where Louise, Jean Guy, and the children had snuggled under the hay. "Are you all right, *mes enfants*?" Pierre asked.

"Jeanette is with me. We're fine. It rather prickles but we can breathe," Louise answered in a muffled voice. She had scarcely spoken to him since the evening he sent her to her room, although she had been exceptionally helpful to her mother and never again mentioned not leaving France.

I'm sure the idea of being in La Rochelle with Marc for a time makes it bearable for her, he thought. It worries me though. I'll have to watch that situation.

"I'm fine," said Jean Guy, obviously in excellent spirits. "I'm going to tell stories to the twins. It will keep their minds off their discomfort." He dug himself in as close to them as possible.

Pierre smiled to himself as he mused. At least he will be all right. I'm sure he sees this as a great adventure. He has always looked up to Marc and now, I'm sure he feels quite grown up experiencing this himself. He's far more like his uncle and his cousin than he is like me. I'm glad the twins are young enough to be adaptable about where they live, and I suppose Baby Andre will never even remember this place.

Claudine, with tears still running down her cheeks, took one last glance at the house. Then, she lay down on the cart beside her youngest child. The little lad had fallen asleep on his blanket. Pierre piled extra hay over them all, so it looked like a regular load.

A sound on the bridge made him look towards the river. It was Marc's brother arriving in another cart. With him were the middle-aged couple, who would look after the farm, while he finished his university training. Pierre gave Philippe last-minute instructions about the livestock, and handed over the keys.

"Don't worry, Uncle," his nephew said. "I've always loved this place. We'll take good care of it and, if things ever change, you can come back."

"*Merci*, my boy. *Au revoir*," he replied, embracing the younger man. He smiled bravely, although in his heart, he knew he would never see this farm or the village again. Fighting off his own tears, he clambered up on the seat beside Marc, and they started towards the coast.

The first part of the night went by without any danger. Once or twice, Pierre thought he heard the muffled sounds of travellers further along the road. However, at no point did they catch a glimpse of anyone walking. "Most likely, they hide in the forest whenever someone comes by," he remarked.

Eventually it occurred to him that the children might be ready for their picnic supper and asked Marc to stop. They turned off the track into a barely discernible break in the trees. There, in a little clearing, another group had finished their meal and looked ready to leave. Pierre recognized them as fellow Huguenots from a neighbouring village. He noted they carried little with them. The father came over to the wagon and helped Pierre's family out from the layer of hay.

"Thank you, brother," Pierre said. "You're moving on tonight? Where are you heading?"

"We've been resting here for awhile," the Huguenot said. "It's best to travel at night. We're going to a secret beach not far from Aiguillon. We must be there by the middle of August to meet an English ship. They've promised to take any Huguenot, who makes it in time, to the Americas—to a settlement called South Carolina. It's our only hope. We can't give up our beliefs."

Pierre's eyes again filled with tears. What faith these people have to leave everything behind and walk all the way to the coast, he mused. Here am I, feeling sorry for myself and I have so much support from Jacques and Marc.

He gripped the father's shoulder. "May God be with you, my brother. We both have a long and dangerous journey ahead of us. I'm sure He has a plan for us all in allowing this, perhaps to spread His message abroad. I pray He will keep us safe."

Chapter 7

Ever since, they left the farm, Pierre had felt the tension between himself and Marc. It was almost palpable. The younger man answered some of his questions about the Chateau Colbert, but for the most part remained silent. Even in the clearing, he stayed by himself near the wagon, as Pierre kept Louise busy handing out the food.

Now, as they progressed through the moonlit night, the forest sounds quieted, and even the small hoots of the owls stilled. Pierre, agitated as he was, could no longer hold back his concerns about the couple's plan. Speaking softly to keep his family from hearing the conversation, he said, "Louise tells me, she's going to marry you. Did you put that idea into her head, Marc?"

Marc started in surprise. He turned to Pierre. "I love her, Uncle Pierre. I always have. I think she loves me, as well. I meant to speak to you on this visit; but so much has happened that I thought I'd wait until we reached La Rochelle."

"I don't like the idea of this going on behind my back. You might as well know I will never sanction a marriage of my daughter to a Catholic."

"I haven't revoked our Huguenot faith. It's true that the monks gave me most of my education, but they've never asked me to sign anything. Perhaps they take my choice for granted. I don't know."

"Nevertheless, I want you to say nothing more to Louise about this. She's still young, and I've no desire to discuss any marriage plans for her until we are safe in England. Do you understand me?"

"I understand what you say. I don't understand why, though. My parents expect it. Our families have always been so close; it never occurred to me, you would feel this way. However, since you do, I'll keep out of her way for the time being." With that, he snapped the whip in an effort to hurry the team through the woods, discouraging further conversation.

Soon the forested areas of pine and oak vanished, and they passed mile after mile of healthy looking vineyards. A silver grey dawn was breaking in the east, and Pierre could make out clusters of luscious, dark purple grapes hanging low on the rows of leafy plants.

"It's going to be a fine harvest," was his wistful comment, thinking of the delicious *pineau* he made each year. Once more, his heart sank as he thought of how much he would miss the peace and security of the fabulous life he and Claudine had made together.

❦

Around six in the morning, they arrived at the chateau of the *Comte and Comtesse de Colbert*. Marc drove the hay wagon straight into a large barn attached to the immense chateau, where Jacques and the couple came out to greet them. The aroma of hot chocolate and warm croissants wafted in from the adjoining winery. Pierre and Marc cleared the hay from the wagon and, stiffly, they all crawled out.

"Welcome to Chateau du Colbert. I am *Aimée* and my husband is *Édouard*. We thought you would appreciate a small breakfast. It's right through here." The *Comtesse* smiled at them as she guided them into the spotlessly clean distilling room.

"After you eat and wash up a little, it's necessary you stay inside the chateau," explained her husband. "If the harvesters see you, they may be suspicious and say something to the dragoons. My own servants are completely loyal and do whatever I say, so I'm not worried about them. You will be quite safe here until tonight. I'm sure the local authorities would never suspect me of such a terrible crime."

"We realize the risk you are taking, my lord. We hardly know how to thank you," Pierre said.

"Well, I'm not happy with my Catholic brethren right now. I can't understand the way King Louis reasons at all. It's distressing to think that so much talent must leave this country. There will be sad consequences of this in our future, I fear."

"I agree," Jacques spoke up. Then turning to Pierre, he said, "Try to get a little sleep, if you can. I'll be back later this afternoon. With the wagon, it's about a four hour drive to La Rochelle, and I'm afraid this evening will be somewhat more dangerous than what we've faced so far."

"You think we'll run into the soldiers on the way to La Rochelle then?" Pierre asked.

"Most of the dragoons are between here and the seaport, so, yes, I'm afraid we will. I must think of a plan to smuggle you into the city without alerting them. Taking a wagonload of hay into the city would certainly arouse suspicion. They're wary of large numbers travelling together. We'll have to keep in two groups. In the meantime, you'll be safe enough here until tonight when I return."

After saying *adieu* to the *Comte* and gallantly kissing the hand of the *Comtesse*, Jacques and Marc mounted their waiting horses and galloped off towards the coast. Pierre watched until they rode out of sight, and then trailed after his family toward the chateau.

☙❧

On the way to Sugères, Marc had answered Pierre's questions about the Colbert estate. The family had owned it for over four centuries, and it was vast. Over fifteen hundred acres of vineyards, fields, and forest surrounded the main buildings. The chateau itself was a handsome residence rebuilt in the fifteenth century, after having suffered a great deal of damage during the Hundred Years War. A moat, left over from its medieval heritage, still surrounded it.

As Pierre looked around, he noted that the chateau and the attached buildings formed a large L-shaped structure, with the main entrance facing into the square. From the barn, they followed the *Comte* and *Comtesse* across the wide courtyard and in through a doorway, surrounded by four Ionic columns, inlaid with marble.

Inside, to the right of the entrance hall, he observed the *grande salon,* an enormous space with a massive marble fireplace. The room was opulent with magnificent wool carpets strewn about a floor of inlaid wood. With his artist's eye, he particularly noticed the walls coverings—four huge, richly coloured tapestries featuring hunting scenes, which rose almost from floor to ceiling. Knowing the price his own, much smaller tapestries commanded, the size of them astounded him. They were approximately twenty feet high and about two-thirds as wide. Surely, the group would cost as much as his earnings for half a year, he thought.

The *Comptesse* ushered them up the majestic staircase to a suite of three adjoining rooms in one wing of the house. In the master room, stood a stately King Louis style bed made of warm oak with curved boards at the foot and head. On either side of this room, doors led to lesser quarters, with smaller beds, where the young people could sleep. Andre, now clean, dry, and fed, settled down to his nap in the main bedroom.

Aimée showed Pierre a slightly darkened brick in the main bedroom fireplace. "Press there," she instructed him. As he pressed it, the wall of books slowly began to turn allowing an opening the width of a large man. Behind it was a room with enough space for about ten people.

She smiled at him as she explained, "This part of the house was left over from the One Hundred Year War. I imagine the ancestors hid here many times. If you hear any commotion downstairs, you should all go in there. Just pull that cord inside to make the bookcase return to its position. Then do the same to get out."

Pierre reached in and tugged on the cord; the door swung shut. "That's astonishing," he exclaimed. "Your ancestors were well prepared."

"Yes. Well, it was how they survived, I imagine. We don't expect any trouble today, but it's best to be ready. Jacques asked that dinner be early tonight. The maid will come and wake you about an hour before to give you time to freshen up. Now have a good rest, and I'm sure all will be well."

After she left the room, Pierre walked to a window overlooking the courtyard. He placed a chair where he could look out at the scene below. Speaking quietly, he cautioned, "As much as Jacques trusts these people, I feel we should be on guard. We'll alternate sleeping, I think." He turned to Jean Guy, "Get some rest now, *mon fils*. I'll take the first watch and wake you in about three hours. After you, your mother can take a turn. Jacques may be right about them. Nevertheless, I'm taking no chances."

Chapter 8

Sugères, France, August 1, 1685

As he had promised, Jacques returned with Marc just before the informal meal was served. The two men gladly accepted the Colbert's invitation to join them. Jacques was now dressed in the height of fashion. He wore a stylish royal blue velvet jacket with a ruffled shirt and silk breeches. His pointed shoes had high heels and his legs were covered to his knees by silk stockings. Over his curly black hair, he wore a powered, white wig in the style of King Louis's court. While they dined in the elegant, frescoed room, he explained his plan for the rest of the journey.

"I have our travelling carriage, and I'll take Claudine and the children with me. It will look as though I'm driving my family home from a visit here, which I've often done. I've brought the proper clothing for them to wear, so I see no problem there."

He turned to his cousin. "Pierre, Marc will take you and Jean Guy in the wagon with the wine barrels. It won't be unusual coming from this chateau with wine and cognac—all the barrels have the Chateau Colbert crest on them."

"So the dragoons are on the lookout then?" Pierre asked.

"Yes, they don't let much get past them, but they know I do business out here. Marc will tell them, he's transporting wine to my warehouse in La Rochelle. That's nothing new, and the absolute truth. Dressed as peasants the way you are, they'll take you two for workers."

He turned to Marc with further instructions. "You'll do all the talking. You have my papers. Explain you are my son and these are workers from the chateau. They'll know of the Colberts, and coming from here, Huguenots would be the last thing they would suspect. So I pray this will work. But you should leave right away to reach the warehouse before dark. We'll follow an hour or so after dinner."

As soon as they finished eating, the Garneau men with the exception of Claude left the table and went out to the yard. Jacques watched as they clambered aboard the wagonload of wine barrels.

"I think we've covered everything," he said to his son. "Watch yourselves. I pray we all arrive safely in La Rochelle."

With a nod, Marc started in a northwesterly direction towards the seaport city. As Jacques watched them depart, the late afternoon sun disappeared behind menacing, black clouds. He found himself shiver as the western horizon turned a strange, blood red.

It's a good thing I'm not a superstitious man, he thought. If I didn't know better, I'd certainly think that was an ill omen.

Before long, Jacques returned alone to the dining room with the four stylish cloaks and bonnets he had brought from home for Claudine and the girls. The bonnets hid their faces quite well. He also gave young Claude a pair of breeches, along with a silk jacket and ruffled shirt to wear. Dressed in the new outfits, they looked like one of the typical, affluent families who often visited the Chateau. Seeing them, he felt confident he could get away with this part of his plan. Around La Rochelle, the citizens recognized him as a prominent merchant, and it was unlikely he would arouse suspicion. He was grateful the Colberts were helping them, well known as they were in the Sugères area as faithful Catholics.

It's beneficial for Pierre to realize that, in spite of the king, individual Catholics are not bad people, he mused.

He was more concerned about Marc and Pierre, and the load of barrels. He had put a few genuine barrels of wine on the outside of the wagons in case the dragoons wanted to test them. Friends told him the soldiers would sometimes run their swords through to see if anyone were hiding inside. More than one Huguenot had died in this manner. Even, though, it was only the looms, it worried him. If discovered, it would be suspicious and put them at risk. Under his breath, he mumbled, "I'll certainly be glad when this night is over."

"*Sacre bleu*" Jacques muttered to himself. "What is that?"

He had been driving for a couple of hours when he stopped the carriage. Ahead in the filtered moonlight, he could see a strange, grotesque-looking tree. Two odd-shaped shadows hung limply from a low branch. A shiver ran down his spine, and he broke out in a cold sweat.

"*Allez droite*" he called to the horses, pulling on the reins, so they turned into a small clearing from which his passengers couldn't see the trees.

He opened the coach door and asked Claudine to come out for a moment. When she had stepped down and closed the door, he spoke to her. "Claudine, there's something ahead on the road I don't want the children to see. It would frighten them terribly. So somehow, can you get them to keep their eyes closed until I tell you? His tone was urgent. "You too. I mean it, dear. Whatever happens—do not look out the window."

Claudine got back in the carriage, and Jacques drove past the tree. When he was about two hundred feet beyond it, he stopped and walked back. It was as he had dreaded. Two people hung like rag dolls from the lowest branch of an old, bent oak tree. A man and a woman, middle- aged and dressed in dark, peasant clothing. He breathed a sigh of relief. For a few terrifying minutes, he had feared it was Marc and Pierre.

He looked at their blackened faces. So horrified, he spoke aloud, "*Fichu!* Another Huguenot clergyman, no doubt. How many of them must they kill? What a horrendous sight. No wonder Guilliame was in such a hurry to leave the country."

The acrid smell of smoke assailed his nostrils. Back from the track, in a little clearing in the fir woods, the embers of what had been a modest farmhouse smouldered. Some of the outer buildings were still ablaze. The crackling of burning wood broke the silence, and there was the smell of roasting meat and the frenzied squawking of dying chickens.

"*Maudit,* this was just done. They won't be far away. Pierre's family is getting out of here barely in time. The terror has definitely reached us."

Shaking his head in distress, he stumbled back to the coach. With trembling hands, he drove on for about fifteen minutes. In his travels, he had often witnessed violence. Nevertheless, this scene—such a horrible murder of innocent people—had stunned him more than he would expect. When they were quite far away from the farm, he stopped again. He motioned Claudine to climb out of the coach once more. Then as gently as he could, he told her what he had seen.

"I hope none of the children looked?" he queried.

"No, I—I expected the worst. I had them play a game of remembering our house. They all had their eyes shut trying to picture their favourite room." Her voice was shaky, as if she could cry; however, she smiled bravely at him.

"Very clever, dear girl." He patted her arm. "No doubt we'll meet the men who did this. However, I'll do the talking. They'll want to look inside the coach, but don't worry. We'll be fine. Just warn the children to say nothing."

Again, Claudine climbed into the coach with the children, while he once more jumped up on top. He flicked the whip, and they started forward.

It wasn't long before he saw a band of soldiers riding towards them. He had been all over the world and, in New France, had come face-to-face with the natives they called Indians. He had never been a coward. All the same, fear gripped his heart as they came nearer.

Knowing now, what they are like, I'm sure they would have no pity, he thought.

"Declare you," the leader called to him.

"*Bonsoir, Capitaine,*" he replied. "I am Jacques Phillipe Garneau, merchant of La Rochelle.

"From the *Maison du Garneau* in La Rochelle, you say? Do you always do your own driving, monsieur?" The man appeared suspicious.

Jacques hesitated before answering. The question took him by surprise. The family employed a coachman for the times when he was gone, but he was too much the adventurer to allow someone else to take the reins while he sat inside a coach. It had not occurred to him this might arouse their doubts.

His quick mind came up with the answer. "Our coachman took ill only this morning, *Capitaine*. I didn't want to disappoint my family. They've been looking forward to this visit."

"So who *do* you have in the carriage, Monsieur?"

"Madame Garneau and the children."

"We'd better check this out, Sergeant," the captain ordered, turning to one of his men. "Get them out of there."

The soldier opened the carriage door and with his musket pointed at them, he motioned them out. Louise came out last, and he grabbed her roughly. "Now here's a pretty piece of baggage, *mon Capitaine*," the man said, glancing at his superior with an evil smile. "Perhaps we need to see her credentials, *non?*"

Jacques spoke up. "I think I should inform you, I am in the service of the King's French East India Company. And a sworn Catholic," he added.

"This is your family then, monsieur?" the leader asked.

"*Mais oui*. We have been enjoying the evening with our friends, the *Compte et Contesse de Colbert*." The thought ran through his mind—at least most of it is true. He had a hatred of liars. "We are now on our way home to La Rochelle."

"And you're with the *Compagnies des Indies Orientales*, you say?"

"That is correct."

"Well, Marcel. We mustn't molest the family of a loyal servant of the king. Let them get back in the carriage." Turning back to Jacques, he stated. "This isn't a good time to be travelling around the country, *Monsieur Garneau*. I would suggest you keep your wife and children at home from now on."

"I understand, sir. I'll keep it in mind although I, myself, have business out here often. By the way, I sent a wagonload of wine barrels ahead of me by a few hours. My son was driving the load. Have you seen anything of it?"

"*Oui, Monsieur.* We stopped him, and he showed us the papers he carried. He did tell us, you would be coming along later. However, I had to be sure of you. We haven't harmed him. I'm sorry to have bothered you, but those Huguenots are everywhere trying to flee our glorious country. My men and I can't be too careful. You're free to go now with the King's blessings."

Inwardly, Jacques breathed a sigh of relief. His clothing was damp with sweat. His fear was not for himself, as he had never flinched from danger; however, he cared a great deal for Pierre's family and their lives had been in his hands.

"We'll be on our way then, Captain. *Bon soir et merci.*"

Again, he pulled on the reins and the horses began the final lap of the trip to La Rochelle.

⋈

That evening, in the safety of his mansion, Jacques' discussed the events of the day with Pierre. Over their glasses of cognac, he nodded as his cousin praised the Colberts for their assistance.

"I'm amazed Catholics would do such a thing for us. Risk their lives like that," Pierre stated.

"Yes," he replied. "The Colberts are special people. I've represented their cognacs in every large city, in Europe. Even though, they believed me to be a Huguenot, they trusted me with all their financial affairs in these transactions. I'm glad you have discovered there are decent people in the Catholic Church, Pierre."

"To be honest, it surprised me."

"I've discovered there are upright and honest people in every faith—Protestant, Catholic, or Jew. Even amongst the heathen, I've met, for that matter. Sadly, the problems are most often with the leaders. Sometimes, they aren't seeking truth at all, just looking for power. That's what corrupts—power and greed—even in religion. Well, it's nothing you and I will see resolved in our time."

He poured them each another glass of cognac. The fact his cousin, who believed wholeheartedly in moderation, took a second glass of distilled spirits gave Jacques some idea of his state of mind. Pierre, too, had viewed the old oak tree with its grotesque burden.

"My main concern now is to move your silks to London and get your gold account established with Paul Thibault," he continued. "Once we load everything on our merchant vessel, that's where Marc and I will go. I estimate another week. While we're over there, we'll arrange with various people we know along your route. No ship's captain would dare to take you all the way to London right now, Pierre, and that's God's truth."

"No? How will we get there then?"

"You'll slip in via a closer port—likely Plymouth. It will take a little planning, so Marc and I'll be gone about two weeks. Keep a low profile here in the city but, please, treat this as your own home. And, Pierre, keep praying that, with God's help, we can get you safely to England."

Chapter 9

La Rochelle
August 1685 (Gregorian Calendar)

The medieval port of La Rochelle was lovely with its cobbled streets, high stone-wall, and ancient buildings. In the more than half century since the siege, it had recovered much of its grandeur, although both the wall and the large, round towers, built in the last century, showed signs of the battles they had seen. However, no matter how hard Louise tried, she wasn't happy there. Compared to her peaceful village, it was noisy and hectic, with people bustling along the streets; peddlers shouting out their wares; and coaches dashing here and there.

Her mother cried every day; and her father, usually so placid and content, had little to keep himself occupied, so he was often in a surly mood. Louise had spent her entire life at the lovely, old, family farm, and now she yearned to be there—riding free through the forest on her favourite horse, or sitting dreaming on her rock by the slow-moving river.

To add to her discontent, Marc kept so busy he had no time to spend with her. She saw him only during the family dinner. Finally, he and Uncle Jacques sailed off to England taking the bundles of silk they would market there. They also took the looms, still hidden in wine barrels, which they would leave in Jacques' London warehouse until Pierre could claim them.

It was only her fascination with the ocean that made life tolerable. Each afternoon, when she finished her lessons and the few chores Aunt Marie assigned her, she donned a modest, unadorned dress and wound her way to the city gate. There, she slipped out to the harbour, walking through the entrance and beyond the massive towers. The guards were now familiar with her as a maid belonging to the *Maison du Garneau*, and since Jacques was a well-known and honourable merchant of the city, they dared not bother her.

Venturing further west, past the old lantern tower marking the edge of the city, she reached a point where the marshes converged with a beautiful sand beach. There she stripped off her boots and let the cool softness ooze beneath her feet. A little of her homesickness ebbed away, and she accepted the fact she should be obliged to her aunt and uncle. They had done so much for her family, who were, consequently, in a far better position than most of the Huguenots fleeing France.

It was late Wednesday afternoon in the third week of August when Louise once again headed through the city gate. She was almost at the harbour when someone put a hand on her shoulder. It startled her out of her reverie and frightened her for a moment. Shocked, she turned and confronted the man. It was her cousin.

"Marc! *Zut!* I thought it was a dragoon. I'm so glad you are back."

"Are you, *Cherie?* I'm so happy to hear you say that. I've longed to talk to you again. The parents, though, they have made it difficult, *non?*"

"Yes, especially Papa. He's still unhappy with your father's choice to revoke his faith, and now he's not certain about you."

They reached the harbour and found a stone stairwell close to one of the large towers where they could sit without being seen. It was nearing the dinner hour and, with the exception of some officials, most everyone had left the area for their evening meal.

Marc put his arms around her and drew her close. Then his lips found hers and, for a few moments, they were lost in their longing for each other. Finally, he drew away and took both her hands in his. "Louise, I have told how much I love you. I'd hoped we would at least be betrothed by now. Things are changing so fast, and with you going to England, I'm afraid we might lose each other. You do love me, don't you? You still want to marry me, *non?*"

"Yes, Marc," she said, with a tremor in her voice. "I love you with all my heart. Must we wait for your return from this trip? You will be gone so long. Can't we arrange something before you leave? Then at least I could stay here with your mother."

"We go too soon, I'm afraid. The ship leaves in mid-September. Already we load the cognac to take to the colony in India. And to marry here in France, it must be by a priest. You'd have to become a Catholic. We both know your father would never permit such a thing, and I don't think you want it either, do you?"

"No, you're right. I can never be a Catholic. But what about you? Have you made a decision? I mean about religion," she persisted.

"With regard to faith, I am like my father." Marc looked up at the sky where Arcturus, one of the brightest stars, had already begun to show itself. "I really don't care what religion claims me. I have read the Bible from cover to cover, and for a certainty, I believe in God. Strangely, though, it is in the middle of the ocean I feel the closest to Him. It's easy to find faith on the high seas."

"In what way?"

"Sometimes I sit alone on the deck at night and look up into the sky. You would not believe the stars when it is all dark on the sea. It makes me feel so small I know there must be a creator. It's only that I haven't found the right way to worship Him yet."

Suddenly he smiled down at her, dimples playing at the corners of his mouth, his dark blue eyes, twinkling. "And also, I'm afraid I'm much more sinner than saint."

"Well, I don't think so," she said, smiling back at him. "Of course, what Papa believes is another matter."

He laughed, and then quickly turned serious. "About us—your father and I discussed it on the way to the chateau. He didn't exactly say 'never;' however, he definitely won't let you marry until you're settled in London."

"Did you ask him if we could at least be betrothed?"

"I didn't press the subject. We both got rather heated, I'm afraid." He sighed audibly. "I'll have another talk with him in the morning. I don't see why we can't announce our engagement to the family. Anyhow, I'll come to London as soon as I'm back from the orient. I'm sure I can get work there. We certainly can't live in France as Huguenots."

"Well, I think I could put up with England if you were there." She again smiled into his eyes.

"Then London is where I shall have to be. Now, I think you should go back to the house, Louise. You shouldn't be wandering about alone down here. The sailors frequent the taverns and they can get dangerous when they've been drinking. I'll walk with you as far as the city gate, but I have to come back as I have business at our warehouse."

When they reached the large arch that opened to the city, he suddenly stopped walking and looked down at her, eyes bright as if an idea occurred to him. "Could you get away tomorrow early do you think?" he asked. "I'll get the little gig and take you to the ocean proper. There's a beautiful beach where we can look across to Ile de Re, and I'll tell you all about the siege of La Rochelle. It's an interesting story that involves our great grandfather. I'll have the cook pack some food for a picnic. It will be just like when we were children. We always had such good times together."

"Oh, Marc, yes. I'd love to do that. Shall I meet you here then? What time?"

"I'll be here at ten. Don't worry if it's difficult to get away. I'll wait for you. Good night, *Cherie*. Tomorrow we will make many plans for our future together." He dropped a kiss on her forehead and headed back towards the harbour.

Louise found Marc waiting at the gate with the gig the following morning at precisely ten o'clock. He was frowning. Her heart dropped at the look on his face. "What is wrong, Marc? Did you speak to Papa?"

"My father and I both have been with him all morning. However, it's of no use. He won't give his permission—not even to be betrothed. He's worried I will succumb and become a Catholic while I'm with the French East India Company. He won't make a decision until I come back from this trip."

"Oh, Marc. That's terrible. How can he be so cruel?"

"Sweetheart, don't be upset. Let's not spoil our day together. Come; we'll go for our drive and our *piquenique*."

"Do you think it is it safe?" She asked as she climbed aboard the gig. She was almost crying from disappointment. "What about the dragoons?"

"Unless they suspect something, they wouldn't go that far from the harbour. The beach we're going to is about a league away from the city, so it will take a while to get there. I hope you are not too uncomfortable," he enquired as they bounced along.

"No, I'm fine. I'd love to hear about the journey you took with your father. Can you tell me what it was like?"

"I thought it was great. There were two ships, neither of them large. We slept in a small cabin along with the ship's officers—behind the Captain's quarters. Alas, there's no place for a lady on board most of these merchant vessels. Otherwise, I would take you with me when we're married." He smiled down at her.

"I'd love to go. I think it would be so exciting. Why two ships, Marc?"

"Because of the Corsairs—the Barbary pirates. They're all around the entrance to the Mediterranean Sea as well as down in the Spanish Main. For safety, we go in pairs. We followed the trade winds south to the Canary Islands and across the Atlantic to the Caribbean where we visited the Island of Martinique. How I would love you to see that sea. It is a most magnificent blue—azure I think they call it. It's so warm; we swam every day. And on the islands, they grow these amazing trees—with large fronds—they sway in the wind like gigantic fans."

"It does sound wonderful."

"The trade winds blow all the time, so you're never too hot. The breeze keeps it comfortable. And the flowers, Louise, you cannot believe the colours—so vivid. Strange, though, the white ones have the most magnificent scent. Jasmine, I think they call them. There's no winter, so there are blooms all year long."

"It must be like paradise. I long to see such places."

"Someday, I'll find a way to take you. From there we sailed north through the Caribbean Sea, again with the trades, and stopped at a Spanish settlement called St. Augustine, which used to belong to France. It's pretty but hot and humid in the summer. I don't think you would survive long there, *Cherie*. Once summer arrived, we sailed north again. A long, rough voyage along the American coast, until we reached a river called the St. Lawrence. You cannot believe how wide that river is—more like a channel until it gets to Upper Canada."

"What is Canada like then? Papa had thought to go there. It was Uncle Jacques who discouraged him."

"It is rough, my petite. There are many fur traders there. They call them the *Coureur des bois*. They are explorers who travel the rivers of North America, and trap the animals for their beautiful pelts. We met with one who is a distant relative of ours—yours also. Did you ever hear of him? His name is Henri Garneau."

"Not that I can remember. Who was he, then?"

"He's sort of a cousin, I guess. His great-grandfather was our great-grandfather's brother. The two of them were so distressed with life in La Rochelle after the siege, that they left for the new world. Their silk business here was ruined, and they wanted to get away from the reminder of all the death and horror. Great-grandfather left his three sons with his father on the farm. So he eventually came back, but the brother stayed. This Henri Garneau was born in New France. He's part native and quite uncivilized. But most interesting."

He stopped speaking for a moment to urge forward the little horse, which had stopped to eat some grass.

"In Ville Marie, we traded cognac for fur, some of which we took to Versailles. As you heard, King Louis was pleased with our gift. I still have a few left. When I get back, I'll have a cloak made for you to survive the London winters."

She nodded up at him. In her entire life, she had never felt happier. She was certain he was the only man she could ever love.

"We stayed there through the winter, and I've never been so cold in all my life. No, no, your family would not have liked it there. In any event," he smiled down at her again, "you must be where I can come to you. As soon as this next trip is over, I'll come to London, and you and I will marry. Oh, *Cherie*, it's going to be so difficult to leave you again."

By now, they had come to a place where the track ran close to the ocean. "Here we are. This is where we can have our lunch, so let's not think any more sad thoughts. Today we are going to be as happy as children, eh?"

Chapter 10

Marc jumped down from the small buggy and held out his hand to Louise. Even dressed in her simple Huguenot clothing, her long skirt made walking in the sand difficult.

"Do you have something decent under that?" he asked. "Maybe you could take off that dress?"

"Well, I do have my chemise," she said, her face turning red. "It covers me quite well, but my ankles will show."

"Well, I've seen your ankles before." He laughed. "Today we will be like back in the village when we were young. I want you to see the tide pools with all the astonishing sea creatures they hide. Maybe we'll want to swim in the ocean. You can't do that with that long skirt. It would weigh you down too much. You'd better take off your boots too."

She still looked doubtful, but he laughed at her embarrassment. "Just pretend it's five years ago, and go as we used to. Here, I'll take off my top and be barefoot, as well. It's difficult to walk in the sand."

It was years she had seen him without a shirt and vest. With his darkly tanned body and rippling muscles, he looked so masculine and powerful she was once again breathless. "What will the people say?" she managed to whisper.

"There are no people here now. All the peasants, who live around here, have gone over to the island, to help with the salt harvest. After that, they rake the oyster beds and dig for clams. And the fishermen have gone off to sea for the good fishing season. They all work hard now to get ready for the winter months ahead."

"Where do they live then?" she asked. "In those little grey shacks?"

A few feet away, stood a small structure built up on stilts. A short ladder stair led up to the door. When the tide was in, water would surround the building.

"No, no. The peasants live back in the marshes along the river. Those are the fishermen's shacks," he explained. "If the weather turns bad they can go up into them and stay for awhile. They usually have a small cot as well in case they have to spend the night."

Wearing only her chemise, she felt rather undressed. However, it was certainly easier to get around. They left their extra clothing in the little carriage. Marc unhitched the horse, so it could eat the small grasses growing along the marsh.

"I'll tie him to this post, and he'll be fine there," he stated. "Now try the stairs. Can you make it?"

"Oh yes. It is quite easy even without my boots. Whew. It smells a little of fish in here. Look there's a table and a couple of chairs. If we were younger we could play house, Marc." She laughed.

He came and stood close to her, and she was aware of a sudden tension between them. She quickly stepped away from him as his body touched hers. She was not naïve as to the nature of men. Helping her mother look after little Andre had prepared her for growing up, and her mother had explained to her about marriage and babies.

"It is right to have much passion for your husband," Claudine had told her. "Although one should restrain these feelings until you are truly married in the eyes of God. Then it is blessed, not a sin."

To her relief, he turned to the door and motioned her to follow him outside, down to the water's edge. For an hour or more, they explored the beautiful rock pools, examining the tiny creatures inhabiting them. Finally, they left the rocky shore and returned to the glorious curve of sandy beach near the little shack. The sun was high in the sky and quite hot by now.

"Do you want to go in the water, Louise? The ocean is cold, though. It's much different than swimming in your lazy river."

"Let's try it, Marc. It looks so refreshing, and I must say I am rather warm now."

Laughing like a happy child, she ran into the rolling surf. Feeling quite buoyant in the salty ocean, she swam further out to the deeper water where the ledge dropped off. At first, it was fun as she floated on the waves. However, she suddenly became aware of a strong current dragging her away from the shore faster than she could swim. Having spent much time in the river on the farm, she was a good swimmer; however, she had never experienced anything like the pull of these ocean waves.

Panic gripped her, clenching her muscles. "Marc, Marc. I can't get back," she cried. As she thrashed about, her strength waned. She could no longer fight the tide, and felt certain she would drown.

"Hold on," Marc called to her, "it's a riptide. Stop struggling. Just tread water."

Then he was beside her, his muscular arms around her, guiding her along the shoreline and away from the current. He was an excellent swimmer, and finally they were free; however, he kept his arm around her until they reached the safety of the sand.

In spite of the heat of the sun, she started to tremble. With his arms still around her, he turned her until she faced him. Her wet chemise clung to her the curves, and she felt almost naked. He drew her against him, so she could feel the warmth emanating from his body.

"*Dieu Merci*, you are safe, my darling," he whispered. "I was so afraid of losing you. I couldn't bear it if anything should happen to you. My beautiful Louise, I need you now. What if I never see you again?"

He took possession of her mouth in a way that made her tremble even more than the fright she had received. In his arms, she no longer felt cold. Her whole being seemed to be slowly melting from some fire deep within. For a moment, her conscience smote her, yet she could not resist him. The feelings he awoke in her betrayed the years of principles her mother had tried to impart. All awareness of right or wrong left her, and she had no thought of anything save the sound of the surf and the pounding of his heart against hers.

Later, they swam again, staying close to the shore, and when they were exhausted they dressed in their dry outer clothing and ate their picnic lunch, sitting on the steps of the little grey building.

"Louise, sweetheart, I am truly sorry about this," he said. "I honestly didn't mean for that to happen yet. I wanted everything perfect for you. You should have had a magnificent wedding. However, we are truly one now. In the eyes of the Catholic Church, you are my wife; and I promise, no matter what your father says, the minute I get back to London we will make it legal. You'll be old enough then to make your own decision."

"I can never be Catholic, though, Marc," she whispered. "Even if I have disobeyed my faith, I could never stop being a Huguenot." She had begun to feel guilty and slightly bereft.

"Then it will definitely be England where we will settle. I have no problem with that and my family will at least be happy we are together. It is what they have always wanted. In the meantime—you have made me the happiest man alive."

The ride home passed quickly. As he dropped her off at the servant's entrance of the house he said, "Tomorrow I must help father supervise the loading of the merchandise for the trip south. We have to make sure everything gets aboard the ship safely. However, I can't bear not to be with you once more before you go. You leave after midnight Saturday, so the family won't be astir very early. Meet me here again, an hour before midday. We'll have our last day together. Be careful, though. I fear your father will be watching to keep us apart before you sail."

Louise lay a long time awake that night debating whether she should go on Saturday morning or not. She knew what would happen if she did. There could be no turning back now. And, even if Marc did not think so, she realized her father would say that what they had done was morally wrong. She had begun to feel a degree of remorse, and had not been able to face her parents at dinner. Instead, she pleaded a headache and went straight to bed. Thinking about it, she recognized a sense of shame. Still, overshadowing that feeling was the wonder of finally belonging to him in that mysterious way, and already she longed to be with him again.

Could it truly be a sin, she asked herself. She remembered her father's warning that the heart could be a treacherous thing. Yet in her treacherous heart, she knew she would go.

On Saturday morning, he again was waiting at the gate with the small gig. This time they spoke little on the trip to the beach. The thought of the long separation ahead of them saddened them both. Finally, they came to the location of the strange-shaped small building near where they had sealed their love.

"Here is where we will eat our farewell meal, Louise."

They climbed the few rickety steps to the door of the shack. He opened the door, and she looked in with amazement. Instead of the smell of fish, the scent of roses engulfed them. The shack inside was now miraculously transformed into something quite comfortable. There were flowers strewn everywhere as well as several bouquets of red roses set in vases. A luxurious piece of fur and some soft blankets hid the sagging cot. Covering the rough-hewn table was a pretty cloth set with two plates and two wine goblets. Marc put the basket of food down beside a bottle of red wine.

"Why, Marc" she exclaimed in astonishment. "Did you do this? It looks like a bridal bower."

"You *are* my bride. We are bound to each other now. I wanted you to have a wonderful wedding. What happened the other day was not what I meant for you at all. But today, *Cherie*—I promise you—today will be entirely different." He took her in his arms and gently closed the door.

PART III

Consequences

"Repentance is not so much remorse for what we have done as the fear of the consequences."
Francois de la Rochefoucauld

Chapter 11

La Rochelle, September 2nd, 1685
(Gregorian Calendar)

"We'll have to walk to the meeting point," Jacques said. "It's on a beach about a league away, so it will take over an hour."

Claudine tried to hide her tears, as she listened to his instructions. It was a few minutes after midnight, Sunday morning. The whole family had gathered in the salon of Jacques' mansion where he outlined the escape route to them. They all wore the basic, dark clothing of a peasant, with their feet shod in felt boots to mute the sound of their footsteps.

"I'm sorry we can't take the carriages," he continued. "That would make too much noise. Once at the beach, we'll light a small fire to signal the ship's captain. He'll be on the lookout for us between one and two in the morning."

Claudine literally trembled in her boots. The moment she dreaded, the time when they would leave the soil of her beloved France forever, drew near. She sat with her arm around Jacques' wife. Although Marie wouldn't be going to the beach with them, she was there to wish them well. The two women had been like sisters for over twenty years and, of all her friends in France, Claudine would miss her the most.

As they stood to take their leave, Marie hugged her, tears running down her cheeks. "I'll come to England to see you one day," she said, as they bade each other farewell. "I shall miss you so much, Claudine. You have always been like one of my own family, and I shall never forget you. May God be with you, my dear sister."

Jacques had some final instructions for them, "There'll be soldiers watching the harbour tonight, as they know a ship is scheduled to leave. We must be cautious, so we'll take the back alleys. There's a small gate in the western wall that's not well known. We'll go in two groups. Marc, you take Louise, Jean Guy and the twins. Wait about fifteen minutes, and then follow us."

He looked down at Andre and Jeanette who were both fast asleep on the floor. "Claudine you and Pierre will come with me. You'll have to carry the little ones. I'll take the lanterns for the signals, but we can't light them yet, so we'll have to watch our step. Quiet now. Make no noise at all. All right then, we go."

With Jacques in the lead, the first group slipped out the side door of the house and headed in the direction of the harbour. Before reaching the main gate, they turned down a series of short alleys, which lead to the wall. No one was about at that time of night, and the windows of the buildings were in total darkness. They followed the wall west for about a third of a league; then Jacques motioned them to stop at a small opening out of the city.

"Wait here for a minute until I see if anyone is on the beach," he cautioned.

Andre whimpered, and Claudine shook him a little. "Hush, you must be quiet, Andee," she urged. "The bad people will hear us." Her own heartbeat sounded so loud she feared it would give them away, in any case.

Jacques soon returned and motioned them forward through the gate. Now they were in the country, and the only sounds were the lapping of the waves on the shore, and the distant croaking of frogs in the marsh. They, themselves, made no sound as they walked through the drifts of sand. It was almost totally dark. The moon had not yet risen, although the sky was ablaze with stars, which helped to show their way. As she looked back towards the city, the ancient towers framed the entrance to the harbour— large and looming in the darkness. In front of their black shadows, the *lanterne* tower, which served as a lighthouse, shed a small beacon of light.

She took one last look, and experienced a great sadness at the thought of leaving this country and the life she had loved so much. However, she had given her heart to Pierre when she was young, and for over eighteen years, she had done whatever he thought was right. As well, her belief it was God's will for them calmed her a little.

They reached a curve of white-sand beach where Jacques told them to stay by a small fishermen's shack with wooden steps. "We'll wait for the other group before I light the fire," he said. "Then you can all go inside the shack. Marc and I will remain out here, to watch for the signal from the ship. As merchants, we can defuse their suspicions if we're discovered. However, they'd be aware of our plan, if they see all of you here."

Because of the twins, Marc's group was slower to negotiate the sandy coast than the adults had been. It took at least another twenty minutes before they arrived at the meeting place. Claudine sensed the men's anxiety. When they finally appeared, Jacques motioned them all into the shack.

"It will be crowded," he said. "And a little fishy, but in case we're seen by the patrol, it's safer for you to stay in there until the boats come. No noise at all, please."

Claudine heard her oldest daughter gasp and saw her clutch Marc's arm.

"Everything's fine, Louise," she overheard him whisper.

How strange, she thought. What could that be all about?

Standing in the little shack that had served as her love tryst, Louise was aware of a feeling of panic. Her heart pounded so hard in her chest, it almost hurt. Returning to the scene forced her to think about her guilt. If her Papa knew what had happened, he would be appalled. Her mind affirmed that what she had done was wrong. Would she now be condemned to hell? If a person sinned, though, didn't it mean they were destined to do it? Thinking about her father's doctrine of predestination always confused her. It must have been my fate, she reassured herself.

At any rate, she still couldn't feel completely sorry about it. Intimacy with Marc had been so incredible—more so than she had ever imagined. She had wanted to stay with him forever, and now her heart ached at the thought of the long separation ahead of them.

Abruptly the door opened. It was Marc. "The boats are on their way," he whispered. "Come now, they won't be long."

Jacques stood down at the water's edge, where the sailors were just beaching the two longboats. "When you get on the ship you will have to go into the wine barrels immediately," he explained to them. "No matter what happens you must make no noise. It's likely the soldiers will board, and search the ship as it nears the end of the island. When the captain allows you out of the wine barrels, stay under the ships beams. Once out in the Bay of Biscay, they could board again, and those soldiers will do anything to keep one Huguenot from escaping. In the past, they've even put their swords through the deck. But if they do, you'll be safe beneath the beams. Oh, my dear family, I wish I could do more for you, but I'll pray for your safety."

Louise watched as Jacques and Marc hugged all of them in turn, and handed them into the boats. She saw the look on her parents faces as they stepped off the shore. She had never seen them so sad and drawn. They appeared to have aged twenty years since they left the village. Realizing for the first time, how this affected them, she felt devastated. I've only been thinking of me, she thought.

Looking back towards La Rochelle, she got a last glimpse of the splendid harbour towers rising behind the city wall. To her they represented

France. It was possible she would never see this land again, and there was no doubt her life from now on would be altogether different. She was the last to leave the shore, and Marc hugged her as he helped her into the boat. There were tears in his eyes as he whispered, "Remember, you are mine now. I will come for you."

The sailors pushed the two little boats into the water. It didn't take long for them to row to the ship moored in the middle of the channel. They held the small craft steady as each member of the family in turn grabbed on to the sturdy, rope ladder. Two of the men carried the little ones. As Louise reached the top, one of them grabbed her hand and hauled her to the deck, where the officers, including the captain, stood waiting for them.

The vessel was not large—only eighteen tons. Louise had heard Jacques tell her father that he had already paid the master of the ship twelve hundred francs for their escape; and that Pierre would pay him the balance when they arrived in the English port. She realized all their lives now depended on this gallant man.

"*Bonsoir, Monsieur Garneau.* I am Captain Trudeau." The man held out his hand to Pierre. "Our plan is to head north-west towards Ireland, which is the destiny for some of our cargo. We'll sail in that direction, keeping quite far out to sea as we round Brest on the Brittany Coast." He gestured to the north. "There are many patrol boats in that area. Once I'm fairly far north, I'll turn towards the south coast of England. We'll sail into Plymouth, just before dark. I'm sorry the trip won't be comfortable for you, but we hope to be in Plymouth in three days. Now, we had better hide you in the hold. You'll all have to go into the cognac barrels for a while, I'm afraid."

Crouched uncomfortably inside the large wine barrel, Pierre had never before felt so out of control—of both his life and that of his family. They were all in grave danger now, and he was powerless to do anything about it. He thought he would rather be facing an army, with a sword in his hands. His heart went out to his poor wife, with little Andre in her arms, and the young twins, just eleven years old, all stowed in similar barrels. Jeanette and Louise were together in another. Would Andre cry out and give them all away? Jeanette at least understood there was danger. What thoughts must be going through the minds of these young ones? Would they ever get over the ordeal of this trip?

Suddenly the ship weighed anchor, and he could hear voices yelling. He presumed the soldiers from one of the King's patrol boats had stopped the ship and would soon be boarding. How far would they go in searching for the Huguenots? He had heard that they even struck the wine barrels in the hold with their sharp swords. Some of his Huguenot brothers had died in such a manner. Would he have been better off to have recanted his faith and become a Catholic? No, even for the sake of his wife and children, he could not have done that. There must be a purpose to all this. It must be God's will for us, he reflected.

He almost stopped breathing as the sound of the men's footsteps and their muffled voices came close to his barrel.

"This is our cargo, *Monsieur Capitaine*," Captain Trudeau said. "We have cognac, which we will deliver to Dublin, plus the salt for the colony at New France."

"Here, Roger" the officer commanded one of his men. "Thrust your sword into some of those barrels—we'll see if that actually is cognac in there."

Pierre held his breath for what seemed like forever. He heard the sound of swords crashing through the tops of at least four of the barrels and there was the distinctly fermented, smoky odour of the cognac.

"*Voila tout*," the soldier cried. "That's good enough for me. I don't want to waste anymore of your expensive cargo. I think we are through here tonight. Thank you, Captain. We'll let you proceed on your journey with the King's blessing."

The soldiers shuffled out of the hold, and then one by one clambered up the ladder to the decks above. Just when he breathed a sigh of relief, there came a little whimper from the barrel beside him, and Claudine's hushed "shh, Andee, please." Again, he stopped breathing for an instant, but the steps above never faltered, and finally he heard the scraping sound of the men climbing down the rope ladder to their boat alongside. Their swords bumping against the side of the ship confirmed to him that they were safe for now. He heard the anchor being hauled up, and they were once again on their way.

In the confinement of his cramped barrel, he thanked God for this narrow escape. He was aware it might not be the last time the soldiers boarded the ship, so he repeated his entreaty that his heavenly Father would continue to look after his little family. That they would find their way unharmed to a new life, where they could worship Him in peace and security.

He knew they were far from safe yet.

Chapter 12

Captain Trudeau raised the lid of the oak barrel and Pierre climbed out, stretching his aching muscles. "How do you feel, *Monsieur?*" the master mariner asked. As he spoke, he worked swiftly with a metal lever on the cover of the next barrel, his face clouded with a worried frown.

"I'm fine, Captain. Anxious to see the rest of my family, though," Pierre replied, recalling it was Claude's barrel.

"Good lord, lad, you're bleeding," the captain exclaimed, as he yanked off the top. "Are you badly hurt?" He turned to one of the sailors and handed him the tool. "Here, you, help the rest of them out." To a second one, he shouted, "Get the first mate. Tell him to bring a needle and bandages. He'll have to stitch this up. Hurry now."

Pierre gasped and rushed to the captain's side. He peered into the barrel to see Claude weeping convulsively, as he clutched at his left shoulder. Blood poured from a gash on his arm. Together the two men lifted him out of the container, trying not to hurt him. Pierre tore off his shirtsleeve and wound it around the boy's upper arm to staunch the bleeding.

Claude tried to speak through his sobs. "I didn't cry out, Papa. I knew they would kill us all. But now, it hurts so much."

Pierre held him close to his chest. "You are very brave, my son. I'm so proud of you." Turning again to the master, he asked, "Captain Trudeau, wouldn't the soldier realize he had hit something other than cognac?"

"*Oui, Monsieur.* That he would. I'm thinking there were two brave souls here tonight. The wound is not deep—only the tip of his sword. Almost immediately, he must have realized there was a body in there."

"*Dieu merci!* He didn't say anything. Isn't that strange?"

"He must be a sympathizer. There are still some of them in the King's army. It takes real courage. If the Dragoon Captain realized what he'd done, they'd charge him with treason, and it would cost him his life. I wonder how he concealed the blood."

By now, the others were out of their barrels and crowding around young Claude. His mother looked as if she would faint. "Oh, my poor boy," she cried. "Will he be all right, Captain?"

"It doesn't look too bad, *Madame*. Here, is the man who can better tell us," he said, as a pleasant faced, older man with a full beard pushed his way through the small group of family and sailors.

"Make way, please. Let me look at the young fellow," the first mate said, as he took a cloth and dipped it in the open barrel of cognac. "The alcohol keeps it from putrefying." He wiped the wound with the dampened material. "I don't think any muscle's been cut. You'll still have the use of it, lad."

Turning back to the captain, the older man spoke, "We'd better give him a glass or two of the cognac. It will dull the pain while I sew him up. I think we'll take him upstairs to do that."

"Good idea, Didier. Don't worry, *Monsieur Garneau*. He's going to be fine, and Master Marceau will take good care of him. The rest of you should try to get a little sleep now. Stay under the beams. We'll give you plenty of warning if any of those rogues come back."

The first two days of the voyage were agonizing for all of them. The weather in the Bay of Biscay changed for the worse and the ship, buffeted by the waves, never ceased its relentless rolling. The captain kept Claude in the officer's quarters on the main deck to make sure the wound didn't become infected. In the event that the soldiers might return, they dressed him in sailors clothing. "They'd not be suspicious. We often get cabin boys that young," he assured Pierre.

Louise and Andre were the sickest of the family. The air was foul with the smell of vomit and unwashed bodies. Even so, Captain Trudeau only allowed them out on deck in the darkness each night, for an hour or two. There they took in the fresh air and a meal of hot soup. Their breakfast of bread and cheese they had to eat in the stuffiness of the hold. The second day, Pierre begged the captain to let them out during the day.

"The King's patrol ships are everywhere," the captain explained, shaking his head. They'll sight you for sure if you come out in the daytime. We're away from the French coast now, and you'll soon be safe. Only one more night will do it, so please, *monsieur*, listen to me, or we will all be drawn and quartered." He handed Pierre a pewter cup. "Give them all a little of the cognac the soldiers opened. It will settle their stomachs. Even the little ones."

That night Pierre and Claudine sat huddled close to each other on the deck, breathing the fresh, salt air. It was the first time the two of them were alone. Usually they came out of the hold separately bringing two or three of the children with them.

"It's too much to have you all out at once," the captain had made clear to him.

Once the storm they encountered in the Bay of Biscay had abated, the young ones all fell into deep sleeps. Even Louise, who had been ill since the first night, said she was too tired to get out of her makeshift bed.

Pierre gazed at the star-studded sky, a large, deep-blue velvet canopy filled with billions of tiny glimmering lights. It gave him the impression he could reach right up to heaven and touch them.

"I feel so sorry for Claude," his wife spoke up. "He must be in pain."

"He's a remarkably brave little fellow, Claudine. You realize he saved all our lives."

"Yes, I know. And to think he's only eleven. I'm not even sure what I would have done.

"I'm so thankful it wasn't one of the little ones. They would never have understood they couldn't cry out. Our God was certainly with us that night."

"Oh, Pierre. Do you not miss our home?" She sighed.

"Yes, sweetheart, I do. It feels like a big hole in the pit of my stomach. However, there's no use longing for what cannot be."

"What will you miss the most, do you think?"

Pierre thought he would rather not dwell on these memories. The loss of all he had strived for was far too painful. The future and, what that might bring, concerned him now.

Still, talking about their home seemed to sooth Claudine, so after considering for a moment, he said, "Of course, I loved the farm house. It's so beautiful and so old. Grandfather said it was built over one hundred years ago. However, perhaps I'll miss the manufactory even more. After all, I built that, myself. And my mulberry trees. Jacques said they were as healthy as any he saw around Lyon. Well, I don't suppose I'll have any silk worms to feed in London."

His smile was sad.

"What will London be like, Pierre?"

"Big and noisy—worse than La Rochelle—I expect. Mind you, a huge fire about twenty years ago destroyed most of the old buildings. Many areas will be fairly clean and new. We'll be living in Spitalfields where many of the French have settled. We'll hear our own language all the time. At least it won't be strange in that respect. What about you, Claudine? What will you miss?"

"The lovely river winding by our door; such a pretty spot, with the ducks and the swans nesting in the rushes. Louise often used to sit on a rock there and day-dream. I really had to get after her about doing her chores. I guess she was thinking about Marc. I used to dream like that when I was young. Well, not about Marc, of course." She laughed.

"Humph. She should have thought about improving her soul, or at least learning her lessons. Anything but Marc."

"Why, Pierre? You always loved Marc as a boy. Why have you changed so? I thought he was like another son to you."

"Yes, my dear. In many ways he still is. I simply don't want him as a husband for my daughter."

"But why ever not?" she persisted. "His parents have always wanted it. I thought we did as well."

"As you say, Louise is a dreamer. She needs someone steady—someone firm. Marc is like his father—fun-loving and adventurous—perhaps, even, a little selfish."

"Pierre, how can you say that? Jacques risked his life for us."

"Of course, what he did was splendid. We are forever in his debt, and I don't mean to sound ungrateful. However, I mean about his wife. He had always been a little self-seeking in pursuing what he wants in life, and not worrying about what Marie wants."

"Why, Marie has a wonderful life, don't you think?"

"In some ways, yes. It's true she has everything of a material nature she could ever want. Nevertheless, it's not good for a marriage—this being away all the time. I have sensed they have grown apart over the years. Did you not see it?"

"I—I never thought of it. She has so much—a grand house—elegant clothes. She has everything she could want, no?"

"I never meant to speak to you about this, Claudine. However, I'm sorry to say I don't suppose you will ever see Marie again. So I'll tell you this. Jacques is an extremely good-looking man. A charming man. And he likes woman. I've noticed how he looks even at you sometimes. Do you think he stays faithful when he is away from his wife for two or three years at a time?"

"Oh, my, Pierre! It never occurred to me."

"In fact, he has admitted to me, he doesn't. That's not what I want for our girl, Claudine. Wealth isn't everything. She is beautiful, and I think she can do better among our people. Someone who's a sincere Huguenot. And I'll see to it, she does. After all, I am her father."

He softened his tone as he looked fondly at her. "Now, you were telling me who you used to dream about." He didn't wait for an answer; but leaned over and kissed her with passion. He loved his attractive wife intensely and, unlike his cousin, not once in all his married years had he ever desired another woman.

"Well, Monsieur Garneau. We are in sight of England," Captain Trudeau said to Pierre on the morning of the third day. He had come down to the hold to speak to him. "The weather is perfect, so we'll be there by nightfall. We'll go into Plymouth just at dusk. I can't let the French see me make for an English port. They believe I'm heading towards the Celtic Sea."

When the ship finally docked, and the family allowed up on the deck, Pierre thanked the first mate profusely for his care of Claude.

"Your boy will soon be as good as new," Master Marceau said. "I suppose he could get a twinge in the arm when the weather is bad. Other than that, he'll be fine."

Pierre then turned to the captain to thank him for his bravery. He was well aware what a chance the man had taken. From under his jacket, he drew the remainder of the gold they owed for the trip, and handed it over. The officer looked pleased and kissed Claudine on both cheeks as he said 'good bye' to her and the children.

"May God give you a good life, Madame," he said, smiling at her. Like her daughter, she was a lovely woman, which he apparently had not failed to notice.

Dry land never looked so good. They hurried down the gangplank onto the dock. The only light they could see, as well as quite a lot of noise, came from a small tavern near the quay. They had no luggage, only the clothes on their backs, so it was easy enough to hail the lone carriage in sight, which stood in front of the tavern.

"To the home of Jean Bourdon, the Huguenot, we wish to go," Pierre said to the driver in his accented English. "Far, is it?"

"No yer honour," the man said in a thick dialect. "'Tis tuller side o' town. We be there shortly. Maister Garneau 'tis it then? Oi been waiting most nights this week for you to cum. The French curate asked me ter look out for ye. Well, brave ye are, and lucky to be 'ere, away from them murdering Papists over yonder. 'op aboard then. Lots of your friends cumin' over these days. Almost every week oi waits here for someit."

"I ask your pardon, me. I do not speak the English so well yet," Pierre replied.

"Well, if yer goin' to learn a language, I tell ye, boy, the old Devon dialect 'tis the best, oi say."

He went off into a gale of laughter at his small joke while Pierre looked somewhat askance at this speech. It was like no English he had ever heard, and he could understand little of it. In any case, he smiled at the man as his family climbed aboard. Once inside the carriage, he undid the belt hidden under his coat and breeches, where he had stashed a large sum of gold. The children showed amazement at seeing so much coinage.

"We've still got a long trip ahead of us to get to London," he explained. "We'll need this money until we see Paul Thibault. Thanks again to Jacques' foresight, we should have enough. Tonight we'll stay with the curate of the French Chapel here in Plymouth. He'll help us see about getting a trustworthy coach driver to take us to London. Jacques told me, it would take several days as the roads are slow and dangerous—muddy and full of highwaymen."

He did not show them the other item Jacques had given him for the trip. Stowed under his shirt and jacket was a small pistol. Although he was a peaceful man, for the sake of his family, he would use it if the need arose.

Chapter 13

Plymouth, England, August 26, 1685
Julian Calendar

Plymouth was not a large town, so it did not take long for Pierre and his family to arrive at the English church where non-conformist groups were allowed to hold their meetings. Tired as they all felt, they clambered sprightly down from the carriage, while Pierre paid the driver. Next to the building sat a neat little house, which Jacques had told him was where the Huguenot curate lived. At his knock, a mild-looking man in his mid-forties answered the door.

"Well bless my soul. Pierre Garneau and family is it?" He spoke in French. "*Bienvenue.* Jacques has told me all about you. *Grâces soient*, you are safe. We hear some have not been as fortunate. Well, we're happy to have you here, and I'm sure you will all want a wash up and a good night's sleep."

He turned and called to someone in the background. "Martha, come and meet the Garneau family from home."

A plump, middle-aged woman with a happy, rosy-cheeked face came to the door and greeted them warmly.

"A dish of your good lamb stew, and some fresh, hot bread, and a warm bath. That's what they all need, Martha. Take care of these brave souls," her husband said. "They are some of God's chosen for sure."

After they had all washed and been fed, and Claude's wound attended to, Claudine and the children elected to go straight to bed. Pierre sat in the kitchen with Jean and Martha Bourdon discussing the rest of the trip.

"You could set up shop right here, Pierre," Jean Bourdon said. "We have a good French community, and merchants arrive here from many lands all the time. We're not isolated."

"It looks like a pleasant enough town. However, my cousin has already arranged a house in Spitalfields, and Jacques deposited my money, with a goldsmith in London. I'd have to go there in any event. I think we should all go together and see how we like living in the city. Although it will definitely be a big change for my family. Our village was small."

"Well, then if you must go, I know a trustworthy coach driver who normally goes as far as Salisbury. However, he'll be happy to go the distance for you. You'll have to pay for his lodging both there and back, for the unscheduled trip; but it is to your advantage to have him take you. Some of them would gladly deliver you into the hands of the highwaymen. They are not all honest, I fear. This fellow is of French descent, so he can be a big help to you with language at the coaching inns. We Huguenots do stick together you will see." He smiled.

"Good. My English is limited, so I will appreciate his help. At the moment, money isn't a big worry. My cousin took care to think this thing out carefully. All he asks in return is I lend my support to those who come after me. As you say, it is the way of the Huguenot brethren."

"Then we'll speak to the driver tomorrow. After everything you've been through, you should consider staying at least two nights here in Plymouth. We're happy to have you and I think your wife and young Claude need to rest up. I know my Martha will enjoy hearing all the latest news from France, even if most of it is bad. But right now, you look as if you could use a good night's rest. So go to bed now and tomorrow we plan."

The following day, the curate and Pierre, met with the stagecoach driver named Luc Le Blanc. Like many Huguenots, Luc's family had left France during the siege of La Rochelle in 1628. Although he was born in England, he had a slight French accent, and he spoke both languages fluently.

Pierre thought him to be a strange-looking fellow, with a long face and ears that stuck out from his head. A large, black hat covered his hair, but it didn't hide the fact it was thin and pulled tightly away from his face, in a sad-looking ponytail. His nose was gigantic and quite crooked. It stood out like a monument between mottled, rosy cheeks.

"I'm the one who brought your cousin and his son out this way from Salisbury last month," the driver explained. "His captain had agreed to pick him up here in Plymouth. He told me to expect you along in about two weeks."

"Well, we're certainly relieved to have arrived here safely. Now, we must get to London. Can it be arranged, do you think?"

"Yes, I could do it. I usually run a distance of approximately eight leagues a day—mostly between Plymouth and Salisbury. But my grandfather told me what it was like to escape France in his day; so for fellow Huguenots as brave as you folks, I'll be happy to go all the way to Wandsworth. There's a

French settlement there where I have family, and I'm always ready for a visit with them."

He looked at Pierre through sad, coal-black eyes. The eyelids drooped and under the large nose sat an equally droopy moustache. Even his clothes had the nondescript look of a man without a good wife. There simply wasn't a handsome feature to be found, and yet Pierre took an immediate liking to the man. It appeared he didn't smile often, but when he did, it lit up his entire face.

"I'll need to arrange to borrow a change of horses at our stopover in Salisbury," he continued. "We'd better plan on a two-night stop there. Then I can get you to Wandsworth altogether in six days. It will be another day into London, but you can hire a coach there. How does that agree with you?"

"I don't mind stopping at Salisbury. Jacques told me about their astonishing cathedral, and the lace trade established there. I've always been interested in architecture since I went to the Huguenot University in Saumur. It's in the Loire Valley. And both my wife and my oldest daughter are expert at making lace, so we'll visit their guildhall as well."

"That's a little more than half way to London. There's an excellent inn where your family would find comfort for a couple of nights. Compared to most of the places along the way it's exceptionally clean, so it'd be well worth the money. Shall we plan on it then? Day after tomorrow we will leave—very early. We never want to be on the road after dark, so we must always get a good start."

"I understand. We'll be ready. So tomorrow is September 7th. We should be in London by the 15th then. That will be just fine."

"Excuse me, Monsieur. This is still August. Tomorrow is August 28th."

"How can that be?" Pierre was mystified. "We left France on September 2nd."

Luc and the curate both started to laugh. "You forget, Pierre," Jean Bourdon said. "England is still on the old Julian calendar. You've just gained eleven days, my brother. Do you feel any younger?"

"*Zut alors!* I had forgotten about that. Jacques did tell me, but my head has been so full of everything. Well, even better. By Friday, we'll be rested and ready to go. So far, on this adventure we've been truly blessed. I pray it continues."

On the way home, the curate told Pierre that Luc Le Blanc surpassed as a storyteller, and knew almost everything that went on in the west counties. "With Luc driving, it won't be a boring trip," he stated.

Friday Pierre awoke to find the town shrouded in fog. The breeze smelled of seaweed and somewhere down in the harbour a bell clanged to warn any ships of the presence of rocks. The clattering of the carriage, and the iron-shod feet of the horses rang out long before Luc Le Blanc and the team came into sight through the swirling mist.

"The fog comes in from the ocean," the curate explained to him. "But don't worry. Your driver's used to it and it'll burn off long before your reach Ashford. By then, the sun will be out and most likely, it's going to be a hot day. Here now, my wife has packed you a lunch, so you won't have to stop at an inn along the way."

"That's so kind of you. But you have done so much for us already," Claudine exclaimed.

Madeame Le Blanc was adamant. "You'll be spending enough of your gold as it is. I've loved having you here to talk about France. I miss it so much. I hope you'll come back this way. You are welcome to stay with us anytime."

"And you must come to our place in London." Claudine gave Martha a hug. "We have so much to thank you for. I never felt as miserable and dirty in my life as when we arrived here. I'll truly never forget the kindness you've shown us."

The two full days' break from their travels had given them a new lease on life. Now, they were all anxious to get to their final destination. The Huguenot congregation had managed to come up with changes of clothing for all of them, so they looked fresh and clean. In return, Pierre donated to a fund to help other Huguenots on the run.

"I'm sure there will be many more of us arriving on your doorsteps over the next few months. I fear life in France has become intolerable for followers of our faith," he said.

Pierre showed Luc the Flintlock pistol Jacques had given him and offered to ride up top with him.

"That's a good idea. How about your oldest boy? Can he shoot as well?" Luc asked, as he pulled a couple of more pistols and a carbine rifle out from under the seat.

Pierre nodded. "Yes, both he and my oldest daughter can; my wife as well, for that matter. We often went hunting in the forests surrounding our home."

"They are familiar with the recoil of these things then. I think they each ought to have a pistol. I'll use the carbine, of course, but if they attack us, it would good to have a surprise element from inside the carriage. If it happens, you and I will have plenty to do, Monsieur. Of course, there may be nothing to worry about at all. It's just that—well—you never know..." His words hung in the air.

"In any case," he continued, "I'm glad to have you up there with me. There's room for the oldest lad as well, if he'd like. It gets rather dull talking to the horses. Good to have some company for a change. Perhaps I can brush up my French a little."

Claudine and Louise, each armed with a pistol, along with the four youngest children clambered aboard the large coach with its team of four horses. Pierre and Jean Guy hoisted themselves up beside Luc on the driver's seat. Luc snapped the six-foot whip over the horses' rumps, and they started at a good pace. Pierre found he rather liked being up in the front, but he kept his eyes roving from side to side in case of an ambush from some unknown quarter.

Mile after mile of English countryside rolled by: grassy meadows; then undulating farmland; and finally forest, where a few trees already showed their autumn colors. The sun had burnt through the mists, and the weather had indeed turned warm. However, the breeze blowing in from the Channel to the south gave a hint of the cooler days to come. Pierre knew that a cold wind in August often meant a long, cold winter; so he was glad they had left France when they did. It meant he would have his family settled in London long before the rains and the constantly overcast skies set in. The inclement weather in that dreary city was one of the things about which Jacques had warned him. After the brisk but sunny winters of his native Charentes, he wasn't looking forward to it.

Soon he began to notice a change in the landscape. There were no more farm buildings, and the cultivated plots gave way to wilder meadows. The mist was again dropping in around them in areas. There were strange grey rocks, some of a large size, and instead of the thick woodlands, sparse growth here and there with low bushes and odd-shaped trees. Somehow, they looked sinister.

"We're into the moor now, *Monsieur*," Luc answered his unspoken question. "This is where the fun will begin if we're going to have any today. In case you haven't heard, there's a lot of mischief goes on around here in Devon. Both the north and south coasts of Devon and Cornwall are full of wreckers."

"Wreckers? I've never heard of them. What are they?" Pierre queried.

"They are cruel, hard-hearted vultures. They have no pity on the poor travelers at sea. They'll deliberately put up lights on the rocks, so the ships' officers think everything is fine. It causes a shipwreck, of course, and then the wreckers take the spoils off the ship. They don't give a damn about the poor folks drowning right in front of them. They are a wicked and heartless bunch. And these highwaymen aren't much better."

"Yes, Jacques did warn me about them."

"Well, we'll keep a sharp lookout for the next few miles. Once we are in Ashburn, it's not so bad. By the way, these pistols are only good up to about eighty yards so don't start shooting the minute you see one of them fellows. They usually come in pairs so I'll tell you when I want you to fire.

It's not in my nature to kill them. Let the sheriff take care of that. I always alert him if I see any, and simply knowing we have arms usually puts a stop to whatever they're planning. You understand?"

"But, of course, Luc. You well know what you're doing and I do not. Up until this summer, my life was peaceful. I certainly didn't foresee all this trouble. You have met my cousin, Jacques. He loves adventure, but me—I can well do without it."

A slight movement drew their attention to the rise in front of them. There on the hill, the shadow of a man on horseback stood out against the blue sky. Then slowly the shadow split, revealing two individuals. As he saw Luc straighten up, Pierre's heart gave a sudden lurch. Jacques had been right about England. Their troubles were not over yet.

Chapter 14

"There, up on the hill, Pierre," Luc pointed. "That's two highwaymen. In another few minutes, we'll start shooting. Better let your family know."

"There are highwaymen on the ridge," Pierre called down to Claudine."Get your pistols ready."

"Alright then," Luc yelled. "Fire!"

Five shots rang out and echoed through the low hills. As suddenly as the two horsemen had appeared, they took off over the ridge and disappeared from sight.

"I think it's going to be okay now," the coach driver exclaimed. "They prefer a surprise attack, and it's the poor, unarmed travelers they go after, especially if they're alone. They know we've got firepower now, so they'll most likely leave us be."

"*Zut alors*, that was exciting. What type of people are these 'highway men' anyway?' Pierre inquired once his heart had slowed down, and he could breathe again. "I had never heard of such criminals until Jacques mentioned them."

"What? You've never heard of your famous countryman, Claude Duval?"

"No, I'm sure I haven't."

"He's considered the most dashing of all the highwaymen," Luc began, looking pleased to be telling a story. "A fellow by the name of William Pope wrote a book about him not long ago. You should read it when you get to London. It's quite famous."

"I'm afraid I'll need a few English lessons before I do that." Pierre laughed.

"Anyhow," Luc continued, "this Duval lived in Normandy. He was working in Rouen as a groom, when a group of English royalists hired him to tend their horses. During the time of the commonwealth, most of the English nobility fled to France, as I'm sure you know?"

"Yes, I have heard that."

"Well, after Oliver Cromwell died, parliament recalled Charles II to restore the throne; this French fellow came to England with one of them noblemen. By then he was quite the gentleman. He had picked up all their ways. He dressed in high fashion and was most gallant with the ladies. Somehow, he drifted into a life of crime and became known as the 'gentleman highwayman.' Apparently he was an expert card player and gambler and lived a life of wine, women, song, and thievery."

"Is he still around then? Maybe that was him?"

"No. Unfortunately, for him, he got drunk in a London pub one day. They managed to capture him, and send him to Newgate Prison. Now there's a hellhole to be sure. I'm not sure if there was ever a fair trial, but they hanged him in any case. It all happened about fifteen years ago, so you won't meet Gentleman Claude out here on the moor anymore unless it's his ghost." Luc laughed and gave the horses the whip, as they headed down the ridge and out of the moor.

The remainder of the trip to Exeter passed by without event. They stopped at a town called Ashburn, and while Luc changed the horses, the family sat by the small river and ate the lunch Martha Bourdon had provided. Pierre found it quite peaceful there and, for the first time that week, he relaxed. Since there was still some time after they ate, he and Jean Guy walked around the town, looking at the woolen mills along the river, and the fine merchant houses on the main street.

"I could live in a town like this," he stated. "Perhaps England won't be so bad after all. If we find we don't like living in London, there's nothing to stop us from moving on in a few years. How do you feel about the city, my son?"

"I'm not so sure I'm going to like it. I didn't like La Rochelle much, and London is even bigger and dirtier, so Marc tells me. I have been thinking that once you and Maman settle in, I might like to go to the Americas. Maybe with Marc. He believes there's a lot of an opportunity for young people there. Land is still cheap."

"Why, Jean Guy, it's nothing but wilderness. It would never occur to me that you would want that sort of life. Well, something to think about I guess. However, we'll give it a few years, eh. You won't be sixteen until next spring. Now, it looks like Luc has the horses ready, so we'd best find the family and be on our way."

They stopped overnight at both Exeter and Yeovil, where they stayed in coaching inns. The food was cold and greasy, and the beds full of fleas; but at least it served as a rest from the constant bouncing of the coach on the rough track. They found it refreshing to lie in a bed and stretch their legs after the long hours on the road. Nevertheless, on the third night, they were pleased to arrive in Salisbury and find a newer and more luxurious inn.

Pierre agreed with Luc that they should stay at the legendary George Inn, where a few decades earlier Oliver Cromwell had spent some time. They found the food excellent, and the rooms and bedding were spotless and new. It gave them all a chance to have a bath and a decent night's rest. He could tell that Claude, as well as the little ones, had gone through as much as they could stand for now. Surprisingly, Louise looked rather wan, as well. Strange she doesn't travel better, he thought. She always seemed so strong back on the farm.

"I'm so thankful we're staying over an extra night," Claudine mentioned to him in their room that evening. "We all need a rest, and it will be nice to see a little of the city. We'll not get this way again anytime soon."

Listening to his wife, Pierre felt it was well worth parting with a fair amount of his gold to see them all looking a little brighter. "You're right. I'm afraid we'll be busy for the next few years just getting by. I pray we will be able to make a good life in London eventually. Then you and I will travel, my dear."

The following morning they set out to explore the charming, medieval city. They went first to the Guild Hall and had a look at all the newest patterns of lace. Claudine asked how she could join the guild in London, as she thought since she and the older girls were skilled at lace making, they could augment their family income that way. They then spent an hour or so exploring the magnificent 13th century cathedral. By the time dinner was over, they were thankful for another night's rest in the inn's comfortable beds.

⚭

In later years, when Pierre would recall the long, arduous journey from France to England, he remembered the Salisbury visit best. Not so much for the cathedral although, with its lovely stained glass windows and soaring spire, it certainly impressed him. Nevertheless, it was all too reminiscent of the eminent Catholic churches of France for him to enjoy. It reminded him too much of why he had left his home.

No, it would be because of the strange and wondrous sight of the stone henge eight miles to the north of the city, and the events that took place that day because Luc had suggested the diversion.

"In case you never get this way again, Pierre, you should see this, and it won't add much time to the trip. It's a sight you can hardly credit, believe me. Your cousin asked me to take him up there earlier this month"

"I'm not surprised," Pierre answered. "He's always interested in seeing anything out of the ordinary."

Therefore, on the fifth day of the journey from Plymouth, they turned north and headed towards the Salisbury Plain, the ground on which stood a strange circle of monolithic, upright stones. Luc had arranged for an early start, so the sun was still high over the eastern horizon, but it was already warm. It was the first exceptionally hot day the family had encountered in England.

They had been travelling about thirty minutes, when Luc stopped the coach at the side of the track, bordered by a farmer's field on one side, and a wooded area of scrub brush, on the other. "We'll have to climb to the mound from here," he explained. "It's rough going through the bush, but it's not high. I think even the ladies can manage it. Everyone fine with that?"

"I think so," Pierre replied. "I'll tell the others."

While Luc unhooked the horses from the carriage, and tied them to a tree so they could graze, Pierre jumped down and opened the coach door. "Luc says we have a small climb through the bush to see the stones, but it's worth the effort," he told his family. "We all better take a look at it now as we're not likely to get back this way again."

Claudine and the twins jumped out of the coach, but Louise sank back against the cushions. She looked pale. "Oh, Papa, now we are travelling like this, I'm queasy again. It's comforting to sit here with no motion for a change. May I please stay and rest?"

He looked at her with some alarm. We must get her to London as soon as possible, he thought. I hope she's not getting the ague. That can be a killer.

"All right then, daughter. It may be too rough for Andre and Jeanette anyhow, and I don't think any of us feel much like carrying them in this heat. You keep your eyes on them now. Don't let them wander out of the coach."

Louise smothered a small yawn. "I'll watch them. They can play with the box of toys Monsieur Bourdon gave them." Smiling up at him, she once more reclined against the pillows.

The small path up the slight slope of the mound was overgrown with gorse and wild rose bushes. They pushed their way carefully through them, but it was impossible not to be scratched. Suddenly they spied a gap in the brush and the party stepped out on to a large flat space. In the centre of the square, stood around twenty or so gigantic upright stones. They were at least twenty feet tall. There were a few, which had fallen, as well as some placed horizontally on top of the others. Pierre could see that originally it had been almost a perfect circle.

"*Zut alors*," he exclaimed, as he stopped in his tracks astounded at the size of the stones. "How could they possibly get here? Those things must weigh several tons. What is this? Some sort of temple? It looks rather pagan to me"

"No one knows for certain," Luc said. "They call it The Henge. It goes way back in time even before the Romans came. They make mention of it in their histories. A few years ago, a writing man, by the name of John Aubrey, came here to explore. He was doing a book about it. He thinks the Druids first worshipped here. That flat rock in the ground was likely used for human sacrifice. It's thought they would choose the palest child in the community; supposedly to honour the family."

"My word, it's horrible to imagine people went along with that sort of thing."

"Even in this day and age, there are whispers of the things that go here; things like Celtic rituals and devil worship. Especially around midsummer's day when the first rays of the sun hit the stones. Some say at that hour, you could walk into the rocks and simply disappear."

Pierre felt a chill run down his spine, and the hairs on the back of his neck seemed to rise. "You mean devil worship is still allowed?"

"No, no. They outlawed it, but it wouldn't surprise me if it still goes on secretly. In fact, it's not many years back that they hanged a few women around here, who were involved in black magic. Just let me show you something." He thrust out another item he had carried up from the coach. It was a thick wooden stick with a forked end.

"What have you got there? I've been wondering why you brought it along," Pierre said.

"They call it a dowser. They say it has magical powers. See what happens when I move it towards the ground. If there's water under, the force will be so strong it pulls the forked end down."

Another cold chill went down Pierre's back. "Well, I'd rather not test it out, if you don't mind. I don't like this place. Jean Calvin always warned his followers to stay far away from witchcraft, and now I can see why"

He looked to where his wife and children stood silently, looking at the stones as if they were mesmerized. "Not that I'm sorry to have seen such an amazing sight, and I can certainly see why Jacques enjoyed it. He's a great adventurer. But I think I'll feel better when we get my family away from here."

By now, the sun was high in the sky. It was excessively hot, and sweat poured down Pierre's face as he and the others made their way back through the gorse bushes. He was relieved to see the coach still sitting there, shimmering in the heat, with the horses cropping the short grass at the side of the track.

There was no motion or sound from inside the coach, and as Pierre opened the door, it horrified him to see Louise and Andre both sound asleep, but Jeanette was nowhere in sight. His tiny, fair-haired daughter was gone.

Chapter 15

"Louise, Louise, wake up," Pierre cried, shaking her awake. "I told you to watch the children. What is wrong with you, girl? Jeanette isn't here. Where did she go?"

Louise's eyes flew open; she yawned then jumped up in her seat looking startled. "Oh, no! Oh, Papa. I'm so sorry. I just can't stay awake. I don't know why. Oh, where could she have gone?" She was white with terror.

Young Andre opened his eyes and looked up at his father. "Jenni go *pipi*," he announced proudly in French. He pointed to the gorse bush from where they had all just emerged

"I'll speak to you later, young lady," her father shouted at Louise, looking daggers at her. Then turning to Luc, he asked, "What should we do?"

"I don't think she could have gone far, none of us saw or heard her on the way down. Let's spread out." He looked over to where Claudine and Catherine were standing, wringing their hands. They both looked terrified. "Catherine, you go with Louise along the track, back the way we came. Keep looking into the brush and calling her name."

"Jean Guy, take Claude and do the same thing that way." He pointed to the road ahead of the carriage. Turning back to Claudine he instructed, "Madame, you and the little boy stay here inside the carriage. Jeanette may find her way back herself. Someone should be here for her. In the meantime, Pierre and I'll do a thorough search of the bush around here. Whoever finds her, yell as loud as you can, and we'll all meet back here. One moment, Pierre. There's something we'll need."

He climbed up to the driver's seat. In a moment, he returned with two cutting tools—one for each of them. He stepped into the bush and began slashing a swath through the gorse. Pierre took the device Luc handed him and followed his example.

Five minutes had passed when Luc stopped cutting and put his hand to his ear. "Shh," he cautioned Pierre. "I heard something."

From the top of the mound, they could hear a child's wailing. *"Non, non*, leave me alone. I don't want to go with you," the little girl cried out in French. "I want my maman. Oh, I want my maman." The wailing started again.

Both men rushed through the gorse, ignoring the prickly branches slapping at them and leaving scratches on their faces. There, on the mound, a strange, stooped old crone was dragging the weeping Jeanette along by her arm. From her odd, pointed hat to her heavy men's boots, the woman was dressed in black, relieved only by her dirty-grey hair, which straggled down her back. A rank smell of dirt and sweat, and something else unpleasant emanated from her.

"Madame," Pierre yelled at the top of his lungs. "*Halte—halte*, I say. That is the child of me!"

The woman stopped in surprise and let go of the little girl's hand. Jeanette immediately ran to her father. "Papa, I want to go home," she cried out. He picked up the weeping child and covered her tear streaked face with kisses.

"There, there, *ma petite*. You're fine now. Maman's waiting for you."

Luc yelled at the old woman, waving his cutting tool at her. She backed away and hobbled off towards the gigantic stones. Before she disappeared between two of the standing monoliths, she cackled wildly and shook her right hand at them. Once more, Pierre felt a cold tingling down his spine.

"What is she doing?" he asked. "Putting a curse on us, you think? Let's get back to the carriage, Luc. I don't think I'll be back to this place anytime soon. I'll keep my distance from black magic from now on to be sure."

"Yes, I agree. After seeing that woman, I don't think I'll be back soon either, Pierre. There's no good to come from any dealings with that old hag. The very smell of her is evil."

⁂

By the time they arrived at the outskirts of Winchester, it was almost one o'clock, and they were all extremely hungry. "We can stop awhile here, Pierre. There's a good inn past the town square, so you can take your time getting something to eat. We'll have no trouble reaching Reading tonight, and by tomorrow afternoon, we will be at my brother's home. You are almost at your destination, *mon ami*."

However, as they got nearer the town center, they found the track crowded with people. Luc looked puzzled. "I wonder what's going on," he said. "It's never been like this before." Their progress was constantly impeded, so he finally halted the team of horses.

"Monsieur," Pierre called out to one of the men in the crowd. "Why goes everybody to the city? What 'appens there?"

"Haven't you heard, stranger?" The man looked at Pierre with interest, obviously noticing his accent. "They're finally going to chop the head off of Alice Lisle today. It's about time too."

"A woman—beheaded? 'ere in England?" Pierre was stunned. "For what?"

"They caught her harbouring a group of Protestants who rebelled against King James. Good riddance to her, I say!"

Pierre gasped, and Luc looked over at him. "I guess you never heard of the Monmouth Rebellion then," he stated.

"No, I did not. What is that?"

"Well, when King Charles died last February, his brother, James inherited the throne. However, Charles had an illegitimate son whom he has acknowledged and given a title—'The Duke of Monmouth'. This son felt the throne should be…"

"Just a minute," Pierre interjected. "King Charles is dead?"

"Yes. Didn't you hear that?"

"No, I did not. Isn't this James a Catholic?"

"Yes, but at the moment, he tries to appease everyone. He even attempted to stop the beheading of Alice, but it had…"

"*Maudit.*" In his agitation, Pierre cut him off again. "Jacques never told me that Charles had died. That's the reason I came here. King Charles offered us all sanctuary. He promised to protect Huguenots. And now there's this Catholic to deal with? And they are beheading a Protestant? Will this hatred never end?"

"Do you want to see it then, Pierre? It looks as though it will start in the town square fairly soon."

"No, Luc. In France, I saw sufficient horror to last me a lifetime and now, at that Henge place, I've experienced enough terror for one day. Me—I think we'll simply find the inn you spoke of, and have our dinner. Then let us be out of this city as fast as possible."

There was little excitement on the rest of the trip to Wandsworth and Pierre found himself relieved to be finally close to London. Luc told them, they were to stay overnight at his brother's home, which was large and comfortable.

"I'm sure he would be most happy for you to stop over longer. I think you all need another rest, Pierre. You might find life in London quite difficult at first."

Luc was right. Robert Le Blanc wanted them to stay longer. He had many questions about France and remembering the stories his father had told of their own families' flight, he was delighted to help any Huguenots escaping from the long sword of King Louis. The Le Blancs owned a mill that produced a superb scarlet-coloured dye and was already becoming famous all over England as being perfect for dyeing hats. Particularly since they guaranteed the colour would not run in bright red rivulets down the face of the wearer in wet weather. As Luc had told Pierre, his brother was a wealthy man because of it.

"Coming to England has been a great blessing to many of us," Robert Le Blanc explained to Pierre. "And this is a great area to get established, if you find you don't like Spitalfields. Some of our people are hat makers and some make wigs, so I'm sure you could do well here as a silk weaver. We are free to hold our meetings as we please.. It's much nicer here than being in the city. I'm sure you would like it. Stop awhile and see for yourselves."

"No doubt my family would like the country better. However, I have a house waiting for me in London and money established with Paul Thibault, the goldsmith, so I suppose we had better start for the city as soon as possible. Luc has to take the horses back to Salisbury tomorrow, so we'll have to find another mode of transportation to the city. Have you any idea how we can get there?"

"There's a hackney coach leaves every morning. If they can't oblige you tomorrow, you can reserve for the next day. For the appropriate amount of money, they'll take you right to your final destination."

"Well then, we'll plan on the morning one, if they can accommodate us."

"But we're glad to have you here with us, Pierre." Robert LeBlanc continued. "Your family is exceedingly brave. In fact, there's a meeting tonight. Perhaps you could say a few words to the group about your experience. Most of their ancestors escaped from France over the last century, so they all understand some French, and I think they should be aware of what our brothers from home now have to go through to get here. I could go and arrange it with the pastor right now, and I'll see about a coach for you, as well. Do you mind telling your story?"

"No, not at all. I know there'll be many fleeing France that won't have had the assistance I've had, and I'm happy to say anything that would help them."

That evening, Pierre gave a stirring talk in French to the Huguenot group, which Robert translated into English. He hoped it would rouse them to action to help the many refugees who would certain to be arriving over the next few months. Afterwards, the members of the congregation crowded around him, asking questions about his life across the channel, and assuring him, they were ready and willing to help their French brothers.

Lying in bed in the comfortable room Luc's brother had given them for the night, Pierre found it difficult to sleep. The excitement of being with fellow worshippers, as well as wondering what his journey's end the next day would bring, left him tossing and turning far into the night. No matter what London or the house is like, we must stay there a year, he thought. My family needs some stability after all this uncertainty.

With that settled in his mind, he finally fell asleep.

Chapter 16

London, September 4, 1685
Julian Calendar

The following morning, Pierre and his family set off in a hired coach from Wandsworth to London. Following the instructions given him by Jacques, he directed the driver to the house of Paul Thibault, in an affluent area called Soho. His cousin had told him, Monsieur Thibault was one of the many Huguenots whose ancestors came to London during the heated persecution in the 16th century. There, his family had done well in the gold trade, and Paul was a man of property. Jacques assured him the goldsmith had a reputation for total honesty, and well known to be most reliable in caring for the assets of others.

Even from outside, the house at #14 Soho Square appeared attractive. Although built since the great fire, it was in mock Tudor style, with lovely, leaded glass windows and a half-timbered façade. Pierre's impression was that Monsieur Thibault was indeed a wealthy man.

While the rest of his family waited in the commercial carriage, he climbed the steps and rang the bell pull beside the massive oak door. After a few seconds, it was opened by a footman. Giving the man his name, he asked if it would be convenient to see Monsieur Thibault.

"The monsieur 'as been in expectation for me, I believe," he explained in heavily accented English.

"Oh, then come in, sir," the servant replied. He ushered him into the large foyer and motioned him to a chair. "Mr. Thibault is upstairs, but I'll ask if he can see you now."

As Pierre waited, he took the time to look at his surroundings. The entry hall was enormous with an archway to the left leading off into an elaborate drawing-room, beyond which he could make out a generous-sized dining area. At the back of the hallway, a wide wooden staircase ascended to the second floor. To the right and front of the stairs were two doors, the nearest of which was closed. However, the one to the rear was wide open and, from his seat, Pierre could view a smaller withdrawing room with two cosy chairs in front of an elegant marble fireplace. The floors were parquet covered with a multi-coloured Turkish rug. All the visible furnishings looked expensive to Pierre, but not ostentatious, and he thought they would be comfortable.

The sound of light footsteps alerted him, and he looked up as Monsieur Thibault descended the staircase. He was a tall man with an athletic body. Pierre thought that he might be a little younger than he—perhaps in his late thirties; but he had a serious face, so it was difficult to determine. Modifying this severe look was a large dimple in his chin and gentle brown eyes. As Pierre stood up, Paul came forward with his arm held out for the English custom of shaking hands.

"*Bonjour, Monsieur Garneau,*" he said in admirable French. "How glad I am to see you. We've been most concerned about your safety. It's a long and dangerous trip, and what you have done is exceedingly brave."

Feeling immediately at ease with the man, Pierre responded with a firm handshake, and answered in English, "Monsieur Thibault, to make your acquaintance I also am 'appy. I 'ope you don't mind we continue with the French. I am not so—so—how you say—fluent with the English yet."

"*Mais oui, mon ami.* French is fine," Thibault said, again in Pierre's language. "Since I was able to talk, my mother insisted I speak her family's native tongue. It's a great blessing for me now to be able to help the compatriots of my great grandparents, who also came to this country because of persecution, so long ago. Here, let's go into the library. I have some legal papers for you to sign."

He opened the door on the immediate right and escorted Pierre into a room that astounded him. His cousin, Jacques' house in La Rochelle had also conveyed an ambiance of luxury, but in quite a different way. This had a feeling of English solidity about it—a place of warmth and safety. Dark oak paneling lined the walls and the large brick fireplace had an oak mantel and surround, as well. The carpets, again, were in a red Turkish pattern, with the lush sensation of a deep, expensive pile. Bookshelves filled with leather-bound books lined one entire wall. There was no doubt the goldsmith had made his mark in life.

Monsieur Thibault pointed to a chair in front of a massive oak desk stacked with several piles of paper, while he, himself, took a seat behind it. "So now, Monsieur Garneau, Jacques has told me much about your excellent family, and how you refuse to convert to the Papists. I admire you for that. I'm sure it hasn't been easy. You'll be glad to be safe in your own comfortable house?"

"Yes, Monsieur, that we will. We loved our home in France, but our faith was of far more importance. So, of course, we're happy there is a community here where we can now worship our God in peace."

"I imagine you're disappointed Jacques doesn't feel as you do about the faith. Even so, he has shown great generosity and courage to others, as well. I'm sure he wouldn't say, but I can tell you, he's helped many Huguenot refugees. Perhaps our God won't overlook that fact. Now, I'm sure you're eager to see this house he's arranged for you."

"Yes, we're all anxious to be settled. It's well over a month now since we left our farm and we're tired."

"Here then, these are the leasehold papers for you ready to sign, and it is yours. The lease is for one year and, if you find it satisfactory, you can purchase it at any time. Jacques also arranged for a minimum of furniture, so you can move right in. Later you and your wife will be able to make some purchases of your own choice. Were you able to bring anything from France?"

"Jacques brought over some of my looms, of course," Pierre said, as he signed the papers. "They are extremely important for my vocation. And some household items, which meant a great deal to my wife. He left them for us in the warehouse he owns here in London."

When he had finished signing all the papers, he handed them back to the goldsmith and set the quill back in the ink pot. "Well, Monsieur Thibault, our hired carriage awaits me, so I think we should go directly to the house. I certainly appreciate what you have done for our family, and I know my wife will want to thank you personally."

Monsieur Thibault's shrug was entirely French, which rather amused Pierre.

"It is nothing. But where are my manners? Where will you eat tonight? The inns around Spittlefields are all rather too rough to take your young family. You should stay here and have dinner with me."

"Oh, no, Monsieur, we wouldn't want to put you out like that. And my wife and children are all rather tired. I'm sure we'll find something quick."

"Well, wait a moment then. I'll see what I can do."

He left Pierre sitting for about ten minutes, finally reappearing with a large picnic basket full of food as well as a jug of wine.

"Here we are, Monsieur—here at least are a few items for tonight as well as breakfast tomorrow. I would hate for you to starve on your first day in London."

They both laughed and Pierre spoke. "Well, thank you again. It's most kind of you. I do hope we will have occasion to see you soon."

"Yes, for a certainty. In fact, I'm having a small dinner party here one week from this Saturday. I would be most pleased if you would come, and bring your family—the children too—it will be quite informal. My maids can take care of the younger ones for you. There'll be others of the French community here, and I'm sure they'll want to make your acquaintance. We are all aware of the magnificent silks you weave. Some of London's wealthiest patrons are anxious to acquire them. Will you be able to come do you think? Today is Thursday, so it gives you a little time to settle. I'll have an invitation delivered to your wife as a reminder."

"I'm sure she will appreciate it very much. Being new in this city, my family will be lonely for a while."

"Well then, it is arranged. You will join us here, and it will be a celebration of your safe arrival," said Paul, again shaking his hand.

By the time they reached Spitalfields, they were all exhausted. However, the dwelling on the corner of Fournier and Brick Lane was a welcome surprise to Pierre. Overall, including the attic and the kitchen in the basement, there were ten rooms. Although not comparable to the house in Soho Square, it was large for a townhouse in that locale. It seemed considerably wider than the other homes in the area and, being a corner house, had windows on three sides, which brightened the interior. This was especially essential for the large room on the third floor, where Pierre would do his weaving.

"Well," he said, rubbing his hands together in satisfaction, "it's not like the light at home, of course, but I think it will do nicely for awhile. Jean Guy, we shall take a short rest for a week and then we'll set up the looms. Sooner or later we'll run out of the money from Jacques, so we need to see if a Frenchman can make a living in this strange country."

The Garneaus found the party at Monsieur Thibault's both enjoyable and reassuring. The group, mostly of French Huguenot descendants, were welcoming and cordial.

One of the maids whisked the children, with the exception of Louise and Jean Guy, away to a nursery. Pierre had been wise enough to pack dressy outfits for each of his family in the wine barrels. In France, the Huguenots dressed simply and without embellishment. However, here, it would be important to make a favourable impression from the beginning. He needed people of fashion to see and talk about his silks. In Paul's stylish Soho House, he knew he would meet such individuals, and he was confident his beautiful women would show his work to an advantage.

Claudine and Louise agreed they didn't wish to wear wigs, so Pierre hired a maid for the day who washed, brushed, and styled their hair in the latest London fashion. Even young Catherine had hers arranged. Spectacular looking, as they were, they created quite a stir. Louise looked particularly grown up and striking. Her green eyes flecked with gold were shining, and with her golden blonde hair and luminous skin, she stood out as a beauty. Pierre had never seen her with such a glow.

Well, he thought, she'll be seventeen in November. It's time to be thinking of a husband. Fortunately, Marc is far away now. He also noted the way Paul Thibault, who he had discovered was a widower, could hardly take his eyes off her. The goldsmith had seemed almost stunned when Pierre introduced her and had stared at her from time to time with a pensive look in his gentle, brown eyes.

Unfortunately, I think he is rather too old for her, Pierre mused. However, I'm sure we'll meet some suitable younger men among his friends.

During the evening, the talk drifted to the death of King Charles back in February. Pierre had only heard about it that terrible day in Winchester, and at the time, his heart had dropped at the news. He assumed that Jacques did not know about it. He would have been in the Americas at the time and too busy when he came to England in August. Since Jacques and Pierre had chosen England partly because of King Charles' promise of sanctuary for Huguenots, it had been a shock to discover that James, a staunch Catholic, now ruled and was regrettably an unknown quantity.

A gentleman by the name of Richard Hoare, whom Paul had introduced to Pierre as a fellow goldsmith-turned-banker, brought up the issue of England's new king at the dinner table. "I think King James has already gotten himself into much trouble," he stated. Turning to Pierre, he went on, "He's been trying to give civic equality to Roman Catholic and Protestant dissenters and got into a quarrel with Parliament over it. To them, it showed favouritism towards the Catholics, and it did him no good, I can tell you."

"I would say not," Pierre replied. "I, myself, experienced profound disappointment to learn of his kingship. I'm afraid I don't know much about how your English parliament works. Do they have much power?"

"Well, not at the moment. The king's working to terminate it. He's already in the process of appointing Catholics to important senior military and political posts, which, of course, alienates many of his subjects. We fear he's definitely trying to turn the country back to the old religion. I think the next few years here in England will be quite interesting. You have come at a good time, to see how our political scene works."

In deference to the Garneaus, the group spoke a mixture of French and English, and by the time the evening was over, Pierre was pleased to find he fit in quite well with the group. It was a relief for him to find ready-made friends, and he already felt a distinct affinity with Paul Thibault. He was positive they would become close friends.

In the whole party, there was only one man about whom Pierre experienced uncertainty. A Monsieur Mathurin Mercier, another goldsmith, who also seemed enamoured with Louise. The man was younger than Paul and quite handsome in a dark, brooding way. However, Pierre felt an immediate distrust of him. Behind Paul's back, Mercier spoke in a disparaging manner about his host, which he thought was extremely poor manners. He wondered if there was indeed animosity between the two. Time would tell, he thought. In every rose, there is always a thorn.

Nevertheless, he considered himself indeed fortunate to have escaped King Louis' long sword, and deliver his family, almost unscathed, to this new life to which, he had no doubt, they were destined.

Chapter 17

Spitalfields, September 26, 1685

They had been living in Spitalfields only three weeks when, late Saturday morning, Claudine went into the girls' room and found Louise still in bed, weeping into her pillow. A sick, sour smell permeated the room.

"Are you ill, Child? You look dreadful."

"Oh, Maman, I'm in terrible trouble. At first, I thought it was the dizziness left over from the voyage and the coach ride. Now, I'm throwing up every morning and—Maman, I didn't have my flux this month. You know I've always been regular with that. I don't know how to tell you this, but I—I think maybe I'm going to have a baby. I'm so ashamed. What can I do?"

"But, Louise, I explained to you about babies. You have to have been with a man in that special way I..." She paused at the look of guilt on her daughter's face. She had seen the same look the night they waited for the ship in the small beach shack. "Oh, daughter, no. Whatever have you done? Not Marc—my dear, you didn't? You were never alone with him, were you?"

"Yes, Maman," she whispered. "We were together twice. Right before, we left La Rochelle. He took me out to the ocean and it—well, it—just happened. I loved him so much. I wanted to be with him; and we planned on marriage anyhow, so he said it was all right with the Catholic Church. Then I went with him again. I knew what we would do the second time. I—I couldn't help myself. Now he is so far away—oh, what will Papa say? He will turn me out. Whatever will I do?" She broke into a wail.

"No, of course not. He would never do that." Claudine took her in her arms and tried to sooth her. Nevertheless, she was extremely upset. Pierre would be furious at Marc, and so disappointed with his daughter, as well as herself. He had left it to her to tell Louise the facts about being a woman and the Calvinist Bible-based belief that sex without marriage was a sin. Did I not explain it well enough? Did I not tell her the consequences of such an action? I'm sure I did. How could she have forgotten our discussions?

It made her sick at heart that Marc would betray them like this, and now he was gone for at least two years. She didn't for a moment think Pierre would turn their daughter out, but it certainly was a dire situation. Whatever *would* they do? She tried to calculate exactly how long it was since they left La Rochelle. How far along would Louise be in her pregnancy now?

"My poor little girl," she continued. "We will have to tell him about this, of course. He will be terribly hurt, and angry with Marc. He should never have taken advantage of you. How could he be so selfish?" She wanted to cry herself.

"Please don't blame Marc, Maman. It was as much my fault. We loved each other too much. To wait for two or three years seemed unbearable. Couldn't I go back to France to Aunt Marie and wait for him? She would keep me safe, I know."

"I don't think that's at all possible. It's far too dangerous for one thing. Moreover, Papa would be even more distraught if his own daughter were to become a Catholic. Stay in bed today, if you're not feeling well," she continued. "I'll approach him this evening, and we'll decide what is to be done. Still, he'll be greatly distressed, and there's nothing we can do about that."

Claudine waited until the children had all gone to bed to speak to her husband. He had picked up the English book he was trying to understand: '*Paradise Lost.*' It was a volume he had borrowed from Paul, to help him with the language. She admired his determination to master this new tongue. She, herself, found it a most difficult language to learn.

It's a shame to interrupt him, she thought. However, the sooner he knows, the better.

'Pierre, I'm afraid I have some terrible news for you." She spoke softly; only her words expressed her urgency. "Something we must deal with right away."

"Is it money, Claudine? Since Paul's dinner, I'm receiving some good orders. I don't think funds will be a problem here at all, and we still have a large amount in the account. In fact, we could purchase the house now if you wish."

"No. This is much more critical than money. It's news I'm afraid will hurt you desperately. It's Louise." Her voice trembled. "We think she is pregnant."

"W-w-what!" He appeared utterly stunned, as his face turned pale.

"Oh, my dear, I'm so sorry." She quailed at his look. He had taken such pride in his beautiful daughter.

"Pregnant—Louise—but how?" As comprehension of the situation hit him, he turned beet red. "Claudine, no. Not Marc?"

Claudine worried he might have an attack of apoplexy. She couldn't speak to answer him, only nod miserably.

"*Maudit*, I'll kill that boy. How could he do this to us? And the girl— you explained everything to her about the sexual matters? The seriousness of such a step—she understood it?"   She nodded again.

"How could she risk her eternal life like this? And destroy our family's reputation as well." His face registered horror as this new thought hit him. "Claudine, we are ruined. Just when things are going so well, now in this community, we are ruined.

As swiftly as the anger had risen, it was gone. In its place was an expression of anguish. The lines of his face sagged, and he seemed to have aged twenty years. For a few moments, Claudine glimpsed the old man Pierre would become. She crossed to where he sat on the couch, and put her arms around him as she did when the children were hurt. His eyes had filled with tears. She thought he might cry. She had never seen him like this, even when his beloved grandfather died.

"Don't worry, Pierre. We'll think of something. Things will turn out all right. Perhaps I can take her back to France."

"Of course, you can't," he said. The anger had returned, and Claudine wasn't sure which was easier to deal with. "The babies need you here, and you'd never get back. I've been much too lenient with the girl—all that daydreaming. I should have beaten it out of her years ago. Believe me; I shall have a few strong words with her in the morning." His voice rose.

"Please, Pierre. You mustn't be too harsh with her now. She's rather fragile I'm afraid. She found the journey extremely gruelling. It may be she will lose the child."

She paused for a moment before saying, "I've been thinking; she's not too far along. Here in the city there will be women. You know—the kind that knows how to take care of these things." She heard the desperation in her own voice.

"Wife, no, no. Have you lost your mind? That is far too dangerous for the mother, and I'm certainly not going to add murder to our daughter's sins." The look of anguish had returned.

"But—now—wait—I have an idea. It means that I will have to lie. *Fichu,* that will be damnable enough."

It startled her to hear him curse. "Whatever are you thinking?"

"The dragoons. Everyone's heard how they've treated our women. Rape, Claudine. Think of it. Our beautiful, virgin daughter raped by those evil men. Such an appalling thing. And ironic, *non?* Still no one will fault her— or us— in that case. Jean Guy will have to be in on the deceit, of course. Not the twins though."

"Could we possibly tell such a falsehood? It is so unlike you. You hate liars."

"Yes, and I shall hate myself for this. Except that, I see no other way." He put his head in his hands. *"Maudit*, how could that girl do this to us? Well we must act fast. I shall go to Paul. I'll start with him. He's been exceptionally kind. He's a compassionate man, and I think he will stand by us. I can only pray we will be forgiven for this—but, Claudine, what else can we do?"

Louise's nausea and weakness kept Pierre from lecturing her for several days. In the meantime, he decided to make his first move in the deception. Since their arrival in London, his family had spent a number of evenings in the home of Paul Thibault and, once they were comfortably settled, he had been back to their home for dinner. They found him a charming and stimulating companion. Monsieur Thibault's ancestors had come from Paris, during the terrible persecutions of the early sixteenth century, and he related stories handed down to him of his own great grandparents' time.

It had seemed to Pierre strange that the goldsmith always included the children in his invitations. He did notice, however, that he kept looking at Louise whenever they were together. The widower acted like a love-struck, young swain.

It's no wonder, though, he thought. It even astounded him to see how beautiful she was becoming. At home in France, she had been his sweet little girl. However, thinking of her need to be married now, he saw her as another man might. She was indeed lovely with an oval face, a milk-white skin, thick, golden blonde hair, and luminous green eyes, which lately seemed exceedingly large and sad.

Three days after his wife's announcement, Pierre called at Paul's shop on the pretext of needing funds from his account. He didn't try to hide the worry eating away at him, and as he expected, Paul, being the astute man he was, noticed it.

"Monsieur Garneau—perhaps I may call you Pierre now—and you must certainly call me Paul—I feel we have become quite good friends over the last few weeks. But I notice something troubles you today. Are you not happy with the Spitalfields' house?"

"Yes, please do call me Pierre. You are by far my closest acquaintance in this community, and I value your friendship. But no, no, it's not the house. That's exactly right for our needs. My cousin did a tremendous service to get us settled like this. I suppose I'll seldom see him now, and we were the best of friends. I'm rather afraid I'm in need of a good friend right now."

"Then, please, feel free to confide in me. I find we have much in common, and I, too value this bond that has grown between us. Can you tell me what troubles you so?

"I'm not sure where to turn with this problem," Pierre said with a sigh. "I find my family to be in a very difficult situation. The last thing I ever suspected would occur to us. My eldest daughter ran into some trouble in La Rochelle, and it appears she is with child. A little over a month now, we think. I'm afraid it will quite ruin us in the community. The situation is, of course, particularly troubling to my wife. She is quite ill over it."

"Zounds. What a terrible thing for such an attractive young woman. She is truly beautiful, you know. Breathtakingly so. How dreadful for her. They say those dragoons are no better than animals, and now the king has revoked the edict, they will get away with even more than rape. The poor child!"

He shook his head in distress at the situation; his brow furrowed, as if in deep thought.

"But think how fortunate you are to be away from France. As for your charming Louise, there must be a way out for her. Can you leave it with me for a few days?"

"Yes, certainly I will. I'm relieved to have unburdened myself. As I said, I truly did not know whom to turn to in this mess. The only solution I can think of is to send her back to our family in France, and I'm not willing to do that. She'd have to disavow her religion, and, in any case, I fear the journey would be much too dangerous. My wife would have to go with her and how would she get back?"

"Well, Pierre, perhaps there's another way out of the problem. Call on me at the beginning of next week—but not here—come to the house. I am going to ponder the situation. It bears some thinking about."

Quite hurriedly, Paul handed Pierre his chapeau and ushered him through the shop and out the front door.

Chapter 18

London, September 1685

L ater that evening, Paul sat in the library of his large, empty house. He took a sip from the goblet of excellent brandy he twirled in his hands, and contemplated the lovely Louise and her situation. He supposed he looked calm enough to his servants, yet his mind was in turmoil.

It's over five years since my beloved Diane passed. There is no doubt I am often lonely. What will my future be like in this large house, with no one to share it? I could give the girl a home and security for her child. Am I actually in love again at my age? It seems improbable with one so young. However, she is so exquisite, and I think, in spite of this misfortune, truly innocent. She quite enchants me.

He reflected on the single ladies of his acquaintance. Pretty and charming as many of them were, he had never once thought of remarrying until now. This was the first girl who had stirred his heart since his wife died. From the moment he met her, he had felt like this. It was the same sensation as when he was a youth and first met Diane. He was normally a confident man and yet around Louise, he became giddy and hesitant, like a schoolboy. He had tried to put the thought from his mind, supposing such a beautiful, young girl would never be interested. Now it seemed she was being handed to him, on a silver platter.

He sipped a little more of his brandy and continued his reflection.

Am I a silly, old fool? After all, I'm twenty years older than she is. Although, many men my age marry younger woman; and now, perhaps she will be glad of my offer. Yes, I believe it is the right thing to do. I'll have to consider this some more. I have until Friday to put the idea to Pierre. He's a decent man. After all he's experienced lately, he doesn't deserve this stressful situation. I think he might well be happy to have an answer to his problem.

He finished his drink, picked up one of the candleholders, snuffed out the others, and headed upstairs to bed. *I will certainly be giving* this much consideration before Monday, was his final thought before he fell asleep.

Louise, Claudine, and Pierre were alone in the large front room on the first floor of their house. Pierre displayed his silks up front, near the entrance, but he had turned a corner of the room in the back into an office. Tonight the three of them were there, away from the other children, discussing the proposal Paul had made to him that morning. Pierre was adamant that marrying him was the only solution for her.

"But, he's so old and he's bald. I don't think I could ever love him," she said, wailing loudly.

"He isn't old. He's three years younger than I am—not quite thirty-seven. You will be seventeen next month, which is certainly old enough to marry. And he's not bald. He cuts his hair short and wears a wig because that's the custom here. It's a safeguard against lice in the city. In any case, it's not a time to worry about love. Your condition will soon become apparent, and it will be far worse for you if you are not married. People will consider you completely immoral."

"Oh, Papa, do you think I'm wicked? Marc said we were truly married by church common law?"

"Well, he should have known better than that. You are not a Catholic, even if he thinks he is." He held his temper thinking of his own deception to Paul. Let him without sin cast the first stone, he remembered.

"I'm not saying either of you was intentionally wicked. Nevertheless, what you have done is against our faith. Marc should have never taken advantage of your vulnerability. He was a beloved member of our family, and we trusted you with him. Now you have put us in this serious situation, and Paul, who is a kind and good man, has offered a solution. So you *will* obey me, girl."

She wailed again.

"You've always been taught there are consequences for wrong actions," he continued. "And now you see that's true. Things are different here in London than if we were still in France. If you do not marry Paul, the whole Huguenot community will brand you as a harlot. Your life will be ruined, and you will have ruined this family, as well. Do you understand me?"

"Yes, Papa." Now she sobbed, her shoulders shaking. "Oh, what have I done? Will I go to hell?"

Pierre closed his eyes, heartbroken by her agonized crying. The thought of his beautiful daughter tortured forever in a fiery hell shook him to his core. What can I tell her? Since leaving France, I'm not even sure what I believe anymore.

For the first time in his life, his faith wavered. He could not rationalize how his beloved child's destiny was to commit this sin, and suffer the consequences of hellfire. For once, doctrine was beyond him. Besides, there was his own transgression. He didn't feel comfortable deceiving Paul, the way he had. What would his destiny be now?

"I don't know, child. What is hell anyway? Your Uncle Jacques doesn't believe there is such a place of torment. I'm afraid lately theology has become a mystery to me. Nevertheless, we must contact Monsieur Thibault and accept his proposal. Truly, it is all we can do, and I know he will be kind to you. If I didn't think so, I wouldn't go along with this. I am most disappointed with you, but I still love you, my child."

It pained his heart to put his beloved daughter through all this. However, he reasoned, she has brought the situation on herself, and it's our only option. "Go to bed now, daughter."

He turned to Claudine, "Maman, will you go with her? She is rather distraught, so perhaps a sleeping draught for her tonight. I'll contact Paul in the morning to make the arrangements. It must be done as soon as possible."

With a heavy heart, Louise went to bed in the room she shared with Catherine and Jeanette. In spite of the opiate her mother gave her, she lay awake for hours in her narrow bed. Although it was late, the noises of a London night, outside her window, filtered through the pane. She counted as the Baroque clock, so carefully packed and shipped from France, struck the second hour past midnight. Unhappily, she tossed and turned, mulling over her father's ultimatum. She reflected back to when, sitting beside her enchanted river and dreaming of Marc, she had imagined what her future would be. The life they would make together.

I wonder if I could go back and relive these past few months, could I change the direction things have taken? If Papa is right, I couldn't and this must be my fate. I could do away with myself. However, I think God would consider that even more wicked, and there's Baby to think of now. Nothing is more important than Marc's baby. I must learn to like Monsieur Thibault. He is a pleasant man but, oh, I shall never love him the way I love Marc.

Chapter 19

The marriage of Paul and Louise took place on the 15th of October 1685 in the English church. Only the Garneau family and two of Paul's closest friends, Dr. Rene Martin and his wife, Lorraine, attended the ceremony. Outside of the family, only Paul and Rene knew the situation, and they both thought it was the dragoons.

Louise wore a special dress in the palest of pink silk Pierre had woven. With her blonde hair covered in a small lace cap of the same shade, she looked breathtaking. Paul could hardly believe this incredible girl would be his. Still he was well aware she did not love him. When he and the family had met to discuss the wedding plans, she scarcely looked at him although she thanked him and declared how honoured she was for his offer.

"I'll try to make you happy, Monsieur Thibault," she said. "I have so many new things to learn in this country, I hope I'll never embarrass you."

"Well, Louise. The first thing you must learn to do is call me Paul. I could never abide this custom of my wife calling me Mister. That will be a start and we'll go on from there."

After the ceremony and a small dinner party at the Garneau's, they drove back to his house in silence. As he sat beside her in the coach, he was aware of her trembling like a frightened child. They arrived at the front entrance and, feeling sorry for her, he took her icy hand and led her into the house. They passed through the spacious foyer and up the elegant staircase to a large, magnificently decorated bedroom where a coal fire burned in the fireplace.

"This is your room, Louise," he said, smiling kindly at her. "You will stay here alone until the baby is born. I won't be coming in here at all, for now. Do you understand what I'm saying?"

Louise blushed; nevertheless, she looked up into his face and smiled. "Yes, I do. It's most kind of you. You've been so wonderful to all of us. I'll always appreciate it."

"You're going to make me a very happy man, but we'll take time to get to know each other. You've been through a lot in the last few months. Now you must think only of the child and its welfare. I always wanted a family, but my wife was not strong, and none of our babies survived. So, we must take good care of you and this little one. While you're waiting, is there anything you would like to do?"

"Why yes, I should like to learn English. Now this is my home, I must be able to speak the language properly.

"That's a splendid idea. No time like the present. Tomorrow, I'll enquire about getting a tutor for you. Now you go to sleep, and stay in bed in the morning. I'll see you at dinner. Perhaps by then, I'll have arranged something for you. Good night, my dear."

As he was about to leave the room, she reached up and kissed him on the cheek. "Thank you, Paul. My father was right. You truly are a good man."

Louise gave birth to a sweet little girl in the early morning of May 22nd. She was tiny with a mop of black curly hair and bright, blue eyes that sparkled with joy from the moment they opened. She was as much like Marc as a girl could be, and she hadn't cried once since her first desperate breath. Louise could not believe how much she could love this little bundle, after all the pain she had caused her; although both the mid-wife and her mother said it was an easy birth. They hadn't needed Doctor Martin, who had come to sit with Paul and Pierre, just in case. Claudine was also there, to oversee the birth of her first grandchild.

Just after lunch, there was a knock on the door of her room. She heard Paul asking the nurse if he could see her and the child. "Only if she's not too tired," he added.

"No, no sir," the woman said. "I'm sure she will want you to see your little girl."

Louise, who had watched her mother nursing Jeanette and Paul, did not intend to leave the feeding of her baby entirely to the wet nurse. She was holding her to her breast, when he entered. Using discretion, the nurse left the two of them together. Paul bent and kissed her cheek.

"Your parents and Doctor Martin have gone. They want you to rest," he said, taking a seat beside the bed. "Well, now—you have a beautiful, little girl. Claudine told me, she's quite tiny; so perhaps people won't look too askance at her coming early. They say there's no telling when a first one will arrive in any case. So I think I'll get the credit for her, even if the gossips think I rushed things a little."

Louise laughed along with him to hide her embarrassment, both at her state of undress and the turn the conversation had taken.

"She looks much like your Uncle Jacques, as I recall him," he continued. "A true Garneau. However, I have a favour to ask you, if I may. I wondered if you would mind calling your little girl, Alice. It was my mother's name, and she was a special woman. It would be a great honour for me."

"Alice Thibault," Louise tested the name. "Why I think it's a lovely name. I would be happy to call her that. I wish I'd known your mother. I think she must have been special."

"She was an extremely good woman—pretty and sweet like you—and exceedingly religious. A much better Huguenot than I'll ever be, I'm afraid. She named all her children after people in the Bible. Besides me, there was Isaac, Joseph, Hester, and Elizabeth."

"I didn't know you had siblings, Paul. I never thought to ask. Where are they now?"

"Sadly all except two of us died in the great plague of 1665. It killed my mother and father, as well. Elizabeth and I were the oldest, so we lived away from home. I was eighteen and went to finish my apprenticeship with my grandfather in Canterbury. Elizabeth came to live there as well, so neither of us got the sickness. She was fifteen and came to help our grandmother. I guess I forgot to mention I have a sister. Although, I don't know if she is alive now or not. She went with her husband to the Americas." He paused for a moment, as if examining the past.

"You don't hear from her?" Louise prompted.

"Not for a long time. She married a preacher by the name of James Wagner. King Charles was back on the throne, and they thought it might be safer for them in the colonies. They went to Boston, but I have no idea where she is now. My wife used to write to her. They were the same age and best friends even before our marriage. I wrote a few times after Diane's death, but they never answered my last couple of notes. Almost anything could have happened to them. They had children who were young. They probably wouldn't remember to contact me if something tragic happened."

"Oh, that is so sad. Well, now you have a family. My parents think highly of you. As for little Alice, she will always know you as her own father."

"Thank you, dear. I promise to cherish her as if she truly were my own. She looks like such a happy baby. As soon as you are back on your feet, we'll arrange the christening. Your mother tells me, she's already made a beautiful silk and lace dress for the occasion."

"Oh, my parents will be so happy. After all they've been through this last year, it will finally be something they could look back on with joy. You're very good to me, Paul. I do appreciate everything you've done."

"Well, you've brought a great deal of happiness to my lonely life. Never forget that. And now, with the baby here, there's much to look forward to."

Paul was often quite serious; however, she detected a slight twinkle in his eyes with that statement. Not sure of his intent, she remembered the promise he had made, that he would not take her as a wife until after the baby's birth. He had certainly kept his part of the agreement. However, she thought he was warning her now that things would change, and she wasn't certain of her feelings about the idea. He was an honourable man, and a wonderful friend and mentor to her. Certainly, she had grown quite fond of him. However, could anyone ever replace Marc in her heart? She hadn't forgotten how it had been with him at the beach in La Rochelle—the feelings he had evoked in her. She couldn't even imagine such intimacy with anyone else. In spite of her misgivings, however, she smiled warmly at him as he left the room.

The crucial moment came on a Friday evening exactly two months after the birth of Baby Alice. It had been a hot, humid day and the evening was still balmy. Louise bathed, and washed her hair with a mixture of herbs to combat the lice, with which there was a constant battle. As she sat brushing her hair, two maids came to take away the water. "Is there anything else you require, Madame?" one asked.

"No, thank you. I'm fine now. You girls go to bed yourselves. You look quite worn out" she replied in English. She was pleased with herself at how fast she was picking up this difficult language. Even the syntax was odd; so much was backwards. However, for the sake of Paul, she persevered with it. Eventually she would have to host dinner parties, and most of his clients and business associates were English, so she knew she must become fluent in it.

A quiet tap on the door to the adjoining room surprised her. It opened, and he stepped in, carrying a wine bottle and two empty glasses on a tray. It was the first time he had come that way. "I wondered if you would mind some company tonight," he said. "I thought we could finally celebrate the birth of our beautiful, little girl with some champagne. May I join you?

Chapter 20

Louise's heart began to hammer loudly, more from uncertainty than fear. Realizing this night was bound to arrive, she had tried to prepare herself. There was no doubt she had become fond of him, but did she want him as a lover? Wasn't she still in love with Marc? She certainly missed him with every fibre of her being, especially when she looked at his daughter. However, she owed so much to Paul, and she thought that most women would be delighted to have such a caring man for a husband.

Tonight he had discarded the curly periwig he wore for business and, to her surprise; she discovered he had let his hair grow. It was dark—not black like Marc's—but a rich brown with only the slightest streak of silver at the temples. Now it was long enough, he had tied it back with a leather ribbon. How much younger he looked without the peruke, she thought. She wondered anew why men wanted to appear in public wearing those unsightly accessories.

He'd taken off the vest he usually wore; and in his ruffled shirt, with long, full sleeves, he looked quite dashing. For a man of thirty-seven, he was in excellent physical condition. Although he spent long hours bent over a workbench, he did much riding and fencing, which kept his body lithe and lean.

A surprising shiver of anticipation ran through her. She liked him immensely, and having sat with him at his dinner table for nine months, she'd learned a great deal about him. He was extremely intelligent and, even though he'd not had the opportunity to travel, was as knowledgeable as Marc about many things.

She found conversation with him stimulating, and he seemed to take pleasure in teaching her new ideas. They had discussed numerous issues, including the religious beliefs of both Jean Calvin and John Milton; and he had explained how he preferred the theories of Milton.

"My father knew him quite well," Paul explained to her. "John was a fearless defender for Oliver Cromwell. However, he paid the price for his outspoken viewpoints when the monarchy returned. They confiscated his treatise on the scriptures, and forced him into hiding. No one ever saw those papers again. Personally, I think there was even more truth in his teachings than Calvin's; but no one pursued it after his death."

'But still, you always go to the French meetings with my parents. Are you not a believer?"

He smiled, "I guess I pick and choose what I believe. Of course, even if I don't accept all the Huguenot ideas, I'd much rather attend their service than go to the English Church. That differs little from the Papists. It exists only because King Henry VIII wanted to divorce his wife."

"Didn't he have a lot of wives?"

"Yes, six to be exact." He then explained how Henry had managed to marry so many women and murder two of them. "After the birth of the baby, I'll take you to see the Tower where Ann Boleyn was a prisoner. There's much history here in England, and I think you'll enjoy learning about it."

Living with him over those past few months, she'd discovered him to be a gentle man. She was certain he would never hurt her, but she still felt shy at the idea of intimacy with him. Of course, he has the right to be with me, she thought. It's only fair to be a wife to him in every way, when he has been so kind.

Now, here he was in her bedroom, and although she wasn't sure what to expect, she realized the prospect didn't frighten her as much as she anticipated.

"I'm not uncomfortable with you, Paul," she said, with only a slight tremor in her voice. "Please come in."

"Good. I'm not uncomfortable with you either." He grinned at her as he filled one of the delicate glasses from the bottle. "Do you like champagne?"

"I've never tasted it. Papa wasn't much for spirits. We only drank the pineau he made from the grapes we grew on our farm. I would like to try it, though. I think I'd like the bubbles." She knew she was babbling, but couldn't help herself. She felt both excited and nervous.

Paul smiled again, and handed her the glass of sparkling wine. She took a rather large sip, which tickled her nose. She took another mouthful and sneezed.

He chuckled aloud, which rather surprised her. He was inclined to look serious much of the time, rather like her father. However, since the birth of Alice, she'd noticed he often seemed amused and certainly more at ease with her. His laughter had a pleasant sound, and he had a beautiful smile, with noticeably white teeth for an older man. His kind, dark brown eyes were quite beautiful, and his slightly lined face only served to make him more distinguished looking.

Why he is extremely handsome, she thought. I never noticed before.

"I never had the chance to court you properly, dear," he said taking her hand as he sat down beside her on the small fainting couch. "I rather took advantage of the situation, I'm afraid. But I want you to know it wasn't only to save your reputation I married you."

"It wasn't?"

"No, I was already falling in love with you—almost at first sight. However, you were so young and so beautiful, I told myself, 'Paul, this girl won't be interested in you; so don't be a fool.' Then the opportunity presented itself and I took it, hoping you might learn to care for me. Now, the more I see of you—especially with the baby—the more in love with you, I am. You are even lovelier since the birth of Alice, you know."

He refilled her glass and she took another sip. She was beginning to feel considerably more relaxed.

"Are you surprised, little one?"

"Why, yes. I thought you were an extremely compassionate man, and I was in such a dreadful predicament. I always presumed that we rather took advantage of your kindness. I—I never dreamt you might care for me in that way."

"I love you passionately, Louise. I want so much to be a husband to you in more than just name. Since the first time I met you, I've longed to hold you and make you mine. I promise you, though; I won't do anything you don't want me to?"

"It *is* your right. My mother always said that intimacy was never a sin between a husband and a wife. Do you believe that is true?"

"Yes, you and I are bound together before God and man. The only sin would be if I forced myself on you. Believe me, my love, I will never do that."

He took the champagne glass from her; and setting it down on a small table, enfolded her in his arms. It astonished her how submissive she felt, and when he bent and kissed her soft, yielding lips, she experienced a sense of delight. Why, I don't mind him at all, she thought.

Of her own volition, her arms slid around his neck, and she leaned against his warm body. He kissed her tenderly for a moment more, then slowly drew away. "I should say 'good night' to you now, sweetheart," he said. "Unless you want me to stay."

"Don't go, Paul." She pulled him back to her.

"You are sure, dear?" he asked, smiling into her eyes.

"Yes, I'm sure," she whispered. "I think it's time for you to be my real husband now."

As his arms encircled her again, what surprised her most was just how willing she was to be his.

The next morning the maid entering the room awakened Louise late. She couldn't believe the time. Baby Alice would want her. "The master has already left for the shop, Madame," Hannah informed her. "Shall I bring you some breakfast to your room?"

"Yes, 'anna," she replied. "That would be nice. Has the baby had anything to eat this morning?"

"Oh, yes. Nurse took care of her; however, she *is* looking around for her mama. She already knows you, Ma'm; no doubt about that."

"Well, bring her to me before my breakfast then. And could you bring the "London Gazette" up, as well. I know society doesn't approve of women reading the newspaper, but I do like to know what's going on in the world. So although Monsieur Thibault says it is 'dry as dust' I shall try to read it. I don't think he will mind me as he knows I want to learn all I can about this country of his."

She spent the morning playing with Alice and reading the paper. Due to her lack of English, it took a long time. She wrote down several words, with which she was not familiar for her tutor to explain. Most of the information was about various ship arrivals; however, there was one column about business in London. It interested her to read what was happening with the banking situation. It seemed the government wanted a national bank for England rather than have the goldsmiths continue to administer the money. She found it difficult to understand, and decided to ask Paul to explain it to her.

The time passed quickly and soon she began to look forward to his homecoming. For the first time since her marriage, she took a long time with her appearance and asked her maid to arrange her hair in a becoming manner. She wanted to look especially pretty for him.

The crunch of the carriage wheels, as it stopped at the front door, brought her to her feet, and she went to greet him. He took one look at her and drew her into his arms. "I've been waiting all day to get home to you. What a lovely homecoming."

Over dinner, Louise asked him many questions about the banking. "I thought you were a goldsmith, Paul. Uncle Jacques always spoke of you as such. He always talked to us about his business interests here since he marketed so much of Papa's silks in England."

"My family has always been goldsmiths. My great-great grandfather established his business in Paris, but he had to flee for his life during the St. Bartholomew Day Massacre. Like your father, they came to London and started again. It's because of being a goldsmith I got involved with banking."

"That's the part I don't understand. What does being a goldsmith have to do with banking?"

"It's quite straightforward when you know the story. For many years, the wealthy people kept their gold in the vaults at the Tower of London.

When the old King Charles needed some ready cash for the Civil War, he somehow figured it belonged to him, and he took it all. Even when Cromwell came into power, they never got it back.

"So then, people with lots of gold began looking for other places where there were vaults to keep their wealth secure. *Voila*, as you say. We goldsmiths had safes, so they would ask us to keep it for them. We issued certificates to them for the amounts they lodged with us, and, of course, we returned it to them on demand."

She nodded her understanding. She had learned record keeping from her father.

"As it turned out, the amounts the owners wanted to take out were usually only a fraction of what we stored for them. So eventually, we believed it would be harmless to loan out their gold at a good rate of interest. It made us money, of course. Why else would we take the risk?"

She nodded again. She found the concept of earning profit on the gold fascinating.

"In time, instead of actual gold, we circulated paper certificates redeemable in coin. People considered these certificates as good as gold. That's what your father brought to me from your uncle. So then, I transferred the value of what was in Jacques' account into one for your father. Do you understand?"

"Yes I do. That's very interesting," she said as they left the dining room and walked together towards the library. "I always wondered how it worked. I didn't think Papa brought enough gold with him to buy the house."

"It's worked fairly well up until lately. However, this circulating of promissory notes has gone far beyond most of us now, and it's time to have a proper system. It will take a few years but the government plans to establish its own bank. They'll call it The Bank of England. Some of the most successful goldsmiths in the city have been working out the details. I'm fortunate they've chosen me as one of them."

"My, I didn't realize what an important man you are." She smiled flirtatiously.

"Well, not so important yet. Do you happen to remember my friend, Sir John Houblon? He's also of Huguenot descent. You met him at the first dinner I had for your family, but I don't suppose you remember much from that night. After I met you, I didn't remember much either. You were all I could think of."

He turned to face her. Smiling down at her, he took both her hands and held them in his as he continued. "In any case, he is an exceptionally clever businessman and the people in government in charge of this project rely a lot on him. It's most likely they'll name him governor of the bank when it's established. He's enlisted my help, so I'll be busy in the next few years, but not too busy to spend time with my lovely, young wife."

Again, he smiled his beautiful smile at her and hesitated for a moment, then added almost shyly, "Louise, can it be that you could learn to love me—to be genuinely happy here with me?

The question surprised her. She looked at the handsome man who was now, without a doubt her husband. For a few seconds, she thought of Marc. But she had forfeited him by her actions and he was lost to her forever. Even if, he came to London, they could only be friends. Deep in her heart, she sensed a tinge of regret. However, Paul was an outstanding man in so many ways; kind and considerate; strong and virile; and there was no doubting his feelings for her. He was a tender and passionate lover who would shower her with affection as long as he lived. In return, she would be the chatelaine of his magnificent house; give him the family he desired; and deeply respect and ultimately love him, as he so richly deserved

She looked up at him and then, laying her head against his chest, whispered, "Yes, Paul, I can love you. I can be genuinely happy here with you."

Silently she vowed, and no matter what happens, I will always be faithful.

PART IV

Time and Unforeseen Occurrence

"I returned to see under the sun that the swift do not have the race, nor the mighty ones the battle, nor do the wise also have the food, nor do the understanding ones also
have the riches, nor do even those having
knowledge have the favor;
because time and unforeseen occurrence befall them all."
King Solomon of Israel

Chapter 21

Pondicherry, India, April 1687

Life in Pondicherry with the French East India Company was much less glamorous than Marc had anticipated. For one thing, there was the heat—the constant, oppressive, overpowering heat. The Company had built a small fort and a Catholic church in Pondicherry, an insignificant weaving and fishing village in the southeast of the Indian sub-continent. Situated on the Bay of Bengali, fairly close to the equator, the climate was not only exceedingly hot, but also humid, particularly during the summer monsoons. That season fast approached, and Marc did not look forward to it at all.

However, it was not only the heat that got him down but also the smells—a blend of spices, sweat and unburied feces—that pervaded the entire area. There was no escaping them.

Most of the building the company was involved in, at the moment, entailed laying out the grid for the city they were planning, as well as the building of new French-style houses for the soldiers and workers already there. Currently, Indian-style bungalows built within the fort accommodated the more than two hundred members of the company. Marc, Jacques and their East Indian servant called a *nauker*, shared one of these long, low buildings.

There were already fruit and vegetable gardens in various stages of completion, and now, besides the houses, they were erecting bazaars. Eventually there would be a complete French town running north from the fort all along the ocean. The company planned to bring in the families of those men willing to remain in India. Marc assisted his father in drawing up the engineering plans and specifications for the design of the city, as well as the purchasing of the necessary items to build it. Dealing with the impassive Tamil officials was often time-consuming and frustrating.

The sandy beaches all along the Bay of Bengal were pleasant with cashew and palm trees and other lush vegetation growing near the fringes.

Although the ocean was sometimes rough, Marc swam most every day. Aside from that, there wasn't much to do for entertainment in his spare time except to visit the bazaars and watch the people. Many of the women looked quite fascinating in their graceful saris; but with his heart still yearning for Louise, they held no allure for him. In any case, the *commissaire* had forbidden all association with them.

He did think it a pity his Uncle Pierre could not visit the place and see the beautiful silks the locals made. The outfits created from these materials were strikingly vivid in shades of scarlet, royal blue, and turquoise even Lyon's French dyers had not yet been able to create.

He and his father had been in Pondicherry working in the office of Francois Martin, the French Commissaire, for not quite a year when a British trading vessel, *The Malabar Merchant*, not long out of Madras and bound for Amoy, China, stopped in for repairs and fresh water.

Although there wasn't much love lost between France and England, Monsieur Martin invited the ship's officers to an official dinner. Jacques and Marc were summoned, as well. During the evening, Jacques had a long conversation with the ship's master, Captain Arthur Sharp—a large, windburnt man with bushy, red hair and an equally bushy, red beard.

It was after midnight by the time they returned to their bungalow. Nevertheless, Jacques brought up the subject of his conversation with the captain. "Marc, you know my contract here in Pondicherry is for another twelve months, and you have signed on as my aide for that long. But are you genuinely happy here with all this clerical work?"

Marc started to yawn but said, "Why, *mon pere,* you think I'm not pulling my weight? I'm not competent?"

"No, no, it's nothing like that. However, I find you are more and more morose and not the lively companion you were on board our ship. I have an idea if you would like to listen to me."

Marc grinned sleepily. "Your ideas are always interesting, *mon pere.*"

"I spoke to Master Sharp at the dinner. He's quite concerned he has no one aboard who speaks tolerable Portuguese. That's the language the Chinese have managed to learn best, and it's important the captain has someone who can translate for him."

"Is that a fact?" Alert now, to what his father was saying, he listened carefully.

"I told him, you were fluent in the language," Jacques continued, "and he's interested in signing you on with them for this trip. The fact you intend to make your home in England helps, I think. I explained to him about the Huguenot situation in France, and that you don't want to convert."

"Me—go to China and leave you here? How would you manage?"

"There's not enough work to keep both of us busy. Seriously, Marc, on the voyage over I came to realize how much you do love Louise. If you're planning to marry her, you'll have to live and work out of England. Pierre will never allow her to go back to France. If you do well with Master Sharp, it's quite likely he could get you a position with the British East India Company when you get back to London."

Marc sighed. "There's nothing I want more than to marry her as soon as possible. And I must admit I've been worrying about how I could support a wife in England."

"There's the gold account I have with Paul Thibault in London. Of course, a lot has gone to pay Pierre for the farm. But there's still enough to buy a house, I think, and there's also the warehouse. My suggestion is that you take the monies from the sale of our cognac here, and go on this British ship to Amoy. You'll have to change it to silver, though, as Master Sharp tells me, that's all the Chinese will take."

Marc was fully awake now. "Why is that then?" he asked.

"I don't know. For some reason, they aren't interested in gold. However, that's not important. What's interesting is that the English have begun to see the value of tea, and they need merchants in that trade. By going to China, you could learn a great deal about it. And if you purchase a consignment, and ship it back to the warehouse in London, it will give you a good start there."

"You think Captain Sharp would let me do that?"

"Given your fluency in Portuguese, as well as English, I think he would allow you almost anything you want. If needs be, tell him that's the only pay you require. He's going to call on us in the morning, and I'm positive he will ask you to join the crew."

He was right. The English captain showed a definite interest in acquiring Marc's services; and, by the end of April, *The Malabar Merchant* sailed from Pondicherry, with him officially on the payroll as the ship's interpreter.

Sailing southeast across the Bay of Bengal away from India, the prevailing winds were not always with them; and when they dropped, a feeling of lassitude hung over the entire ship. Often the skies were leaden, but it brought no relief from the heat and humidity. Even some weeks later, as they made their way north through the hazy South China Sea, the days seemed heavy and long. Soon the monsoons would come and bring torrential rains and a slight relief from the heat. Then the sea could turn fierce and agitated. Marc had heard of the cyclones that spawned in the hot waters of the tropics and prayed they'd be safely moored, far to the north of the equator in the port of Amoy, when that took place.

It was the end of June, with the ship still bearing in a northerly direction through the China Sea, that the lookout caught a glimpse of the mainland. Marc went looking for the master and found him in his quarters studying a large map. The two men had spent many evenings together over a glass of Cognac or brandywine as the English called it. They were now firm friends.

"We're nearly there, are we sir?" he asked Captain Sharp.

"Yes, we are, Marc," the captain said, handing him a glass full of the amber liquor. "Have a seat, my boy. I've been thinking. It's time I was considerably more honest with you about what I have in mind for this little venture."

"You mean with the translating, don't you?" he asked, taking one of the comfortable chairs. "I'm quite prepared for that."

"That's your main duty, of course. However, I have to confess there's more to it than I originally told you. It's true my instructions are to go to Amoy with this load of metal and pick up tea there."

Marc smiled to himself as Captain Arthur tugged at his red beard as he often did when perturbed; a habit the younger man had noted.

"Actually the best place for tea is Canton," the captain continued. "However, English ships haven't exactly been welcome in that port since there was a disastrous skirmish about fifty years ago. Shots fired from a British ship killed some customs officials."

"Good lord. Is that right? My knowledge of China is quite lacking, I'm afraid. I've some idea of where Amoy is, but I know nothing about Canton. But what would all this have to do with me?"

Captain Sharp moved back to the map he had pinned to the wall of the cabin. He pointed to a small island up the coast near the mainland.

"This island is Taiwan and the dot right across from it is the city of Amoy. A few customs people there speak some English. They don't particularly love us either, but they'll be happy to have this metal; and I'll be able to exchange it for a load of tea. As I said, that's the official plan. The thing is, Marc, I'm actually here on a mission only a few of the company governors know anything about."

"A secret mission?" Marc began to feel mystified.

"Yes, and that's where you come in. Before I go on to Amoy, the company wants me to see if there's any hope at all for us to do business in Canton again. And that's here, ninety miles up the Pearl River." He pointed to a spot on the map west of Macau.

"We don't think there's anyone there now who speaks English. I don't know how those fellows back home thought I would manage it; but then you came on the scene, and that was a fantastic break for me. I needed someone who at least speaks Portuguese to find out where we stand with the Cantonese officials and see what the possibilities are. You, my friend, fit the bill perfectly.

"Because I speak the language?"

"That, and the fact you are not English, and you really do want to buy tea. Even if they won't sell to the British East India Company, they might be willing to do so to a Frenchman. I want you to try to buy a full load of tea in your name. While you're doing business with them, I can get a sense of how they feel about the company now. If you manage it, twenty-five percent of the cargo will be for you. You won't have to pay a cent of your own money."

"My word. That's quite a bounty, and it doesn't seem too difficult a job. It would certainly take care of what I need."

The captain paused for a moment, again fingering his beard before he answered. "Well, I should warn you. There's always the chance, as soon as they see the English flag, they'll start shooting at us. They could possibly blow the ship up. It's the Chinese that invented gun power, you know. So, it's not quite as simple as just sailing in there. I'm going to have to make an alternate plan."

"I see. You're thinking of some sort of a reconnoitre strategy then?"

"Exactly. There's the definite possibility of danger. At least you know now what you're up against. If you're still willing to do it, we'll seal it with another shot of brandy. A drink to friendship and success. Agreed, my boy?"

"Agreed, Sir. I'm always ready for adventure. It's what I do best," Marc replied with a laugh.

As Marc held out his glass, the captain bestowed a friendly slap on his back and proceeded to fill it to the top again with the aromatic liquid.

Chapter 22

Pearl River, China, June 1687

Morning mists rose from the warm, sheltered waters of a large delta, some eighty miles inland from the mouth of the Pearl River, when *The Malabar Merchant* dropped anchor amid a group of well-wooded islands. With the ship hidden deep among the reeds, Captain Sharp and Marc, along with two armed escorts, rowed across to the mainland. There they secured the small craft as best they could in a concealed spot and headed towards the town of Tungkun, a few miles east of Canton.

Finding a man who spoke Portuguese, Marc made enquiries about travel into the city. He managed to organize two sedan chairs for himself and the master. However, there seemed to be a dearth of fancy transport in the town, so the two guards ended up, being shoved along the streets in worn-out wheelbarrows, by a couple of peasant farmers. Even the bearers laughed at the sight of two small oriental men pushing the brawny sailors along the road in their noisy vehicles.

"Never mind, lads," the captain called out to them. "If we can get this business organized with the Chinese customs, I'll send you back to the ship in style."

With Marc doing the talking and Captain Sharp nodding and smiling, they appeared to be Portuguese sailors, so they encountered no problems along the route. By the time they reached the teaming metropolis of Canton, dusk had fallen.

"We'd better wait to settle the customs issue in the morning, I think," Captain Sharp said to Marc. "Ask them to find us some sort of inn as near the harbour as possible."

The flea-bitten inn, the bearers led them to, was noisy and smelled of fish, but they were all so tired no one argued about staying there. Marc asked the two sedan owners to wait overnight, and take the sailors back to Tungkun the next afternoon. The captain agreed to procure rooms and a meal for them. However, he paid the two farmers and sent them on their way, along with their decrepit wheelbarrows. By the time he and Marc finished their meal, and were ready to climb the stairs to their shabby rooms, the sailors and the Chinese bearers were drinking themselves into oblivion.

"Well, I'll let them be. They don't get much fun when we're at sea. I'll consider this shore leave," the captain said, shaking his head in amusement. "I don't see how they communicate, though. Neither of my boys speaks a word of Cantonese." He winked at Marc as they parted at their separate doors.

The next morning, the two of them made their way down to the harbour where they could see several large trading ships moored. The frenzied activity in the port surprised Marc.

"Those two large ones are Portuguese," the captain explained. "Their home port is Macau, but they pick up tea here. And the other big one anchored across the river is a Dutch East India Company ship, out of Holland." He also pointed out numerous small boats called *sampans* and the larger *junks* used by the Chinese merchants. As well, two or three medium sized Arab dhows lay at anchor.

"This is all so amazing," Marc exclaimed. "What are those beautiful white structures along the waterfront?"

"Pretty, aren't they? The Portuguese built those in their Mediterranean style," the captain explained. "They've been more or less in control here for the last one hundred years. Now, of course, our 'John Company' is interested in tea, so things in China are bound to change. The Portuguese and Dutch might as well get used to it."

They headed for the nearest building. Passing along the narrow street, Marc noted how different the people were from those in India. Here, the groups of labourers and loiterers all seemed possessed of a good-natured hilarity, laughing with each other as they went about their jobs.

As Marc and the captain approached the entrance, they stopped a man who looked like an official and Marc asked in Portuguese if any of them spoke English. Marc translated his reply. "No, there is only one tea merchant who speaks any English at all. His name is Li Jang. He's down in that building at the far end of the harbour."

"Well done, Marc," said the captain, patting him on the back. "You're worth your weight in gold. I don't know a word of Portuguese and only a few words of Mandarin. I've only been here in China once before. That was up in Amoy, and I had a Chinaman who was born in India with me. He knew enough English to act as a go-between. Well, you have an aptitude for languages I see, so maybe you'll be able to pick up some of their lingo. But it's difficult because it's not related to anything we know."

By now, they had arrived at the tea merchant's building and, by pointing and mouthing the words 'Li Jang' along with inquiring looks, they managed to find the gentleman in question. He was of medium height with a slim build. His long, straight black hair hung down his back in a thick ponytail covered by a conical-shaped, felt hat. Marc noted his clothes were of pure silk, and he looked quite prosperous compared to the workers they had passed on the dock.

He had a long moustache curving down to his chin, which sported a neat, pointed, little goatee. He was frowning at a paper he was reading, and the overall effect gave him quite a fierce countenance. Nevertheless, Marc decided to approach him.

"Mr. Li?" he said, speaking in Portuguese, "I understand you can speak the Portuguese language and some English as well?"

"Yes. What you want?" the man replied in broken English. He scrutinized them through slanted black eyes with a hint of a twinkle.

"This gentleman is the captain of an English ship moored down the river near Tungkun. We need to get clearance before we dare bring it here, but Captain Sharp doesn't speak Portuguese. I'm Marc Garneau from France. We've just arrived and I'm looking to buy a shipload of tea for myself. We need an honest man to help us arrange, with the customs men, for an English ship to dock here."

The tea merchant started to laugh, and looked much younger as the frown disappeared. Oh, yes. English not much liked here. But I can help you," he said. "I come from Amoy so learn English pretty good. You pay me well and I be velly honest. Only fair, you aglee?"

"Of course, Mr. Li, we intend to pay you fairly. How much would you suggest?"

Li named a sum that seemed akin to what they would pay in India. The Captain nodded in agreement and held out his hand to the merchant.

With a broad smile on his face and eyes again twinkling with amusement, Li responded, "Okay then. We shake hands now and make 'deal' like English say.

"Good," Marc interjected. "What happens next?"

"You need proper chop from custom fellows to bring ship here. I can do that. Where you stay now?"

Marc told him the name of the inn. Li wrinkled his nose and said, "Best we go see customs men about *chop* fast. You need your ship here in harbour. Much better to live on. Come, we go together."

He led the way down to the customs house where, once the officials discovered they were English, a great deal of excited conversation took place. Wondering exactly what was happening, Captain Sharp and Marc stood back while Li handled the situation. He spoke Cantonese animatedly to the group of men, while one particularly angry-looking man kept glancing over their way. After awhile Li came over to them.

"Not looking good right now, my fliends. Maybe you go now. I have to talk to velly important head official. He not here until later. He owes me big favour, so I think he fix trouble. Maybe look around city and then go back to inn. I come to see you tomorrow after morning meal."

"Well," Captain Sharp said as they left the building, "that didn't look too promising. I'm certainly glad we met this Li fellow. We'd never have been able to handle anything this complicated with no knowledge of the language."

"You're right about that, Captain," Marc said. "Li Jang looks more and more like someone I'd like to have as a good friend."

Chapter 23

Canton, China

The two men spent the rest of the day wondering around the ancient city; then went back to the inn, where the sailors and the bearers waited for them, somewhat worse for their drinking spree. The captain explained to the two crewmembers the problem they had encountered.

"I'll want you lads alert in the morning. No more drinking, you understand. As soon as we get that *chop*, you'll have to rush it back to the ship and give it to the first mate. I hope you can get that across to those lazy louts who brought us here. Since I have to pay another night for them, they'd better be in good shape, in the morning. I want that ship here in Canton harbour as fast as possible. Two nights in this hell hole are enough for me."

⊷⊱⊰⊶

By mid morning the following day, Li and the administrators had managed to work out the formalities. The Chinese merchant introduced them to one of the officials who handed the crucial *chop* to the Captain. He looked somewhat friendlier than on the previous day.

"English ship can enter harbour now," Li advised them. "As for buying tea, you say you need honest merchant who know about tea. I know everything about tea and I sell for decent price. But I must have my commission. We still have deal?"

"Yes, of course. We're certainly grateful for what you've done already," the Captain said. "Are the teas ready to buy yet? Can we arrange to see them?"

"Not much down from mountain yet. Take long time to get here. Best you wait one month. Then much to choose from. I help you then."

"A month?" Mark exclaimed. "What will we do here in Canton for a whole month?"

"You better wait here today for ship to arrive, but tomorrow you come to my house. I have many different teas there. My women do tea ceremony for you, and you see what you like best. You come tomorrow afternoon?"

Mark looked at Captain Sharp who nodded.

"Yes, we can do that," he replied. "Where do you live? How do we get there?"

"I live up river. Not far. Big house with red roof and white pillars. Everyone know it. You come at three o'clock. That good time for tea. I tell you history of tea. I best person in Canton to talk about tea."

"Fine then," Captain Sharp affirmed. "We will see you tomorrow, Mr. Li."

They all bowed, and Marc and the captain turned and left the building. "Well, what do you think about that, Captain?" Marc asked. "You think Zang speaks the truth? We need a go between to get the tea, as well?"

"Yes, I'm afraid so. These city merchants have it all figured out. They belong to a guild called the *Cohong,* supervised by the Imperial Officials, and we can't do a thing without them. We'll probably have to bribe the customs' men something, as well. Well, let's hope Mr. Li is as honest as he appears. He certainly got us out of trouble yesterday, so I'm willing to put my money on him now."

Marc and the Captain had no trouble finding transportation to Mr. Li's house the next afternoon. Everyone on the waterfront knew exactly where he lived. When they arrived at their destination, and the chair-bearer pointed out the house to them, the beauty of the structure amazed them. It was a three-story, tiered, white building with a red tile roof over each portion. The bottom floor was partly built on stilts over the water with a beautifully, pillared veranda overlooking the river. It was surrounded by graceful willow trees with branches spreading above the water. The top roof over the third floor was pagoda shaped with the same red tiles. Small birds floated on the river, once in awhile diving for food. An aura of peace and tranquility surrounded the house.

"No wonder Mr. Li seems so happy." Marc gasped. "What a wonderful place to live!"

"He's obviously successful and not particularly superstitious," Captain Sharp agreed. "This must have been built by the Portuguese. Usually Oriental houses have green roofs to bring them luck. Well, it should be interesting. I've never been invited to a Chinese home before, but I think he likes you, Marc."

"I think I like him."

They rang the large bell on the front portico, and soon an obsequious servant ushered them into a simple, but stunning room. The floor was bamboo, covered in silk mats, and the furniture was of an uncomplicated but elegant style lacquered in black with gold designs. A low table was set with a brazier, five cups, and several teapots. The servant indicated they should wait while he went to tell his master.

Li Jang soon arrived with two slim, pretty women dressed in flowing, silk robes. Their shiny black hair was dressed stylishly and heavily lacquered. They minced along in a strange rocking gait, which drew Marc's attention to their feet.

He was so shocked; he could hardly take his eyes off them. They were abnormally tiny and encased in neat, silk-covered shoes. He'd heard of the practice of feet binding but still could hardly believe what he saw. Although their movements were ungainly, the women had no trouble getting around on these miniature appendages.

Mr. Li introduced the older of the two women first. "This Number one wife," he explained. She good woman but she no make children for me. So I take second wife." He now turned to the younger woman who was exceptionally beautiful. Li Jang smiled appreciatively at her.

"Second wife give me three children. Two boys and one girl. Girl expensive to marry off but she is velly pretty. Her name is Li Ying. Means beautiful flower. You see?"

A servant ushered three little children into the room. The boys were about six and four and exact images of Li Jang. The little girl was held by a nurse and appeared to be not quite a year old. She was like her mother and looked like a little, china doll. Marc was glad to see that so far her tiny feet were not bound. Mr. Li noticed his appraising look.

"Emperor Kangxi allow foot binding now, but Jesuits do not like it. They say it barbaric. Emperor studies with Jesuits. He wants all people to listen about Jesus. I listen to Jesuits; and I think Jesus is velly good man. Maybe I become Christian. So I not bind little girl's feet. But she grow up like Hakka woman with big, ugly feet. Maybe no one want her for wife."

Captain Sharp appeared quite taken aback at Mr. Li sharing this information. However, he shook his head. "No, she will marry," he reassured his host. "She's already lovely."

Mr. Li motioned the children out of the room then indicated his guests should sit at the table, the captain and Marc on one side and the two women beside him on the other.

The ceremony was impressive. The water was boiled in an iron kettle on an attractive ornamental brazier with different inscriptions and Chinese characters. Number One Wife carefully measured out the various types of tea leaves using a bamboo spoon and placed them into small teapots. Then

Number Two Wife added the boiled water with much whisking and stirring. This whole process took some time. When it was finally ready, Number One wife poured it into the exquisite, tiny porcelain cups.

As the women performed the tea ceremony, Li Jang explained it in Portuguese. "My English not good enough to tell about tea ceremony," he told them. Marc, in turn, translated it to the captain in English. In between the boiling and the brewing and the pouring, Mr. Li spoke poetically of the history of the Quing Dynasty and the life of Buddha whom, in spite of the Jesuits and his Christian leanings, he admired a great deal.

After it was over and the women bowed and minced out of the room, Jang turned to the two men. "I go next week to mountain to see about tea crop this year. I look for best tea to sell to my customers."

"Where do you go, Mr. Li?" Marc inquired.

"Please, you call me Jang. We flends now." He smiled at them, his black eyes twinkling. "I go to tall mountains in Fujian Province. Wu-li Mountain. Best tea grow there and so there are many, many factories. I go for one month and then I know which tea to sell you. Some good one year. Some good, other year. I never know until I try myself."

"I'd like to go with you." Marc said, and then looked at the captain. "If that's all right with you, sir?"

"It's fine with me. What about it, Jang?"

"Oh, velly dangerous trip. Mountain trails steep and narrow and full of snakes and bad monkeys. I don't know if safe for you."

"Still, I would like to go. I want to know all that I can about tea, Jang. I need to start by seeing where it grows." After discussing the pros and cons for a while, Jang agreed Marc should go with him.

"Well, if you're going to be gone a month, I'll sail the ship over to Amoy, and get rid of this metal I have in the hold. Perhaps we can stop over in Macao, as well. It'll give my crew a rest. They'll like that," Captain Sharp stated. "They aren't allowed to mix with the women in Amoy, but in the area controlled by the Portuguese anything goes. It will keep them happy for the long trip home. But, Marc, I hope you know what you are getting into here. From what Jang tells us, it's an extemely rough journey."

"I'll be fine, Captain. I've been idle long enough. I'm used to lots of exercise and adventure. I'll be in good hands with my new friend to look after me." He grinned at Jang who looked at him with a rather inscrutable smile.

"We see my young fliend. We see what kind of man you are."

Chapter 24

Wu-li Mountain, July 1687

The journey was every bit as tough and treacherous as Li Jang had warned. After miles of travelling up-river, a gruelling journey by pole-barge, they began the climb to the altitude where the tea grew. It was a magical land of clouds and mist-covered peaks, but getting there had been arduous. The trails were too narrow and dangerous to use pack animals, so their bearers had to carry the heavy packages of supplies on their backs.

Sometimes they crossed swaying, wooden footbridges spanning crevasses hundreds of feet deep. And as Jang had warned, there were cobras and monkeys everywhere. The snakes usually slithered out of the way, so the monkeys were the bigger problem. They jumped around making faces at them, looking quite fierce.

"Do not look them in the eye," Jang warned Marc quietly in Portuguese. "It makes them angry and agitated, and they can be mean."

When there was no danger, the merchant would speak to Marc in English then repeat the phrase in Cantonese. Marc wished to learn as much of that tongue as he could. In the evenings, over the campfire, Jang showed him how to write the Mandarin symbols, and his skill in learning languages served him well. As the trip progressed, their admiration for each other increased. "We make good partners, my fliend," Jang would often say.

It took them two weeks of hard climbing to get to the terraces where the tea grew in abundance, some at altitudes of 4,000 feet. It amazed Marc to discover it was a type of camellia. He had seen the lovely flowering variety in the gardens at Versailles, but this species, which produced the aromatic leaves for tea, only grew at certain latitudes, high in the misty mountains. They were planted haphazardly on the terraces and, as they needed little attention, they grew anywhere from three to six feet tall.

Marc wondered at the number of young girls who worked as tea-coolies. They carried enormous burdens, which hung from bamboo sticks resting on their shoulders. Their feet were the large, unbound feet of the Haaka people.

In every village, Jang would visit the local factory, each with its own teahouse for sampling. After a few days, they came to a jade green river flowing through a verdant valley. Here, in this wondrous setting, was the most incredible town Marc had ever seen—the village of Xiamei, dating back to the Sui Dynasty over one thousand years earlier. The houses, built with exquisite brick sculptures and topped by a sea of green tile roofs, seemed to meld into each other. Patterns of flowers, birds, landscapes, and human figures decorated their facades.

In this town, the government maintained offices to control tea production, and it was the distribution center for what, Jang told him, were China's finest teas. After they had spoken to the officials, Jang took him along a narrow lane to an especially charming house at the edge of town. It was surrounded by high walls, which hid exquisite gardens and delicate, green pavilions covered with graceful, pagoda-shaped roofs.

"This home of Fan Zou. He keeps it as an inn," Jang explained. "You are velly tired now, are you not? We stay here one week before we go down mountain. We can visit other factories from here. I have yet much to teach you."

To Marc's astonishment, he could hardly find the energy to nod in agreement.

"Yes, it's because we high up now. You not used to it. We both need rest, my young friend."

Mr. Fan welcomed them both warmly and immediately ordered a servant to escort Marc into a luxurious bedroom. He had never been more tired in his life and thought he could sleep for days. He supposed the spirit of adventure had kept him going, but now he saw Li Jang was right. They both needed a good rest before attempting the trek down the mountain.

The dinner the inn provided was delicious—delicate, boiled dumplings filled with shredded pork and cabbage; chicken pieces in a tangy, garlic sauce; and delicious steamed vegetables—all served over beds of rice. The cuisine was completely new to Marc.

The dozen or so Chinese merchants besides Marc and Jang sat at the table, while four attractive, young women served them. "They are courtesans," Jang whispered to Marc in English.

The beauty of the one assigned to them astounded him. Her skin, unlike the other girls, was pale, the colour of alabaster. It contrasted sharply with her black hair, piled high on her head, and the equally black, almond-shaped eyes, slanting prettily up to her eyebrows. Her lips were full and red, and he thought he had never seen a woman with such a combination of delicate and yet seductive beauty.

There hadn't been much time to think about Louise since he had arrived in China; and now he suffered a little guilt at the sensations he experienced each time the servant girl bent down to replenish his cup of fermented, rice wine. Her cheong sam fit her neat little body tightly; and she smelled of a combination of jasmine and sandalwood. He sensed he blushed as Jang looked at him with his enigmatic smile. For once, he could almost read the merchants' mind.

After dinner, some of the men decided to play *sic bo*, an ancient Chinese gambling game, but Marc was so tired he wanted nothing more than a hot bath and bed. Jang took him outside to a little bath house in one of the pavilions where there was a tub of steaming hot water. He had no sooner stripped out of his clothes and settled into the water, when the beautiful servant girl appeared. She carried several sponges and some large cotton drying cloths.

"Hello, Mr. Mac. I am Mei Ling. Mr. Li told me to help you tonight. You must rest so you can make long trip down the mountain. After you dry, I will do Oriental acupressure on you. It makes you sleep well." She spoke in the Cantonese dialect but Marc understood enough of the language to know what she said.

"Oh, it's not necessary," he replied, beginning to feel panicky.

"It is my pleasure, Mr. Mac. You must rest and I will help you." She began rubbing his back with the sponges. It felt so calming; he did nothing to stop her. Nor did he later, when she dried him off and took him back to his room to give him the acupressure treatment. After the soothing massage, he watched mesmerized as she slipped off her beautiful silk robe and, dressed only in a short, gauze shift, sat down on the bed beside him. It seemed the most natural thing in the world to turn to her and kiss the alabaster skin.

◦✦◦

Marc and Li Jang stayed longer than the planned week at the house of Mr. Fan. Each day they would visit a new factory and Jang explained a great deal to him about choosing the finest teas. The merchant showed him the complete drying and fermenting process as well as how to determine the various varieties from the smell of the dried leaves. Although he woke each morning heavy-eyed and sluggish, he found himself fascinated by the whole procedure. After sampling hundreds of cups of tea, he finally picked a few he thought the English would appreciate. As his agent, Jang purchased a large shipment for him, which would be loaded on Captain Arthur's ship as soon as they got it down the mountain.

However, he spent the evenings with Mei Ling, and it was then that he felt oddly out of this world and euphoric—as if he had become part of some strange, imaginary fantasy. It was far enough north of the equator that there was a little twilight after dinner. The two of them would stroll around the ancient town, or climb a little knoll to view the valley below. The strangely contoured mountains, rising above the mist-covered terraces, appeared to shift in shape. Even the fragrant, exotic woman standing beside him seemed sometimes to float—like a hallucination—a sensory experience existing only in his mind.

In Cantonese, the girl tried to explain to him some of the history of the Oriental people. She told him, she was from Korea and how, as a young girl, some evil men had kidnapped her and sold her into slavery. Marc didn't understand everything she said but still he listened, captivated by her foreign charm. The feeling was not the love he felt for Louise but, she was so exquisite and desirable, he didn't try to resist her. He'd never been so relaxed and passive in his entire life, and he wasn't sure whether it was the refreshing mountain air; the medicinal quality of the teas; or Mei Ling's nightly therapies.

Somehow, he was glad she didn't have the ugly-shaped, bound feet of a typical upper class Chinese concubine. Although, he thought, it will no doubt keep her from marrying well. Oddly, that idea didn't make him sad.

Jang encouraged him to enjoy the respite and explained it would take the coolies at least eight weeks to get the tea down the mountain, while they would make the same journey in less than two weeks. He assured Marc, there was plenty of time before he would have to help oversee the loading of the ship in Canton. They sent a message to Captain Sharp, not to worry; they had purchased the tea; Jang would take care of the customs; and Marc would be away an extra week.

The trip, down to the city, was much easier than the climb had been. But for some reason Marc didn't feel very well. His dreamlike state had disappeared, but he suffered from cold chills and vomiting attacks. During these bouts, Jang helped him along the narrow tracks and over the dangerous bridges, with a worried frown on his brow. However, after several days, the malady cleared up, and Marc wondered what had come over him in those mountains.

Soon they were back in Jang's attractive house on the river. After a good nights' sleep, Marc hurried to the port just as *The Malabar Merchant* slipped into the harbour. Captain Sharp was relieved to see him as he had made several excursions to Macau and back before receiving the message from Jang.

The captain hadn't wanted to wear out his precarious welcome in Canton; so for a month the ship sailed back and forth along the Pearl River, first waiting for Marc and then for the coolies to bring down the tea. By the time the ship was fully loaded, it was the first of September. The weather had cooled and the trades blew to the west.

"That ought to make our trip back to India fairly speedy," the master told Marc. "Your father will be starting to get concerned just about the time we get you home." He smiled at him.

Marc was pleased. He had successfully completed the captain's mission, as well as the one he had set for himself. He had made some good contacts in Canton. Li Jang, he was sure, would be his friend for life. Moreover, without parting with any money, he had acquired for himself a sizeable share of some of China's finest teas. Teas that were now destined to his father's London warehouse, while he headed back to join him in Pondicherry.

Chapter 25

Indian Ocean, Late October 1687

As the massive British trading ship slipped out of the Straits of Malacca and into the Bay of Bengali, Marc breathed a sigh of relief. Behind them lay the looming, silent island of Sumatra and the always-present danger of the Malacca pirates.

He stood near the bow of the ship watching three fun-loving dolphins racing and diving into the whitecaps breaking from the prow. To the right a forest of green palms swayed on the nearby Island of Nicabar. Ahead, as the sun swiftly sank into a sea of molten gold, the sky ranged from citrus green to pale lemon to a soft pink and finally a burst of bright orange as the large orb disappeared behind the horizon. That close to the equator, there was no twilight and almost immediately, it was dark.

He raised his eyes heavenward, as always fascinated by the brilliancy of the star clusters, and, once again, recognized his belief in a Creator. He wondered why it was only on the ocean that he had this awareness of spirituality. On land, I'm a different person and not always particularly moral, he acknowledged to himself. It seemed that once away from the sea, his God was far off from him. There were too many distractions then. In his heart, he was aware that this was what Louise's father held against him.

Still he was happy. The worst of his long journey to China was over. With a little help from the trades, he should soon be in India with his father. A few more months and they would be free to return to France. Yes, he thought, Father will be pleased with what I've accomplished over the last six months.

Pondicherri, November 1687

The bazaars, with their exotic goods, as usual swarmed with people and activity when Marc finally disembarked *The Malabar Merchant* at Pondicherry harbour and made his way through to the main street. The stalls were crammed with a variety of products: pearls and diamonds, gold and ivory, perfumes and opium as well as an array of Indian textiles. There, too, the women sold their aromatic spices. The odours of India surrounded him, the pleasant aromas of cinnamon, cumin, and coriander, along with the pungent stench of unwashed bodies and unburied excrement. It did not feel like he had been away from India for six months. Nevertheless, he was glad that soon he would see his father.

He and Captain Sharp had bidden each other farewell on the bridge. "Don't worry about your cargo," the captain said. "I know a good broker in London. He's a French Huguenot, so you can trust him to see it gets to your father's warehouse. I would recommend him to anyone. The tea leaves are dried so they don't lose their flavour."

"I appreciate that, Captain. I'll no doubt be there before the end of next year. I'll have to go with father back to France first, of course.

"Then let me know as soon as you get to England," Captain Sharp had said. "I have a fairly long shore leave coming to me after this voyage, so I'm sure I'll still be home. I'm confident the Company will have a place for a man of your abilities, and I'll be happy to do what I can for you. It's been most enjoyable having you on boar, Marc. In fact, I don't know how we'd have managed without you."

He shook Marc's hand then and added, "You must give my regards to your father and tell him, I hope to have the pleasure of meeting him again. *Adieu,* my young friend."

Once through the bazaar, it didn't take long for Marc to find a palanquin, or *palkee*—as the Indians called it—large enough to hold him and the one piece of baggage he had taken with him. Soon they manoeuvred their way through the teeming masses of humanity along Rue de le Francois Martin, towards the garrison of the French East India Company.

It took about fifteen minutes to get there. He paid one of the four bearers the agreed upon rupees for the trip, and headed into the general office. As he entered the room, there was a sudden silence in the buzz of voices. One of the clerks came towards him and, throwing his arms around him, kissed him on each cheek.

"Marc," he said with a catch in his voice. "We are so glad you are back. The *commissaire* will want to see you immediately. Come along with me right now. I know he is free." He marched Marc toward Francois Martin's office.

Monsieur Martin greeted him warmly, and waited until he had settled into a chair to speak. He looked unusually serious. "Well, Marc, did you fulfill your father's wishes? You look none the worse for such a difficult trip."

"It's what I'm best at, sir and, yes, I think I've done well in that regard. Where is my father? Is he not working today?"

"No, my boy. In fact—I'm afraid I have bad news for you. Your father took sick over a month ago. We think it's the Tertian fever. The doctor has tried everything to help him but—I'm sorry to have to say this to you, lad—he says Jacques is dying."

Mark went cold. "Good lord, sir," he said. "You can't mean it. He's so strong and he's not old at all."

The *commissaire* looked at the young man with compassion. "It's true, but the ague is no respecter of age nor strength, I'm afraid. Some get better in a week or so; some succumb, and there seems to be no good reason for the difference. Well, come along, son. You'd better see for yourself." He stood and, with his arm around Marc's shoulder, escorted him out of the office and over to their large bungalow.

Marc's stomach felt as if it had dropped to his toes. His heart was beating erratically. In his whole life, he had never known his father to be ill, and this turn of events terrified him. He had looked up to Jacques as his hero since he was a little boy.

Monsieur Martin opened the front door of the bungalow and ushered him into the darkened bedroom where the servant sat beside the bed fanning his master. Marc could not believe the change in his father. He had always maintained a good, healthy weight for his height and a robust, muscular body even in middle age. Now Jacques looked thin and wasted. His facial bones were prominent, and the skin drawn over them was the colour of saffron, with a slight greyish tinge beneath. His dark, curly hair was streaked with white and matted with sweat, and there was the musky odour of jaundice about him.

"I'll leave the two of you together," Monsieur Martin said. "You will have much to talk over." He clasped Marc on the shoulder again and left the room.

Jacques moved restlessly in the bed and then his eyes opened. He saw Marc standing over him. "*Mon fils,*" he said in anguish. "You are here. *Dieu merci!* I have been praying for your return. I have much to tell you before I depart this life."

"Papa, I've brought tea from China. They say it can work miracles. We'll get you better."

"It's ague, Marc—marsh fever. They have given me quinine and all the old Indian remedies. There's nothing more they can do. For myself, now you are back, I'm prepared to sleep. But there are arrangements I must make for your Maman and the girls. I need you to listen carefully."

A sudden shudder overtook him and he began shivering. The Indian servant rushed to a small dung fire where stones heated on the brazier. He placed a couple in a blanket and hurried back to his master.

"You should be resting, *mon pere*. You must save your strength for the voyage home."

"Listen to me, boy. I will not be leaving Pondicherry. You will bury me here in India, but no matter. We'll meet again on Judgment Day." He chuckled weakly. "It's strange, but in many ways, I'm still a Huguenot at heart. Perhaps I made a mistake in renouncing my faith, but I could never accept that God predestined our destinies before he even created mankind. It wouldn't be just, and above all else, Marc, God is just. He gives us free will and most of the time we make our own destiny. Never forget that, son. Maybe if I had chosen to flee France with Pierre, I would not now be dying. Rather ironic, is it not?"

"Oh don't worry about such things right now. You did what you thought was best."

"Yes you're right my son. We should not look back. Now you must do as I ask. It's extremely important to me."

Marc sat down in the chair beside the bed and took his father's wasted hand. Tears slid down his face.

"Can you get paper and ink, Marc? I want you to write down my instructions and then get two of the men to witness my signature. It will have to do for a last Will and Testament. The old one is not what I wish now, at all. *Allez*. Get the paper and two of the clerks. We have no time to waste."

Marc was gone about twenty minutes and came back with two of the clerks from the office. His father appeared to be sleeping; the spasms had stopped; and he looked slightly better.

Pierre opened his eyes and smiled. "Ah, Marc. You are back. Now write down the following. The farm in the village and all its contents and the stock are to go to Phillipe as I promised him. Maman and the girls will move there with him. I know they'll be happy there. I spoke about the possibility with your mother before we left. You must sell the house and the warehouse in La Rochelle. Together they're worth a small fortune. One third of that money goes to your mother. She'll need some of it to pay dowries for the girls. They will soon be coming of age. The balance is yours." He stopped speaking to rest and give Marc time to write it down.

After a short time, he continued. "I told you about the gold deposits with the goldsmith in London, and there will be monies coming from 'the company' for my work here. There's also the warehouse in London. As my oldest son, you should have your fair inheritance. As I say, Phillip is well satisfied with the farm in the village. It's been in the family for four generations."

Again, he waited until Marc finished writing his last instructions. "If you can get the money out of France, you'll be a wealthy man. Certainly enough to give you and Louise a good start. Of courses, it's against the law to take gold out of the country right now, so I don't know how you'll do it. You'll have to work that out for yourself."

He smiled at his son and for a moment, his look of self-assurance was back.

"By the way, you managed to purchase a load of tea in China?"

"Yes, quite a large one."

"Well, that's yours, of course. You have it consigned to London in your name?"

Marc, his face full of misery, nodded.

"Then that takes care of it. I've done my best for all of you, and that makes me happy. Here—give me the paper. I'll sign and have these two gentlemen sign below that they've witnessed my signature with the date and place. Get it stamped in the office with the official seal. It should be legal enough; I think. You'll need a certificate of death. The *commissaire* will give you one. I've written a letter to your mother. It's in the drawer, but it's sealed. You must take it to her for me."

The effort to sign the Will seemed almost too much for him, and he sank back onto the bed with no strength left. He was damp with sweat. "Leave me now," he whispered. I must rest for a while. Then come back, Marc. I still have things to tell you and I would like you with me when I go."

"*Mon pere*. Don't speak of such a thing. We must get you better. We'll try those teas. They say they even cured Emperor Kangxi when all else failed." He patted the wasted hand and, with the two company clerks, left the room as the servant took the seat by the bed, and once again fanned his master until he fell asleep.

⚭

Jacques lasted only one more week. Even the miraculous teas from the Wu-li Mountains could not help him. It was as though he had only been waiting for his son to return. Marc spent most of the time sitting by his side and, in Jacques' better moments, he told him much about his adventure in China. However, he could not reveal to him his affair with Mei Ling. He had begun to feel guilty about how readily he had betrayed Louise.

Occasionally, the patient would rally and mention something he wanted his son to take care of in France. Sometimes he would simply give him guidance about life. Marc marvelled at how his father faced death as bravely as he had lived his life. He gave no indication of fear.

"I have some regrets in my life, Marc," he said. "Don't make the same mistakes I've made, son. If you truly love Louise, stay faithful to her no matter what. I know it's not normal in our society, but a wife will lose trust if you don't, and somehow they always know. It's my last piece of advice to you, my boy."

Marc's face grew hot with shame. Did his father sense his indiscretion? He wondered about the statement and it bothered him for a while. However, on the final day of Jacques' life, the implication became clear to him. As the day wore on, his father weakened. His breathing became laboured and the doctor came and went, shaking his head. Late in the evening, Jacques clutched at Marc's arm.

"Tell your mother—I'm sorry for many things; but I always loved her—very much."

His father's words were so soft; Marc had to bend to hear them.

"Of course, Papa," he replied.

Then the shuddering began again. He was standing up to get some heated stones from the brazier when he heard the rattle of his father's breath—then silence. It was over. He reached down and closed Jacques's eyes; then quietly knelt by his bed to pray. He stayed there for some moments, privately weeping, before going to tell the servant who was taking a much-needed rest. The realization came to him that he had admired his father more than anyone else on earth.

The French East Indies *Commissaire* arranged for a small graveside service on a rocky outcropping overlooking the harbour. There, other servants of *"la compagnie"* had been laid to rest. Jacques had mentioned, not being a staunch Catholic, he didn't want a priest. Therefore, Monsieur Martin, himself, read a few scriptures from his Latin Bible and offered a short prayer. He told Marc he had an immense regard for Jacques Garneau and was glad to follow his wishes.

To Marc, it seemed a fitting place for his father to remain; forever facing the azure seas, he loved, perhaps even more than his family.

A few days later, Monsieur Martin called him into his office. He explained he had arranged for Marc to take the next sailing leaving in mid-December, a passage that would take five months or more before he would be able to tell his mother. The idea depressed him a great deal. However, he was glad to be going home. He had been away now for over two years, and his thoughts returned to Louise. That he had betrayed her with the lovely courtesan bothered his conscience. Of course, he could not know if she had made it to London. What if he had lost her too? He prayed she was well and still loved him as he loved her. Before going to sleep, he once more gave way to tears of grief, and imagining himself in the comfort of her arms, whispered, *"Cherie.* Please be waiting for me. I need you so."

PART V

Friends and Enemies

"Pay attention to your enemies, for they are the
first to discover your mistakes."
Antisthenes

Chapter 26

London, August 1688

"There's a gentleman to see the master, Madame," Hannah announced. "He wouldn't give his name, so I left him in the receiving hall. Will you wish to speak to him or shall I tell him to go to the shop?"

"Perhaps you should take him into the drawing room," Louise said, somewhat puzzled. Paul hadn't said anything about expecting a caller and, in any case, if it were about business, why would he come here? Aloud she added, "I'll see what he wants before we send him to the city."

She glanced into the hall mirror and patted her hair into place. The figure reflected in the looking glass was every bit the elegant and poised lady of London's upper classes. Motherhood had softened and matured her face. Her golden hair was arranged in the manner of the day, with ringlets and soft curls at her cheeks. Her dress styled in the latest fashion, and tailored from her father's best silks. Satisfied at what she saw, she smiled, and then entered the room.

The man standing there, large feathered hat in hand, astounded her. It was Marc—so handsome she thought she would faint. It was three years since she had last seen him. His remarkable eyes were astonishingly bright in his tanned face, and his black, curly hair drifted well below his shoulders. He looked as dangerous and exciting as a Barbary pirate.

He stared at her in astonishment and his visage paled somewhat. "I'm sorry to disturb you, Madame, but it's important I speak with your husband. Is he here?" His voice held neither warmth nor acknowledgement.

"Marc, Marc" she cried, slipping automatically into French. "Don't you recognize me?"

"Of course, I do, but what do I have to say to you that you would want to hear. I wish no friendship with you. But I do need to see Paul Thibault."

"I see." she said, with a sigh. "Well, of course, you are angry with me for marrying."

"Did you think for one moment I wouldn't be? We were bonded together. We gave each other a solemn promise, which did not seem to be of much importance to you."

Rage blazed in his usually merry eyes. "I've only just arrived in the city, and, by accident, I met your father in a coffee house yesterday. My uncle was most unfriendly, I must say. He told me, you'd married the goldsmith. He seemed to take great pleasure in telling me about it."

"Oh, Marc. I'm sorry you had to hear it like that. I…"

"I would not have come here, but I have urgent business with your husband. He's always handled my father's affairs in London. Again, I'm sorry to disturb you. If you tell me where his place of business is, I'll certainly go there from now on. This is far too painful"

"Yes, for me, as well," she said softly.

"*Maman, Maman* where are you?" called a sweet voice, followed by the sound of little feet in the hall. Alice toddled into the room, throwing herself at her mother's skirt and hugging her. She glanced up with a puzzled look at the caller and then asked her mother in English, "Who zat man, mama?"

"This is your Uncle Marc, Alice. He has come all the way from France."

"Hello." She smiled up at him.

Marc looked down at the little girl for a few seconds with disbelief. He gasped. "You have a child? How old is she then?"

"She turned two in May," Louise said, deciding to be honest. She watched the look of amazement in his countenance, as realization dawned on him. The similarities between the little girl and her father startled Louise as well. She had thought it to be so, but seeing them together confirmed just how much the child resembled him. Alice had his curly black hair—his rosy cheeks—his laughing blue eyes. Even the shape of her face, was the same.

"Louise, can it be? Is she—whose child is she?"

"Sit down, Marc. I'll be right back."

Taking the little girl back to the morning room, she called to Alice's nanny. "Keep Alice here for a while, please, nurse. I must speak with my cousin from France."

"So," she said, as she returned to the drawing room, sitting opposite him, "you see the resemblance then? Yes, she is your daughter. Can you understand there was nothing I could do but marry? I wanted Papa to send me back to Aunt Marie. I thought she would be happy to look after me until you came home from the Orient, but, of course, it was impossible. Paul was wonderful to our family and offered for me, knowing of my folly. He has given Alice and me his name and this lovely home. I owe him a great deal."

"Does he know I'm the father?"

"No. He believes I ran into some trouble with the dragoons in France, and Alice was the result. I'm afraid we haven't disabused him of that idea."

"Well, he's only seen me once. It was a few years ago, so he probably doesn't remember exactly what I look like. Perhaps it's better if he doesn't see me now. It's possible he'll figure it out. Fortunately, I have a broker who can take care of my business affairs with Monsieur Thibault." He put his face into his hands.

She reached over to touch his shoulder. When he looked up there were tears in his eyes. "*Cherie,* I'm so sorry," he said at last. "What a disaster I've caused. I was terribly selfish that day. I took what was not rightfully mine and now I must pay for it for the rest of my life"

"It was not all your fault. I think I knew what would happen when we chose to go to the beach together. I didn't want you to go away for such a long time with nothing between us. Yes, it was wrong, and so we face the consequences. I have a wonderful life now, but in my heart, you will forever be my first great love. The cousin I will always adore."

He looked so downcast she wanted to throw herself into his arms and weep with him. Her heart was beating extremely fast. *Non, non,* she thought, I must not let myself feel like this.

"I agree it might be best if Paul doesn't meet you," she continued aloud. "I didn't realize just how much Alice resembles you. Before you go, though, you must tell me about your family. Your mother and father—how are they? I miss them so."

"My news of my father is sad, I'm afraid. In India, he took the tertian fever, and he didn't survive it. We buried him in Pondicherry."

"Oh, no" she cried, no longer able to hold back her tears. "Did you tell my father?"

"No, as I say, Louise, he was not at all friendly. He certainly didn't want to talk. I understand why now, of course."

"I'll have to tell him. He'll be so distraught when he hears. Dear Uncle Jacques. We all loved him so. He was so charming and such fun. What of your mother? How does she bear it?"

"It's been terribly distressing for her. However, Papa's last words were for her, and he had written a letter, which I delivered. I think it helped."

A small sob escaped from her as she continued to listen to him.

"There was much to take care of. First, there was my father's final business with the government in Paris. Then we sold the house in La Rochelle and moved the family to your old home on the farm. They all love it there.

"Phillip has planted grapevines everywhere. For now, he'll sell the fruit to the *Compte,* but eventually he wants to make cognac himself. Because mother has gone back to her church, the dragoons do not bother them, of course."

"And what about you. What will you do next?"

"I sailed to China with the British East India Company, and they're more than willing to hire me on here. Of course, my inheritance from father is quite large but much of it is still in France. I'm not sure how I'll get it out."

He looked perturbed. There was silence for a few seconds. Then he continued. "However, I brought back a shipment of tea from China, and I have Papa's warehouse here. So I'll have a considerable amount when I sell that; enough to do for a while. I'll need to contact Paul somehow about the rest of father's gold, though. It's part of my inheritance. To be honest, I didn't intend to make any long-term plans until I spoke to you. I had so hoped…"

He stopped and looked at her longingly. "I'm not sure I can bear this, Louise—losing both you and my father. It's too much. I'd better go now. Take care of our sweet little girl. Perhaps when I've had time to adjust to this, I may see her again. At least I must have news of her. I—I already love her although I know I don't deserve a place in her heart."

Louise was surprised at the deep emotion she felt for him in his sorrow. There was no doubt she still loved him in some way, but she kept the thought of what she owed Paul and her vow to always be faithful, uppermost in her mind. It was safer that way.

"I will tell Papa about Uncle Jacques right away, but you must also go to him. Beg his forgiveness and tell him how you feel about Alice. I think he'll stay in contact with you. He loved your father very much. Now, I'm afraid, you are right. You must go. Paul will soon be home, and I don't want him hurt. I pray you find happiness as I have, Marc. There is my pretty little Alice, and my husband treats me extremely well. More than I deserve."

As they parted at the entrance, he kissed her on both cheeks, and then walked out into the street, never once looking back. She closed the door and leaned against it for a moment. Her legs felt shaky, and tears streamed down her face. "Oh, Marc. You've come too late—much too late." A small moan escaped her lips. "You weren't there for me, and Paul was. I must never forget that—never."

Chapter 27

Spittlefields, September 1688

One day in late September, Pierre answered his door to find Marc standing there. Beside him, stood a large oak cask. "I've brought you some cognac, Uncle Pierre. It's the last of what was in our warehouse here."

Pierre had not seen the young man since they met accidently at the coffee house, and for a moment, his arrival took him aback. He realized it required much courage for his nephew to come, but it brought to mind all the agony the young man had caused his family. His anger towards him was still intense. However, they were family, so after Marc and his two oldest sons had carried the cask down to the kitchen, he ushered the young man into his office, closed the door, and indicated a chair.

Looking severely at him over his spectacles, he spoke. "Well, Marc. I hear you have seen our little Alice. I'm sure she was a shock to you. So now, what brings you to us? Do you actually think you have the right to simply show up, and everything will be the same? Do you have any idea what this family went through when Louise discovered she was with child?

"Yes, I can imagine it, Uncle Pierre. Believe me, I'm so sorry."

"Sorry hardly covers the damage. What I don't understand is why you would let us—your own family—down like that. We always loved you just like our own sons. We trusted you with our precious daughter, and you treated her like—like a common harlot?" His voice rose as he gave him an icy glare.

Marc's tanned face paled at his uncle's words. "I beg of you, Uncle, never think it was like that. Please let me explain. I—I loved Louise so much. She meant everything to me. Even before my first trip, I knew I was in love with her, more than as a cousin. But while I was away, I could picture her at your farm, and almost know what she would be doing. I never worried about her."

His lips trembled, but he coughed, and continued. "When we got home that last summer, I planned to ask you if we could marry the minute she

145

turned seventeen. Then my father got the commission to go to India. As well, there was all that trouble in France, which complicated everything. You'll remember, in La Rochelle, I did come and ask if we could be at least be betrothed."

"Yes you did. And I said 'no, not now.' All I asked was for you to wait until we settled in London, and you'd made the trip with your father. I wanted to make sure you would not turn Catholic. Was it too much to expect?"

"I know, but your escape from France seemed so dangerous. To be honest, I wasn't sure that you would all make it out alive. I didn't know if I would ever see my beautiful Louise again. I knew she loved me. She told me, she did. So I planned the day on the beach."

"That's another thing. I don't understand why she didn't ask my permission. She always did before. Of course, I would not have let her go. It was absolutely the wrong thing for a young couple to do without a chaperone."

"At the time, I thought it would be innocent enough, Uncle. You know we were always together as children. Then she almost drowned, and I felt— I needed to make her mine—in case something happened to her. To be with her was all I wanted in life."

Pierre's face burned with anger. Did his nephew have no shame? Did he not realize that the scandal could have ruined Louise's life? He wanted desperately to trounce the young man, and throw him out in the street; but he took a deep breath.

"No, wait, Sir. Please let me finish," Marc exclaimed in response to Pierre's obvious fury. "I loved her so, and I truly believed we had a marriage contract. She came with me—quite willingly. I thought it would seal us, like in the Catholic Church, and then I would come to England and claim my bride. I never thought there could be a baby. And now—now I realize how wrong it was. It was a grievous sin and I got what I deserved, I guess. I've lost them all—Louise and my child as well as my father."

Tears now ran down Marc's cheeks, and Pierre's felt a little of his anger dissipate. For the first time, he could empathize with him. He was certain the boy had truly loved Louise; and hearing his impassioned plea, he tried to understand the situation. However, it was his beautiful, little daughter, they were discussing, not some wanton, street girl. Then he thought of the deception he himself had devised. It had not only been for the sake of Louise he had been willing to lie. In his heart, he knew it was to protect his own reputation in the new community.

"Uncle Pierre, can you never forgive me? I was so in love, I truly never thought of the consequences." Marc's cry broke into his thoughts.

A scripture from the gospels came to mind. '*Judge not, and ye shall not be judged, condemn not, and ye shall not be condemned; forgive and ye shall be forgiven.*'

"Well, Marc. You should not have been alone together. It was extremely wrong of you. However, who is without sin? I have thought it over many times in the last few years. I must admit that your father and perhaps your Aunt Claudine also, were partly to blame. They encouraged the relationship since you two were children."

He stopped to blow his nose, emotion finally overcoming him. "I'm so sorry about Jacques," he continued, his own eyes filling with tears. "Since we grew up together, we were like brothers, and I still can't believe he is gone. How we shall all miss him—he was the best friend a man could ever have. Look what he did for me. So many of our people have suffered poverty since coming to London, and here I am fairly well-off because of his planning."

"He loved you and your family as well, Uncle. I know he considered you as his brother."

"Well, *neveu*, since I left our village, I've learned life isn't as black and white as I used to believe. I see good people can make dreadful mistakes, and people I once considered condemned can do noble and courageous things. If Louise has forgiven you, who am I to hold a grudge. She thinks it is only fair you should get to know Alice."

"That would make me extremely happy, Uncle. I never knew I could feel this way about a child; but from the moment I saw her..."

Pierre spoke at the same time cutting him off. "The problem would be if Paul were to find out. I'm sure it would upset him, and he has been extremely good to her. To all of us, really. I should hate to have him hurt by any of this. Well, I'm sure we'll find some way. What about your future now? Will you be staying in England?"

"Yes, I will. The trouble in France has escalated. Unless one willingly becomes a sworn Catholic, life is extremely dangerous. Because I've been working for the monarchy, they've asked me to sign a renunciation, and I find I can't. I got out of the country just in time, and I don't dare go back. It seems that in my heart, I'm a Huguenot after all."

"It isn't a bad thing, my boy," Pierre said.

"No, I suppose it isn't. In any case, I've made the choice, so here I am. As to what I'll do, while my father was concentrating on the Pondicherry project, I was able to travel to China, and I've made some good connections there. I think there's a great future in the tea market in both England and the North American colonies. It's an excellent drink and already well received here."

"So you would still be traveling quite a lot?" Pierre interjected. "Even if you make your home here?"

"Yes. Because of my experience, the British East India Company has hired me. Right now, there's been some more trouble with a British ship in Canton harbour. The ship fired towards the shore for some reason and killed a customs man. So I won't be going back there for awhile. In fact, for the next six months, I'll be in London working as a clerk and learning about the company. Eventually they'll assign me to travel to North America"

"And where will you live?"

"Just the other day, I purchased quite a large piece of land out in the country—in Hampstead. It's a good investment. In the meantime, until I can build the house I want, I've rented rooms in the city. Uncle Pierre, if you can find it in your heart to forgive me, perhaps you will find ways for me to see the little girl once in a while, when I'm here."

"I'm still not sure you deserve it, but for the sake of your father, I'm going to help you. You're family, and your father's son, and after all, the child is yours. Therefore, between Louise and me, we'll work out something. One thing I would ask of you, though. Please do not try to see Louise alone. She's become especially fond of Paul. He's a good man and I don't want him upset in any way. In fact, I would ask that you keep away from her altogether."

Marc looked hurt, but nodded his agreement. "Well, once I start those overseas trips, I won't be around much. But I'll sure appreciate whatever help you can give me in getting to know Alice. She's such a charming little girl."

"She is. Which means she's like you and your father," Pierre replied with a chuckle. "Well, well. Me—I hope we don't all manage to spoil her too much. She is a darling *petite* for sure. Stay for supper, lad. We want to hear about your father, and what happened to him. *Zut alors*; how I am going to miss him."

Once more Pierre teared up as he put his hands on his nephew's shoulders. Marc was so much like Jacques, he thought.

Aloud he said, "I'll tell Claudine to set another place, and then you'll tell us the whole story."

Claudine looked happy to see the two reconciled. Pierre knew she was extremely fond of Marc. She had always hoped he would be her son-in-law.

During the dinner, Marc told the family about his trip to China; how Jacques had suggested he travel there to learn the tea trade. "He didn't mind being in India without me. He loved the work there. I don't know how he got the ague, but it was a particularly virulent strain apparently. At the end, it seemed a blessing for him to go. His last words were for my mother. At least hearing that brought her a little happiness. She is content now to stay with my brother on the farm."

"And so young Phillipe is going to go into cognac, I hear." Pierre queried, with a catch in his voice.

"Yes, I'm afraid he cut down all your beautiful mulberry trees to make room for the grapes. He's already hired men to turn the manufactory into a distillery. I must tell you something, but please keep it a secret."

He directed his remarks to the young people. "Even here in England, it wouldn't be safe. As you know, Mother recanted her faith, so the dragoons don't bother them. But Phillipe is a secret Huguenot. He attends their meetings when he can. They change the location all the time, so he can't always get to them. It's very dangerous."

"Well, bless him. I thought he was educated as a Catholic," Pierre stated.

"Yes, he was. But he never agreed with it. When we sold the house, he asked me for all father's books on Jean Calvin, as well as his Huguenot Bible. He has to keep them securely hidden. Even from Mother and my sisters. They must never know."

"What about the girls?" Claudine chimed in. "Are they happy then?"

"Oh yes." Marc smiled at her, charming as always. "They are Catholics, of course. They are both promised to young men in neighbouring villages. So soon, Maman will have grandchildren close by to keep her happy. I have just now sent her a letter explaining about Alice. I'm afraid she will be very angry with me."

He stopped for a moment and sighed. "But I dare not go back to see her unless I'm willing to convert. So, for now, I must stay here and sail with the British company."

"Can I come with you when you go to North America, Marc?" Jean Guy spoke up.

The whole family turned to look at him in astonishment.

"You know it's what I've always wanted," the boy pleaded with his father. "Now I'm eighteen, I'm sure I could be of some use to Marc. I'm not that good at weaving. I don't enjoy it for one thing."

"Would there be a chance for him?" Pierre asked.

"I can speak to the company, Uncle. They're always looking for fresh, new recruits and having another language will help him. Perhaps he could go with me next spring."

"Well, I don't think anyone should have to work at something they hate. Perhaps it's not his destiny, which means I'll need a new senior apprentice. Claude, are you ready to take over?"

"Papa, I have to tell you. I have my heart set on something else too. Since the stabbing, weaving makes my shoulder ache. I've been meaning to ask you to speak to Paul about me. The day we all went down to see his shop—I realized I'd like to try making jewellery. He needs another apprentice, and I think he might take me on."

Pierre was thunderstruck, so it was a few seconds before he replied, "Why, Claude, that work is as back-breaking as weaving. Paul's a successful man, but he spent many years over a workbench bending hot metal before he got to the point where he is now. He made a lot of his money from banking gold for his clients; but that will all disappear once the government establishes its own banking system."

"Yes, I know it's difficult. I've been back twice with Louise, and Paul let me try it. It doesn't seem to hurt my arm. When I see those beautiful creations of his—I know it's what I want to do. I'm not worried about getting rich."

"*Zut alors*. You boys have shaken the firmament from under my feet. So that only leaves you, Andee." He turned to the small boy, speaking to him in English, "Do you want to weave pretty cloth like your father?"

"Yeth, Papa. I weally do," said the little boy.

"Andee would be quite happy to jump over the moon if his father asked him to," Claudine said, as they all laughed.

They stood and Pierre led the men into the drawing room for a glass of the cognac from Marc's peace offering. Well, he thought. All's well that ends well, I presume.

In spite of his sadness about Jacques, he hoped that this was the beginning of a new era for the Garneau family and their friends.

Chapter 28

London, November 1688

Paul was unusually quiet at the dinner table. This was generally the happiest time for them as they discussed his day's business and Louise would tell him the about the newest "strangers" to arrive from France. King James had issued letters patent granting the Huguenots a licence to establish one or more churches for the refugees in the City and suburbs. The congregation of La Patents, Spitalfields had been formed, and now met at the Glovers Hall.

Both the Thibaults and Garneaus were involved in setting up the relief center for new refugees, and Louise had taken on the task of helping out several days a week. Paul always enjoyed hearing about her work. However, tonight, no matter what she said, he answered her with only a word or two.

When dinner was over and they had settled into the parlour for coffee and brandy, he picked up the book he had been reading. Louise could no longer stand it.

"Is everything alright, Paul? You seem tired tonight."

"No, I'm fine, Louise. It's just that—well, perhaps I should tell you. I had a rather disturbing encounter this week. I've been debating whether to speak to you about it or not."

"Oh, please tell me, dear."

"A few days ago, I was at Perault's Coffee House. You know—the one on St. James Street."

Louise nodded.

"I met some merchants I know from the British East India Company, and your cousin, Marc Garneau was with them. He's been working for the company here for almost three months. Not only that, he's sailing to North American in the spring and, of all things, Jean Guy is going with him."

He looked at her with a frown on his face. "You must have known about that. I thought it rather strange you've never told me. Marc seemed

151

to know quite a lot about Alice. I got the impression; he must have seen her somewhere."

Louise's heart sank. "Why yes, he has quite often visited with my father and mother," she replied. "I was there with Alice, so he did meet her. He seemed to take to her, as she looks so much like his father."

"It's a long time since I've seen Marc. I thought she looks remarkably like him, as well. You don't look like that side of the family at all, do you?"

"Well, no. I'm like my mother. It's not unusual, do you think? Really, this is a curious conversation, Paul."

"I find it difficult to understand why you wouldn't have invited him to come and see us here. I thought you and Jacques' family were devoted. Even though, I didn't know the son, I always admired Jacques Garneau. In fact, we were good friends." He stopped for a moment to pick up the decanter and pour another glass of the brandy wine.

"Marc told me he died in India. It seems extremely strange that no one mentioned that to me. He also said he has a signed paper from his father, with instructions to me that Jacques' account should go to him. I thought that was odd too. Why didn't he bring it to me right away? There's quite a lot of money involved."

Her face grew hot with embarrassment. Nevertheless, she said nothing, stirring her coffee with a small spoon.

"Anyway, the whole encounter puzzled me, and when I met your father for coffee this morning, I asked him about it. He seemed uncomfortable and tried to change the subject. When I pursued it, he made some comment about the lad being so busy since he got here; and suddenly remembered he had to meet a client. It wasn't like your father at all. The more I think about it, it doesn't sit right with me."

He finished his drink in one gulp. After scrutinizing her expression closely, he continued, "Louise, have you and your father been honest with me? I think Marc is far more interested in Alice than most second cousins would be. I want you to tell me the truth now. Is Marc the father of Alice? And, if so, why did you keep it from me? I thought you trusted me completely."

She started to weep. She sensed her husband's hurt and she had never wanted that. Over the last three years, his tenderness had completely won her heart, and she cared intensely for him.

"Yes, it's true, Paul," she said, through her sobs. "Marc is Alice's father. At the time, I...I thought I loved him. It was a young girl's fantasy. Can you ever forgive me? "

His expression was impassive.

"We've always known each other," she continued. "We were together every summer since we were little children. He was my first love, and when Papa decided to leave France, I thought I would die without him. So I—I succumbed. But none of that has anything to do with what I feel for you now. Please believe me."

"But why did you both deceive me? It is so unlike your father. That's the part, I can't understand. He knew I thought it was the dragoons, and never corrected me. I was so in love with you, the truth wouldn't have made any difference to me at the time. It might even have been better. I have hated the thought of your beautiful body ravaged by those evil men. What hurts me the most is that neither of you trusted me enough to tell me what actually happened. It makes me wonder if I can ever again have confidence in what you tell me—you or your father. Can you not see, Louise?"

"Yes, I do understand and I'm so—so sorry." She started to cry uncontrollably. "M—Marc learned about Alice, and he wanted to be able to see her once in awhile. Pa—Papa promised he would arrange it at their home. Only if Marc consented not to come near me. He agreed, which is why he's never been here. I—I should have confided in you after you married me— when Alice was born and I realized you loved me. Is it too late, Paul? Can you not forgive me?"

"I love you. That much will never change. So shall we'll leave it for now?" To her despair, he returned to his reading.

A month had gone by since Louise's admission to Paul about Marc. Since the night of their discussion, Paul had never come to her room, nor once taken her in his arms to kiss her. He seldom spoke to her other than at the dinner table, and meals were now a solemn affair. Often he worked late at the shop and only came home in time for bed. She was well aware of this change in him, and it hurt her immeasurably. It was the first time since she met him that he had been anything but kind.

On this particular morning, she had gone to the Glovers Hall to help as she did three times a week. However, she had taken a sick spell and had to come home early. Over the last month, she had lost weight and now looked decidedly peaky.

By the dinner hour, she was still not well and picked at her meal. Half way through, she lay down her fork and said, "I'm afraid you'll have to excuse me, Paul. I think I'll go up for an early night. I'm feeling quite ill." She stumbled to the door, but overtaken by the dizziness, she sank to the floor.

"Louise, what is wrong?" he cried, ringing for her maid.

She heard him but was too ill to answer. He carried her upstairs to her room, with Hannah following. "Get her in bed, Hannah," he instructed the woman. "I'll send for Dr. Martin."

Louise had somewhat recovered from the dizziness, by the time the doctor came. He spoke to her quite severely. "You have not been eating enough, Louise. You're far too thin. And tell me, when did you last have your monthly bleeding?"

She considered the question. Since Paul had not been sleeping with her, she had not given it a thought. "Why—I think it was over two months ago," she said.

"Yes, I thought as much. Then it's likely you are with child. You had better make sure you have enough to eat and some bed rest for the next month. We don't want to take any chances. I treated Paul's first wife you know. Their babies never survived past childbirth. It could be something in Paul's family, so you'll have to be careful of your health. I leave it to you to tell your husband. I'm sure it will please him."

After he left the room, she sat up in bed trembling with excitement. Could it be, she wondered. It would make Paul so happy. He has the idea he can never have a child of his own. Oh, I must have this baby. Nothing must happen to it. He is such a good man. He deserves to have his own son.

❧

Dr. Martin walked down the stairs where Paul anxiously awaited him in the library. "I don't think it is too much to worry about," the doctor said to him. "Make sure she stays in bed for the next little while. I'll check back in a month." Rene looked at him with a slight twinkle in his eye. "Don't worry, old friend. It might be the greatest thing that ever happened to you." He clapped him on the shoulder as he left the house.

Louise was sitting up in bed when he went into the room. "Sit down, Paul," she said. "I have something to tell you."

"Are you alright, sweetheart? Rene says to keep you in bed for a month. Louise, I'm sorry I've been so foolish. I was hurt that's all. To know you'd loved someone before me. It was my silly pride."

"But, Paul, you loved someone before me," she reminded him gently. "It's truly possible to love more than one person, I've discovered. It seems each love is entirely different."

"Yes, I realize it now, and I should never have acted so miserably. I should have been happy it wasn't by force. That could have scarred you for life. Now I can't stand you should be sick like this. You mean the whole world to me."

"If things go well, perhaps I won't be the only thing in your world for long. Rene thinks I'm pregnant again." She smiled tenderly at him. "This time, believe me, it could only be yours."

"Louise," he exclaimed. "Is it possible? You know Diane lost several babies. I don't think I could bear it if it happens again." He took her in his

154

arms, and covered her face with kisses, tears of joy flowing down his cheeks. "My sweetheart. We must take care of you."

⋘⋙

It wasn't an easy pregnancy this time. Dr. Martin was quite concerned Louise might lose the baby, and urged her to stay in bed past the first two months. She felt drained of energy, and found even going up and down, the stairs wore her out. She suffered greatly from nausea and, even when that stopped, her appetite didn't improve. However, the doctor was insistent she should eat.

"You must keep up your strength, Louise," he told her. "I'm afraid this might be a difficult birth."

"I don't understand it," she later confided to her mother. "My pregnancy with Alice was so easy. Of course, she was small. I can feel this baby is already quite large, even though I'm thin. Did you ever have any problems like this, Maman? I don't remember."

"Well, the birth of Claude and Catherine was rather gruelling. Maybe you are going to have twins. They say it runs in families. I got so large I hated even for your father to see me. But, I must say, every one of my children was worth all the tribulation." She smiled fondly at her before continuing, "And the only problem I ever had with you was after you were born, trying to keep you down-to-earth all those years. That was the real challenge."

Claudine hugged her and they laughed together. Still, Louise noted a look of concern on her mother's face.

⋘⋙

"I wish I could have kept on with the work at the church," Louise said to Paul one spring morning at breakfast. "It meant so much to me to help the Huguenot strangers. They arrive with so little compared to my family. But I simply don't have the energy."

She regretted giving it up, but she found anything beyond managing the servants too much for her. Not only did she find the slightest exertion tiring, but also her back ached constantly even though she stayed in bed a great deal.

Paul didn't reply but his face held a look of apprehension. He spent most of his spare time with her now, as if he were afraid what the future might hold. His concern rather frightened Louise when she remembered he had been through this several times with Diane, until it finally claimed her life. She tried to shake off the feeling of calamity, thinking it might not be good for the baby, but it persisted.

155

Chapter 29

London, 1689

It was mid-July when Louise went into labour. As she and Paul sat in the morning room having breakfast, she suddenly gave a startled cry. "Oh, Paul. A pain—a bad one. I think the baby is ready. I wonder if you should send for the midwife. Oh—oh."

"You'd best get back to bed. I'll send the coach driver immediately. Is that another one?" He took her arm and helped her out of the chair as her face twisted with pain again.

"Yes, ohh. They're already strong and coming quite fast, Paul. She'd better come right away."

"Don't worry, dear. It won't take long for Oliver to bring her. After that, I must get him to go for Rene, as well. I know the midwives don't like doctors at the birthing, but I'll feel better if he's here on the scene, and he said he wanted to be. Your mother and father also wanted to be with us. You go right back to bed now." He rang for Hannah, Louise's personal maid, who came scurrying.

"Quickly, Hannah—help Madame upstairs to the confinement room. Her pains have started. I think it's time." Then he turned and ran swiftly towards the coach house to alert Oliver.

Contrary to what Louise had supposed, her labour was long and hard. Paul, Pierre, and Rene Martin had gathered in the library where Paul had opened a bottle of brandy to help settle their nerves. They each tried to read, but they could not ignore her groans and cries of pain, which carried all the way downstairs. Paul's clothing was soaking wet with perspiration.

"Renee, can't you do something? I can't bear it when she screams. Do you think this is normal?"

Doctor Martin walked out into the hallway and looked up the stairs, shaking his head. "I'll be honest, Paul, I don't like the sound of it. But I don't feel I can go up there until the women ask me to. It's their domain."

Paul went back to the library. "Dear God, please don't let her die," he whispered, cradling his head in his hands.

Finally, around the dinner hour, the midwife came downstairs and spoke to Dr. Renee. "I can't think how to help her anymore, doctor," she said. She's in agony—her body just arches with the spasms, but the little one won't come. I'm afraid it's turned wrong."

"Has she lost her water?" he asked.

"Yes—a long time ago. That baby should be coming by now, with the pain she's had, but I can't see a head. I think you'd better take a look, sir."

"Yes, you are right. She should have had the child by now if everything were normal. I'll come up."

It was about fifteen minutes later, when Dr. Rene came hurriedly down the stairs to find Paul and Pierre still waiting in the library, growing more and more alarmed with each new session of shrieking.

"Rene, please tell us. What is happening? Has something gone wrong?" Paul asked frantically grasping his friend's shoulders.

"The baby's definitely turned the wrong way. It's breeched. We can't bring it out like that. It would kill her," Dr Martin said grabbing up his cloak and sword.

"Why are you leaving then? What are you going to do?" Paul demanded.

"Generally we have to make a choice. We can save either the mother or the baby. Not both.

"Oh, dear lord. Please not again." His head dropped to his hands.

"But don't despair yet, Paul. I've thought of someone John Houblon told me about. He's an associate of his who's apparently something of a genius. For some reason, he's working with John on the government's new banking system, but he's also a doctor. Medically trained in France, John told me, and apparently skilled in mid-wifery. He has some sort of apparatus, which helps in cases like this. I'm going to Houblon's home now to see if we can find the man right away. I've given Louise an opiate to make her sleep and stop the contractions. It will work for a couple of hours, I think, but there's no time to lose."

The doctor rushed out of the house, leaving Paul and Pierre to console each other with their bottle of brandy. In spite of their anxiety, neither of them dared to go upstairs.

Two hours had passed before Rene returned with a strange man carrying a large, black bag. By that time, Paul was beside himself with worry. "Paul, this is Dr. Chamberlen," the physician said. "He has recently returned from a hospital in Paris. It was fortunate John knew exactly where to find him."

A sudden cry of anguish from upstairs proclaimed the fact Louise had woken from the effects of the drug. "We mustn't waste any more time," Renee said. "We'd better get upstairs and see what can be done."

"First, though, Monsieur Thibault, you must immediately have your servants bring me up boiling water," Dr. Chamberlen instructed Paul. "It's extremely important."

Both doctors rushed upstairs as Paul rang for a maid, who bustled out at his directions. It wasn't long before she ushered two footmen up the stairs, each carrying a bucket of boiling water. Paul, along with his father-in-law, went with trepidation back to their vigil in the library.

It was after midnight when the high pitched, jerky wail of a newborn startled him out of his stupor. Louise's agonizing cries had ceased some time ago and, terrified of her fate, he had sat helplessly, along with his father-in-law, waiting in the library. The maid brought them some food, which neither had the appetite to eat. Except to go to the water closet in the back of the house, neither man had left the library for the last twelve hours. Each cry from the upstairs room had been like a knife in Paul's heart. Several times, he had stood up wanting to run upstairs, but Pierre had stopped him.

"They won't let you near her, Paul. You know what these mid-wives think about men at a time like this."

Now he didn't believe he could face going upstairs. He sat at his desk with his head in his hands no longer pretending to read. His lips moved in silent prayer. Pierre lay back in a large chair with his eyes closed. After some time, a door above opened followed by the soft tread of feet on the carpeted staircase. Both men jumped up and hurried into the hallway, anxiously looking up as the two physicians descended the stairs to meet them.

"Well, my friend," Rene Martin spoke first. "You have a big, sturdy son, and I'm delighted to tell you, they will both survive. He has a few marks on his face from the instrument, but they will go. Dr. Chamberlen has performed another one of his miracles."

Paul wept openly at the news. "Louise, she is safe?" he managed to gasp.

"Yes, she will be fine, but you'll have to take good care of her, Paul. I fear it will take a long time for her to heal mentally. It has been a terrible ordeal for her, and I'm afraid turning the baby damaged the womb. It is doubtful she could ever become pregnant again. In fact, even if it were possible I would certainly advise you to take steps against it. I have explained this to her. I'm afraid it's made her quite unhappy so she'll need your reassurance."

"I have my son, and all that matters is that Louise will live. Thank you both so much," he replied, emotion still chocking his voice. "I couldn't ask for anything more. There's nothing I can do that would begin to show my gratitude for you, Monsieur Chamberlen. You must send me your bill."

"I am so delighted to have been successful yet again, Monsieur. This apparatus has been handed down through our family from my great grandfather, but not too many are willing to risk it. I'm sure it could save the lives of numerous women and their babies. Well, at least I'm glad to have been able to help your family."

Chamberlen looked up at the picture of Louise hanging on the wall beside one of Paul. It was a superb painting of her. Paul was particularly proud of it. The physician shook his head in admiration. "She is exceedingly lovely," he continued, "and I'm happy we could save her. My great hope is someday the world will know what these forceps can do."

He sighed. "Goodbye, Monsieur Thibault. Tell your servants to keep everything in the room spotlessly clean. Use boiling water. It stops the childbed fever—another of my little secrets they can't seem to accept. God bless you and the little one. It's been my pleasure to help."

Picking up his bag holding the mysterious instrument, he left the house. Rene Martin shook Paul's hand, clasping him on the shoulder, and followed the other physician out the door.

In spite of the difficult birth, Pierre Charles Thibault was a chubby, healthy infant with a soft down of blonde hair. He resembled Louise noticeably, and his father couldn't be more delighted. He looked at the lovely, pale mother clasping her son to her breast. He could hardly believe they were both safe after their dreadful ordeal. He admitted to himself, he hadn't expected either of them to survive, and he couldn't imagine what his life would be like now without Louise in it.

"What a wonderful gift you have given me, sweetheart," he spoke softly, trying not to wake the sleeping infant. "You have made my life perfect in every way. I only wish it hadn't been so gruelling on you. You must take it easy for a long time—until you get your strength back."

"He's worth all the agony. Oh, but, Paul, I wanted to have more babies for you. I'm so sorry." There were tears of grief in her eyes.

"Don't feel that way, dear. I am truly elated with this little fellow. To have a son of my own, after all this time—and our pretty, little Alice—and to have you safely beside me—it's all I need in this life."

She looked exhausted but smiled up at him and pulled his hand to her lips to kiss it. "But our little boy doesn't look very French does he?" Paul continued. "It will be confusing to call him Pierre. However, your father might be hurt if we call him by my father's name, Charles. I suggest we start calling him Peter immediately. I don't think Pierre will mind the Anglicized version too much, do you?"

Louise nodded, nuzzling the top of her son's head.

Paul looked down again at his new son with pride. "He looks too happy to be a banker—perhaps we need a lawyer in the family. We'll work on it. Oh, Louse, this is the happiest I've ever been in my entire life. You, my darling, have made me complete."

Chapter 30

London, October 1689

It took a few months for Louise to regain the stamina she had before her pregnancy. During that time, Paul was careful not to burden her with social obligations. However, he and Pierre met now and then for lunch to discuss family matters. Over the four years they had known each other, the two men had forged a strong friendship.

The Garneau family, in due course, had settled into their new lives in England. France would never be forgotten, but they no longer pined for it. When occasionally they mentioned they missed their cousins and the old friends in the little village, Paul readily empathized with them. They had no way of knowing whether their Huguenot neighbours managed to escape, nor where they had gone. It reminded him of his lost sister.

A year earlier, in 1688, the unpopular Catholic King James had been forced to leave the country. He and his family now lived in exile, in France. After the debauchery of the Stuart court, the British, for the most part, were satisfied with their new royals—James' eldest daughter, Mary and her pious Dutch husband, William of Orange. Since the king was a staunch Protestant, this new turn of events elated the Huguenot community. All fear of reprisals against them from forces within England had disappeared.

In the spring of 1689, Marc Garneau sailed with a shipload of tea destined for the North American colonies of Boston and Jamestown. Jean Guy went along as his assistant. Like his cousin, Jean Guy was quick to learn a new language. In only over four years, the young man spoke perfect English, and Marc planned to teach him Portuguese and Spanish, as well. He seemed to be well-suited for a career as a merchant.

"How are your new apprentices faring?" Paul asked his father-in-law one day in late summer. They were enjoying lunch together at a coffeehouse near the goldsmith shop. "I guess they keep you busy since Jean Guy left? Zounds, is it already six months he's been gone? I'm sure you miss the lad tremendously."

"Yes, we do—but we knew we must let him try it anyhow," Pierre replied. "I feel a man should love his vocation. Otherwise, life isn't worthwhile. It saddens me, but Jean Guy was never meant to be a silk weaver. It's tedious work for anyone who doesn't like it."

"How long will they be gone then?"

"Until next spring, I think. Marc said they would have to stay a month or so in each place to get the idea of drinking tea established over there. A voyage to America is a lot shorter than going to the Orient, so Jean Guy can see if this really will be the life for him. He's the only one who didn't get seasick on the way over from France which is a good sign."

As they both stopped talking to sip their coffee, it occurred to Paul that Marc hadn't converted any of the family here to tea drinking yet. It struck him as amusing and he smiled to himself. However, he didn't think his serious father-in-law would see the humour in it, so he continued their conversation. He expressed his satisfaction with Claude, now installed in the goldsmith shop as an apprentice.

"He seems to have a gift for this work, Pierre. He's already better at making the jewellery than Henri who has been there for a few years. I think he'll be an excellent goldsmith. So now, all you have to worry about are the girls and little Andre. What are your plans for him? He can't be considered a baby any longer, can he?"

"No he'll be six in February. We've hired a tutor who'll come in to teach both him and Jeanette their lessons each morning. I already let him do a little work on the small loom, as well. He's quite deft for a little boy."

He smiled over at Paul. "I content myself with the thought; here might finally be my silk weaver. But he must have a full classic education, and I've saved enough money for that. There should be at least one scholar in the family."

"Any news about Catherine's romance, Louise will be anxious to know the latest?" Paul asked. A young wig-maker from the area was courting Claude's twin sister, and they planned to marry as soon as she turned seventeen.

"Oh, they're still very much in love. The wedding will be next summer. They'll live with us for a while. He's never going to be wealthy, I'm afraid, so it's good that she's satisfied to stay home with Claudine, and learn how to be a good wife and mother. I must say she's a lot easier to handle than Louise ever was at that age."

Paul grinned at Pierre, but again said nothing. He privately thought his wife was quite easy to handle. Although, perhaps it is she who handles me, he mused. Once more, he had to stop himself from chuckling audibly at the thought.

Aloud he said to his father-in-law, "So we'll soon be looking forward to a wedding in the family. You know, if you intend to invite quite a few people, you are quite welcome to have it at our house. Louise will certainly be up to helping her mother with a party by then. I assume she'll be coming to see you about some material for another new dress. As my wife always tells me, 'it's very helpful having the best silk maker in London in the family.'"

Even Pierre laughed at that, as they finished their coffees, and bade each other a fond farewell.

While the Thibault house on Soho Square was spacious and elegant, and Louise seemed happy there, Paul realized, with so little to do, she was sometimes bored. There were several servants as well as a wet nurse for Peter and a nanny for Alice. She read a great deal, played the spinet, sewed beautiful outfits for the children, and kept up her English lessons, but, nonetheless, he could see she sometimes found the days dragging without something to challenge her mind.

Even, though, her strength was returning, he didn't want her to go back to the church to help with the refugees from France. Those who managed to make their way to London, often arrived with fevers and illnesses, and what she might bring home to the baby concerned him. However, he appreciated she was not the kind of woman to be satisfied with just needlework and giving parties. She clearly wasn't the usual type of English upper class bride.

He decided to compromise by bringing the accounts from the goldsmith shop home to teach her how to keep them for him. She had told him that, on the farm in France, she helped her father with his accounts. More and more he was involved in the plans for the new Bank of England and was quite happy to have her take over that part of the business. Having a natural ability with figures, she learned quickly and, since she could do it unobserved in the house, no one could accuse her of being unladylike. Gentlewoman in society simply didn't do things like that but, outside the family, Paul thought, no one had to know.

As they breakfasted together one day in early autumn, Paul asked his wife, "How would you like to do something different for our marriage anniversary, Louise? I was thinking we might go to a play in town. I know it's the custom to celebrate only exceptional anniversaries like the twenty-fifth; but this is such a special year for us, I feel like doing something out of the ordinary. And anyhow, I'll be fortunate to be around for our twenty fifth anniversary." His smile was slightly sad.

"Why I've never been to the theatre, Paul. There was no such thing in our little village in France. In any case, I'm not sure my father would ever have thought to do something like that. He's always been rather pious about entertainment. Have you been to the theatre much then?"

"Yes, many times. I've seen most of William Shakespeare's plays. They were spectacular. During the reign of King Charles, it was the thing to do in London Society, even though the plays got quite ribald sometimes. In fact, it got so bad the women wore masks to hide their identity."

"My, that must have been something to see. I suppose then, they could flirt with whomever they liked—married or not."

"That was the general idea, but now, of course, King William, being such a strict Protestant, has cleaned up the theatre somewhat. Most of the plays are quite decent, so ladies don't need masks anymore, and I wouldn't hesitate to take you."

A few days later, he told her he had arranged for them to see a play at the Drury Lane Theatre. The name had rather intrigued him. "It's an old comedy called 'A Chaste Maid in Cheapside' about a goldsmith climbing the social ladder. Thomas Middleton wrote it nearly fifty years ago, but it's still relevant. Most of us in the guild don't mind a laugh at our expense. It is a little on the cheeky side I'm told, so I hope you don't mind."

"Of course not, Paul. I think it would be amusing."

Because it was their first social outing since the birth of Peter, he also invited Louise's parents. He arranged for a comfortable box in the theatre for the four of them, and afterwards they would go to dinner together, so it promised to be an elegant evening. .

Pierre, although explaining to them that, in his Huguenot heart, he would most likely feel guilty, nevertheless agreed to attend. He admitted that, as a young apprentice in the city of Tours, he had gone to the occasional drama; but neither he nor Claudine had seen one since getting married.

The evening of the event, Paul instructed his coachman to go around to Fournier Street to pick up Pierre and Claudine, and the four of them arrived at the entrance to the theatre in grand style. They made their way to their reserved box, and looked around at the audience to see if there was anyone in the audience, they might know.

"It's unlikely I'll see anyone of my acquaintance," Pierre said. "Even here in London our Huguenot friends are fairly strict when it comes to entertainment."

"Well, I see a lot of guild members I know, and there's someone you may remember," Paul replied, after surveying the crowd. "See the box two back from the one directly across from us. There's a gentleman in a long black wig and the bright green and gold silk jacket. And his wife is the lady in a white wig beside him."

"Oh, I see who you mean, Paul," Louise spoke up. "Isn't that Monsieur Mercier? He's another goldsmith, Papa. He's also French."

"Yes, that's the one. Do you remember him, Pierre? You met him at the first dinner you came to at my house. He showed a lot of interest in Louise at the time. I'd heard he's gotten married since then. In fact, I know the lady quite well. My friends always tried to match me up with someone or other, and she was one of them. Thank heavens I waited." He smiled at his wife who looked particularly attractive in a new turquoise silk from her father's collection.

"I remember him." Pierre replied rather dourly. "I've met him once or twice since then, but I must admit I've never been particularly impressed with him." He frowned as he made the statement.

"Why, Papa. It's not like you to speak unkindly of someone. He must have really annoyed you."

"Yes—well—it's in the past. Let's not ruin our evening by discussing Monsieur Mercier."

The conversation changed to another topic, but Paul filed it away in his mind to find out why Pierre disliked the man so. As Louise had remarked, it was so unlike him.

The play being about a goldsmith using his daughter to move up the social hierarchy, at the beginning of the seventeenth century, proved quite amusing. As Paul explained, all these years later, it was still quite realistic. Many members of the guild were now held in high regard, and the upper classes accepted wealthy goldsmiths such as himself, as gentlemen. Some had already received knighthood, and others expected such an honour would yet come to them. They could afford to laugh at the biting wit of the story.

They all agreed it was an enjoyable way to spend an evening. Claudine and Louise decided that the theatre was an excellent form of entertainment, especially if the playwright kept his work within the bounds of propriety.

"Well, I for one am not quite sure he managed to do so," Pierre informed them, as they sat in the coach on their way to dinner. Paul had arranged for them to take their meal in a private room in one of the better inns in town. "There were a few times when I felt downright uncomfortable. I rather hoped none of my friends saw me there. But all the same—I must admit—I found it interesting."

Paul smiled to himself. Pierre had obviously caught some of the inferences that it was as well, the ladies did not understand. "But Pierre," he said, starting to chuckle. "Your friends would only see you if they were there, as well. So wouldn't it be rather hypocritical for them to look down on you for being there?"

For a moment, Pierre looked puzzled. Then he said, "Well, yes, that's true. I never thought of it that way." He joined in as they all laughed at his bewilderment.

Good for Pierre, Paul thought to himself as the coach stopped in front of the inn. Perhaps we'll elicit a sense of humour in him yet. He's a first-rate friend and that's really all he's lacking. Still smiling he led the party in to dinner.

⚜

After the meal, Pierre invited them to stop off at Fournier Street for a nightcap. "Our families don't get enough time for visiting anymore, Paul," he mentioned. "That banking business keeps you so busy now."

Claudine took Louise up to the attic workroom to show her the innovative silks Pierre and his new apprentices were making. The two men sat in the drawing room enjoying a glass of cognac from the precious stock Marc had left with Pierre. "I noticed you seemed inclined not to discuss Mathurin Mercier tonight, Pierre. Do you have something against him?"

"I don't like the man, Paul. Nor trust him for that matter. I've met him in the community a few times since that first evening, and I'm afraid my opinion of him hasn't changed."

"I do remember you enquired about him. You still have some doubts about him then?"

"Yes, even that first evening in your home, his comments were most malicious about you. Then the next time I saw him, he smirked quite insolently when he asked me how you were doing. The word was already out that Louise was pregnant, and I remember exactly how he looked. He raised his eyebrow and said 'I hear there's a child already on the way. The virtuous Paul has quite surprised us all.' I didn't like the way he said it at all."

Paul laughed. "Well, then, perhaps I should take it as a compliment to my virility. Anyway, I suspect he was jealous over the fact that I won the beauty. Did you get a glimpse of his wife tonight? Believe me, the lady is no prize. Not gentlemanly of me to say so, though, is it?"

Pierre shook his head, smiling discreetly behind his cognac glass as he spoke. "I know he seems harmless enough, Paul. Nevertheless, I would look out for him. I think he could be a dangerous enemy."

Chapter 31

"Come into the library, darling. I have something for you," Paul said to Louise.

It was late when they reached their Soho mansion, but Paul had one more surprise for her. Motioning her to a seat in front of his desk, he opened a secret drawer from which he pulled out a small box; the type he gave to clients with their purchase of quality jewellery.

With a shy smile, he handed it to her, his heart beating rapidly in anticipation of her response. It was many months since they had been together as husband and wife, and he found himself longing for her. Sometimes he wondered if she ever felt that way about Marc. However, he tried never to show his jealousy over her handsome, young cousin.

"Why, Paul," she exclaimed, as she opened the box. Inside was a beautiful gold filigree pendent set with an emerald the size of a small rock. "It's exquisite. Oh, but my dear, it's too much. It must be worth a fortune."

"Well, I remember a proverb that says 'doctor's wives die young and shoemaker's wives go barefoot.' I don't want them adding that 'goldsmith's wives don't have beautiful things.' Louise, this year you gave me the most wonderful gift ever. I'm not a poor man by any means, and no amount of gold or jewels could ever be worth the value of our small son. So let me do this for you—this small token I have fashioned with my own hands for the woman I love more than anything in this world."

He took it from her and placed the exquisite piece around her neck. As he fastened the clasp, his hands brushed the soft nape of her neck. Beneath his fingers, he felt her shiver at his warm touch.

The gold filigree shone against her milky skin and the emerald reflected in her grey-green eyes. He had never seen her look more breathtakingly lovely. "It's stunning on you. I should have you model all my jewellery. This particular piece enhances your true loveliness. If it's possible to make a beautiful woman even more so, then I think I have managed to do that."

Her large, luminous eyes shone with pleasure. Putting her hand in his, she looked up at him and murmured, "This has been one of the most unforgettable nights of my life. I don't think it should end, do you? I think it's time you came back to my room."

"Why, Madame." He chuckled. "I think you are trying to seduce me?

"Seduce you? *Au contraire.*" She smiled into his eyes. "I think *you* have been seducing me this whole evening. But, I am perfectly well now and it's lonely in that big room by myself."

She threw her arms around him and kissed him. Then taking his hand, led him up the splendid staircase. All envious thoughts of Marc Garneau, as well as the warning Pierre had given him about Monsieur Mercier, went completely out of his mind.

However, Paul was to recall Pierre's words a few months later when he and Louise attended a banquet at the Goldsmith's Hall.

All the goldsmiths in the city belonged to the Guild and several times a year they met at their beautiful hall. The most important of these meetings was the annual Trial of the Pyx, the procedure for ensuring that newly minted coins conform to required standards. It was a great honour to be one of the jurymen and Paul had served in the position twice before. His peers considered him an honest man and one of the foremost goldsmiths in the city.

The Trial began the first week in February, although the actual testing of the coins would go on for two months and the final verdict given in May. On opening day, the Pyx, or large boxwood chest holding random samples of coins of the realm to be tested, was presented to the jury. There were thousands of these coins representing one coin from every batch of each denomination minted, so it was a tremendous job for the six assayers.

The goldsmiths had first to check the number and denomination of the coins and then weigh the coins in bulk, to ascertain if the average weight was within the tolerance allowed by law. They also had to measure the diameters of the coins to make certain they were within the tolerances allowed by the Coinage Act.

Paul knew he would be busy for the next two months and would not have much time to spend with his family. However, at the end of opening week, the guild held a banquet in one of the Hall's magnificent rooms, and he and Louise attended. His wife looked fetching in a pale cream-coloured silk. At the neckline of the dress, she wore the filigree pendant with its magnificent emerald. Paul believed he would burst with pride at the beauty of the woman by his side.

The feast was a lavish affair served in the new, informal French buffet style. They could choose what they desired from tables laden with salmon and oysters and lobster meat; roast chicken and pigeons; fricasseed rabbit and roast lamb; along with salads of sweet herbs, capers, dates and raisins, figs and almonds, and slices of orange.

Finally, there was the sweets table with every type of pudding and baked tart. Paul and Louise were standing there enjoying an after dinner brandy when Mathurin Mercier and his rather podgy wife approached them.

"We haven't seen you since the night at the Drury Lane, Madame Thibault. Did you really enjoy your evening at the theatre, then?" the man enquired slyly. "I'd have thought the play would make you uncomfortable." His face was mottled and his speech somewhat slurred as he looked at Paul with a leer.

"What's that supposed to mean, Mercier?" Paul spoke up sharply.

The man swayed and grasped the table. "Why, Paul, the title of the play—'The Chaste Maiden of Cheapside.' It must have been embarrassing for Madame in view of her own conduct. And I hear, once again the new baby looks nothing like his father."

Louise gasped and Paul went livid. In his entire life, he had never experienced such an insult or such anger. He would gladly have put a bullet through the man's heart. His hand reached back to the sword it was the custom for gentlemen to carry at their side. "I should call you out for that, sir," he said with a dangerous tone in his voice. "You are despicable."

"Paul, please. It doesn't matter." Louise spoke softly, putting her hand on her husband's arm. "I'm sure Monsieur Mercier isn't responsible for his speech right now." Mercier took an unsteady step towards her, but his wife stopped him.

Louise's smile was extremely sweet as she turned to her. "I'm afraid your husband has been enjoying the superb refreshments well but perhaps not too wisely. If I were you, I would persuade Monsieur to go home as soon as possible, Madame." Her sugary tone belied the dig. She curtsied briefly to the couple as she dragged Paul away from the explosive situation. To have a duel was against the law and there would be no winner in such a contest.

"I'm so sorry you had to go through that," Paul said, as they awaited their carriage. "Although you handled him magnificently. Your father warned me about him, and it seems he was right. I'm afraid we have an enemy. Perhaps a treacherous one."

Chapter 32

London, April 1690

L ouise sat in the morning room eating a late breakfast when the butler brought in an important-looking envelope. "Sir John Houblon's coachman just brought this to the house, m'am. I thought the master might want to see it immediately. It could be quite urgent."

"Oh, thank you, Herbert. You're right. The postal service is so corrupt these days I'm sure Sir John wouldn't rely on it for anything important."

As it was addressed to both Mr. and Mrs. Thibault, she opened it to find an invitation to a ball. Paul's close friend, James Houblon, was to be knighted, and his older brother, Sir John, was hosting a ball in his honour. She knew that her husband had gone to school with James, and he had often been a guest in the Houblon home.

Although Sir John was sixteen years older than the two boys, he had taken a keen interest in his brother's friend. As the years passed, he became Paul's counsellor and gave him a great deal of practical advice. The knight, a successful London merchant, now served as Sheriff of the City. Louise didn't understand the English political system, but she knew many of Paul's friends were well-placed in London's hierarchy, and Sir John was one of his favourites.

The function, being formal, would require special clothing, so thinking that Paul would like to know about it as soon as possible, Louise decided to visit the shop in Goldsmith's Row. She seldom went there if she could help it. The one square mile known as The City, wasn't a part of London that appealed to her, although, in the four and one-half years she had lived in England, she had learned to appreciate many of the other areas. There were regions of exceptional beauty in the county of Middlesex: especially along the River Thames and in the many tracts of land set aside for parks. However, in the heart of the city, it was noisy and crowded; the streets were rough and filled with litter and manure from the horse-drawn carriages. Street cleaners were rare, so it was hard for them to keep up with the heavy traffic. To Louise, the smells of the city seemed intense, a combination of raw sewage, fresh manure, and choking smoke from the chimneys.

As well, all classes of people inhabited these streets: beggars and merchants; servants and labourers; businessmen and lawyers. The few women found among the throngs of busy people were mostly of a lower class; street mongers who clustered on the corners calling out their wares, or even prostitutes making bold eyes at the men passing their way.

Nevertheless, she felt she needed to speak to her husband straight away, so she asked Oliver, who had only arrived home from taking the master to work, to drive the carriage back the one-mile ride to the shop in the busy financial district. At least the buildings in that area were comparatively new. They were rebuilt after The Great Fire had burned through the area. She passed by the old Goldsmith's Hall, which had not escaped the conflagration. While it hadn't burned to the ground, a great deal of restoration had been necessary to bring it back to its former glory. Now, it was once again a magnificent, stone edifice with Corinthian columns adorning the front entrance and curved windows facing the main street.

From their home in Soho Square, it took about twenty minutes to reach the shop located in a new brick building on the corner of Goldsmith's Row and the Hackney Road. She stepped out of the carriage and asked their coachman to return in one hour. It was difficult to get a public carriage in this part of town as most of the owners, like Paul, had their own transportation and their wealthy patrons certainly did. The apprentices, who worked in the shops, and the seedy characters, with illicit wares to pawn off, were more apt to walk.

She entered the front portion of the shop, which held a glass-covered case containing intricate gold pieces and sparkling jewels of every description, all inlaid in exquisite settings. The black velvet lined case set off the dazzling colours and clarity of the magnificent stones. Since Paul had a reputation for both honesty and the quality of his merchandise, he catered to some of the highest and richest of London's society.

As she stepped through the door, a small bell above the frame announced her presence, and he emerged from his office behind the showroom. His eyes lit up when he saw her. "Hello, sweetheart." He bent and kissed her on the cheek. "What brings you here? I thought you didn't like this part of town much."

"I really don't like coming here, Paul, I'm a country girl at heart." She smiled teasingly at him. "I find the city much too busy and dirty for my liking. But this invitation was delivered to the house today, and I thought you would like to know about it right away. It's from Sir John Houblon—an invitation to a ball in Kensington. He addressed it to both of us, so I opened it. I hope you decide we should go. I think it would be most exciting."

"Well, let's have a look at it. Wait, I'd better wipe my hands."

She followed him into his office where there was a large desk and the huge iron cast vault that contained the gold. He pointed to the small, leaded pane window." I've been trying to fix that window. The latch doesn't work right. It looks as though I'll have to get it taken care of by a locksmith. I certainly don't want unscrupulous people finding a way in here with all the gold I have in the vault."

"My word," she replied. "You'd have to be pretty small to get through that window. I don't think even I could squeeze through it."

He laughed at her as he wiped his hands on a cloth sitting on his desk. "Alright, let's see the invitation, then. If it's from Sir John, we most certainly should plan on going." He took the gold-rimmed invitation from her and scrutinized it closely.

"Hmm. So, it's in connection with the investiture of his brother, James. Well, the three of us go back a long time together. I'll be glad to be among those who pay their respects to my old school friend."

He laughed again at her expectant look. "Yes, for a certainty we'll be going, Louise. It's a most important event and an honour to be invited. We'll both need to be properly clad for such an elegant affair. Is that why you braved the wilds of London's financial district to come here? You want to talk to me about another new dress?" he added, with a chuckle.

"Yes, husband." She laughed, feeling slightly abashed. "You know me too well. In fact, I'm planning to go to see father today and look at his latest silk collection. He's hired a wonderful new dressmaker who just escaped from France. She was a secret Huguenot who worked for some of the nobility. But she was afraid they'd find out about her faith, so she decided to flee."

"No doubt she's familiar with all the latest court fashions then. We'll get her to make up apparel for both of us, shall we?"

"Yes, I merely wanted to make sure it's fine with you before I go there. Oliver is coming back for me at noon, so I'll probably eat something with them."

"Well, since you have a few minutes more, would you like to see Claude? He's in the middle of bending the gold for a necklace, I'm making. It's his first try at something complicated, and if he does a good job of it, I'll add a sapphire. Perhaps you could wear it to the ball before we sell it."

Paul motioned her into the large workshop in the back where her middle brother worked at a high desk fashioning the metal. He smiled up at her as she approached and spoke to him in French.

"Well, brother. You seem happy. You really enjoy working here don't you?"

"I love it. Since the first time Paul brought us down here to see his shop, I've known this is what I wanted to do. I think it disappoints Papa a little that neither Jean Guy nor I wanted to be silk weavers. However, there's still Andre, so perhaps he will be the one to carry on the family tradition. For me—to make these beautiful pieces—it's all I ask in life."

"Hmm," she said, with a laugh. "I'm sure you'll want a wife and family someday, as well. That will come in time. You be sure to make a good job of the necklace. Paul tells me, I might be able to wear it to a ball. And then I shall tell everyone my young brother is the artist, and he is going to be one of the finest goldsmiths London ever had."

She hugged him and then made her way out to the front of the shop where Oliver now awaited. Feeling quite light-hearted, she kissed her husband 'goodbye' and instructed their coachman to take her to her father's house. Her life with Paul had turned out extremely well. Marc was often away from England and even when he was home; she rarely saw him. Gradually her old feelings were becoming a distant memory. It seemed that, since the birth of Peter, nothing could mar her happiness.

A few days later, the jingling of the shop's doorbell alerted Paul to the fact he had a visitor. He stepped into the showroom, with a smile on his face, to discover his potential customer was none other than Sir John Houblon.

"Well, good morning, Sir John." He welcomed his friend, shaking the man's hand. "How good to see you. Soon your brother will be 'Sir James,' as well. He's done a lot for this country and certainly deserves the honour."

"Well, to you, Paul, it will always be John and James. But there's something I need to discuss with you. Something important. I wondered if you could have luncheon with me today. I've made an appointment at Lloyd's Coffee House for a private room around half past noon. Do you think you could get away for about two hours?"

"I don't see why not," Paul replied, quickly mulling over his day's schedule. "The two lads can look after the shop. They're both proving to be real assets."

"Good. Just present yourself to the steward at the door as my guest. He'll take care of you." Sir John smiled at him. "It's good news, so don't worry about it."

Paul watched him leave the shop. What could be so momentous that it would merit a luncheon at Lloyds, he puzzled? Only the city's wealthiest citizens frequented that particular coffeehouse. Well, well. This promises to be an interesting day.

Chapter 33

When Paul arrived exactly at twelve-thirty, Lloyd's Coffee House was already crowded with some of London's most influential and powerful people. He gave his name to the steward who ushered him into a private room at the back. Sir John sat perusing a sheet of paper listing the daily menu. He looked up as Paul approached.

"Well, you're a prompt fellow, Paul. I appreciate that in an associate. I've ordered a brandy for you. Is that acceptable?"

Paul took his seat, smiling at John. "Ahh, yes. Always look forward to a good *aperitif*. It's part of my French heritage, I guess. "

John passed him the menu and, after they had made their decision and the house servant brought their drinks, he looked at Paul. "No doubt you've heard the government is ready to implement our ideas on The Bank of England."

"Yes, of course. It's all they write about in *The London Gazette* these days."

"Well, this is all confidential right now, but once we get the subscriptions needed to start, they've asked me to take over the post of Governor. We've been discussing who the directors will be as well, and I'm happy to inform you your name is among about twenty that we're considering. You have an honest reputation in this city, Paul. And that fact has not gone unnoticed."

Amazed, he took a small sip of brandy to compose himself before answering. "Well, thank you, Sir John," he said. "It certainly would be a great honour, and I'd be happy to do it. Who makes the final decision?"

"When the time comes, I'll hand in my suggestions to the King and the Prime Minister, and they'll no doubt pass whomever I want. But that's not my main reason for speaking to you right now."

"No?" He raised a querying eyebrow.

"No, this is about another position—the City of London Sheriff. I'm going to end my term soon, and the livery companies need an upright man to fill the position. They've asked me to come up with a suggestion. I'd like to put your name forward. They'll announce the name of the new man on Midsummer's day."

"Zounds," he exclaimed. He almost choked on his brandy.

"So would you be interested? It's another step up the ladder. A knight-hood usually follows, and an opportunity to become London's Lord High Mayor, as well. I think you have a good chance of getting the appointment. I hear the only other serious contender is Sir Geoffrey Watson. He has the money and the title, of course, but you know his reputation."

"Good lord, man. That *is* extraordinary. Well, yes—I believe I could handle it. As I say, I have great help at the shop with those two lads now. Since we're speaking confidentially, I'll let you in on a little secret; Louise does all my bookkeeping for me. She'd rather I didn't tell anyone, as she doesn't think it's ladylike. But she seemed bored, and she likes doing it and, as it turns out, she's good at it."

"Your wife is a remarkable woman, Paul—brains as well as beauty. I don't know how you got so fortunate in your old age. Well, I'll keep this little gem to myself unless I ever desire to blackmail you, my boy."

With a laugh, the two men turned to their meal in earnest.

The ball at Sir John Houblon's palatial home in Kensington was the grand-est Louise and Paul had ever attended. Even King William and Queen Mary made a brief appearance. Louise thought the queen was quite beauti-ful, but she was surprised at the mien of her husband. He was shorter and smaller than his wife, and his large, periwig-covered-head looked out of proportion to his hunched, narrow body. With his hooked nose and down-turned mouth, he wasn't a particularly appealing looking man at all.

The royal couple stood in the receiving line, along with the three Houblon brothers, as the guests were presented to them. Although Louise felt quite intimidated by him, she curtsied and responded to the King's greeting. "It *ees* my *pleas-zure* to meet you, sire." In her nervousness, her accent was obvious.

The King noticed it and looking intently at her, questioned her in French, "You are not long here from France, Madame Thibault. Are you a Huguenot then?"

"*Oui*, Your Majesty," she replied in her own language. "My family escaped in 1685. We were fortunate to arrive safely in this country."

"We would say, Madame, it is England that was fortunate. France's loss is definitely this country's gain. We look forward to meeting you again." His strange lips turned up ever-so- slightly in a smile, which didn't quite reach his eyes.

Louise curtsied once more to him then moved on as he turned to the next couple in line.

"Well, my beautiful lady," Paul whispered. "You have made an impression. King William is said to be a harsh, stern man and not given to flattery. So he means what he says. I always knew you would be my greatest asset."

In her new dress made up in an ice blue, brocaded silk, she felt every bit as grand as any of the other ladies in attendance. Claude had made a truly professional job of finishing the necklace and, with the sparkling diamonds and sapphires Paul added, it was the perfect embellishment to her couture.

How fortunate I am to have all these talented people in my family, she thought.

Paul also had a fine-looking jacket made from one of Pierre's silks, which he wore over a ruffled, white silk shirt and a royal blue, velvet vest. Since it was such a formal occasion, he also sported a white powdered wig, which, in spite of her dislike of hairpieces, she decided suited him. In fact, they both looked spectacular, and this could without doubt be the salient social evening of their lives together.

As she looked around the luxurious salon, she marvelled at the famous and prominent people she could see. Imagine it's only six years since I was hauling water from the well in our little French village, she thought. What has happened to me is all so unbelievable.

Shortly after their presentation to the King, a middle-aged couple approached them. It was Sir Geoffrey Watson and his fashionable, but extremely gaunt wife. Her emerald green, satin dress was skilfully styled, as was her white, powdered hair. However, her sallow skin, which was mottled and rather wrinkled for her age, spoiled the effect. She had likely been quite attractive at one time, but her prettiness had faded, and it was rumoured that her husband now kept a young courtesan in an apartment near The Vauxhall.

Paul had told Louise that Sir Geoffrey was in the running for the office of city sheriff. However, as he approached, it was obvious to her he had imbibed more than his share of champagne. His florid complexion was beet-like in appearance. He looked as though he could succumb to apoplexy at any moment.

His glance at Paul was contemptuous as he spoke. "Well, Thibault, You seem to be the only serious opponent I have for this city sheriff position. Since I've already been knighted, it s gives me a bit of an edge, would you not say."

Paul smiled at him. "It is a great honour for me to be even considered, Sir Geoffrey. I'm happy, whichever one of us wins, and if it is you, I'll gladly drink a toast to you then." He lifted his glass to him. "May the best man win. In the end, it's about the good of London; would you not say?"

Sir Geoffrey harrumphed and, along with his wife, strode haughtily off towards the supper table.

Later, sitting in a small alcove eating their meal, Louise looked over the crowd and saw Mathurin Mercier and his wife. The man glared at her, but turned away quickly and walked to the opposite side of the large salon.

We seem to be accumulating enemies faster than I like, she thought. It turns out that Society can be rather a quagmire. However, she did not mention her concerns to her husband.

After the champagne supper, the dancing started. Paul bowed to his wife, and led her onto the floor for the set. He smiled down at her as their hands met and said, "Do you realize this is the first time we've ever danced together in public?"

She frowned at something behind his back. "What's the matter, Louise— you seem perturbed?"

"I'm looking at Sir Geoffrey. He's over in the corner rather hidden behind a large plant. I think the man with him is your assistant. Why would Henry Du Bois be here—with Sir Geoffrey?"

"I don't suppose that is too odd. Henri's father must be here as well, although I haven't noticed him yet. He's a prominent member of the French Community. Sir John always includes many Huguenots in his entertaining. Like me, he never forgets his background. And I suppose the Du Bois family would know Sir Geoffrey, as well. No dear, I don't think it's anything to be concerned about. Let's just enjoy ourselves tonight. Who knows when we'll get another occasion like this?"

⁂

The dancing lasted until well after midnight. When it was over, Louise stood with Paul, under the mansion portico, waiting for the arrival of their coachman. An odd-looking figure moving furtively down the curved driveway caught her attention. The man kept as much in the shadows as possible, but, as he walked under one of the lantern posts he turned his head, and she had a good view of him. He was quite stooped and probably the thinnest person she had ever seen. Thinner than Lady Watson, Louise thought, smiling to herself.

He wore no stocking and his bare legs looked like match sticks. However, what she noticed most was the striking pair of breeches he wore under a gold silk cloak. They were a bright, peacock blue shade. An odd colour combination for someone who didn't look anything at all like a gentleman, she thought.

"Look at the peculiar little man," she said to Paul. "Who is he? Why he looks like a little rat—and look at his odd breeches. Whatever would a man like that be doing at a ball like this?"

Paul's eye caught him as he reached the next lantern post, just before he ducked back into the shadows and turned the corner onto the street. "Yes,

180

I see him. He's a pawnbroker we all know. His name is Walter Roberts, but we call him 'Wally the Weasel.' He has a rather dubious reputation, so none of us likes to do business with him. He's been under suspicion by the Pyx jury for distributing underweight coins once or twice; but we've never managed to prove it. I can't think why he would be here. I know Sir John would never invite him to an affair like this."

At that moment, their coach drew up and she gave it no more thought.

Chapter 34

The Monday morning, one week after the ball, found Louise lingering over her coffee and reading the newspaper, when there was a frantic pounding at the front door. After a few seconds, the butler appeared, looking perturbed. "Madame, your father, and young brother are here. They need to speak to you immediately."

Oh, whatever is wrong? This is so unlike them, she worried as she hurried into the receiving room. One look at her father made her heart stop. "Papa, what is it? You look ghastly."

"Louise, dear, please sit down. We have something to tell you. Something I don't really quite understand, but it is bad news. Claude, you explain what happened. You were there, and you comprehend the situation much better than I do."

"It's Paul. The police have taken him to jail. Sir John Houblon and a constable came and arrested him early this morning. Sir John is still the city sheriff until the new ones take over in July. He was extremely apologetic, but said he had to do it. It's his job. They went into Paul's office and found proof in his desk he's been involved in coining."

"Coining? I don't know what that means."

"It's a serious offence, Louise," Claude continued. "It's when they shave off some of the gold, and pass off the coin as being legal when it doesn't really have the true value. I hate to say this; but they hang people for this crime. It's considered treason. I know Paul would never do such a thing. He's far too honest. He told Sir John he didn't know how those items got there. I think Sir John believes him, but still he had no choice but to make the arrest."

"Arrest him! They've taken him to jail? I must go to see him." The room seemed suddenly to whirl around, and Louise could hardly get her breath. I mustn't faint, she thought, dropping into the nearest chair.

"Definitely not," Pierre said. "He's in Newgate. Under no circumstance are you to go to that place. Paul would never allow it. Claude and I will find Marc and Jean Guy. Thanks be, they got home from their voyage this week. Marc may know what to do about something like this. I have no idea, myself."

"But, Claude," she turned back to her brother, "what about the shop? Who's there? You must be the one to take charge of it for now. You're the one Paul trusts. He said you learn remarkably fast, and—oh—what about the vault. All the gold is in there."

"It's alright. Paul locked the vault before they took him away. He told me not to leave the key in the shop, but to bring it to you for now."

"Well, I already have one, but you must keep that one with you at all times. Don't let it out of your sight. Wear it around your neck, I think. I must depend on you, Claude. I know Paul would not wish Henri Dubois left too much on his own in the shop. Since I saw him at the ball the other night with Sir Geoffrey, I don't quite trust him anymore. You'd better go back to the shop right away. Get Oliver, our coachman to take you right back."

"Yes, you're right. I'll go back, and, don't worry, I promise to look after everything until this is all settled. I'll keep my eyes on Henri. Come, Papa. You'll have to find Marc and Jean Guy. They're most likely at the East India offices on Leadenhall Street."

"It's a good idea for us to split up now," Pierre agreed. "Once we decide what to do, someone will come back to you, Louise. Don't you take it into your head to do anything foolish, daughter."

"But—I must see…"

"I know how you feel," he broke in. "But you simply cannot go to that place. It's best for you to stay here with the children. Although, I wouldn't mention anything even to Alice yet—she's far too young to understand."

They both gave her reassuring hugs and went out the back entrance towards the coach house.

"Monsieur Marc Garneau to see you, Madame." It was much later in the evening. Louise sat in the library, quietly weeping to herself, when Herbert entered to make the announcement. Marc was right on the butler's heels.

She stood up, dabbing at her red-rimmed eyes with a handkerchief and Marc, crossing the room swiftly, put his arms around her and pulled her close. It was the first time she had seen him since he and Jean Guy returned from their yearlong trip to America.

"Louise, *Cherie*. Please don't cry. Your whole family is in this together, and we are all going to help Paul be acquitted. We all know he's an upright man, and certainly not the type to do this thing. Even Sir John Houblon said so."

She couldn't seem to help herself. It was so comforting in his arms, she relaxed against him; suddenly he was kissing her, and she was responding. For a few moments, time stood still and she was back in France. Then she remembered herself and gently pushed away from him. Not wanting to hurt him, she took both his hands in hers. "Marc. What am I to do? I can't even go and see him in that ghastly place. And I'm afraid it will be the death of him."

"Don't worry, sweetheart. We have it all planned. Uncle Pierre will be in the shop each day to help Claude, and they will watch Henri carefully. He's the only one who had any access to the place other than Paul and Claude. It's almost certain no one broke in. There's no evidence of it anywhere."

She let go his hands and motioned him to take a seat opposite her. "The other night at the ball—it was strange. Henri was there having a discussion with Sir Geoffrey Watson. I had the feeling they might be up to something. But it would only be our word against theirs, I'm afraid."

"And that is certainly circumstantial. It wouldn't stand up in court at all. Well, it will be up to Jean Guy and me to do some investigating. We've already been to see Paul at the prison—yes, yes. He is all right," he assured her, as she was about to break into his story. "Thanks be, Sir John is such a good friend of Paul's, and he definitely believes he has been framed."

"But I need to talk to him."

"He said to tell you not worry too much, and don't tell the children anything about this. If Alice asks, he's just away. We're going to take him decent meals, so he doesn't get sick. And some paper and quills, so he can write to you. That's the problem with the place. You have to bribe them for every little comfort. However, Sir John Houblon has spoken to the head warden, and we gave him some money so they will treat Paul with some decency. And at least he has a room to himself."

"Marc. I *must* go to see him."

"No." His voice was firm. "It definitely would not be safe for you to go there—even with one of us. Louise, you can't even imagine the horror of the place. The worst people are there and that includes the jailers. However, we're going to look after him for you. He asked us to get in touch with Sir Francis Hoare. He has a friend who is a barrister. We must have one, they won't allow your solicitor to argue a case in the Old Bailey. But, whoever it is, they'll have to work together."

"Thank you so much, Marc." She wiped her eyes again. "I haven't even asked you how you are. And I haven't seen you for well over a year. It's so wonderful of you to do this for Paul when you must be tired from your trip. I'll never forget it."

"Well, that kiss was a nice welcome home." He smiled, teasingly. Quickly his faced turned serious. "*Cherie*, I like Paul. He's a fine man, so I don't usually say anything. For one thing, I don't wish to make your father angry. However, perhaps it's not for him I do this thing. Louise, you have to know I love you still. It's something I have never been able to get over." He sighed deeply. "Perhaps I never will. However, don't worry. For now, I only want what makes you happy. So, if I can help it, nothing bad will happen to your husband."

"Thank you, Marc. I understand." She gave him a wan smile. "Did he tell you the other things we saw at the ball?" she asked quickly, desiring to change the subject.

"About that ferret-faced fellow, Walter Roberts? Yes, he told us everything he could think of. In addition, there's that other Frenchman doesn't trust. Another goldsmith, I think."

"Yes. Monsieur Mercier." She nodded. "He really hates Paul for some reason."

"Well, tomorrow I'll speak to Sir John, as well. Perhaps he can give us some clues. Anyhow, you must go to bed early tonight. Get some rest, dear and try not to worry." He kissed her again, this time chastely on each cheek, then let himself out the front door.

After Marc had gone, Louise sat in the withdrawing room sipping a small glass of brandy the maid brought her to help her sleep. She reflected on the statement he had made to her—that he was still in love with her. *Oh, I'd hoped he'd gotten over it by now. It was all so long ago, and so much has happened to both of us since then. If only he would find a pleasant mistress for his beautiful house. He needs to settle down with a wife and children.*

A terrible thought struck her. *He wouldn't do anything to harm Paul, would he? No, no—he couldn't. He's only been back two or three days. He wouldn't have had time, and anyhow Marc is honourable. Even if, he thinks he still loves me, he likes and admires Paul. I'm sure he wants to help him, so I had better put the thought right of my mind before I say something to Papa. He's inclined to think the worst of Marc anyway. He doesn't need any prompting from me in that regard.*

"I believe we've eliminated Henri as being part of any plot against Paul," Marc said to Louise. The men of the family had gathered with her at the Soho Square house, late one evening, to discuss their findings. "Your father has had some strong talks with him, and he swears he had nothing to do with it. He thinks highly of Paul and doesn't mind Claude getting so much commendation. He wants to help us in any way he can. Can you add anything, Uncle Pierre?"

"No. Other than, I'm inclined to believe him. I think he's sincere, and he definitely wants to finish his apprenticeship there. Paul says he'll never be as naturally good at the craft as Claude is, but he does know the business end very well. He's a journeyman now."

"I'm glad," Louise said. "I've always rather liked him. But that eliminates the possibility of someone in the shop, and how could anyone else get in there and leave the evidence?"

"Well. There is the window in Paul's office. Henri reminded me the latch was broken. Paul meant to get it fixed but they never got around to it," Marc answered.

"But, Marc. It's so small. Paul showed it to me and I thought even I couldn't possibly get through it."

"Ahh, but luv. You are inclined to be curvy, eh." Marc smiled fondly at her. "A young boy might—or that skinny, ferret-faced fellow you mentioned—he might be able to slip through."

"You mean the pawnbroker, Walter Roberts," Claude interjected. "I think we have to consider the possibility he was involved somehow, although he wasn't particularly an enemy of Paul's"

"Yes, but Paul says he's been involved in illegal activity, in the past," Pierre spoke up. "I'm inclined to think he's mixed up in it somehow. But how do we get him to own up to such a thing?"

"The best thing to do is to give the solicitor our list of suspects. He has spies working for him who know how to talk to these seedy characters," Marc continued. "I'll set up an appointment to see him as soon as possible. Would you like to come with me, Louise? He may ask you questions that only you would be able to answer."

"Yes, I'll come with you, Marc. Any day—give me a bit of time to get ready and I'll be happy to go. If only we can find the answer to this. It's so frightening to have Paul in Newgate."

"He's alright for now." Her father patted her arm. "He's as well as can be expected. Being a friend of Sir John certainly helps. We're able to make sure he has some decent food each day. By the way, dear, how could I forget? Here's a letter from him. We managed to get the warden to let us bring in some paper and ink for him."

"Oh, Papa. Thank you so much. All of you. I appreciate what you are doing for us so much. I don't know what I would do without you."

"Don't worry, dear sister." As the men got ready to depart, Jean Guy put his arms around her. "We love you, and we care a great deal about Paul. We'll solve this for you."

They took turns hugging her 'goodbye' again, and Marc said, "Until tomorrow, Louise. I think I can arrange for us to see both the barrister and our solicitor then. Be brave, *Cherie*."

Louise went into the library and poured herself a brandy. She had never taken to drinking spirits, but with all this going on, she felt the need of something to steady her nerves. It was strange to look at the letter and realize it was from Paul. Since their marriage, they had never been apart, so this was the first she'd had from him. She knew she would keep it forever.

My darling wife:

I pray that you and the children are well and that you are not unduly worried about me. Rest assured I am as comfortable as one can be in this godforsaken hole.

The warden has given me a cell to myself and Sir John has managed to bribe them into allowing me a decent chair, a desk and lamp, and some writing materials. He also managed to smuggle in a few books that I have wanted to read to keep my mind occupied so I am not dwelling upon my present distress overmuch.

I must admit the charges were a total shock to me as I have always prided myself on my complete honesty. I reassure myself, however, with the fact that Sir John has no doubt about my integrity and will do everything in his power to prove my innocence.

I will also admit to you that the food served to the inmates is terrible— almost inedible; but each day Oliver or someone in your remarkable family brings me a substantial meal, enabling me to keep up my strength. The biggest surprise to me is your cousin, Marc. I am discovering that he is a remarkably amiable and resourceful young man, and I appreciate his many kindnesses to me. Although I don't flatter myself that, it is because of any great fondness for me.

Please take care of yourself and our beloved children. Keep me in your prayers but, Louise, do not even consider for a moment, coming here to see me. I cannot bear the thought of you coming anywhere near this wretched place, although I hope you will write to me often. I love you more than life itself, and feel confident that I will soon be with you.

Your loving husband, Paul Thibault

As she sipped her drink, Louise read the letter through several times, and then went to bed happier than she had been for some days.

Chapter 35

London, June 1690

The Old Bailey was crowded with spectators of all classes, some quite anxious to see a prosperous goldsmith get his just desserts. Many of the poorer class supposed goldsmiths were wealthy only because they cheated. Therefore, it delighted them when they heard of one going against the law.

The famous courthouse was just outside the western wall of the City of London. This proximity to Newgate allowed the constables to bring the prisoner directly from the jail to the courtroom for his trial. Situated as it was between London and Westminster, it was a most suitable location for hearings involving people from the entire area.

It was Saturday and up in the balcony, where only people of quality were allowed, Louise sat with her parents—one on each side of her for emotional support. Marc and Jean Guy were also there, seated a few rows behind them. From that vantage point, they overlooked the courtyard below, which was crowded with people from all walks of life. Louise's palms felt damp with sweat and her breathing shallow. In spite of the building being partly opened on three sides, there was no fresh air. It reeked of stale bodies and heavy perfume.

She gasped when they brought Paul into the dock, placed in a way that emphasised the conflict between the accused and the rest of the court. The prisoner stood at 'the bar' facing the witness box. Here, both prosecution and defence witnesses would testify looking straight into his face. The judge sat higher up, on the other side of the room, with the jury members below his exalted position.

In only two months, Paul's appearance had altered considerably. His dark brown hair was flecked with grey, and his thin, lined face showed signs of strain and weariness. However, even though he came from Newgate, he looked clean and presentable. His wore no wig, but his shoulder-length hair was tied neatly back with a leather thong. He was dressed simply in dark breeches and a ruffled shirt. Even his white stockings were spotless.

I'm so thankful, Sir John managed to arrange for him to take a bath, and put on fresh clothing, Louise thought. She knew Sir John Houblon believed in his friend's innocence, and even though the law required he be the chief witness for the prosecution, he promised to do everything possible to see Paul got a fair trial. The outward appearance of the accused could weigh heavily either for or against him.

The judge, imperious in his white, tight-curled peruke and flowing, scarlet gown, looked over his spectacles at the noisy crowd and banged his gavel on the bench. Slowly the crowd settled down as he called the court into session. The court clerk summoned the first witness for the prosecution—Sir John Houblon, himself.

"State your name and position, sir," the Counsel for the Crown asked Sir John.

"My name is Sir John Houblon, and I am one of two Sheriffs of the City of London."

"Thank you. And can you tell us what happened on the morning of April 20th this year?"

"Yes, it was a Monday morning, and I was in my office when a note was delivered to me by an unknown person. Apparently, he handed it to my clerk in the outer room and then quickly disappeared."

"I see, and then what happened?

"The clerk brought the note to me and I read it. I was loath to believe it since I know Mr. Thibault to be an honest man, and the actions of the fellow who brought the note were suspicious, but I had to act on the information in any case. It's my job to do so."

"And what did the note say, sir?"

"It accused Paul Thibault of 'coining'. It also said he kept illegal tools for coining in his desk, in the right-hand bottom drawer."

"And for the record, Sir John, could you tell us what 'coining' actually is."

"Yes, it's when a coin of the realm is illegally depleted of its value by shaving off some of the gold or silver."

"It is a serious offence, is that correct?"

"Yes, it is treason—an offence against the King and the realm."

At that, the crowd in the courtroom turned angry, muttering amongst themselves and shaking their fists at Paul. One man called from the lower gallery, "'Ang, him now. A trial's too good for the likes of 'im."

Louise thought she would faint; but her father put his arm around her and her mother took her hand and squeezed it. The judge banged his gavel on the desk and called for order, then indicated the prosecutor should continue his questioning.

"So what did you do after reading the note, Sir John?"

"I found one of our constables and my coachman drove the two us over to Mr. Thibault's goldsmith shop. He had only just arrived and was not yet open for business, but he invited us into his office. We explained why we were there. He looked shocked at the accusation and invited us to look around."

"And did you find anything incriminating?"

"Yes, in the bottom drawer on the right-hand side there were some devalued coins and the "coining" material. It's illegal for a goldsmith to have such things in their possession."

"What was Mr. Thibault's explanation?"

"He was clearly stunned, and said he had never seen those items before, and that someone must have planted them there."

"And was that a possibility?"

"It would need to have been one of his apprentices, since there was no sign of a break-in anywhere. In Mr. Thibault's office, there's only one small, high-up window. It seems unlikely anyone could have gotten through it. We did question the two young men indentured with him. They both could account for their whereabouts for all day Sunday, and into the evening. One is his own brother-in-law."

"Thank you, Sir John," the Crown Counsel said. He sat down. The judge turned to Sir Thomas Kidd, the barrister for the defence. "Do you have any questions for this witness?"

"Yes, mi lord. I do." Facing Sir John, he asked, "How long have you known the defendant, Sir John?"

"I've known him ever since he was a child of about twelve—that would be about thirty years now. He went to school with my younger brother, James."

"And what has been your opinion of his character."

"Paul Thibault has always been one of the finest men I've known. He has come to me for advice in many aspects of trade, and I never thought him to be anything but completely honest. This business goes entirely against my assessment of his character."

"Now, Sir John," Sir Thomas continued. "You mentioned that, when you searched Mister Thibault's office, you saw the small window high up in the wall. Did you look closely at it?"

"No, it seemed to be locked and anyway it was too small to allow entrance by any adult of normal size."

"Do you think anyone at all could get through the window?"

"Well—yes. I suppose a child could."

"Did Mr. Thibault mention to you that the window was not, in fact, locked; that the latch was broken; and that, in the excitement of your brother's investiture, and being invited to the ball for Sir James; he had forgotten to get it fixed."

"No, as I told the prosecution, he seemed rather distraught at the accusation and looked absolutely dazed when we found the coining tools. Aside from denying any responsibility, he merely spoke a few words to his apprentice. Then he locked up the vault and said he was ready to come with us. He never said a word about a window."

"Thank you, Sir John." He turned to the judge. "No further questions, mi lord."

Louise had not taken her eyes off the jury during all these enquiries. They looked happy when the prosecutor made his points, nodding their heads. Now the defence asked the questions, they appeared rather sceptical.

Oh, I hope they haven't already decided he's guilty, she thought.

There were only two more witnesses for the prosecution: the constable who had accompanied Sir John and the office clerk who had received the note. The constable confirmed Sir John's statements. The clerk then took the stand and, after giving his name and position, the prosecutor asked him about the person who delivered the note.

"I couldn't see his features. He wore a heavy cloak, which went over his head and more or less covered his face. The only thing I noticed was under his cloak he had a bright pair of breeches. They were a strange colour and material for a man of his type—a brilliant blue-green. And he was extremely thin."

Sitting listening to this testimony, she gave another audible gasp. Several of the people in the audience including her mother and father turned to stare at her. Sounds of whispering filled the room. People somehow knew she was the wife of the accused.

"Order in the court." The judge said crossly, banging his gavel.

"Did he say anything to you?" the prosecutor continued.

"Very little. He thrust the note at me and said 'Take this'. It had 'For the Sheriff' written on the front. He was so fast, I looked up just as he ran out of the office. That's when I saw the breeches. Anyhow I took the note straight in to Sir John."

❦

When they had all been cross-examined, the judge adjourned the trial to resume on Monday. As Louise and her parents left the courthouse, Marc came up to them.

"Marc, that man must be the same one I saw the night of the ball," she said, grasping him by the arm.

"Which man?"

"The one who brought in the note. The clerk said he wore bright, green-blue trousers. That's the same man Paul and I saw as we left the ball that night—Walter Roberts, the pawnbroker. He wore those strange,

192

peacock-coloured breeches, and I think he is thin enough to get through the window."

"Mmm, interesting. I want to have a look at that window. I don't think anyone has looked at it closely. Have you got the key to the office with you?"

"Oh, yes, I never let it out of my sight now. Papa, let's go with him," she said, turning to Pierre. "I never thought to have a look at the window. You'd have to stand on a chair to do that."

They hurried to where Oliver waited with the coach and told him to drive them directly to the shop.

Chapter 36

Claude was still in the shop when they arrived. They found him in Paul's office, putting all the valuable jewellery into the large iron vault for the night.

"Claude, can you get us something to stand on?" Louise said. "We have to take a closer look at the window. It might tell us something."

He brought in one of the benches from the workshop, and Marc immediately placed it under the window and jumped up. The latch was still broken. He pushed the lower pane up as far as it would go, creating an opening not much over one foot square.

"Louise, look," he cried eagerly. "Can you get up here, dear? Do you mind helping her up, Uncle? There's something she should see."

Her father and Claude lifted her onto the bench, and Marc put his arm around her to keep her steady. Looking to where he pointed, she could see a small piece of cloth caught on a rough piece of wood on the window ledge. It looked as if it had ripped off a garment of some type.

"Marc, that's the colour." She almost shouted in her excitement. "That's the bright peacock blue of Walter Robert's breeches. It's not a normal colour for a poor man's clothing. Aren't those silk threads, Papa? Oh, do come up and see."

"Louise, calm yourself, girl," Pierre admonished as he climbed onto the bench beside her. "You'll fall off." He looked closely at the small piece of torn cloth. "Yes, this is a silk-velvet. As you say, quite expensive material for a man such as Roberts to be wearing."

"Don't touch it, anyone," Marc cautioned, as he stepped down and put his arms out to lift Louise down. Once they were off the bench, he continued. "I think we should get Sir John Houblon here to see this. It's definitely important evidence. And we *must* locate that pawnbroker before he tries to flee London. I suppose Paul knows where he lives. I think I'd better try to see the barrister today and tell him about this. Pierre, you and Louise, take the coach and go to Sir John's office. He may still be there. I'll go to the warden and see if he'll let me into the prison to speak to Paul."

"Have you got your own keys?" Claude asked as he closed up the shop. "In case Sir John wants to come here tonight after I've gone. There's a lantern under the counter in the front office. It might be dark by the time you get back. Don't forget to lock up after yourselves, if you do come," he instructed.

"Don't worry, dear brother. We will take care of everything. We're quite responsible," she reassured him with a smile.

Sir John was anxious to see this new piece of evidence. He brought along his clerical assistant as he thought there should be two witnesses outside of the family. The two of them rode in his coach following Louise and her parents back to the shop. Claude was still in the office, as he had not yet finished putting everything in the vault.

Pierre and Claude helped the older man up on the workbench, so he could see the small, torn piece of material stuck in the corner. "Hmm," he mouthed as if he mulled it over, an idea clearly forming in his mind. "This certainly looks as if it could come from the breeches my clerk described. It's an unusual material for a poor man's everyday wear, isn't it?"

"Could it be someone wealthy gave the man this pair of pants? Someone, who finds it advantageous to have such a man as Walters, in his debt?" Louise inquired.

"Yes, you may be right, my dear. The criminal may have a wealthy backer who isn't above using him for his own nefarious purposes. It sounds reasonable. Anyhow, I'm going to take this piece for evidence." He turned to his clerk, "You are witness to where I got this from, William. We'll both have to make a sworn statement."

The clerk nodded his agreement.

Turning to Louise, Sir John continued. "I'll turn it over to your barrister Monday at the trial. But we certainly do have to find the owner of these amazing breeches to get Paul out of this mess."

"My cousin will visit Paul tonight, Sir John," she said. "Marc thinks he might know where this Walter Roberts lives. That's who we suspect it is. I saw him the night of the ball wearing breeches that peculiar colour. And he's very thin—he could easily slip through the office window."

"Right then. I'll go back to my office and get a warrant out for his arrest. If we can find him, we'll force him into court as a witness for the defence. Well, let's pray this is the answer for Paul. I hate to see a man like him imprisoned in that hell-hole they call Newgate."

Claude locked up the shop and Louise, with her hopes somewhat raised, drove off with her family in the Thibault coach.

They found Walter Roberts. He ran a small, dirty pawnshop in one of the most crime-ridden parts of London. Here, the poor kept to themselves and even developed their own form of language known as *canting*. It was to keep others, outside the area, from knowing what they were talking about—a protection for them against the law. One of the thief-takers of the city, hearing there was a reward for information about the man, happily told the sheriff the location of his shop.

Roberts was still wearing the bright blue breeches when they arrested him. However, they said nothing about them to him. To make sure he wouldn't flee, Sir John had him locked up for two nights.

Monday morning found Louise and her family once more in the Old Bailey courtroom. A rustle of astonishment arose from the crowd when Walter Roberts came to the witness box. His appearance was exceptionally strange. Again, he wore the telltale breeches. However, they were almost entirely covered by a gold, silk cloak, which also concealed his reed-like body. The hood of the cape was down, and nothing could hide the gaunt face with its long, pointed chin and bulging eyes. His grey-brown hair, which he wore to his shoulders, was thin and scraggly and looked like it hadn't been washed in weeks. Even where they sat, they could catch a whiff of the strong, offensive smell of rancid sweat, which emanated from his clothing.

"State your name and occupation," Paul's barrister said to the man.

"I'm Walter Roberts. I'm a pawnbroker in the City of London," the odd little man said. "And I've got no idear at all why I'm 'ere."

"You need only to answer the questions as I ask them, Mr. Roberts, thank you," Sir Thomas replied. "Now, I want you to think back to last spring. The 20th of April to be exact. It was a Monday. Did you take a note to the office of the City of London Sheriff and give it to the clerk."

"It might 'ave been that day, I don't remember dates. I don't 'ave any idear at all wot were in the note. Were a gentry cove give it ter me to deliver it for 'im and I did."

"Did he pay you to do it?"

"Yes, 'e did. He equipt me with five quid ter do it."

"I see. That's quite a lot of money. Can you tell me the name of the man who gave you the money to deliver the note?"

"No, I can't. I swear I never saw 'im before, and I never got a good look at 'im. 'e 'ad 'is face covered and it were dark. It were a real coin, though. I tested it, and it were a proper piece, so I said I would do the job for 'im the next morning."

"Did you read the note?"

"Nope. I don't read words too good. But I knows money and I knows jewellery. I runs an 'onest pawn." He thrust his long chin out as he made this statement, as if to defy anyone to doubt the fact.

"All right then, sir. Now, after you left the man who gave you the money, do you have any recollection of where you were on the late hours of Sunday, the 19th of April or the early hours of Monday, the 20th of April?"

"That's two month ago—'ow do I know where I wuz. I 'ad the money, so I probably went to the ale house and then 'ome to bed—seems the most likely."

"Let me ask it another way then, sir. During any of the times, I mentioned to you—were you in the office of Paul Thibault's goldsmith shop planting the 'coining' items you see on the table there in his desk?"

There was a general eruption of sound from all over the audience, and every eye in the courtroom was now on Walter Robert's face. The protest of voices continued

"Order," the judge shouted above the hubbub, banging his gavel. "The witness will answer the question," he ordered in his sonorous voice.

"Of course, I weren't there. I were home in bed like I told yer."

Sir Thomas took off his spectacles. Looking straight into Walter Roberts' eyes, he said very softly and very sternly, "Mr. Roberts, I want you to take off your cloak, and then I want you to turn slowly around in a circle.

The witness's face went red, but he stood his ground not moving. "That's dim. I ain't gonna do it—what fer?" he said.

The judge again banged the gavel. "The witness will do as asked, or he will be held in contempt of court. Do it now, sir."

Roberts shrugged and took off the gold cloak and tossed it over the railing. As he turned around, everyone could see the small patch on the side of his breeches where it would cover his hip. It was a ludicrous shade of bright orange. The court once again erupted—this time into gales of laughter.

"Order," the judge bellowed, again banging his gavel.

"Your breeches have been patched, Mr Roberts," the barrister said. "You must have torn them. Can you tell me where it happened?"

"How do I know? I go all over the place. It could have been anywheres. I found it out when I took 'em off ter go to bed one night. So I sewed them with a piece of cloth I happened to 'ave. They's the only breeches I've got. Times are bad for my business right now."

"I believe that is true, Mr. Roberts. So bad, that you were happy to take money from someone who paid you to go—late at night—to Mr. Thibault's goldsmith shop, slip into the alley running alongside his shop, and climb through the small window that goes into his office. Not too many people could get through that window, but you could. Then you took the devalued coins and the 'coining' tools and planted them in the drawer on the lower, right hand side of Mr. Thibault's desk. Someone paid you quite a lot of money to do this, and then to take the note to the Sheriff's office. Is that not true, Mr. Roberts?"

"No, of course, it's not true. Wotever makes you fink so?"

"This—Mr. Roberts—this tiny piece of material." Sir Thomas pulled out a small package and showed the court the small piece of peacock blue material they had found on the window, in Paul's office. It was the exact shade of Walter Robert's breeches. Turning to the judge he said, "The defence would like the jury to see this small, peacock blue piece of material, which both Sir John Houblon and his clerk, William Clark have attested to the fact that it was found, caught on a piece of wood, in the small window, in Mr. Thibault's office. We should like it marked as an exhibit in the case, mi lord."

"So be it," he concurred. He then turned to Sir John. "Do you confirm you found the material in that location, Sir John?"

"I do, mi lord. And, as city sheriff, I would like to state that all charges should be dropped from Paul Thibault, that he be released immediately and that Walter Roberts be arrested and held for the crimes of breaking and entering, as well as receiving stolen goods and coining. He will have to stand trial for these charges."

Louise had been watching the entire proceedings, with her heart in her mouth. Her whole body trembled even though her parents each had an arm around her. She realized this was Paul's only chance for vindication. Now, as Sir John finished speaking and pandemonium broke out in the courthouse, time seemed to stand still. She could hardly breathe waiting for the judge's response.

Finally, he once more pounded the gavel. "Order—order in the court," he yelled above the din. "Let the prisoner, Paul Thibault be released and hold this man under arrest. Court dismissed."

The minute Paul was free, he wanted to go to the shop to ensure everything there was satisfactory. Louise, Pierre, and Claudine went along with him. Both Claude and Henri were on hand and were ecstatic to see him and learn of his acquittal. Paul walked all through the building, inspecting the latest creations the boys were making; examining everything in the glass showcase; and finally checking the contents of the large iron vault in his office. Then he looked up at the small window.

"We must get the lock fixed right away," he stated. "If it weren't for my procrastination, this thing would never have happened."

"We had the locksmith in here first thing this morning, Master," Henri replied. "It's got a good, sturdy latch now. However, I worry that the man who hates you so much is still out there. You will have to watch out for him. What he's done shows he will stop at nothing to harm you. I certainly wish we knew who he is."

"I'm pretty sure I know who he is," Paul replied wearily. "But I'm damned if I know why, and I don't think there's anything I can do about it. Walter Roberts insists he didn't see his face. Well, the little rat will go to trial now himself and, if he does know, perhaps it will come out then. I'm simply glad this terrible nightmare is over. And you boys did a fine job of taking care of things." He patted each of them on the shoulder. "You're good lads—both of you."

"Right then, my dear," he turned to his wife, "let's go home. I'm anxious to see the children, and then I could certainly use a shot of brandy." Looking over at Pierre with a smile, he added, "And I'll wager your father could too."

PART VI

Destiny's Weave

"It is not in the stars to hold our destiny, but in ourselves…"
William Shakespeare

Chapter 37

London, September 1690

Midsummer's Day had long passed, but because of the accusation against him, Paul lost his bid for the position of City Sheriff. Sir John assured him, however, the affair would not affect any future consideration for a high position.

Wally the Weasel was dead. His trial had been swift and so had his justice. Paul, Pierre, and Marc drove over to Tyburn Hill to see him swinging on the gallows. Not one of them could find it in their heart to feel sorry for the 'little rat' as they called him.

"At last he got his just desserts," Paul commented. "It's been coming a long time. We always recognized he was on the wrong side of the law, but we couldn't prove it."

"Yes," Pierre said "Although it's too bad he couldn't say who hired him. He went to his grave insisting he never saw the man's face. It's possible I suppose, but I'm disappointed we never got that important information."

There were some good times for the family that summer. The wedding of Catherine to her wig-maker, Edward Renault, took place in August. As Paul had promised Pierre, the Thibaults held the reception at their beautiful Soho mansion. Since both families were well known in the Huguenot community, there were many guests to invite, and everyone agreed it was an outstanding event.

Catherine, although not an outstanding beauty like Louise, looked extremely pretty in her white silk dress. She had the same black hair and blue eyes as Pierre; and father and daughter made a striking picture as they walked down the aisle of the church together. For now, the young couple lived with Pierre and Claudine in the house on Fornier Street. They occupied most of the third floor, where Jean Guy and Claude's old bedroom had been turned into a private sitting room for them.

Claude and Henry had restored Paul's former apartment above the goldsmith shop, and both the boys lived there for now. Paul paid for most of their meals at a nearby inn. Since the break-in, Claude felt it was safer for the shop if they were on hand. Jean Guy also had a bed there whenever he was back in town.

The long, hot summer that brought the family both trouble and joy was almost over, but the atmosphere in the city was still uncomfortable. With the extreme heat, the smells had become abominable; and. Louise noticed that, ever since the trial, Paul had shown an aversion to life in London.

"I'm thinking it's time we purchased a second home—out in the country. I'm tired of spending these sweltering summer days in London," Paul said to his wife, one evening in early September.

Peter was already one year old. He was walking now, getting into mischief faster than his nanny could keep up with him. His father, who had undoubtedly aged in the last six months, and even now looked rather wilted, had just come downstairs from his nightly, bedtime romp with his son. He found his wife playing on the spinet in the withdrawing room. As he uttered the words, he came and stood behind her, putting his hands on her shoulders.

"Are you serious, Paul?" She stopped playing and turned around to look at him in astonishment. "Why only the extremely wealthy have country homes, don't they?"

"Your cousin is building an expensive new house in Hampstead—that's country, and we aren't poor, my dear."

Louise wasn't aware of her husband's actual financial state. She kept the books for the goldsmith shop and Paul gave her a handsome sum each month to look after the household accounts. She knew he was prosperous, but of his total worth, she had no idea.

"But the Hampstead house is all Marc has. He rents the rooms in the city when he's working at the East India office. I think he's quite comfortable, but not tremendously rich; although I suppose he would be if he could get his money out of France. It's only that he hasn't figured out how..."

"Yes, yes. I realize all that. But the point is, we really *are* as you say, tremendously rich."

"We are?" She gave a slight gasp.

"Yes, we are, Louise. As rich as much of the nobility, but we can't be considered gentry until we have a country estate as well as a town house. Both the Houblon brothers have them, and so does Richard Hoare. If one wishes to get anywhere in society, people must be able to see that you don't really have to work for a living. That's how the social order works in this country."

Paul walked over to the butler tray on a sideboard and picked up a bottle of brandy. He gave her a questioning look, but she shook her head. She still hadn't acquired a taste for the distilled wine, and thought of it more like medicine. He poured himself a drink; then took one of the comfortable chairs facing the small spinet bench where she still sat.

"The false arrest and the trial were a bit of a set-back, but I think it will all blow over soon. King William's advisor, Sir William Bentinck, told John Houblon that His Majesty feels quite badly about it. He mentioned that the king might want to do something for me, when he's back from the war in Europe. Consequently, that's my new goal—to rise into the upper classes; perhaps even a knighthood for Peter someday. Sometimes you can buy one, you know."

She thought he must be joking, but he looked and sounded quite serious. "Why, Paul, that doesn't seem a bit like you. You never cared about social standing before. It's not the Huguenot way, is it?"

"Why not? There are quite a few Huguenots high up in the social order. Sir John, and now his brother—and Sir Richard Hoare. Their families came from France originally, and they all started out as goldsmiths. And then there's the Lanier family—they were all prominent musicians at court."

He took a sip of his brandy.

"I'm sure there are many others as well, but, to be honest, I'm not so much thinking of me as I am of Peter. I'd like him to have a university education and be known as a gentleman—not just a tradesman. And someday we'll be looking for a suitable husband for Alice. We would want someone with some social standing."

"Did you get these ideas from the goldsmith play we saw last year? You know I have never been concerned about things like that. I'd rather Alice marry for love than status."

"No, it wasn't that. It's been in my mind ever since Peter was born. For myself, I never much thought of it before either. Now I'm thinking of my son. It does make a difference to how society in London accepts you. Don't forget, my darling, you didn't marry me for love, and look how well that turned out."

The twinkle was back in his eyes, and she realized now he was teasing her. "Yes, but after I married you, I discovered how loveable you are. Now you're telling me that you are extremely affluent too. My, my. What a fortunate woman I am."

"Seriously, Louise, I know we have never discussed this, but we do have a great deal of money. As I say, much more than many of the aristocracy. When I was young, both my father and grandfather left me good inheritances, and

I never squandered any of their money. In fact, I invested it rather well. Then I had the opportunity to become quite prosperous in the banking business, myself."

As he spoke, she looked more and more concerned.

"Don't worry, it was all done honestly, sweetheart," he quickly added at her look. "Of course, I still would like to make the odd piece of jewellery," he continued, "As a hobby, you know. I do enjoy it; but if I never sold another item, it wouldn't matter to us financially. A country estate makes a lot of sense. It would be a good investment for Peter. He will inherit everything I have, so he should learn how to live like a gentleman. As I say, it's more for him and our grandchildren. It takes a generation or two to be accepted by those people, in any case."

He stopped speaking for a moment as a spasm of coughing hit him. He'd had spells like that all summer, ever since his sojourn in Newgate. It worried Louise, but she had not spoken of it to him.

"That's another thing—I can't seem to get rid of this cough. I'm thinking that living in the country—away from the city's bad air, even for part of the year, might be better for me."

"I see." She nodded her head slowly, still somewhat stunned by this revelation about their finances. "Do you have somewhere in mind then. I don't know much about England outside of London, and our trip through the west counties. But I was so sick most of the time, I didn't notice the countryside."

"There is a house I'd like to see. It's being advertised for sale in the 'Gazette'. It's less than a day's drive from the city. I'd like to go there next week—just the two of us. Of course, Oliver will drive, and we'll take one of the footmen for safety along the route. The weather should be a little cooler by then."

"But what about the children?"

"They have Nanny, but I spoke to your father; and he and Claudine would be happy to come over here to stay a few days. Andre and Jeanette will come with them, so the little ones will enjoy being together. And we know Claude and Henri do very well looking after the shop. They'd have to do without me if I retire anyway."

"Then you really are thinking of living like a gentleman. I always thought you loved your work." She paused then, as a horrible thought struck her. "Paul—you would tell me if something was really wrong, wouldn't you? Did Doctor Rene say something?"

He walked over and sat down beside her on the bench, pulling her close. "No, no. Of course not. I'm fine, Louise. However, I do feel tired a lot and, since being in Newgate, I have this cough. I'm forty-three years old—I have two young children, a beautiful wife and more money than all of us will ever need. What I want now is to enjoy everything, before it is too late."

"You've got years ahead of you, darling." She laid her head on his shoulder. "I'm sure the cough will go. You're right though—the country would help. Will we sell this house then?"

"No, we would keep both the house and the goldsmith shop. I'll still have the banking for the next few years, but that will end when the Bank of England opens."

He covered his mouth and stifled a yawn before continuing. "Of course, there's still the chance I'll be named a director. But I *am* tired and living in the country even half of the year would help. We could have marvellous times together, sweetheart. We'll keep horses and ride and go hunting. Didn't you used to do all that in France?"

"Yes, but it wasn't for sport. It was so the villagers had enough meat for the winter. As the mayor, Papa always felt responsible for his people. But if you're going to be able to spend more time with me—that will make me happy. So let's go and see the estate you have in mind. It's only that this is all such a new idea for me. I do find it rather overwhelming."

✣

The following week found Paul and Louise, along with their driver and a footman bound for the village of High Wycombe, about half way between Oxford and London. They planned to stop at that town for the night, as Alston Manor, the property Paul wished to see, was about five miles to the west.

"I like the idea of being close to Oxford," he said. "It's been the seat of learning in England for such a long time, and besides, it's a beautiful old city, with its spires and ancient towers. You'll love it. I hope Peter will go there for his education. He could come home every weekend."

"Oh, Paul. You certainly are looking ahead." She laughed at his eagerness. "He's not even two years yet."

"Yes, but at my age it's good to plan beforehand. You never know what could happen. I might not even be here when he reaches that age. No, it's better I get everything arranged now, for the sake of Peter and Alice and for yourself as well."

As soon as they were out of the city, Paul felt himself begin to relax. Simply being away from the pressures of London, and the terrible memories the city now held for him, helped him unwind. He looked at his wife sitting beside him in the coach. It was almost as though they were on their nuptial trip. He reminded himself, they had not had the honeymoon period the bards sang about. It made him feel young again to be travelling with such a lovely, young woman on this new adventure.

He tried to remember what it had been like with Diane when they were young. She was a merry, pretty girl—not a dreamy beauty like Louise—

and he had believed himself very much in love with her. They met when he worked with his grandfather in Canterbury. After most of his family died from the plague, he'd felt terribly alone. He fancied a wife would be the answer and Diane was the daughter of another goldsmith of Huguenot descent. She had several admirers at the time, but flirted with him in particular; and he fell for her fun-loving cheerfulness. They suited each other estimably and, without a doubt, he experienced an enormous sense of grief when she died in childbirth after four miscarriages. However, he recognized his love for Diane had never been as intense as what he now experienced with Louise.

He had realized just how much he loved her at the time of Peter's birth. He believed he would have gone mad with anguish had he lost her. He wasn't sure whether it was her exceptional beauty or some inner, intangible quality. He had sensed it the first night Pierre had brought his family for dinner. Young as she was, he became almost instantly obsessed with her and now, after almost six years of marriage, she had matured into an exquisite woman, and a delightful companion. He perceived she was a match for him in every way.

They stopped for the night at an expensive and comfortable lodging called The Chequers Inn. It was extremely romantic to drink champagne and eat dinner, in the delightful, candlelit dining room, off the main entrance; then go hand-in-hand up to the snug, canopied bed in their cozy room.

They stayed in bed late the next morning, something that never happened at home where Paul had so many duties. They ordered breakfast sent up to their room, and finally, looking every bit like lovebirds, and giggling like naughty children, descended to find their coachman, Oliver, waiting patiently for them in the public room. Paul had not felt so carefree and light-hearted for many years. In spite of the new grey streaks in his hair, the image he saw in the mirror looked ten years younger than back in London. Many of his recently acquired worry lines had disappeared.

"Well, now, Oliver," he directed the driver. "We'll head west, my good man, and see what awaits us at this Alston Manor. I hope it's as first-rate as the advertisement in 'The Gazette' made it out to be."

Chapter 38

Clipped bay trees lined the approach to the principle entrance of the manor. It ended in a large circle surrounding a Venus fountain. As they drove up the drive, Louise gasped at the loveliness of it. "Why, it's beautiful, Paul," Louise said. "So much grander than our farmhouse in France. It's huge."

"It's not so big," Paul replied. "Not compared to most country houses these days. But what's important to me is that it's well built and can be added onto without looking odd."

He went on to explain that while built in the Jacobean era at the turn of the 17th century, its half-timbered frontage, and crisscrossed beams showed it was constructed in the Tudor style. The white plaster between the beams, and the timbers painted a dark brown made it look Elizabethan. The frontage, he figured, was about one hundred and fifty feet wide, but it was hard to judge the depth of the house from that angle.

There were three large gables evenly spaced along the facade as well as several chimneys. He counted the number of chimneys to estimate the likely taxes he would be required to pay. It was on these the king's Inland Revenue men calculated the amount.

They emerged from the carriage, and he stood back, sizing it up for a few moments before they walked to the front entrance. The numbers 1606 carved into a large beam over the front door proclaimed the year it was built.

"That's not very old, though, is it?" Louise asked. "Our house in France was built in the 16th century, and there was nothing at all wrong with it. Of course, it was made of stone."

"But they used the best timbers for these old Tudor-style houses. With care, they should last a few centuries. Of course, a lot will depend on what we see inside." He smiled down at her as he rang the front door pull. A portentous-looking butler opened the door and, after Paul presented his card, escorted them with great dignity into the large reception hall.

"Mr. Buckley is Lady Alston's steward. He will be with you shortly, sir," he said, indicating two comfortable chairs in the spacious hall.

It wasn't long before the steward showed up, and after shaking Paul's hand and bowing courteously to Louise, he asked that they follow him. There were seven large rooms including a ballroom on the main floor—all elegantly furnished. A curved, flying staircase led up to the second floor, with eight bedrooms, as well as a nursery and a large playroom for children. On the third floor, there were smaller bedrooms for the servants.

"It's marvellous, Paul," she whispered. "It's all so imposing inside—it reminds me of the old chateau in our little French village. I never pictured myself living in anything like this. Do you think we need it?"

"No, we probably don't need, it." He laughed. "But I think it's what I want, Louise. For the generations to come, don't you see?"

When they finished the tour of the house, Mr. Buckley took them outside to the grounds. Directly behind the house a path led through magnificent gardens to a picturesque lily pond. Beyond was a hedge that separated the floral and vegetables gardens from the outer buildings, the working pastures, and other small fields. In the distance, a woodland formed a semicircle around the cleared land.

"There's one hundred acres right now, and lots of work to be done here yet, as you can see. There are a few milk cows but no horses, although there is a paddock. I have five tenant farmers working the land right now. Their cottages are in the village, beyond the woods." He stopped walking and waved his hand over the land stretching away to the horizon.

"We only have half of the area cleared as yet, and there are surrounding properties, which could be purchased if it's not large enough for what you have in mind. Since the restoration, Lord Alston kept too busy looking after the king's affairs to get everything he wanted done. He passed away shortly before King James fled to France. There are no heirs, and Lady Alston only wants to end her days in the city where she was born, and where she has an unmarried niece. So she's willing to sell it for much less than it's actually worth."

"Yes, of course," Paul replied. "But, as you say, there's much work to be done. Perhaps we could hire transient workers. You have no interest in staying on as the steward?"

"No, I'm sorry to say I have not, sir. I've wanted to retire for a long time now, but his lordship was so ill I didn't have the heart to leave him. And, after he died, I felt I must stay out of loyalty to my lady. But once a sale is arranged, I have my dear wife and a little cottage in Abington waiting for me."

"Well, Mr. Buckley. I thank you for your time." They turned to walk along the side of the house where they passed through another imposing, landscaped garden.

"It's a marvellous layout, and I am certainly going to consider the idea of purchasing it. I have the name of her ladyship's solicitor. Please inform him that mine will be contacting him as soon as my wife and I make some decisions."

Mr. Buckley gave Louise a quick glance, looking a little surprised, that Paul's wife would have any say in the matter, but tactfully made no reply. "You're very welcome, sir. It's been my pleasure ma'm." He bowed again to her. "I'm positive you would find the farm everything you desire in a home. I have spent many happy years here myself."

By now, they were back around the front of the manor, and Oliver was ready for them to board. Louise took one last look around at the magnificence of the estate. Paul heard her sigh as she entered the coach.

∾⋎∾

That evening, back at the inn, they enjoyed another succulent dinner in the peaceful dining room. Over their meal of ham, baked with cloves and served with applesauce; buttered, green beans; and a small salad of lettuce and cucumber; they discussed the management of such an estate.

Although she tried to be enthusiastic, Louise still had a few qualms about such a venture. "You definitely would need a steward, Paul," she declared.

"Yes, I have been giving it some serious thought. I'm thinking about Pierre."

"My father? Why would you think of him for such a position?" she asked, breaking off a piece of bread.

"I don't believe either of your parents like the city, do you?" They are both so sweet and unworldly, and I feel some of the things that go on there disturb them. Your father loved the farm in France, but he didn't do much of the actual work, did he?"

"No. He had to be careful of his hands because of the weaving, so he hired the villagers, which actually helped them out. The king didn't make it easy for Huguenots to get work. But Papa always told them what he wanted done, and how to do it, and he paid them well."

"That's what I gathered. So you could say, in a way, he's already been an estate manager. This would be a much bigger property, that's all. They could live there all year. When they want to come to the city, they could stay with us. Perhaps Jean Guy or Claude will eventually want the house on Fournier Street. That is, if they don't sell it."

"But what about their church? There's no French church in Oxfordshire is there?

"No, but I'm sure there are Protestant groups. They're all based on the teachings of Luther and Calvin, so there's not much difference in their beliefs. Both your parents have a good understanding of English now.

They'd fit in anywhere, I think. Well, of course, it's just my idea. We'll have to wait and see how they feel about it."

"What would you plan for the property, Paul? I mean, it's so much land."

"The house will do fine for now; and I think it's the type of house that could be added onto and still look nicely balanced. As for the land, it will always be a work in progress. We'll see about buying those adjacent properties. One hundred acres isn't much. We'll want orchards and we'll need to acquire more horses. Perhaps more cows also." He paused to refill their goblets of claret.

"You can never go wrong owning land, Louise. It's real—real estate. The whole idea is that we will do some things now, and then when Peter inherits, he can do what he wants. As I said, it's an absolute necessity to have land to become a peer of the realm in England."

She looked into his face. He had never looked happier. Oh, I pray nothing ever happens to Peter, she thought. I'm afraid it would kill him. Aloud she replied, "If it's what you want for Peter, then I'll help in any way I can."

"But you have reservations? Is that what you are telling me?"

"I suppose I do, but they are not important, dear." Her lovely smile reassured him.

❧

A few days following their return to London, Louise asked their coachman to drive her to Fournier Street. Her parents were rather surprised to see her again, so soon and unannounced.

"Will you have lunch with us?" her mother automatically asked. "Although it's nothing special, today. Catherine has gone to visit her mother-in-law."

"Whatever you're eating is fine with me. It's important I speak to both of you right away. Before you see Paul again."

"My word, child," Pierre interjected. "Is something wrong?"

"I don't know really. It's only that Paul has changed. It goes back to his time in Newgate, I think. Since then I almost don't know him anymore. He's gone rather—well—acquisitive is the only word I can think of."

"Acquisitive? Whatever do you mean?" her father asked.

"All of a sudden, he wants things. Large things. Things he never talked about before. Now he wants to be in society—the gentry. He even spoke about purchasing a knighthood for Peter. I didn't know you could do that. And he is serious about buying an estate called Alston Manor way out in Oxfordshire. Papa, the house is huge and there are one hundred acres of land."

"A hundred acres isn't much. Not if you want to make money farming. Is Paul interested in agriculture then?

212

"That's the thing I've come to warn you about. He's suggesting that, since you know something about farming, you might like to live there and be the steward. It's way out in the country, Papa. Almost a day's drive from London."

Pierre and Claudine glanced at each other—astonishment on their faces.

"He would want me to be the steward of a hundred acre estate?"

"Yes, but he said we don't have to worry about making money right away. It's all for the children. For their future. So Peter can be considered a gentleman, and Alice can marry into the nobility. Papa, you don't think he is going mad, do you? Do you think the time in prison did something to his mind? I know he's coughing a lot, but it's not just that—he's different—in the way he thinks."

"*Zut alors*. It's not what I would want, but I don't suppose a man has to be insane to desire to get ahead in society. Even though, he isn't a particularly religious man, Paul is a good person." Pierre pulled at the hairs of the small goatee he was growing; his forehead furrowed, which she knew, meant he was deep in thought.

"He certainly believes in God, although he does have a few doubts about doctrine. Paul reminds me of Jacques in many ways. He believes we make our own destiny, and it's not all pre-planned by God. We've had some deep discussions about Calvin's teachings, and we certainly differ on that point. But I believe he's an exceptionally fine man and quite sound in mind."

"You don't think it's strange to have all these grandiose ideas then, Papa?"

"Not if he has the money from an honest source, and he isn't going to put his family at risk by doing so. And, who knows. Perhaps this is God's plan for him. Luther always said God blesses those he loves. So we can't judge him on that. Maybe, because of the cough, he *is* worried about his health to some extent. I can tell you that living on a farm, away from this dirty, odorous city tempts me."

"You mean you wouldn't mind being his steward?"

"It would depend a lot on what he plans to do with the land but, you realize, I do know a lot about it. I lived on Grandfather's farm all my life, and made a study of agriculture at the university in Saumur, before I met your mother and decided to get serious about the weaving."

He looked over to his wife. "What would you think, Claudine? Would you even consider moving there?"

She looked thoughtful. "Now, you're older, it would be easier on you physically than making a living over a loom, wouldn't it, Pierre? I've never gotten used to the ways of the city. I love the country, and horseback riding, and walking in the woods—breathing country air. It would be wonderful to live like that again." Her eyes appeared wistful.

Louise glanced from one parent to the other in amazement. "Why, I never considered you would want to go back to it. Paul definitely means to ask you, but please, don't tell him I warned you about it. I think he might be angry with me for interfering."

"All right, daughter, we won't let on we know anything about it. I don't suppose that would be lying in any way—just evasive. I'm glad you told us. It means your mother and I'll have time to think things over and discuss it thoroughly. Now, let's have a bite of lunch, Claudine. I'm starving. And, Louise, you'd better tell us more about this Alston Manor."

Chapter 39

London, October 1691

The summer of 1691 saw significant changes for the families of both Paul and Pierre. Paul purchased Alston Manor and Pierre accepted the position of estate steward. He and Claudine planned to move there permanently the following spring. Eventually there would be a dower or retirement cottage built for them, but in the meantime, they had their own suite of rooms in the manor house. Mr. Buckley, Lady Alston's steward, had changed his mind, and promised to stay for one year to help get them settled.

Paul, Louise, and the children spent the three months of summer on the farm and declared it the perfect retreat from the city. Much of Lady Alston's furnishings and paintings were included with the sale of the manor; so Louise had little to do in the way of decorating except to change the position of some pieces, and add their family's personal touches here and there. By the time she finished, the house was exactly right for them, and they had all fallen in love with Oxfordshire.

In August, Louise's parents arrived for a month's stay. Paul and Pierre spent countless hours planning what they would do when the land was ready for cultivation in the spring, and Pierre would move there for good. Both he and Claudine showed their pleasure at being back on a farm and threw themselves into the various activities. They picnicked in the woods or took drives into the country as far as the scenic Cotswolds.

The children loved the farm. Alice was only five, but Paul promised her that when she was eight she could learn to ride a real pony. She and her brother took turns galloping around on the small wooden horse he had bought for her. He assured the little boy he too would ride a large 'horsy' when he was bigger.

The two men supervised the construction of the new outbuildings, which included stables for the promised horses, a large dairy cow shed, two small greenhouses, and other various tool sheds. They turned one of the existing buildings into a private office for Pierre. It had a small kitchen with a fireplace, and another larger room where his desk, along with a cabinet for his papers, would go. As well, it had a space large enough to set up the two looms he planned to keep. Like Paul and his jewellery making, he didn't want to give up altogether the skill at which he excelled. He planned only to take special orders from his best customers.

The day in September the whole family headed back to London, they all felt rather sad to be leaving the country.

❧

Once they returned to the city, Paul spent much time working with Sir John Houblon on the government-banking project. As well, Claude and Henri needed additional training before he could turn the business totally over to them. Already he missed the life of a country squire.

It was early October, and Paul was back in his shop when he looked out the window to see a coach with the royal crest, drive up. Immediately, an important-looking, slightly pompous, gentleman stepped out. The doorbell jingled and, to his astonishment, in walked one of King William's top advisors—the Earl of Portland, Sir William Bentinck. After greeting Paul, he declared, "Perhaps we could go into a less public room, Mr. Thibault. I must converse with you on a matter of great importance." He spoke with a strong Dutch accent.

"Yes, certainly, sir. Right this way please."

He ushered the earl into his office and motioned him into the best chair there was. "Would you like a little brandy, your lordship? It's all I have to offer here, I'm afraid."

"Nr, Nr," the king's man replied. "I have business elsewhere, and this won't take very long."

He looked up at the ceiling as if trying to recall lines from a speech then proceeded to recite. "The King has only now returned from fighting on the continent, and he has asked me to extend the government's deepest apologies for what happened to you last year. He remembers your lovely wife, and that she had to flee for her life from France; so he feels extremely sorry about the whole situation." He stopped speaking for a moment to clear his throat.

"It has come to his attention that your business has suffered because of the accusation and he would like to make amends. I'm here to commission you to make a necklace for Queen Mary in time for the 12th Night celebration."

Paul was stunned.

"Zounds," he exclaimed in astonishment. "Excuse me your lordship, but this overwhelms me. I never dreamt I'd receive such an honour. How-

216

ever, the King is correct about my business suffering. I'm afraid some of my old customers did lose confidence in me. Certainly, this would let people know I can be trusted."

"So, then It's settled. His majesty would like it made in gold set with diamonds and rubies. If you will be good enough to draw up some designs and have them delivered to my office, King William will look and pick the one he would like. Could you have the piece ready in two months do you think?"

"Yes. Once the king approves the design, I can have it finished within a month. I'll concentrate on that and leave everything else to my assistants."

"If the king likes the design, you will receive a substantial sum at that time, and full payment upon completion to His Highness' satisfaction. We will shake on it now, *nr*?

Paul could hardly believe his good fortune. It was a tremendous honour to be chosen by the King. However, he realized it would take a master craftsman to do it. As good as his apprentices were, it was too big a responsibility for them. Henri was soon to become a freeman, while Claude still had four years of apprenticeship left. Moreover, Henri was sometimes a problem. He was bright enough, but he was inclined to be lazy; and Paul suspected he actually was a little jealous of Claude's abilities in design work.

Unless I can hire the right person to look after the King's commission, it's back to the workbench for me, he reflected. I'm afraid it might be a while yet before I can retire full time to the country. Those lovely green fields of Oxfordshire will just have to wait.

As so often happened now, he began to cough.

Coincidently by the end of the month, Paul found the right man to help with the job. Lucien Robard had made an impressive reputation for himself as a goldsmith in Marseilles when his enemies discovered he was a secret Huguenot. It took careful planning on the part of friends to smuggle him out of the city before King Louis' soldiers could catch up with him. They were fortunate to get him on a British ship, recently out of Venice, which brought him straight to England.

Upon landing in London, he went to the French Chapel in Spittlefields. There, he met Pierre who took him to see Paul. He was a gifted designer and had excellent qualifications, so Paul employed him immediately. They decided he could stay with the other two boys in the apartment above the shop.

That solved Paul's problem of the extra work and together the two goldsmiths spent long hours making drawings of designs until they had several which they felt were good enough to submit to the king.

Paul and Lucien had the necklace ready before the end of the year. It was such an enormous success with King William that before Twelfth Night, his Royal Advisor came again to Paul's shop.

This time, the earl looked a trifle uncomfortable as he asked if they could once again go into the small office. Even with the door closed, he spoke softly. "Mr. Thibault, King William was so pleased with Queen Mary's necklace that he has another commission for you. However, in this particular matter, I must ask for your utmost secrecy and discretion." He cleared his throat, looking markedly ill at ease.

"Yes, of course, your lordship. What would His Majesty like me to do?"

"He would wish you to make up another necklace. The king has—ah—a special fondness for a lady at the court. It is no secret among his courtiers, of course. And I tell you in confidence, even the queen is aware of it, although she turns a blind eye. However, it is not generally known here in England and perhaps Her Majesty would not quite appreciate the gift of jewellery to the lady, *nr*? So, we would need to have your total silence in this matter. It is understood?"

"Of course. I may have to confide somewhat to my chief designer, but no one else need know."

"*Goed*. Then once again submit your designs and we will let you know, which one he chooses. You understand it must be quite different from the other one. Perhaps, a less valuable stone such as amethyst, and not as large as the other one. *Begrepen*?

Paul wasn't sure of the Dutch words, but the message was clear. He ushered the earl to the door and closed it behind him. What have I gotten myself into, he thought. Thank goodness, I have Lucien. I'm sure he can be totally trusted in this.

King William was so pleased with the second piece of jewellery that he appointed Paul as "Goldsmith to the King." Queen Mary had taken a notion to collect dinnerware, and it had become the latest trend with the upper classes. Therefore, the royal couple commissioned Paul to design and create a distinctive golden dinner service for Windsor Castle, in honour of the fifth anniversary of their reign the following year. Because of these privileges, the Crown allowed him to add a special phrase to the name of his company. To include all his young assistants, he decided to rename it: 'Thibault & Associates, Goldsmiths to King William."

In April, this led to a surprising announcement from Windsor Castle. As one of the King's specialists, and for his services to the Bank of England, Paul was to be made a Baronet—a step above knighthood—with a heredi-tary title, which would go to Peter at his death. The investiture was to take place in Windsor in the first week of May; and Sir John Houblon once again planned a large ball at his home in Hyde Park to honour the new baronet.

A baronetcy was not considered part of the nobility, but as Paul remarked to his wife, "It is a step in the right direction. Peter will automatically become a knight at majority, and he will inherit the title. If he distinguishes himself in some way, he can move up to the peerage from there. So at least I've given my son a decent start."

In some respects, Louise was glad Paul's dreams were finally coming true. He was undoubtedly worthy of the honour, she reflected. Everyone else was thrilled about this turn of events; however, she had reservations. She explained her doubts to her mother as they planned their wardrobes together.

"I never particularly wanted any of this, Maman. I liked the peaceful life we had when we were first married. Though I don't have the heart to tell him that I'm not fond of all this socializing with the aristocracy and, of course, I must do it now. It will be expected of me."

"I know, dear. We brought you up in France in such a simple way, it's difficult to get used to all this fan-fare. But Paul has been so kind to us. We must all do what we can to make it the most special day of his life. So many of his lifelong friends have made good in this fashion that I think he felt driven to do so as well."

Paul was allowed three guests for the investiture ceremony at which the king would officiate. Aside from Louise, that honour went to Pierre and Claudine. However, a much larger party, which included Claude and the two other goldsmiths; Jean Guy and Cousin Marc; and Catherine and her husband, Edward, had invitations to Sir John's ball in London later the same week. The entire family was in a flurry of excitement.

Chapter 40

April 1692

The investiture was a unique experience celebrated with pomp and circumstance. Paul and his party travelled to Windsor the day before the event and spent the night at The Crown, a quaint Elizabethan Coaching Inn, arranged by Lord Portland and paid for by the monarchy. Since it was already dark by the time they arrived, they could just make out the gigantic outline of the castle across the road from the inn.

The two suites the earl had organized for them were elegantly furnished in Jacobean style with comfortable four-poster beds. Both couples were exhausted from their long trip in Paul's coach, so after an excellent dinner of fricasseed rabbit with leeks and asparagus, and a dessert of fresh spring berries, they retired for the night.

Louise awoke early the next morning and, hurrying to the window, looked out onto the cobbled street. Directly in front of her stood the ancient citadel started in 1070 by William the Conqueror. "Oh, come and see the castle, Paul. It's unbelievably huge. Much bigger than Whitehall Palace."

He crossed the room and knelt beside her. "I say, it *is* large, isn't it. Well, I hope there will be someone to show us the way to the king. I don't think I'd want to be lost in that fortress." He smiled down at her, giving her a quick kiss just as the maid knocked on the door, to bring them their morning coffee.

"Do you feel nervous, Paul?" Pierre asked later when the two couples had finished their breakfast. "I am so thankful it isn't King Louis we're going to meet. It's reassuring to remember King William is a Protestant, and I won't be losing my head today."

The four of them laughed heartily and headed across the street to the Norman gate where members of the Yeomen Guard dressed in striking uniforms of scarlet, gold and black, awaited them. One of the men escorted Paul to meet with the other investees while another directed Louise and her parents into the ornate St. George's Hall, where the ceremony would take place.

To Louise it seemed a long time they sat there in silence. It was so impressive, even a whisper seemed out of place, but she took the time to look around at the splendid baroque décor. The area was long, high, and narrow—she could see why they didn't call it a room. Paintings and frescoes covered gilded walls. The grandeur astounded her. Both her Soho house and the manor in Oxfordshire were impressive, but they couldn't begin to compare with what she now observed.

At last, trumpets sounded, everyone stood, and the procession marched in led by the king and queen in glorious regalia. Paul and his fellow honourees followed at a respectful distance.

The royal couple took their places on their thrones while the small group of inductees stood apart looking anxious. Another blast of the trumpets and King William stood with Lord Portland at his side to announce the name of each new recipient. Paul's name was the third one called. He moved forward and knelt on a small, velvet stool before the monarch. King Williams then took his sword and proceeded to impart the "Accolade."

This consisted of tapping him twice on each shoulder with the blade, which dubbed him a baronet. Lord Portland then handed the King the insignia or medal, which His Highness hung around Paul's neck pronouncing him Sir Paul Thibault, 1st Baronet of Alston. Paul bowed to the royal couple and returned to the group.

Well, my dear husband, Louise thought. You now have everything you've ever dreamed of and no one deserves it more. In all my life, I've never met a finer man, but I pray it makes you as happy as you hoped.

Deep in her heart, she wasn't sure wealth and prestige were as important in life as love and contentment. It went against her early upbringing.

The day after the ceremony and the ensuing banquet, the two couples headed back to London. They were still groggy from the amount of food and drink they felt obligated to accept at the royal couple's table. King William sat at the head of the twenty-five foot board, with Queen Mary at the other end. Although the monarch himself ate little, the servants brought in course after course: first, bowls of French onion soup, which they drank; then dishes filled with oysters and lobsters; followed by huge roasts of beef and venison; as well as plates of baked fowl.

There were few vegetables with the exception of salads with herbs and flowers; carrots, which the King apparently loved; and green beans cooked in an almond cream sauce. Footmen who each served only two people kept filling their wine glasses with the finest French and German wines. When they thought they could not eat another morsel, the king escorted them to the "banqueting hall." There desserts of every description were brought in—puddings and tarts; fritters and fresh fruit; as well as bottles of brandy and port. Before the evening was over, Louise felt she was literally going to burst.

Now, as the coach bounced its way back to the city, she mentioned the subject of the dinner. "I don't think I ever ate so much in one day, in the whole of my life. I'm sure most of my clothes will have to be let out."

"I'm thinking that as well," her mother replied with a sigh. "And we still have Sir John's gala affair to attend Saturday. I hope my new gown will fit."

Beside her, her husband nodded drowsily, his head dropping forward. She looked across to her son-in-law. "Did you ever see so much food, Paul?" she continued. "To me, it seems rather wicked when there are so many hungry people on the streets of London. It does appear as though much in the world isn't fair."

"Ah, but that's been going on a long time, Claudine. Since ever Adam and Eve left Paradise, I imagine," Paul replied. "I'm told that many of our French friends don't find it easy to make a decent living here in London. In fact, while we were waiting to come into the ceremony, Queen Mary told me about her new charity. It's called 'The Royal Bounty for Refugees' Aid' and it's specifically for Huguenots."

He paused for a moment, and then continued with enthusiasm. "It's definitely time we started thinking about a hospital for our people. Not many of the refugees are as quick to learn English as you folks. Some of them don't know where to go when they're sick. With Lucien in charge of the shop, I plan on getting involved with some of these charitable organizations now."

Deep in thought, he stared out the window for a few moments before sitting bolt upright. "Here's an idea. Perhaps I *will* encourage Peter to be a lawyer and go into government. To work toward the betterment of the poor would be a worthy endeavour. It's so interesting to think about your child's future. I hope I live long enough to see him into manhood."

Pierre, who had fallen asleep in his corner, suddenly snored so loudly the three of them jumped, and then, sharing another good laugh, settled back against the cushions to see if they too could grab forty winks.

The evening of the ball arrived. Sir John Houblon's Kensington mansion glittered with candlelight, while the scent of a myriad of floral arrangements perfumed the elegant ballroom. Louise wore a décolleté dress of forest green silk with yellow roses tucked in the bodice. The emerald pendant her husband had given her for their fifth anniversary lay around her exquisite neck. Paul himself was resplendent in white, silk breeches, a white and gold doublet and vest, and a lace-trimmed, linen shirt. Since it was such a royal event, they both donned fashionable, powdered, wigs.

To show their patronage of Paul, King William and Queen Mary appeared quite early in the evening and stayed for more than an hour. They even danced a set, in which the king requested Louise as his partner and Paul squired Queen Mary. It was a tremendous honour as the royal couple rarely danced in public.

Marc had managed to get his name on Louise's dance card and, when it was his turn, he came to claim her as his partner. She had spotted him earlier standing among a group of younger ladies. He wore no wig but his long black hair curled to his shoulders and, with his chiselled features and flashing blue eyes, he was the best-looking man in the room. Now, as he took her hand, her heart fluttered alarmingly and she smiled rather shyly up at him.

Towards the end of the minuet, there were a few moments when the dance steps brought them close together. "Well, Lady Thibault," he said. "You are certainly the most striking woman here. How does it feel to have a title? Any different?"

"Oh, Marc. It's not anything I ever aspired to. I find London society all rather overwhelming. I often dream that I'm in our farmhouse by the river in France. Life was so peaceful then. Sometimes I wish I could go back."

"Do you, Louise?" he asked, looking into her eyes. "I wish that with all my heart, my darling. If only things could have gone the way we expected that first time we danced in your village. Or even the day I took you to the beach in La Rochelle. We would be living a much different life now, wouldn't we, *Cherie?*"

For a moment, listening to the caress in his voice, and remembering their youth, she felt a little thrill go through her. She longed to be safe in his arms, somewhere quiet and away from all the trappings of English high society. But she remembered her vow, and feeling guilty, she quickly shook off the feeling.

"But we can't, Marc. We must be thankful for what we have and the fact we are all alive." The music stopped. She smiled regretfully at him. "Thank you for the dance, dear cousin. You will always be one of my best friends no matter how many titles I have."

"It's not your friendship I want, Louise." His tone sounded forlorn, but he bowed graciously and took her back to where Paul was sitting.

224

While she acknowledged that both the investiture and the ball had been a wonderful experience, Louise felt glad to have it end. The excitement, which had gone on since they left for Windsor, had taken its toll on her. It was way past midnight and most of the guests had disappeared, so it was appropriate they should now take their leave. She could see that her husband, too, was exhausted; but they both went to thank their host for all he had done for them.

"Think nothing of it. You've deserved this for a long time. And don't forget, you're still going to help me finalize this banking business. There's still much to do." Turning to Louise, he kissed her hand and gave her a warm smile. "Good night, Lady Thibault."

She curtsied. "Thank you for everything, Sir John. You have been so kind."

They headed out to the front entrance, where the coach drivers waited for their masters. A great deal of light emanated from a group of lanterns, but their carriage was nowhere in sight. "Don't move from here, Louise," her husband commanded. "I'll look around the back for Oliver."

As he turned the corner of the building, a coach came tearing up the driveway. As it stopped beside her for a moment, a man leapt out and grabbed her roughly. He threw her into the compartment where she landed on the floor. Two shots rang out, but she could see nothing and then the man jumped in beside her, urging the driver to hasten away.

Chapter 41

They sped away from Sir John's house in a direction unknown to Louise. The events had occurred so suddenly her mind was in a turmoil. More frightened than she had been in her entire life, she broke out in a cold sweat and began to tremble. She tried to scream, but no sound would come.

"Who are you?" she managed to whisper. "Why are you doing this?"

The man looked at her with a sneer. "Well, well—Lady Thibault." He stressed the title in a mocking way. "Don't you know me? I'm saving you from that brute of a husband of yours. He is a killer of woman. Look what he did to my beautiful Diane?"

Louise had her first clear look at him. "Monsieur Mercier," she gasped. "But I don't understand?"

"I told you. I'm saving you. Even, though, you're a slut, you're too good for that man. He killed Diane and he'll kill you too. He's completely evil and why people don't realize that I'll never understand. How can he fool them the way he does? He's the last person who should be honoured like this."

"Paul—killed Diane? Whatever are you talking about?"

"You don't know? He took Diane, my beautiful little virgin, and forced himself on her so often it killed her. All those pregnancies in so few years, and her so delicate. And look at you—just a naive, young girl and he got you with child, so he could marry you too. You think I didn't know, the moment I saw you that first night, what his intentions were. And the baby came too soon. I figured that out. Oh, I desired you too. I'd have courted you properly, but he got in the way again. And then I heard you almost died with this last child, so I had to do something or he will kill you too. Paul is an absolute monster. He's dangerous."

Something in Mercier's eyes made her realize the man wasn't quite rational. However, she had calmed down, and had her wits about her once more. It's best I humour him for now, she thought.

"I didn't realize you knew Diane. When was that?"

"Back in Canterbury. I was a young apprentice in her father's goldsmith shop. My parents lived way out in the country, so I lived with her family.

Diane and I were the same age, and I know she intended to marry me as soon as I finished my training."

"Did you discuss marriage with her?"

"No, of course not. Until I had my qualification from the city, I couldn't think of such a thing. Her father would have been furious if I even suggested it. I saw it in her eyes, though. She liked me. Then Paul came to town to finish his apprenticeship with his grandfather. He was a few years older than I was, so he became a journeyman first. Diane was pretty like you, and it didn't take him long to set his sights on her. I knew I didn't have a chance anymore. After awhile they announced their engagement, and that was the end of me. But she was delicate and he killed her with his lust."

By now, the carriage had stopped in front of a large brick building, but Louise had no idea of where they were.

"All right then, my lady. You can get out here. You'll be living here from now on. You'll be much safer away from that maniac. I'll take good care of you, I promise. But be warned, I'd rather kill you than let you go back to him."

"But what about your wife?"

"Oh, this isn't where I live. This is my shop. There's an apartment upstairs where I keep my lovelies. My wife doesn't need to know. I take care of them, myself, and as long as they treat me right, I'm good to them. I've saved more than a few fallen ladies from their terrible existence. I make them fit for heaven before I send them there."

His eyes had that strange, blank look again and, once more, she began to feel alarmed. His cold, calculating madness terrified her. Who would ever find her here? They would never even think of Mercier. I'm sure they don't realize he's insane, she thought.

"Oh, please, Lord, let someone find me," she whispered.

Mercier pushed her forward with the small pistol pressed against her back. The door of the shop was ahead of them. There appeared to be nothing she could do. The surrounding buildings were all in darkness—the street empty.

Suddenly she heard a swishing sound and, several things happened at once. Someone came flying through the air straight at them. The man, swinging in on a rope looped over the building's overhang, struck Mercier with his feet. As her capturer staggered backwards, Louise flew away from him, and landed on her bottom. There was the clinking sound of something metallic landing not far from her. It was the gun Mercier had been holding. She reached out and grabbed it and, still sitting there, looked around at the unusual scene.

The coachman jumped down and ran towards Mercier as if to help him, but the man on the rope swung back again. He appeared to lunge into the driver, with the weight of his whole body, sending him crashing to the ground. With that, he let go of the rope and landed lightly on his feet. To her utter amazement, she saw it was Marc. Like a pirate, he had swooped in on them ready to do battle.

How did that rope get there? she wondered.

The driver still lay where he had fallen. He looked unconscious. However, Mercier now stood with his body in a fighting stance. Both men unsheathed their swords; Marc yelled *"en garde"* and the contest began.

Marc was tall and at least ten years younger, but Mercier was solid and strong as a bull, yet light on his feet for such a heavyset man. Louise watched—her heart pounding furiously—as the two men thrust and parried, their swords clashing repeatedly. She held the small pistol but didn't dare shoot for fear of hitting Marc.

Watching the men duelling, she became aware of a disturbing thought. It was the unwelcome but unshakable knowledge that she loved Marc Garneau, with all her heart and soul. If he perished now—fighting for her life—she didn't think she could bear it. She reasoned it was quite natural not to want Marc to die, but this was more—much more. She had felt the same way earlier in the evening as they danced. The yearning to be once more in his arms—far away from here—to experience again the absolute joy she had known with him on the beach in La Rochelle.

This is terribly wrong, she thought. I mustn't feel like this.

However, the emotion persisted so there was no doubt. She loved him still—the way she had ever since she was fourteen. It wasn't a happy thought—it hurt her conscience that she could love someone, other than her husband, like this. Yet, strangely, loving Marc didn't lesson her feelings for Paul at all. Oh, but Marc must not guess. And Paul—he must never find out. He is such a good man. He doesn't deserve this from me at all.

She heard a groan of pain, and the sounds of fighting stopped suddenly. She looked up. Marc stood above Mercier with his foot on the man's chest—the tip of his sword against his neck.

At that moment, a carriage pulled into the square, and four men jumped out—Jean Guy followed by Sir John Houblon along with the new city sheriff and a constable.

"Here, Jean Guy," Marc called. "Get this fellow tied up. He tried to kidnap your sister for some reason. Better see to the driver—I hope I haven't killed him. I've got to help Louise." He turned to where she still sat with the weapon in her hand.

"Are you all right?" he asked, helping her to her feet. "I'm afraid your dress is ruined."

"Yes, I think it is," she said ruefully. But I'm fine, Marc. Where on earth did you learn that rope swinging trick?"

"I've spent a great deal of time on ships don't forget. When there's a storm at sea, you become skilled at whatever you need to do to keep yourself alive. They call it "learning the ropes." He smiled at her. "Thankfully, being a merchant, I usually keep one handy in my coach."

"But what made you think it was Mercier?"

"I've been keeping my eye on this fellow for a long time. He was at the Old Bailey for Paul's court case looking quite smug that first day. He didn't look very happy when they identified Walter Roberts, and I've never really trusted him since then. I suspected he was the little rat's mystery man, and figured he might not be finished with Paul yet."

"You knew where he might take me then?"

"Yes. Jean Guy and I came spying around his shop now and then. We've both noticed some curious goings on here. I saw him grab you tonight, and when the coach took off, I knew exactly where to come. I took a shortcut he obviously didn't know about. Gave me time to figure out how to use the rope. Good thing I remembered that overhang." He grinned again, cheekily moving a little closer.

"Did he injure you at all?" She asked, stepping back, trying to avoid an embrace. Even to herself her voice sounded aloof.

"Nary a scratch. Can't say the same for Mercier, though. Cut him up in a few places."

He began to look puzzled. She knew her attitude bewildered him.

I can't do this to him, she thought. He risked his life for me. I can't let him think it meant nothing to me.

"Well thank you, Marc. You saved my life. It seems you're always doing that in one way or another." She gave him a brief hug then stepped back again quickly, trying to avoid his gaze.

He still looked perplexed but, as he continued searching her face, their eyes met. She could no longer hide what she felt for him. As they stared silently at each other, his pupils suddenly widened in wonder. His expression softened, and a look of incredulous joy took over as a discerning little smile lit his face.

"Ah, I see," he said, sounding breathless.

"Marc," she whispered. "I—I have to tell…"

He put his finger on her lips. "No, *Cherie*—don't. Don't say anything you might regret. I understand. Just remember, mi'lady. I am at your service—always." He took her hand in his and kissing it, bowed before her. Then still smiling, he turned to Jean Guy. "Here, cousin. Take Louise back to her husband. I'll attend to matters here. She can make her statement to the Sheriff another day."

When Jean Guy and Louise reached Soho Square, they found the whole household in turmoil. One of the bullets from Mercier's pistol had bounced off the stone facing of Sir John's mansion, and hit Paul in the back. They had rushed him to his own home where Dr. Rene and another man set up an operating table on the big desk in the library. The door was still closed, but Pierre explained to the two of them what had happened.

"They've got the bullet out clean, but they're afraid of infection. Louise—brace yourself, girl—I have to tell you. The doctors don't think he will ever walk again. There's too much damage in the lower back area."

"Oh, no. Not Paul. He's such an active man and now just when he has everything he ever wanted. Papa, this is too much. I can't bear it." She felt her father's arms encircle her before everything blacked out.

∽❧∾

Louise discovered no matter how difficult things got, life did go on. They turned the big library on the main floor of the Soho house into a master suite for Paul. There, his loyal customers, including the King's representative, could call on him. Together, he and Lucien worked out the designs for the pieces that the three young men would create at the shop.

Pierre had the estate under control. He and Claudine had admitted to their daughter this was the happiest they had been since leaving France. If it weren't for Paul's condition, it was the ideal solution for their old age.

Mathurin Mercier had not hung at Tyburn as one might expect. The sheriff's men discovered he had murdered several prostitutes who had gone missing in the area. They judged him to be criminally insane and sentenced him to rot in Bedlam Asylum for the rest of his life. Marc told Louise such a thing was a fate worse than death.

"I could almost feel sorry for the fellow," he'd said. "Bedlam is the worst thing that can happen to anyone. They're shackled and whipped; caged up liked animals; and kept naked on beds of straw. I honestly think the man might have been better off dead. Anyhow, he won't be bothering you or anyone else, anytime soon."

Marc never spoke to her about what had passed between them the night of the shooting. For that, she felt thankful. At the end of August, he and Jean Guy left on a merchant ship for Virginia. They would be gone until the following spring. Once they left, she experienced a sense of relief. Her secret was safe, at least for a few more months.

The routine of the family had changed forever, but they all became exceptionally adept at the parts they had to play. Keeping Paul comfortable and content was now their main concern.

Chapter 42

Hampstead, England, May 1693

It had been a cold spring. Now, in Hampstead Heath where Marc had built his mansion, the hills were finally white with hawthorn trees in full blossom. Louise thought it was one of the loveliest and most peaceful areas around London. Marc is so fortunate to live here, she mused.

Alice would soon turn seven, and the whole family, with the exception of Paul, was there to see the pony Uncle Marc had bought for her. When it was a little older, it would go to the manor stables at the Oxfordshire farm.

Louise sat on the portico with Marc, newly returned from America. They watched as Pierre led the little horse around and around the riding ring with Alice sitting sidesaddle. Peter galloped about the ring on his hobbyhorse. The children and Pierre were always content together. It reminded her of her own happy childhood in the French village.

It's good that Alice and Peter have such an active grandfather now that Paul was immobile, she thought. Marc was good with them as well, which, for a bachelor she found rather surprising.

She turned to him and spoke. "You've made a wonderful home here, Marc." Then, without thinking of the consequences, added, "Have you never considered marriage and children?"

"So far my lifestyle has not lent itself to courtship, Louise. I'm too much away from home. I won't pretend there haven't been women. After all, I am a man—and a Frenchman at that," he added. His spontaneous, impish smile lit up his face.

"In any case, I've never met anyone I can care for as much as my first love. Perhaps as long as she haunts me the way she does, it wouldn't be fair to wed another. I still can never smell a rose without thinking of a certain day on the beach at La Rochelle."

Her eyes widened in astonishment at this proclamation. She knew her face had given away how she felt about him the night he rescued her from Mathurin Mercier. However, that was over a year ago, and since he learned

233

that Paul could not walk, he never mentioned the incident. She dreaded
what he might say to her now.

Drawing a little closer to her, he continued, "And I have a sweet, little
girl who has learned to love me as a dear uncle, and who fills my heart for
now. But what about your future, *Cherie?* What do they say about Paul's
progress?"

"He's as healthy as he'll ever be, I'm afraid. There is no hope he'll ever
walk again. Dr. Renee says he's lucky to be alive, although I sometimes
think Paul doesn't feel that way. There was so much he wanted to accomplish to help society. Now he often says he would as soon be dead. However,
he does enjoy being at the farm. He's always happier there."

"Yes. It's a wonderful place. I can see why he loves it. But what about
the shop?"

"We're fortunate all three boys have turned out to be such wonderful
goldsmiths. With Lucien doing much of the designing, and all of them
working hard, they keep King William satisfied. They don't take on too
many other commissions. There's no need."

She stopped to wave at Alice who had completed another circle on the
pony.

"Of course, I do the books, and Henri helps me with the banking duties. That's his expertise, but it will be finished when the Bank of England
opens. Papa loves running the estate and it's doing fine now. So everything
is well taken care of."

"Outside of the farm, does Paul have any interests?"

"He loves to read and, when he's tired, Maman or I read to him. He
likes books on theology and history. His brain is as good as ever although
physically he weakens a little each day. Nevertheless, they've rigged up a
sort of pallet so he can be on a horse and they lead him around the farm
with Papa. He loves that. Rene Martin says he could live for many years yet.
I can't say he's happy though. I'm afraid he's a changed man in many ways."

"And what about you—are *you* happy, Louise? A beautiful, young
woman like you should not have to live like a nun for the rest of her life."
He looked intently into her eyes the way he did when they were young. "It's
true I've never forgotten that time in La Rochelle—can you say you have?"

She hesitated to answer and looked over at young Alice still sitting on
the brown pony. Both she and Peter were laughing delightedly at something their Grandfather had said.

"No, Marc. How could I forget? I have my charming little reminder
over there."

"I'm not speaking of Alice, my dear. I'm thinking of how we were
together. For me, it has never been the same with anyone else. You know,
Louise, we are in this intolerable situation. I love you passionately and I
know you love me too. You can't deny it. Your eyes told me so, the night I

fought Mercier." He reached up and picked a red rose from a bush climbing up the porch. Coming close to her, he bent and carefully tucked it behind her ear—his fingers gently stroking her face. She shivered at the contact.

"Red roses are for love, *Cherie*. Do you remember the first time I kissed you? Have you really forgotten how we were, when we were young? We belong together, Louise," he continued, with a rather sad smile. "Of course, I know you must never leave Paul but, could you consider being my lover? My mistress?"

The question was so unexpected she stared at him in shock, her eyes wide, and her hand covering her mouth.

"It goes on with the nobility all the time," he assured her. "Even your sanctimonious friend, King William has his affair with the infamous Elizabeth Villiers. They haven't managed to keep that a secret." He moved closer, urging, "Tonight, darling—come to me—let me be with you again as I have so longed. I think we need each other right now."

His declaration left her breathless. Was he serious in suggesting they should begin a liaison? That would break her father's heart all over again; and even in his present condition, she was positive Paul would know. She thought of the vow she had made to herself all those years ago. That she would always be faithful to her husband.

She answered him quickly. "Dearest Marc, ask me anything but that. You know I have a Calvinist father and, the heart of a Huguenot myself. It may be common in royal households but not among our community. I almost destroyed my soul once for passion. Am I to do that again? No, no, I couldn't, Marc. It would be a sin against both my faith and my husband."

He stared at her with such a sorry look, she could hardly bear it, but she continued. "It is true; I never stopped loving you. But I also love Paul deeply, and I owe him so much. He was there for me when you couldn't be. As long as he lives, I'll be true to him. Can you understand how I feel?"

"No, Louise, I can't. However, I do respect your decision. It is final I take it? "

"Yes. It has to be. There's no way I can do what you ask."

He nodded his head ruefully but said nothing more. After a few seconds, he turned from her and leaned against the railing watching Alice, the little girl who could never know she was his. Louise was afraid she'd hurt him keenly and put her hand on his arm.

"When is your next trip, Marc?"

"At the end of summer. Jean Guy and I will finally sail to China. We'll be gone for well over two years, but I think it will be my last trip. It won't be an easy one, if I go back up that mountain, and there's someone I want to see again."

He sighed before he went on. "After that, I'll stay in London. The company has a job for me in the city, if I want it. There are younger merchants like Jean Guy who are quite willing to do the traveling. I've already seen much of the world, and I seem to have lost my taste for roaming the globe. It's strange, but I find I like England after all."

"So you plan on settling here, then?"

"I think so. Perhaps I will take your suggestion and start looking for a mistress for my house. I'll need a good strong son one of these days to take over everything I've built up here. I'm sure Paul has taken care of Alice's future?"

"Yes." She nodded. "He always thinks of her as his own daughter. He's been exceedingly fair to her."

"I know, and I appreciate it. Anyway, Louise, I'll be off now. I have some business to take care of in London, so I don't think I'll be back in time for dinner. I'll most likely stay over. I'm sure Uncle Pierre will act as host for me. You'll be going back to Soho tomorrow? Please give my regards to Paul. I hope he knows what a treasure he has."

Kissing her on each cheek, he bid her '*adieu*'.

Yes, I've hurt him, she thought as she watched him leave. But he asks the impossible and he knows it. Will I mind dreadfully if he finds someone he can love? He deserves to be happy. Why does life have to be so complicated?

"Come in now, children," she called aloud. "I think you've all had enough for one day. You should say 'good bye' to Uncle Marc. He is going to town; and you all need to have a nap before we eat. Including your Grandpapa," she added with a smile.

With that, she entered Marc's house for what she imagined might just be the last time for a long while.

Louise did not see Marc again before he and Jean Guy left for China. At the end of June, the household moved to Oxfordshire for the summer. The country was cooler and much more comfortable for Paul. Talking every day to Pierre about the farm, and touring around the property held on horseback by his special gear, seemed to revive his spirits.

Lucien and the two young apprentices took care of the goldsmith shop, and Louise went back into town once or twice a month to do an inventory of the gold on hand and reconcile her books. She heard no news of Marc until one day while in the shop with Claude.

"Did you hear the latest about Marc?" her brother asked her.

"No, I only hear anything when Jean Guy comes out to Oxford once in a while. He tells me how the plans for their big trip are progressing."

"I guess Marc keeps quiet about it, but I heard he's squiring Lady Elizabeth Fitzgerald around town now. She is gorgeous and the daughter of one of the directors of the East India Company. One of our customers is a vintner, and he delivered a large order of wine to the lord's house for a ball last week. The servants told Monsieur Montague that Lady Elizabeth spends a great deal of time with Marc Garneau. It's rumoured, they'll announce an engagement as soon as he returns from the Orient. He's to have a good position with the company here in London, and won't have to travel anymore."

A cold chill ran through her and her heart felt like a ball of lead dropping to her boots. But you knew this could happen, she thought. You can't be so selfish.

She turned to Claude with a fake smile pasted on her face. "Well, wouldn't that be lovely for him. He deserves to find a nice wife and settle down."

Chapter 43

Oxfordshire Twelfth Night, 1695

The winter had been cold and wet and, after travelling from Oxfordshire to London on a damp day in November, Paul came down with a fever he could not shake. Two months had passed with no improvement; and now Rene Martin told Louise there was nothing more to be done. Paul was dying.

"It's that phlegm humour in his lungs I'm afraid. He's had the asthma symptoms ever since he was in prison. While he led a healthy way of life—riding and exercising—he could fight it. But now I'm afraid he can't anymore."

Each day his body weakened a little more. His cough was ragged, and shortness of breath made it difficult for him to speak. Now death seemed inevitable, he appeared almost relieved. He would smile lovingly at her as she read to him, or sat quietly by his bed with her needlework.

However, one day he seemed agitated. He indicated that he had something urgent to discuss; but his constant coughing made speaking almost impossible. The maid brought a drink of hot tea with honey and brandy, which he sipped slowly. Finally, he had enough breath to speak at length.

"Louise, there are things I need to tell you. Things you must know before I die."

"Paul, don't say that. In the first place, you are not going to die."

"Sooner or later it happens to everyone, Louise, and I'm not afraid. I think the Lord will find a place for me on Judgment Day." He managed another bright smile. "However, I need to speak to you about my Will. Pierre and our solicitor are in charge, of course, but I wish you to know what I've arranged and why."

"I think this could all wait, darling. It's too hard on you, and I'm sure anything you have done is fine."

" Nevertheless, you need to understand. It will help your father if you do. The estate all goes to Peter, of course. It's the law of entailment. I've asked Dr. Renee and your father to be in control of all the assets until Peter reaches majority. There's no one I trust more than those two men."

He stopped speaking for a moment. Louise helped him take another drink before he continued.

"The goldsmith shop isn't part of the estate, so it doesn't have to be handled that way. I've instructed the solicitor to break it into shares now—five shares of twenty percent each. Peter won't need it, so I'm giving you two shares—forty percent of the company's worth. Then each of the lads—Claude, Henri and Lucien—will all get one share. That means that you and Claude together will hold the majority, which should keep you safe enough."

"Oh, darling. That's extremely generous of you."

"Well, it's not unusual for a wife to take over her husband's business. You understand the financial end of it, and this way you'll at least be a lady of some means. It's important for me to know you're looked after. But I also thought the boys should have shares for all their hard work. Lucien and Claude are true artists, and Henri is a nice enough lad. I hope they will all stay. If they want to go, then you must buy their shares."

He coughed again, and Louise helped him with another drink of the honeyed tea.

"That's very kind of you, Paul, and a wonderful opportunity for Claude. But you shouldn't talk anymore right now. The rest could wait."

"No, no. I must tell you these things now. There's more. We've arranged for Peter to go to Oxford in time. Perhaps he will want to be a lawyer. That's what I would like for him."

"Papa and I will try to persuade him that way, dear. But I do wish you would think about getting better. You must think positive thoughts. They say it helps."

He looked amused. "I'll try sweetheart but, in case it's of no avail, I need to talk about your future. Besides the shares, there's an annuity, which will bring you a nice income each year. Even if you marry, it will continue. I don't want you to be totally dependent on some man. In case, he's not good to you."

"I can't bear it when you talk like this, Paul."

"But it needs to be said, Louise, so we must do it now. We've arranged the annuity in such a way that, if you die, it would go to Alice and not your husband. There is also a sum set aside for Alice's dowry. Pierre will have control of that. Do you think that is fair?"

"You have always been so good to both Alice and me, Paul. Better than I ever deserved." She could no longer hold back her tears. He patted her hand.

"There's something else I need to say. It's concerning you marrying again. Not right away of course but, Louise, in the fullness of time, you *should* marry."

He hesitated, coughed, and said, "And when you do, I want you to consider marrying your cousin. At first I thought he was a selfish, young man; but I've been watching him for a few years now, and I don't think any man could love someone more than he loves you. I've seen the look of longing in his face sometimes and pitied him. In spite of his youth and his looks, I had something he wanted and could not have."

"I don't even want to think of such a thing right now. We can't let you go, Paul. You must be here for your family."

"I wish that I could. But I don't think it is to be. I'm so tired now. Too tired to fight anymore. And when the inevitable happens, I don't want you to be alone too long. You are beautiful and you will have income. There will be many men wanting you and some won't have your best interest at heart. Sadly, there are other men like Mathurin Mercier around. I know Marc would take care of you and Alice. You must also think of her, as well. Stepfathers can be devilishly evil sometimes. It would be much better for you to marry her real father. We know he loves her dearly."

"I can't promise you that, dear. I think there's someone else he cares for now. But please, just stay with me as long as you can."

He squeezed her hand with what little strength he had left. Then exhausted, fell into a sound sleep.

❦

Paul rallied for a few days after their discussion, but by the end of the week, the extreme lethargy returned. He no longer gave the impression that he understood what she read to him and, crossly, he would waive away his meals. All he could manage was a little broth and some water. On the first day of February, Renee Martin came for his weekly check of his patient and, after feeling his forehead and his pulse, he shook his head.

"I don't think he can last more than a day or two, Louise. It's definitely pneumonia, and he has no strength left to fight it. We could bleed him, but I don't think it would help. You better prepare the children for the worst." There were tears in the doctor's eyes. "I'm so sorry, my dear. You know I love him too. He has been like a brother to me." He brushed her forehead with a kiss.

Louise shook her head, too overwhelmed with sorrow even to answer him as he turned to leave the room.

After she had explained to the family and the servants, she sat beside his bed far into the night, eventually falling asleep in the big chair. Sometime past midnight, a sound startled her awake. One look at her husband's face was all she needed to see. Sir Paul Thibault, at the age of forty-seven, had passed away quietly in his sleep.

The day after Paul's funeral, Claudine and Louise, went looking for Pierre in order to discuss an estate matter with him. They thought they would find him in the large building that accommodated his workshop and the farm office. Young André, busy at the loom, barely looked up. He loved weaving, and often neglected his studies to concentrate on the small tapestries he was gifted at making.

"Where's Papa?" Claudine asked her son.

"I saw him go into his office not long ago, Maman. He seemed so sad; I thought I'd leave him alone."

They opened the door to the office quietly and peeked in. Pierre sat, elbows on the desk, with his head in his hands. His shoulders shook with silent sobs. Louise stopped, appalled at her father's grief. She stepped back letting her mother go to him. It surprised her to see the depth of his feelings for the son-in-law who had been such a loyal friend. Even the death of Jacques had not affected him this way.

"Why, Pierre. You're crying." Claudine spoke softly. "Oh, my dear, I know how much you must miss Paul."

"He was such a good man." Pierre looked up with a sad smile, wiping his eyes on his sleeves. He seemed not to notice Louise standing in the background. "A kind and generous man and a wonderful friend—and far too young to die like this. That's the problem. I can't comprehend his death. I loved Jacques, but he was an adventurer. I understood his death—almost expected it. But Paul—what did he ever do to deserve this? It shakes my faith in our God somewhat."

"Pierre, *non, non,*" she replied lapsing into French, as she often did at an emotional time. "You must never blame God for such a thing. Only Satan bears the responsibility for a thing this evil. For such jealousy to eat away at a man like Martin Mercier, and cause him to do this bad thing, that can only be the work of the Devil."

"But why would God allow it then? It must have been Paul's destiny. But why?"

"I am not clever like Jacques was. He was so well-travelled, and I certainly don't have his education. But he told you, he didn't accept Jean Calvin's strong belief in predestination. Many Huguenots don't, you know. Paul didn't, and I'm sure that Louise and Marc don't anymore either."

"Louise too? I recall she used to argue with me about it when she was young. What has happened to my authority?"

"They grow up, Pierre. They think for themselves. For me also, predestination no longer makes sense. When Paul was so sick, Louise and I and would sit by his bed, and he would talk to us about his beliefs. He said he could not accept a God that would deliberately cause all the terrible things that happen to people. He didn't believe that is what the scriptures teach at all. And Louise agreed with him."

Her husband stared at her with a look of amazement. "How can you say these things to me?"

"Pierre, I have to tell you—I have always gone along with you on our beliefs, but now I think there are other factors. Things like the choices we make; time and unforeseen occurrence; being in the wrong place at the wrong time. Terrible things happen to so many good people. I can no longer accept that all these things are their destiny."

"But Claudine," he replied, shock in his voice, "it is the faith of our fathers. Why would dreadful things happen then?"

"Don't you remember the story of Job? I have often read it to the children. Satan taunted God that he could turn Job, a good and righteous man, away from worshipping Him. All he had to do was make things go wrong for the man. So, God told the Adversary, 'Go ahead then. Do whatever you want to him. Only don't kill him.' But Job stayed loyal. He would not turn against God just because so much went wrong."

Louise stood perfectly still. Her mother's bravery stunned her. In matters of faith, her father's word had always been law. Pierre's family had looked to him for guidance in doctrine, and yet now it was her submissive mother, who counselled her father. She waited breathlessly for Claudine's next words.

"I believe that is the answer," her mother continued. "This was not God's plan. If anything, the evil one arranged it. He took over Mercier's mind to try to turn us away from our God. Do not give in to him, husband. Our daughter and our grandchildren will need all the help and all the spiritual guidance we can give them. Let us be strong for them. Let us never lose our conviction, Pierre."

Pierre sat still for what seemed to Louise like an agonizingly long time. When he spoke, it was with neither sorrow nor anger. "Claudine, you are always so compelling in your quiet and modest way. No matter what has happened to our family you have been there for us, providing the comfort and wisdom we all needed."

He stood and put his arms around her, kissing her firmly on her lips. "Thank you, *mon coeur*. I will ponder your words. You are certainly correct about one thing. We must remember our grandchildren. And we must make sure this estate succeeds. For Louise and Alice—but especially for Peter—we must protect his heritage."

He stepped back and reached for his cloak hanging on a hook. "I should go and speak to the farmhands to see how the livestock are managing. I haven't checked for a few days now. Spring will soon be here and the new babies are due."

Louise slipped out the back door before her father could see her standing in the shadows. Tears streamed down her face as she hurried to the house. She would never want him to know she had seen his moment of weakness. But what she witnessed gave her new admiration for her mother. Claudine's fearlessness in speaking out to her husband reminded her of some of the stories she had read about courageous women in the Bible. She thought of Sarah, who at a time when women were mostly subservient, had bravely told her husband to send Ishmael away for persecuting her own son. Instead of rebuking Sarah, God had told Abraham, "Listen to the voice of your wife, Abraham."

I hope Papa remembers those words, she mused.

She thought back to the events of the past ten years. Unheralded by the family, this small, quiet woman had shown remarkable resilience through it all. She had left behind much she held dear without a murmur of discontent. Not once did she think to renounce her faith to save her life, nor argue against making a long and dangerous journey to be free to practice it.

When her unmarried daughter became pregnant, Claudine had taken the situation in hand, and guided the entire family through it. She had worked tirelessly at the Spittlefields Chapel to help the new refugees from France. She made the best of life in London, even though secretly hating the city. And during all their tribulation, she had never once turned her back on the God of her ancestors.

At that moment, Louise made the determination: no matter what lay ahead for her own little family, she would try to emulate her mother—a strong, unselfish, and devoted woman. My mother is exactly what a Christian ought to be, she thought.

Chapter 44

London, January 1696

The first day of 1696 dawned a cold and drab day in London. Feeling
rather depressed, Louise made pretence of eating a late lunch in the
morning room. Although the governmental ban on Christmas established
by Oliver Cromwell was no longer in effect, as strong Protestant dissenters,
the Huguenots took no part in the pagan customs that had crept into the
celebration. Nevertheless, Alice and Peter were spending the winter school
break with their grandparents at Alston Manor leaving Louise alone in the
Soho house with only the servants.

No matter the season, the children loved their time on the farm. This
year—with the cold and the snow—there would be ice-skating on the
frozen millpond as well as delightful rides on horse drawn sleds. Louise
pictured them; dashing over the silent, silvery meadows and through the
hoary, pine-scented forests, tucked snugly under fur covers.

It cheered her immensely to know they would experience a far more
enjoyable vacation than the same period last year, when the inevitability
of Paul's death blanketed everything. She desired that her children put all
sad thoughts behind them and get on with the joy of living. However, she
sensed a feeling of solitude in the house without them, which added to her
dejection over her loss.

On Twelfth Night, her parents were hosting a gala dinner at the farm,
their first social gathering since Paul's death. She would travel out to the
farm to attend but, in truth, she felt little like celebrating anything. It was
nearly a year since his death, and it surprised her how much, even now,
she missed him; his keen intelligence; his charming tenderness with her;
his warm, easy laughter. There was no doubt that he had been a wonderful
companion. Their life together was completely different from what she had
expected, at the time of their marriage.

So far, Paul's vast fortune was intact. The country estate under Pierre's
stewardship thrived and paid for itself. He had not taken any money from

the trust fund to run it. The goldsmith shop also prospered. The boys had all opted to stay realizing how fortunate they were to be part owners of such a successful shop. She lacked for nothing, but she missed the devoted and kind man very much. Although it was not the all-consuming, passion she felt for Marc, there was no doubt she had loved Paul at some deep level.

How fortunate I was to have known such a man, she thought, and to have had those amazing years with him. He taught me so much about life and always made me feel so cherished.

She looked at her reflection; sad eyes with dark circles under them stared back at her. She had recently turned twenty-seven, but she looked older now. What had Marc said to her the last time they were together?

She remembered his exact words. "You are too young and beautiful to be living like a nun," he had said. She laughed bitterly. I'm sure he wouldn't feel that way now, she thought.

She remembered what Claude had told her before he left on his last trip; that Marc planned to marry the beautiful Lady Elizabeth Fitzgerald as soon as he arrived home. Prior to going to China with Jean Guy, he had come to the house to say 'goodbye' to Paul. However, it was on a day when she was at the shop. She was convinced it was deliberate on his part. He was well aware of her schedule.

The doorbell jangled breaking into her thoughts and, a few moments later, the butler came in to announce her father had just arrived. "Shall I seat him in the drawing room, Madame?" he asked.

"Bring him in here, Herbert. He won't mind being informal."

"Shall I bring fresh coffee?"

"Yes, that will be nice. And some of those warm pasties we had for breakfast, as well. If he's come from the manor, he probably hasn't eaten since very early." Inwardly she worried that something might be wrong with the children. Her father almost never came to the city without a good reason.

"*Bonjour*, Papa," As he entered the room she stood and gave him a hug. "You must have left terribly early. Are the children well? Why are you in the city when the party is this weekend? Don't you have to help Maman?"

"Everyone's fine. The children are enjoying themselves immensely. Catherine and Edward are already helping your mother, and along with the servants, they have everything under control. However, there's something rather urgent that I must speak to you about. You won't know yet, but Jean Guy and Marc are home from the Orient. They arrived a few days ago. Jean Guy is at the farm now, and we've invited Marc to the dinner on Saturday. I felt I should warn you."

"Oh, that's exciting." Her heart skipped a beat. She hoped her father would not see that she was somewhat shaken by the news. "Are they both well? It's been a long journey for them. Did Jean Guy say whether or not he liked China?"

"Jean Guy loved everything about it. I feel definitely, that it's his destiny. I must ask you something, though, Louise. Please don't be angry with me. Do you still think about Marc? I mean other than as a family member?"

"Why, I don't know, Papa," she replied, rather stunned. "He helped us so much in clearing Paul's name over the coining. And he saved me from whatever Martin Mercier had planned. I'm sure I owe him my life. But all the time Paul was alive, I never thought about Marc as anything but my dear cousin."

That wasn't entirely true, but it would be difficult to explain to her father what she had discovered about herself the night Paul was shot. She continued, "I mean—things are different now with my situation. However, I don't know what his thoughts about me are now. There was all that talk about him and Lady Elizabeth before he left."

"Well, Jean Guy gives me to understand that Marc still cares a great deal for you. It's not quite that simple, though. There's another problem. And I don't want you hurt by him any more than you have been."

"Another problem? Why? Are he and Lady Elizabeth already married then?"

"No, no, not that. But he has brought a little boy home with him. He's part Chinese or some type of Oriental and Jean Guy tells me, he's Marc's son."

"Marc has a son! My goodness, Papa!" They'd been standing until now but, at his words, she dropped into a chair. Pierre also took a seat just as a maid appeared with a cup of coffee and some warm biscuits. He helped himself and began to eat.

"Does he have a wife then—in China?" she finally asked.

"Jean Guy says not—at least, not a legal wife. Apparently, on his first trip there, his friend, Li Jang, took him up the mountain to where the tea grows; and he had a—a—liaison—I guess you would call it—with an oriental girl."

Pierre looked so uncomfortable telling her this; she had to suppress a smile, even though the news shocked her.

"I see," was all she could say aloud.

"It appears that the boy's mother died, and Li Jang brought him down to his home to look after him. He would have seen to the boy's education, so I don't know why they didn't just leave him there in his own culture. However, Jean Guy says the women in the household were not kind to the boy—knowing his background, I guess—and Marc decided not to leave him."

"Well, Marc has already given up one child. I can see why he would want this one—his own flesh and blood."

"I suppose so, but I don't know what will happen to him here in England. People don't take kindly to these sorts of mixed children. Anyhow, Louise, it's not something in which you should get involved. There's been enough controversy in your life. That's what I wanted to tell you. When you're ready, you'd best look for a husband elsewhere. It wouldn't do the goldsmith shop any good if society finds a reason to look down on you."

"Papa," she said, feeling quite angry with her father. "We can't think like that—it's not Christian. First, we aren't even sure Marc is interested in me anymore. But the poor little boy. We must consider him. Never knowing his own mother; and being ill-treated by those women; and then having to make that terrible sea voyage with a father he doesn't really know; and to come to a place where everyone and everything is so different."

She stood again and walked to the window, looking out at the dreary weather. Turning back to him, she continued, "It's so sad. Let's not make Marc's life any more difficult than it is. Let's welcome him, with open arms. I think he has more than made amends to our family for any harm he ever did to us."

"If that's the way you feel." His tone sounded slightly chagrined. "But I thought I would warn you what to expect when you see him. Now at least you know."

Her tone softened. "I understand, dear Papa. You always want to take care of me and I thank you for that. Well, we'll see how it goes when we meet. Don't you and Maman worry about me. I'm all grown up now, you know." She laughed, and, walking over to him, bent down and kissed him on both cheeks, not wanting to offend him.

"But you know how the French feel about their children? You'll understand when Peter and Alice are adults. Well then, I'll bid you *adieu*, daughter. We'll see you tomorrow then. You're coming a day ahead?"

"Yes, I'll leave early in the morning. I'll be there before dinner."

He stood up to go; however as she followed him to the front door, she remembered his lengthy trip home. "But what about you? You should have a proper meal. It's a long trip home. Don't you want to stay here tonight?"

"No, no. I have to meet our solicitor in The City. I'll eat dinner with him and then I must return to the estate this evening. Don't worry. I can sleep in the coach. So, I'll see you tomorrow evening."

Taking a long look at her, he added, "The party will be good for you, dear." Then, giving her a hug, he swept on his large feathered hat and went out the door.

⚔

After watching her father's departure, she ran up the stairs to her room. Strangely, she now felt full of energy, and the party began to be important to her. Her heart pounded like a drum, and she could hardly get her breath. "Oh, Marc," she whispered. "Why do you always affect me like this--even after all these years?"

Hannah was busy elsewhere, so she went into her wardrobe and took off the black dress, which didn't complement her delicate colouring. She took out some of the new frocks her father had ordered made for her. Her year of mourning would soon be over, and she could soon wear colours again. She certainly had no plan to wear black forever as some widows did. Finally, she settled on a stylish, deep plum coloured silk that gave a superb effect with her green eyes and translucent skin.

It's dark enough to be suitable for a widow of almost a year, she reflected.

She twisted the little curls over her ears the way Hannah did her hair; and applied some powder to her cheeks, and then pinched them until they were rosy. Her eyes sparkled and the frown on her face relaxed. Already she looked years younger.

Yes, she thought, there's no doubt I still have strong feelings for Marc. But be careful, Louise. He may care nothing at all for you except as a dear cousin, and you don't need another broken heart.

⚭

The Alston Manor house glittered with a festive atmosphere. It was the family's first social gathering since Paul's death and Claudine, along with Catherine and the household servants had worked wonders with the decorations and the menu. In the large entrance hall, a hired flutist played Baroque music.

Claudine permitted the children to stay to see the guests arrive; then they would go upstairs for their own small party. Young Andre had taken Alice and Peter in tow and acted every bit the gracious host, although it was actually Peter's house. Fourteen-year-old Jeanette, looking astonishingly like a young version of Louise, was allowed to stay with the grown-ups for the first time. She confided to her sister how delighted she was, as she secretly held romantic feelings for Lucien Robard, the handsome, young goldsmith.

"I think he is so elegant," she whispered to Louise.

Many of the guests had already arrived. As they entered the ballroom, the servants offered them French champagne, caviar and other *hors d'oeuvres*. Louise stood with her mother and father in the foyer ready to greet the newcomers. She kept eyeing the entrance nervously. Her footman, brought in from the London house for the occasion, announced the visitors as they entered the hall.

"Mr. Marc Garneau and Master Lee Garneau," the man at last proclaimed.

Her hands were clammy and once again, her heart pounded in her ears. Marc entered the room, as striking as ever. His black, curly hair still fell to his shoulders, but Louise immediately noticed a subtle difference in him. The boyishness was gone. There was now an older, more distinguished look about him. Here, was a man, completely sure of himself, and yet without an air of arrogance.

The intense gaze he gave her utterly stunned her. He extended his hands and held on to both of hers as he kissed each cheek. "How are you, dear Cousin?" he asked. "Please accept my condolences about Paul. He was a good man. I admired him a great deal. I'm sure that he is sorely missed in the city."

"Thank you," she said rather breathlessly. "He had a fine funeral, and even King William attended, despite his own grief over Queen Mary's recent death. It was gratifying to see how well liked Paul was in so many quarters. But, Marc. How wonderful to see you. We're so glad you're home safe."

Her eyes dropped to the little boy beside him, and she almost gasped at the exquisiteness of him. He reminded her of an exotic painting she had once seen. His black hair was as curly as his father's and his eyes as blue, but they slanted provocatively in a pale, alabaster face. He looked a little frightened; even so, the almond-shaped eyes held a twinkle, as if laughter would come easy to him.

"This is my son," Marc said, looking straight into her eyes. "His name is Lee Marc Garneau."

"He is stunning, Marc. Does he understand English?"

"Yes. At least enough to be polite." Marc laughed. "We had time to give him a lot of lessons on the ship. French, as well. This is your *Tante* Louise, Lee—Jean Guy's sister. Didn't I tell you, she was a beautiful lady—like an angel?"

"I happy to meet you, *Tante* Louise. It is great pleasure."

With tears in her eyes, she bent down to the boy and hugged him for a second or two. "The pleasure is all mine, Lee," she said, smiling at Marc, who flushed, but returned her smile with his familiar, impish one.

"Thank you, *Cherie*," he replied softly. "And now perhaps he should meet his cousins. They will want to take him upstairs for the evening, I believe."

She nodded, and the man and boy moved on. Her father was watching her with a bemused look, but she smiled placidly at him, and then turned to greet two new guests who had just arrived.

250

The dinner was an enormous success, and it appeared no one thought it odd that Marc should be there with a young son. He was a fine-looking child and the eastern blood seemed only to have enhanced his beauty. Louise was convinced that London Society would take him to their hearts. However, even if they didn't, she certainly planned to do so. She loved him at first sight and would have no qualms about including him in whatever her relationship with Marc was to be. It seemed the children had all gotten along remarkably well, which pleased her. Alice and Peter's nanny told her that Lee, although being a quiet and well-behaved little boy, laughed a great deal and eagerly joined in the games. He reminded her of Marc as a child.

Before the evening was over, Marc approached her. "Louise, my son and I are staying at the house in Hampton, and I'll be there with him for a week or so. He's an adaptable little boy for one so young, but I don't want to leave him right away. After I get him settled, I'll go back to the city to do some work, and I'd like to visit you. I do want to hear about Paul. I hope he didn't suffer too much at the end. May I see you then?"

"Of course, Marc. I still go to the goldsmith shop for the bookkeeping on Friday's. But I'll look forward to seeing you at the house, whichever other day is convenient."

They appeared so formal with each other she didn't know what to make of this upcoming visit. He certainly didn't sound like a suitor.

Chapter 45

London, February 1696

It was over a month before Marc made an appearance. Louise had almost given up on him. The anniversary of Paul's death passed and, once again, she felt lonely and depressed. She had stayed at the manor with her parents during that time, but now she was back in the London townhouse. The children had returned home with her to continue their schooling.

Sitting with a cup of chocolate after breakfast in the morning room, she picked up her embroidery. She was decorating a special dress for the new baby her sister expected. The day after the dinner party, Catherine and Edward informed the family that a new little member would arrive in the summer.

At least the rest of the family is happy in this new life, she mused. Coming to England was advantageous for all of us in many ways; but I do miss Paul so much. Will it always hurt like this?

She sighed, and turned to her needlework.

The front doorbell jangled and shortly afterwards the butler came in to announce, "Monsieur Marc Garneau is here to see you, Madame. I had him wait in the parlour for you."

"Thank you, Herbert." Her heart began those unpredictable palpitations again, and she found it difficult to reply. "Would you tell him I'll be down in about five minutes and ask cook for fresh coffee for him?"

She ran up the stairs to her room. Don't get too excited, she warned herself. He may have come to tell you, he is marrying the beautiful Lady Elizabeth. Although I don't know, what her family would think about the little boy.

Hannah helped her change into a pale pink dress that complimented her colouring. Her cheeks looked flushed, so she dabbed a little powder on them, but it didn't seem to help. When she could no longer avoid going down, she descended the stairs and entered the parlour. It reminded her of the day he had first come to visit Paul here at the house and discovered

Alice. Once more, she felt shy with Marc. Having a husband had protected her from his charm.

He put down his cup and stood as she entered the room. He took both her hands and kissed her in the French mode. "Hello, *Cherie*, I have missed you so." He let her go and stepped back to look at her.

"I imagine that you have been kept busy since your return from the orient." She spoke rather quickly to hide her agitation. "Please have a seat, Marc. I'm anxious to hear all about your adventures. Did your little boy adjust to the Hampstead house?"

"Yes, but it took longer than I thought," he said, sitting directly across from the settee she chose. "Everything here is so different from China and he's not quite eight. There have been many arrangements to make. I've finally found a nanny he's taken to and a tutor for his lessons. I'm beginning to understand that children take quite a lot of one's time." He grinned at her then, roguish as always.

"What about your future? Will you still be gone a lot?"

"No. I've decided I no longer wish to travel so much. Although some day, I'll take Lee back for a visit to China, and I'll continue to import the teas from there. My good friend in Canton—Li Jang—can look after the buying for me. Jean Guy will contact him each trip he makes. The problems the East India Company had with Canton have all been sorted out."

He picked his cup and quickly drained it. "I've learned a good deal about the Company over the last few years; so I've been given a good position here in head office. I also have plans to build up a business here in London. It will be costly and challenging, but I think it might bring in a great deal of money in the end."

Louise stood and poured him another cup of coffee, nodding for him to continue.

"I've bought four coffee houses—all in excellent locations—but I am going to try promote them as tearooms, which is a new concept here. I suppose I'm taking a bit of a chance. But Li Jang knows tea better than anyone else in Canton, so these will be extra fine blends. I think the drink has great potential. It seems to aid people's health."

He stopped to take another sip and one of the petite fours the maid brought. It occurred to her that he wasn't as poised as she remembered him. He seemed to be babbling, she thought. Why, he's as nervous as I am; I've never seen him like this.

"It's because you have to boil the water," he continued. "Helps the humors they say. I've been working on my ideas since I got home, which has kept me busy, as well. I'm sorry I didn't get here as soon as I had hoped—I have so much to say to you…"

"Well, of course I understand and I'm glad to see you now," she broke in to forestall him. There was a moment of awkward silence, then, "Marc...?" Her tone implied a question.

"Yes, Louise?" His reply, the same.

"Perhaps it isn't my business. However, I *am* your cousin and Alice is Li's half-sister. Do you feel like telling me about the little fellow's mother? She must have been exquisite."

"Yes, she was—in an eastern way. I met her when I went up the mountain to the villages where the tea grows. Actually, she was Korean, not Chinese. Li Jang tells me that some of the most beautiful women in the Orient are Korean. She certainly was."

"Did you seduce her?" She blushed at her audacity, but she needed to know.

"No, dear," he replied with a slight smile. "I would say she rather seduced me."

He paused as if groping for words. "I don't mind telling *you*, but for the sake of the boy, I'm not mentioning it to anyone else. Society in this country can be cruel, and I don't want him scorned. His mother was a courtesan. Do you know what that means?

"Yes, of course I do. Well, then, can you be sure that you are Lee's father?"

He laughed out loud, looking relaxed for the first time since he arrived. "You won't understand how funny that is, Louise," he replied. "You've seen his head of curls and his eyes. I can assure you, it's most unlikely that there was another tea merchant in that village—at that time—with anything but straight, black hair and even blacker eyes. Oriental men seldom have curly hair. Nor blue eyes. No, there's no doubt he is mine. And, you understand, Mei Ling would have known how to prevent a child."

Her hand went to her mouth. "Oh, I see. So she wanted your baby. Well, yes, he certainly looks like you. And quite a lot like Alice."

"The friend I mentioned, Li Jang—the Cantonese merchant, goes up the mountain to the factories every summer. When he went back that next year, Mei Ling had this baby. He was only three months old, but Jang recognized immediately he had to be my son. She had called him Li Mac. She never could say Marc. She was very ill when he found her, so he had both of them taken down the mountain to his house in Canton. He has two wives, and they weren't happy with the situation, but they looked after the baby when she died. In any case, they would never have dared go against Li Jang's wishes. Needless to say, it pleased them when I wanted to bring him back to England."

"Were you in love with her, Marc?"

"I'll be honest. Outside of you, she is one of the few women who ever totally intrigued me. I'm not sure what I felt for her. The trip up the mountain was more difficult than I had ever imagined and I was exhausted. The higher altitude had something to do with it, they tell me. Although, I've often wondered if it wasn't more than that. Perhaps I was drugged—maybe opium. I felt drowsy all the time. Jang and I discussed it, and he thinks that Mei Ling would do that to get what she wanted. Everything seemed so strange and unreal at the time—somewhat euphoric. Something like what the Hindus call nirvana, I guess." He paused, looking into the distance.

"She had a depth to her that went well beyond her status and she was remarkably intuitive. I don't think she was really amoral, just a victim of her circumstance. She had been kidnapped as a child and forced into slavery."

He took another sip of his coffee before continuing.

"I missed you so much, and she was more than willing—perhaps she wanted the child of a Caucasian. So—it happened. When I see my son, I'm not so sure I'm sorry. I love him tremendously, Louise. Can you understand that?"

"Yes, of course I can. I wouldn't give up Alice for the world, although being pregnant with her terrified me at the time. I felt so guilty. But yes—somehow the results alleviate the problems encountered."

"Louise." Suddenly he put down his cup and was on his feet. He crossed over to her, and sitting down beside her on the settee, took both her hands in his. "I can stand this no longer—all this—this little talk. I must speak to you once again about the great love I have for you. Try as I might, I cannot disregard my feelings for you. I know you sincerely cared for Paul. But I've been positive the night he was shot that you loved me, as well. More than as a cousin. Do you still?"

He looked into her eyes with a pleading look. "I—I tried to wait a decent length of time from the anniversary of Paul's death, but I can no longer keep silent. Oh my darling, could we start again? Of course, there's my little boy now, but is there any way you could love me, and my son as well?"

His urgency surprised her. She felt he deserved an honest answer. She looked directly into his eyes. "Yes. I love you, Marc, Definitely more than a cousin does. Perhaps I never stopped. And I already love your son. But everyone was talking about Lady Elizabeth. They told me, you were going to be married. I assumed that's what you came to tell me."

"I like her very much. We've been great friends and before I left on this last trip, she honoured me by being the hostess at some of my business functions. But we have never been in love. She's soon to marry a lord who's overseeing the East India Company in Bombay. A good comrade of mine, in fact. Elizabeth knows how I feel about you. She's told me not to give up this time."

She started to speak.

"Wait, dear." He put his finger on her lips. "I once told you, I am more sinner than saint, and you have seen the truth of that. Over these last few years and especially during the trip back from China, I've had time to think about my life. And I find that having a son has changed my viewpoint on many things."

Louise smiled at that. "Yes, I know what you mean. Children certainly do that."

"I want the boy to grow up with the moral and spiritual values of our people. I know in order for that to happen, I'll have to do better myself. I'm many things, Louise, but I'm not a hypocrite. Will you marry me, and help me bring up my son in our faith? I'll soon be an old man, and I want only you to be the mother of any more children I might..."

He stopped speaking as she gave a startled cry.

"Why, sweetheart, what's wrong? What have I said?"

"Oh, Marc. I'm sorry, but I can't marry you. It wouldn't be fair. Of course, you don't know—you weren't here for Peter's birth. Things went wrong—the baby was breeched. They used a tool to turn him. Otherwise, I'd have died; but it ruined me—inside."

"My poor darling. No, I didn't hear that. By the time I got home, you and Peter were both fine and Paul was in prison. We were all so concerned about him."

"I can't have any more children, Marc. At least the doctor didn't think it would be possible. That was over five years ago and—well—I didn't get pregnant again even before Paul's injury."

He looked shocked for a moment. Then both his arms went around her, and he held her to his heart, kissing her tear-filled eyes to erase her sorrow.

"*Cherie*—don't cry. It wouldn't matter to me. We know Alice is ours—you have Peter and I have Lee. We'll be a family. It's all we need if we have each other. Say you'll marry me soon. Louise—please, darling—I need you so."

For the first time in many months, joy swept through her. It was certainly what she wanted. But for some reason, she was still hesitant. "If I am to marry again it would only be you. But we should be cautious. We have both experienced so much, and it has altered us. Perhaps you won't love this older, wiser me as much as you did the young, romantic version. And, as you say, there will always be Peter."

"You think I haven't seen the changes in you and marvelled at them?" Mark sighed. "You have gotten more beautiful and desirable with time. As for Peter, I promise you that I would love and care for Paul's son the same as he cared for my daughter. I'll do it gladly."

He still held her against his breast, while they sat in silence for a few minutes. Finally, he spoke again. "I'll make you a promise, sweetheart. I am going to court you quite properly, and in six months, I shall make you mine forever. I don't think you can escape me this time."

She looked up at him, so virile and handsome. She did not believe for one moment that he was through with travel. She had known him all her life, and he had always sought excitement over ease. If she said 'yes' to him, her life would be totally different. With Paul, she had found safety and contentment with a kind and gentle man. He had loved her dearly and she had responded to his tenderness.

With Marc, she would travel to the ends of the earth, if he wanted, and would soar to heights yet unknown. The feelings she had for him as a girl came flooding back. He was as exciting to her now as he had always been and it was impossible to resist him. Suddenly, she laughed with glee. "I don't want to escape you, Mark Garneau. You make me happy. You always have. Perhaps we don't have to wait too long. After all, we do know each other extremely well and my mourning period is over. People won't consider it improper. I think a May wedding would be most appropriate."

Mark looked at her as if to make sure she meant what she said. Then, bent his face to hers. This time their lips met and the pent-up longing for each other overwhelmed them both. When they pulled apart, they were breathless.

"Louise—girl, I love you so much." He sounded ecstatic. "I can't offer you a title or extreme wealth. Until I can get my money out of France, I'm little better than a middle-class merchant."

"Do you think I'm concerned about those things? I told you the night of Paul's ball that I don't care for the *beau monde*. He strived so hard for wealth and prestige in the world, and in the end, where did it get him. No Mark. All I want is you—to wake beside you—every morning for the rest of my life, and to bring up our children together in our faith. It's a good way of life."

"Then it shall be. Now I know you will be mine, I have something I have longed to give you. I found it in China on my first trip, and I've kept it all these years. I hope you will wear it now."

He pulled a small case from the pocket in his coat and opened it for her. It was a magnificent smooth, royal blue stone with tiny, white embedded fragments. She had never seen a gem of that shade. It was set in beaten gold and surrounded by diamonds.

"It's exquisite. It's so different—what is it?"

"It's lapis lazuli—from Afghanistan. The story is that Marco Polo took it to China as a gift to Kublai Khan. I suppose it could be true. It's unique enough to give to a goldsmith's widow, I think." His smile held just a tinge of sadness as he slipped it on her finger.

"It's a wonderful ring." She held her hand out to see the effect of the light. "I'll love wearing it. Shall we tell the family right away?"

"Of course, my love. In fact, I already let your father know what I planned to do, and he was quite calm about it. He truly gave me his blessing. You know, Pierre is quite a different person than the one we grew up with in France. I think Paul helped him to see the amusing side of life. He is far more understanding than he used to be. But still, I had to make him a solemn promise that I will never again do anything that would hurt you in any way."

She laughed merrily. "And I suppose he said that, after everything we've both been through, it must be that you are my destiny after all."

"Yes, *Cherie*, he did say that." He smiled down at her, drawing her once more into his arms. "But then, don't you think, just this one time, he might be right?"

Epilogue:

Oxfordshire May 1696

Pierre stood beside Claudine at the door of Alston Manor as their oldest daughter and her new husband drove down the lane away from the house. Their two grandchildren, along with young Andre and Marc's son, Lee, chased after the coach, shrieking with laughter and excitement, trying to throw flower petals at the couple.

The children at length gave up the pursuit and returned to the house where the dancing was still in progress; however, Pierre and Claudine lingered awhile in the twilight, mulling over the events of the past decade. He had resigned himself to the fact that Marc and Louise belonged together.

"Well, Claudine." He turned to his wife with a smile. "I'm sure this is a particularly joyful day for you. You always wanted Marc as a son-in-law, didn't you? Even before those troubled days in France. Well, he has turned out to be a far better man than I ever dreamed he could be."

"I'm glad to hear you say that Pierre. I've worried a little that you would not see the changes in him. Can you feel the least bit happy for Louise in her new life?"

"I'm not so pigheaded that I can't admit when I've been wrong about someone. There's no doubt that Louise loves Marc fervently. She looked radiant today. I expect she never stopped, in spite of what I tried to do about it."

"Yes, she tells me that, as much as she adored Paul for his great kindness to all of us, she has always loved Marc with her whole heart and soul. I think a devotion like that will help them through life's challenges, don't you, Pierre." She slipped her arm through his.

"I can't deny Marc has good qualities. He was always a bright young man and no one could accuse him of cowardice. In fact, he seemed to crave adventure and danger. Probably that's what put me off him in the first place. Well, I hope that he is finished with all that now he's married. I don't fancy my daughter chasing half way 'round the world after her husband. Although, I expect if she decides to do it, we'll go along with it."

"And I'm not so sure that won't happen. Louise is also inclined to be adventurous." She laughed and throwing her arms around her husband's neck bestowed a kiss on his lips. "So you and I had better get used to the fact that we might have another young family to raise."

"I'm glad we have been blessed with two healthy and happy grandchildren; and now there's Catherine's child on the way; and Marc's son as well. We've not done too badly in this strange country, would you say, my dear? Can you agree that life here in England has been good to you after all?"

"Yes, husband, I can," she admitted. "Much better than I ever imagined on that day you told us, we'd have to leave France. That was one of the worst moments of my life. I think we have much to be thankful for, and especially to those two splendid men who did so much for us."

"But of course—Jacques and Paul. How I miss them both. In some ways they were much alike, those men. Their wealth didn't deter them from putting others' welfare ahead of their own. I imagine that was what they were destined to do."

"Oh, Pierre, will you never agree that we have freewill to determine what we make of our lives."

"I have given it some thought. It seems rather haphazard to me. How do explain what has happened to us then?"

Claudine gazed up to the sky with a far-off look in her eyes. It was a few moments before she spoke. "I see the design of our lives rather like one of your tapestries. When you start the pattern, there are certain threads already in place—the warp. The weaver stretches them tight across the loom, parallel to each other. Once those warp threads are in place, they move up and down, but they never change, do they?"

"Well, it's a lot more complicated than you make it sound, but I suppose basically that's true."

"You could liken them to the things in our lives that can't be altered— the way our body is made; the colour of our hair and eyes; even our character to some extent. And most of us can't change the world we are born into either. We ostensibly go up and down with its flow. For example, we couldn't change what King Louis decided to do."

"No, we couldn't—most likely because it was his destiny. But go on."

"On the other hand, the weft threads are wound on spools or bobbins, and the colours you pick, and the way your work them through the raising and lowering sequence of the warp, determines the weave structure or pattern you want."

"Claudine, I know how to weave. What are you trying to say?"

"The weft threads are like the choices we make and the things that happen by chance—time and unforeseen occurrence. Those things can change the pattern of our lives. We could call it 'destiny's weave." All these things working together make up our final life's pattern, our destiny."

"Hmm. It's an interesting comparison. To some extent, it appears you are right. However, I've remembered a proverb by an old French poet. It goes like this: 'one meets his destiny often in the road he takes to avoid it.'"

"And what does that prove?" she asked.

"Do you not see? I went to all that trouble to get Louise away from Marc and, *voila!* Now they are married. So don't you think there are events that, no matter what you do to try and change them, they will turn out the way they are meant to be?"

He smiled playfully at his wife knowing what her reaction would be.

"Pierre, you can be such a stubborn man..."

"Well, who really knows," he cut in with a laugh, as the sound of dance music wafted out from the ballroom. "Perhaps Jacques and Paul were right. Perhaps I am. In any case, my dear, we have the rest of our lives to argue about it. For now, I suggest we go in and see how our guests are faring. Me—I think it is destined to be a very long night."

Author's Notes

Much of the information for life in the city of London in the last half of the 17th century comes from a book entitled "Restoration London" by Liza Picard and published by Phoenix, an imprint of Orion Books Ltd. published in 1997.

The information on the British East India Company and the incident in Canton comes from a book entitled "The Honourable Company" by John Keay and published by HarperCollins Publishers in 1991.

"A Chaste Maid in Cheapside" is an actual comedy written in 1613 by English Renaissance playwright, Thomas Middleton. It is considered among the best and most characteristic Jacobean comedies.

My ancestor, Pierre Gastineau was a Huguenot who made the decision to flee to London from the Poitou-Charentes region of France in the late 17th century. He was a silk weaver, whose family apparently did quite well in Spitalfields. I discovered his son's last Will and Testament, in the Prerogative Court of Canterbury, which is a reliable indicator of a person being well off at the time. His grandson married into a prominent, upper-middle-class family.

Some of the characters in my story, such as the brothers, Sir John and Sir James Houblon; the banker, Sir Richard Hoare; and the doctor, Hugh Chamberlen, are actual historical figures who were all of Huguenot descent. Dr. Chamberlen's family is credited with inventing the forceps as far back as the late 1500s, but for some reason used the instrument in secret until the end of the 17th century. However, I have taken the liberty of also crediting Dr. Chamberlen with the knowledge that boiling water was useful in the birth of babies. Sadly, that wasn't realized until a much later time.

Of course, King Louis XIV, Queen Mary, King William of Orange, Sir William Bentinck, and Elizabeth Villiers are all well-known historical figures. The opinions expressed about these characters can be backed up by history.

However, all the Garneau family members along with Paul Thibault, and most of the characters in this story are fictitious, and any similarity to anyone living or dead is purely coincidental. While many of the things in this novel did happen to some Huguenots, the story is a figment of my imagination. The premise came to me when I happened to 'meet' on-line a descendent of my ancestor's brother living in France, who was also researching his ancestry. His family decided to risk staying in the country they loved, but remained secret Huguenots—a very brave and dangerous thing to do. He was able to give me several generations of the Gastineau family going back as far as the 16th century. With that in mind, I began a series of "what ifs" and came up with the idea of Pierre Garneau and his cousin, Jacques, and the heart breaking choices they each had to make.

Above all, dear reader, please understand that writers of historical fiction are allowed to use a certain amount of verisimilitude, which means the 'appearance of truth,' and forgive me if you feel I have done an injustice to history, in any way.

Author Biography

Elizabeth Kales began her career by writing television and radio adver-
tising for the Canadian Broadcasting Corporation. Later, she worked
in the travel industry for many years and had numerous travel articles
published in newspapers and trade journals. Five years ago, at age seventy,
and after spending time in France and England, she began to research and
write her novel based loosely on the Family History she has done for over
twenty years.

She currently lives in Western Canada with her husband and their cat.

Printed in Great Britain
by Amazon